Hunted

Escape from Dollhouse Manor

Book 1

Also Written by Nicole Coverdale

"F-E-A-R has two meanings:

'Forget Everything And Run'

or 'Face Everything And Rise.'

The choice is yours."

—— Zig Ziglar

Chapter One

"No!"

"Please!"

"Someone! Help us!"

The shrill screams split through the air, and Ashleigh Carlson started. She snapped her eyes open, blinking, as her eyes adjusted to the darkness, staring up at the pebbled ceiling high above her. What was it? Nine? Ten feet? Where the hell was, she? Better yet, what the hell had happened to her?

She slowly rolled from her back to her stomach, wincing as her body ached. Her muscles felt like they were on fire. Her head was pounding like she'd had a few too many drinks, and she had no unearthly idea what had happened to her.

Come on, Ashleigh. Think. Think!

She pressed her hands into the thin carpet, shoving herself to her feet.

"Whoa..."

Her knees buckled, and she staggered backward. She slammed back into the wall with a hard thud, her vision blurring momentarily as her head pounded once more. Dots swam before her eyes, and she dragged in deep breaths.

I will not pass out. I will not pass out.

She chanted the words to herself, drawing in another deep breath, and above her, the lights flickered. She lifted her head, watching as they danced in the darkness. They flickered once. Twice. Then in one swift motion, they flicked on in a gush of white light.

"Whoa. Now that's some serious brightness!" she cried, holding a hand over her eyes, shielding them from the light, and turning to look at the room around her.

What the...

Her eyes widened, as she stared around the small, square shaped room at the weapons that hung on the black walls surrounding her. There was an axe. A chainsaw. A ball and chain. A crossbow, even a set of swords. *Just where the hell am I?*

Again, the question crossed her mind and she desperately tried to retrace her steps. She'd been working, hadn't she?

Yes. She had.

She blinked, suddenly remembering the busy night at Francesca's, the Italian restaurant she worked at in Los Angeles. It'd been late. Way after close, and she'd sent everyone home for the night. She'd been taking out the last bag of garbage before heading home herself.

Oh. Why did I tell Steph to go home? I know better. Rule number one, never take the garbage out after dark alone.

And now look at what had happened to her. She swallowed, rubbing her fingers along the inside of her wrist, and she winced. *Ouch!*

Pain pulsed from the spot, just underneath her fingertips, and she lowered her gaze, staring at the bruise that lay on the inside of her wrist. There was a matching mark on her other wrist. Were those fingerprints? Had someone dragged her?

She froze, fragments of her memory starting to come back together. Someone had been waiting for her in the car. She hadn't seen them, it'd been dark, and she'd only seen them when she'd been halfway down the road...

She gasped, remembering glancing in the rearview mirror. He'd been dressed like a clown, and he'd had a knife. He'd scared her so badly, she'd driven off the road. The car had hit a pole, and her head...

She rubbed her forehead. It'd slammed against the steering wheel. She'd been in and out of it, but she remembered them getting out of the car. She remembered their hands grabbing her, tossing her to the ground, and then...

She swallowed. They'd dragged her across the ground. It was the last thing she remembered.

Oh my God. Someone had kidnapped her.

Confirmation of what she'd thought had happened set in, and fear filled her as she stared around her.

Why had they been in the car? Where was she? Was she still in California? Did anyone even know she was missing? Was she... going to die?

Her breath caught, and she gasped, suddenly feeling like she couldn't breathe. She dragged in deep breaths, struggling to pull air into her lungs. *Oh my God*. She was going to die!

Ash, stop it. Don't think like that. You are not going to die. You're fine. Everything will be fine. Just breathe.

Ashleigh snorted. *Fine? As if. How could things possibly be fine? She'd been kidnapped!*

She shoved away from the wall and took a step forward, then another, her legs slowly steadying with every step she took.

She exited the room and started down the long hallway. The walls were painted a dark shade of red. The awnings, a shade of black, and pictures lined the walls on each side of her. Each elegently framed with portraits of Adolph Hitler, Jeffrey Dahmer, Ted Bundy, Jack the Ripper, and so many more.

"Well, I see someone has a fetish for serial killers," she muttered, shuddering, and suddenly wondering if she was in the presence of one herself. She needed to find a way out of here. Her sisters were counting on her, and she could not let them down.

"Ashleigh…"

A mysterious, raspy voice echoed through the air, and she jumped. She spun around, a shiver racing down her spine as she stared down the dark hallway. Above her, the crystal chandelier flickered. Each light flickered out one by one, before turning on once more.

This is starting to feel like a freaking house of horrors! she thought, turning and trudging down the hallway, ignoring the voice. "It's going to take a lot more than some flickering lights and a creepy whisper to scare me, asshole!"

"Ashleigh…"

Once again, the voice sounded, and she stopped. She turned, glancing over her shoulder.

"Ashleigh…"

Now she was getting annoyed.

"What!" she shouted, spinning around, clenching her hands into fists, as she stared into the darkness of the house. "Who's there? What do you want? Show yourself!"

But all that greeted her was silence.

"Just what I figured. Silence. You think this is funny, don't you? I mean, you knock me out, kidnap me, take me away from my home, my family, and now you want to play mind games? I don't think so! I am not some puppet you get to manipulate, because I am getting out of here… now!"

She turned and raced down the hallway. She glanced to her left, to her right, desperately trying to find a way out, and then she saw it. The window at the end of the hallway.

"Told you I was getting out of here," she said, sliding to a stop in front of it. She gripped the edge of the espresso-framed window and shoved it open.

Except, it didn't budge.

"What the hell?"

She tried again, and again, using all her might, but still, it wouldn't budge. She sighed, leaning forward, and pressing her forehead against the cold glass of the window as she stared out across the courtyard.

It's pretty, she thought, staring up at the dark sky sprinkled with stars, then below at the trees and flowers that bordered the pebbled pathway. Her eyes followed the pathway to the arch that lay at the front of the entrance, leading up to the tall, white manor, and in the distance, she could see the city lights of Los Angeles.

"Well, at least I know I'm still in California."

"Indeed, you are."

The voice echoed behind her once more, and she narrowed her eyes, spinning around to glare into the darkness. "Alright, asshole, you got me. I'm not escaping this place. Now, tell me. What do you want from me?"

"Why, to play a game, of course."

"What kind of game?"

"This game."

A switch sounded, and she turned, just as the wall behind her slid open. A large, flatscreened television rolled forward. It flicked on, and an image of a man filled the screen. He grinned at her, his red lips curling into an evil smile, as he stared into the camera. His face was painted a pale, bright white and he was wearing a wig. The curly blue and green strands dangled around his face as he stared at her with gleaming, dark eyes.

"You've got to be kidding me." Ashleigh stared at him in dismay, barely believing what she was seeing. "Seriously? A clown? Do you really think that's going to scare me?" she asked, even though deep inside she was trembling with fear. The fear of what he wanted with her. The fear of what he had in store for her, but she would not show him that. She refused to let him have that much power over her.

"Oh, I know it does."

"You're wrong," Ashleigh said, lifting her chin. "I know everyone thinks clowns are these scary, scary things but I love clowns! Their funny... sweet... artistic... and fun!" She smiled, crossing her arms in front of her chest. "You picked the wrong girl, Clowney, because I do not scare easily."

The clown laughed. "Oh, aren't you a feisty one. I like that. It's going to make things so much more fun, but you're wrong about one thing," he told her as he stared at her through the camera. "You are scared of me. You might be trying to hide it. Trying to fight it, but you can't deny the fear filling you every moment you're inside this manor."

"You know nothing about me," Ashleigh said, swallowing, as she returned his gaze. "Who are you?" she finally asked after a long pause. "What do you want from me?"

"I told you. I want to play a game."

"I don't play games," Ashleigh told him. "And you didn't answer my question. Who are you?"

"Oh, this one you'll be playing, Ashleigh," the clown told her, grinning devilishly at her. "Because you won't have a choice. As for who I am? Well, that doesn't matter. All that matters is you, Ashleigh," he said, lifting a long knife into view and running a white, gloved finger across the blade. "Oh, and of course... them."

He pointed the knife, and the camera switched. That's when she saw them.

"No."

Ashleigh felt the blood drain from her face as the camera focused on the three women sitting in the wooden chairs just behind him. Their arms and legs were bound to the chairs, duct tape was slapped across their mouths, and fear was etched in their eyes.

"You asshole."

"So, I take it. You remember them?"

"Of course I remember them!" Ashleigh cried. How could she ever forget them? They were her best friends from childhood. She, Sydney, Addison, and Nikki had been like sisters, but it had been years since she'd seen them. What were they doing here? And why had he brought them all together? "Please, let them go. I don't know what you want from me, but my friends have nothing to do with this. Please, just let them go!"

"Well, you see, that's where you're wrong, Ashleigh. They have everything to do with this, and as far as letting them go, well that's out of the question. They're stuck here, just like you are. The only question is, are they going to live or die by your hands?"

"What are you talking about?"

"I told you I wanted to play a game, Ashleigh, and the game is..." He held up the hourglass in his hand. "Can you find your friends before they're sliced in half?" He flipped the hourglass over.

"Before they're..."

She trailed off, as a loud noise suddenly filled her ears, and the camera switched. It zoomed in on the other side of the room, as the panel slid open, and a large, circular saw appeared. It roared to life, spinning, as it slowly made its way across the room. "You wouldn't!"

"Oh, but it's all part of the game, Ashleigh. Now, can you do it? Can you find them in time?"

The screen faded to black.

"You asshole!"

Ashleigh swore, spinning on her heel and racing down the hallway. "I'm coming! I'm coming! Just hold on!" she cried, inwardly seething as she thought of the madman who had brought them here. Just who did he think he was? Playing with their lives for his own amusement? It was sick! Deranged! Inhuman.

She raced down the hallway, ducking her head into the room next to her. Her eyes widening when she saw the ropes, chains, whips, and other contraptions scattered throughout the room.

Looks like some sort of torture room, she thought as she backed out of the room, cringing, as she thought of what he might do to her, to her friends. She needed to find them, but where were they? This place was massive! Finding them was going to be like finding a needle in a haystack.

"Tick. Tock. Tick. Tock."

The sound of a clock filled her ears, and she glanced at the clock on the wall behind her. She was running out of time.

She turned, racing down the hallway, ducking into another room. This one, looked like an interview room, similar to what they used in the police station. She stared into the small, gray room at the metal table and two chairs, eyeing the gadget on the table. Was that a polygraph?

She shook her head. *Nope. They're not here either. I have to keep moving.*

She continued down the hallway, ducking her head into the next room.

This room was painted a pale pink, and a large, rectangular table sat in the middle of the room. A floral teapot sat in the center of the table, and five matching teacups were set in front of five wickers chairs. Each wicker chair had an initial on the back. One for each of them. An A for her... Ashleigh. An S for Sydney, an N for Nikki, an A for Addison, and an X for their unknown captor.

Does he really think the five of us are going to sit in a room and drink tea together? she wondered in dismay as she stared around the room. After everything he'd done to them? Ha! She'd rather toss hot water on him than ever sit in the same room with him willingly.

She hurried down the hallway and the next room chilled her to the very core.

It looked just like her bedroom back home. The full-sized bed sat, leaning against the wall on the other side of the room. The walls were painted a pale yellow... her favorite color, but how could he possibly know that?

She gripped the edge of the doorway, feeling sick to her stomach, as she stared at the black and purple floral bedspread lying on top of the bed. She had the same one on her bed back home.

She took a step forward, walking into the room, and wrapped her fingers around the knobs of the white closet doors. She slid them open, and a gasp escaped her lips when she saw the same clothes she had back home. The purple dress she wore for special occasions. The sundress with daisies she loved to wear in the summer, and a set of cashmere sweaters she preferred when the weather got cooler. They sat among the dozens of articles of clothes that lay on the hangers, and just below them lay dozens of shoes she'd purchased throughout the years.

She swallowed. How had he gotten his hands on these same clothes? The same bedspread? An even better question, how did he know what her bedroom looked like?

She turned away from the closet, crossing the room, and running a hand along the white dresser. She stared into the oval mirror, remembering the days she'd sat there, brushing her hair, applying her makeup, even doing her homework. Then she froze when she caught sight of something in the reflection of the mirror.

She spun around, a gasp escaping her lips when she found herself staring at her name written in dark, cursive letters on the wall behind her.

He'd been planning this, and by the looks of it, he'd been planning this for a very, long time.

She turned, racing out of the room. She ducked her head into each of the next three rooms, her breath hitching when she saw a bedroom for each of her friends. It was so eerie... so creepy!

"Ashleigh..."

His voice sounded from somewhere inside the manor, and she glanced behind her, as the television flicked on. An image of the hourglass filled the screen. It was nearly half gone already. She didn't have much time left.

She neared the end of the hallway, wrapped her hand around the doorknob and shoved it open.

"Whoa!"

She slid to a stop, staring at the pit of dirt far below her. "Oh, Jesus! What the hell is that smell?" She pinched her nose, staring down into the darkness, trying to make out what was below her. The smell was nauseating, like manure. But why would he have manure? And why did he have this pit?

She stared down further into the pit, squinting, trying to see into the darkness, and a light switched on above her. It shone down brightly into the pit and she screamed when she saw the skeletons scattered amongst the dirt.

Holy crap! Did he bury people alive in here?

She shuddered, her breath coming out fast and sharp. The image of someone standing in the pit as he poured dirt over them, chilling her to the very core.

Breathe, Ash. Breathe.

She dragged in a deep breath, then another. *Was this how they felt, as the dirt filled their lungs?* she wondered, feeling her chest tighten. She drew in another breath, then another. With each breath she took, the tightness in her chest eased. She closed her eyes, focusing on her breathing, and when she opened them again, she found herself staring at the door on the other side of the pit.

"Let me guess. That's the door I've been looking for." But how was she going to get over there?

She glanced below her, contemplating walking through the nasty pit, but there was no ladder.

She glanced to her left, at the narrow ledge that stood between the wall and the pit. Could she fit? She was petite, but that... that might be asking a little too much, but she at least had to try.

She stepped onto the ledge, gripping the wall for support. She started across, taking one step, then another, when her foot suddenly slipped. She screamed as she fell downward, and she lunged forward. Her fingers wrapped around the small groove atop the pit, and she pulled herself back up.

Well, that wasn't going to work.

She sat there, staring across the pit at the door, knowing her time was running out. Were her friends going to die, because of her? There had to be another way across.

Finally, her eyes landed on the rope hanging from the ceiling above her. Maybe she could swing her way across? But how was she going to grab it? It was hanging from the middle of the pit!

She glanced around her, looking for something, anything to help her grab it. Then she saw it. The three buttons next to the door. They were labeled one, two, and three.

"You really like your mind games, don't you?" she muttered, scrambling to her feet, and studying the buttons. "Well, here goes nothing." She took a gamble and pressed the button in the middle.

A loud buzz filled her ears, and she turned. The rope slid forward, and stopped, right in front of her.

"Wow. That actually worked!" She gripped the rope tightly in her hands and backed up as far as she could. She closed her eyes, saying a silent prayer, before racing forward and leaping across the pit.

She swung across, and above her the ceiling opened. Dirt poured down into the pit, drowsing her in the process.

"Ugh! That's disgusting!"

She cringed, as the dirt and manure washed over her. Her hands slipped, and she tightened her grip around the rope, as she swung to the other side.

She let go of the rope, jumping down onto the platform, and raced toward the door. She had to hurry. Her friends were counting on her!

She dragged the door open, flinching, as it scraped against the concrete floor, and snuck through the opening. She trotted down the old, rotting stairs and they creaked under her weight.

Oh please! Please don't cave under me! she thought, gripping the wooden railing. She swore, wood splintering through her flesh, and she shook off the pain, continuing down the last set of stairs. She shoved the large, metal door open and stumbled inside. Instantly, a large roar filled her ears.

The saw.

"I'm here!" she shouted, racing forward, waving her hands in the air. "I'm here! I'm here! Stop the damned saw!"

Laugher sounded behind her, and she spun around, as the clown stepped out from behind her. He lifted his hands, clapping them together. "Congratulations, Ashleigh. I knew you could do it."

"Damnit, did you not hear me? I said, stop the damned saw!" Ashleigh shouted, snapping her head around, just as the saw's large jaws bit into the chair Sydney was sitting in. "You promised! Stop the saw!"

"Ah, yes. I did promise that, didn't I?" the clown asked, as he lifted the remote in his hand. He pressed the button, the saw shutting off, and stopping, just seconds before slicing into Sydney.

"Oh, thank God!" Ashleigh cried, blowing out a sigh of relief, as she fell to her knees. They were safe. Her friends... they were alive.

"But you don't think that's the end of it now, do you, Ashleigh?"

A hand wrapped around her arm, jerking her to her feet, and Ashleigh gasped. Her body hit the wall behind her, and she lifted her head, staring into the dark eyes of the clown. "What... what do you mean?"

The clown chuckled. "Oh, Ashleigh. You're here for a reason. You're all here for a reason." He raised the knife he was holding, pressing the blade against her cheek. "Because the four of you have sins you need to pay for."

"What... what do we need to pay for?" Ashleigh asked, gasping, as he lowered the knife, the tip of the blade pressing against her throat.

"The four of you did something a long time ago, Ashleigh. Something, that you never paid the consequences for, and I aim to make you pay. For your sins… and for the sins of the past."

"I don't know what you're talking about," Ashleigh whispered, tears rolling down her cheeks. "Please. Please. Just let us go!"

"Oh, that's not going to happen," the clown said, reaching up and twirling a lock of hair around his finger. "You see, Ashleigh. You may not remember what you did, but I do, and trust me, you will remember. One way or another, but for now, the five of us are going to have lots of fun together."

"What… what are you going to do to us?"

The clown laughed. "Oh, Ashleigh. I have so much planned for the four of you. You're my dolls, and while you're here, you'll each endure your own little private hell. Starting with you." He grinned, tracing the blade down her chest, trailing it lower, and lower. The blade stopped and rested against the juncture of her thighs. He leaned in close, whispering in her ear. "Because you, Ashleigh, are going to be my sex doll. You're going to please me any way I want, and if you don't, well then, I guess I'll just have to kill you."

"You're…" Ashleigh's eyes widened. "What? No!" She struggled against him, trying to shove him away. "No! I won't do it!"

The clown laughed, grabbing her by the arms and slamming her back against the wall. He captured her wrists in his hand, holding them above her, boxing her in with his large body. "Oh, Ashleigh, you don't have a choice in the matter. None of you do. This place… it's mine. I built it, specifically with the four of you in mind. I have weapons hidden in every corner of this house, and if one of you gets out of line. If any of you dare to defy me all I have to do is say one word, touch one button, and bam! You're dead." He chuckled. "So, tell me, Ashleigh. Do you think any of you have a choice?"

Ashleigh stared up at him, swallowing as she stared into his evil, dark eyes, then she glanced across the room at her friends. It might have been ten years since she'd seen them, but they were still her friends. She couldn't let them die. He was right. She didn't have a choice. She was his hostage, and she had to do as he said.

"No," she finally whispered. "I don't." She swallowed, hating the next words that came out of her mouth. "What do you want me to do?"

The clown laughed, grinning with glee. "Oh, so much, Doll," he said, jerking her forward. "So much, because you're mine now, Ashleigh. From now, until the day you die."

Chapter Two

Six months later...

"Ashleigh!"

The door slammed opened with a loud bang, and Ashleigh jumped. Oh God, was he back? Already? She couldn't. Not now. Not again.

She tried to open her eyes, but they wouldn't open. They were still swollen from the beating she'd taken earlier, and fear washed over her. Oh, God. What if he was back? He was volatile, insatiable, and never satisfied. The things he'd made her do...

Tears filled her eyes just thinking about it. She'd been stuck in this god-awful place for months now. Or at least she thought it'd been months. Her days were starting to blend together, and she was starting to think that she was never going to get out of this place. That she was never going to see her sisters again, and that, she would be his toy until the day he finally decided to end her. Every day was the same. More beatings. More torture. That awful, clown face leering at her, laughing at her, and she hated the person she'd become. She used to be strong, but he'd broken her. Turned her into a shell of the person she used to be.

"Ashleigh!"

The voice sounded again, and this time, Ashleigh realized it wasn't him at all. The voice... it was feminine. Wait. Was that... Sydney?

She heard footsteps, and she once again tried to open her eyes. Finally, after a bit of a struggle, one eye slowly opened, then the other. Her friend came into sight.

"Oh my God. Ashleigh..."

Sydney trailed off, staring at her friend from where she was shackled to the wall in front of her. She held a hand to her mouth, stifling the cry that wanted to escape her lips. *Do not cry. Don't you dare cry. There will be time for that later.*

"Syd?"

Ashleigh croaked, staring at her friend as she stood before her. She had her long, dark hair pulled back into a ponytail, and there was a look of determination in her hazel eyes. "What... what are you doing in here?"

"Getting us the hell out of here."

"What? No!" Ashleigh shook her head, struggling against the restraints. "Syd, no. You can't! If he sees you in here, finds out what you're doing, he'll kill you. I can't watch you die!"

"Ash, he's gone," Sydney told her. "I heard him leave a few hours ago. Finally. Now we can do what we've been waiting to do for six, long months. Get the hell out of this damned place."

She stepped forward, eyeing the shackles that held Ashleigh to the wall. "Good God. What the hell did he do to you?"

She winced, as she stared at Ashleigh. She had bruises marring her fair skin, both of her eyes were black and blue. There were welts patterned along her ribcage, fingerprints marred across her throat, and there was fear in her eyes. Both for herself, and for them.

"It's going to be so much fun, breaking that spirit of yours."

The clown's words echoed in her ears. He'd said the words to all of them at one time or another, and he'd kept his word. He had broken them. None of them would ever be the same people they'd been, before they'd been taken hostage.

"I had a hard time pleasing him this morning."

Ashleigh's words cut through her thoughts and Sydney winced. God, the bastard! Ashleigh should have never been put in this position. None of them should have, and every time she thought of what they'd gone through it made her mad. She could kill him for what he'd done.

"Well, it's the last time you will have to please him, ever again," Sydney told her, swallowing back her anger, and gesturing a hand. Addison and Nikki stepping into view.

"Addy. Nikki. You're here."

"Of course we're here!" Addison cried, as she stepped up next to Sydney. She looked exhausted. Her light, green eyes looked terrified, and dark circles were evident underneath her eyes. She had dirt streaked down both of her cheeks, through her dark, auburn hair, and she was glancing nervously over her shoulder as if she expected the clown to appear any moment behind her. "We would never leave you here. You're our friend!"

"Exactly. We would never leave you behind," Nikki added. She shook her head, running a hand through her dark, brown hair that was standing on end. "Plus, you're the reason we're all still alive. What you've done... what you've had to endure just to keep us alive..."

"I would do anything to protect you guys."

"And we would do the same for you," Sydney told her, glancing around the room. "Any idea if there's a key to those damned shackles?"

"I think he took them with him."

"Of course he did. Fucking control freak." Sydney sighed, reaching up and pulling a bobby pin from her hair. "Guess we'll have to do this the old-fashioned way."

"How the hell do you have bobby pins?" Addison asked, staring at her in disbelief. "He searched all of us for any sort of weapons!"

"I'm very creative," Sydney told her, crossing to Ashleigh and sticking the pin into the lock. She jiggled it, listening to the lock. It was all about the tumblers.

"You always were very good at picking locks," Nikki murmured. "Who even taught you that?"

"An old friend."

"You're not going to give us any more than that?"

"Nope." The lock gave away. "One down. Three to go." Sydney moved to the next lock. "Two down! Nikki, can you come here? I need you to hold her in place while I get her arms free. I don't want her to fall."

"Of course."

Nikki walked forward, wrapping her arms around Ashleigh, and Ashleigh mentally cringed. Her friends... they had seen her naked. They had watched, while that man had forced her to do horrible, unspeakable things. What must they think of her?

"Ash."

Ashleigh raised her head, staring at Nikki.

"I've got you, okay? Don't worry."

"I... I'm not," Ashleigh whispered, swallowing. "But, Nikki, you have to promise not to let me fall, okay? I've been like this for hours. I'm not sure if my legs will hold me."

"I got you."

"Addy? You watching the door?" Sydney asked, as she worked on the lock. She swore. The thing was being a pain in the ass.

"Yup. The coast is clear."

"Good. That's what I like to hear." The lock clicked, the shackle falling open. "Just one more left to go."

Sydney turned her attention to the last shackle, sticking the pin into the lock. She jiggled the pin, listening to the sound of the lock, and a click sounded. The last shackle fell open, and Ashleigh screamed, as she slid downward. "Nikki!"

"Dammitt, Nikki! What did I say? Hold on to her!" Sydney cried, as she wrapped her arms around Ashleigh, holding her upright.

"I'm sorry!" Nikki cried. "She slid really fast!" She tightened her grip around Ashleigh, draping Ashleigh's arm around her shoulders as she struggled to hold her upright. "We need to get her dressed."

"You brought the clothes, right?"

Nikki glanced at Sydney. "What?"

"The clothes. I told you to bring clothes with you."

"You never told me that."

"Yes, I did!"

"Girls!" Addison rolled her eyes, staring at the two. "Stop bickering. It is not helping." She peered into the hallway. "I'll be right back."

"Wait!"

"Addy!"

"No!"

She disappeared out of the room, and Sydney swung toward Nikki, glaring at her. "Do you ever listen to a thing I say? I had a plan, and now, because of you, Addison is out there... alone! Do you know what'll happen if he comes back? What he'll do to her? We were all supposed to stick together!"

"Syd, chill. I'm fine," Addison said as she appeared back inside the room, holding a pile of clothes in her arms.

"Jesus, Addy, you scared the shit out of me!"

"And apparently being scared brings out the bitch in you," Nikki muttered.

"Nikki!"

"What? I'm just saying."

"You two need to get over... whatever this is," Addison told them, gesturing between the two. "This is not helping. We shouldn't be fighting with one another. We need each other, if we're going to get out of here alive. So, apologize to one another."

"What?"

"I don't think..."

"Now."

Sydney sighed, glancing over at Nikki. "Okay, I'm sorry. I was out of line. I shouldn't have yelled at you."

"I'm sorry, too," Nikki said, shuffling her feet. "I should have listened, I guess, and I'm sorry I called you a bitch."

"Well, I kind of am being one."

"See. Was that so hard?" Addison asked, rolling her eyes. God, she hated playing peacemaker, but the two were like water and oil. They never got along.

She stepped up to Ashleigh, pulling the shirt over her head. Ashleigh winced. "Ouch."

"Sorry." Addison gentled her touch, staring at the welts and bruises on Ashleigh's body. "You need a doctor," she whispered. "Your ribs, I'm pretty sure they're broken, and I wouldn't be surprised if you had a concussion."

"Let's focus on getting out of here first," Sydney said. "Then, we can worry about getting to the doctor."

"Right. One step at a time."

Together, the three of them managed to get Ashleigh dressed. Moments later, Ashleigh stood there, fully dressed in front of them, glancing at one, then the other. "So... what's the plan?"

"The plan is to get the hell out of here. Come on. Follow me," Sydney said, turning, and heading for the doorway.

"Think you can walk?" Nikki asked, glancing at Ashleigh with concern.

"I...I think so," Ashleigh said. She gripped the arm Nikki offered her, taking a shaky step forward, then another. "Yes. I can feel the feeling coming back into my legs."

"Good. Now let's go!" Sydney disappeared through the door, into the hallway.

"Damn, she's still quite bossy, isn't she?" Ashleigh asked, shaking her head, as she, Nikki, and Addison followed Sydney out into the hallway. "Even after all we've been through."

"I suppose some things never change," Addison said, glancing over at Ashleigh worriedly. "Ash, are you sure you're okay?"

"I'm okay, Addy."

They made their way down the dark hallway, and above them, the lights flickered.

"God, I hate this place," Nikki said, shuddering.

"We all do."

They uttered the words in unison, and a whine suddenly split through the air. They all jumped.

"What the hell was that?" Addison swung around, staring at her friends, her eyes wide with terror. "What the hell was that noise?"

"Just the wind, I think," Sydney said, swallowing, as she tried to calm her own nerves. No matter how hard she was trying to put on a brave face, the noise had scared her too. "Come on. Let's keep moving."

They walked further down the hallway, rounding the corner, and walked even further. Finally, they reached the door she was looking for. She wrapped her hand around the knob and pulled it open. "Come on. In here."

"How is it that you know exactly what to look for?" Nikki asked.

"Because I got to know this place while we've been stuck here," Sydney told her. "Like, I know that every night at midnight, the bastard goes and gets himself drunk. I know that at two a.m., the security system reboots and for fifteen minutes each night, I got to explore this place."

She led them inside, closing the door softly behind them. "There's a hidden room in here, and as long as I didn't get lost inside this damned manor, it leads to the sewers. If we can get there, we'll be free, and away from that bastard... finally."

Addison, Nikki, and Ashleigh followed her through the doorway. They walked down the steps, and through another doorway, walking into the office. They rounded the desk, and Nikki stopped, staring at the files that were scattered along the surface of the desk.

"This is all just so creepy," she said, flipping through one of the files. The file with her name on it. "He knows so much about us. About our families. Look. Here's a picture of me at my graduation. A picture of me, at UCLA. There's even notes about me! My favorite foods. My likes. My dislikes. Even boyfriends I've had. He knows everything!"

"Just because he's done his research on us, doesn't mean he knows us. There's more to us, then what's written in those files, Nikki," Sydney told her. "Now, will you stop snooping? He could be back any moment, and I would prefer not to be here when he does."

Sydney crossed to the bookcase, trailing her fingers along the spines of the books, reading through the titles. *The World's Most Notorious Serial Killers. How to Torture Someone in a Hundred Different Ways.* There were even books on bondage, electrocution, and how to bury someone alive.

She shuddered, gripping the edge of the bookcase and giving it a shove. It slid to the side, revealing the doorway behind it.

Addison's mouth gaped open. "How the hell did you know that was there?"

"I told you. I got to know this place pretty well, and it gave me a chance to devise a plan for the four of us to escape. I was just waiting for the right moment."

"And that moment is today?"

"Exactly."

Thump!

The sound of a door slamming shut sounded above them, and they all froze, staring at one another in horror. He was back, and it wouldn't be long until he realized they were gone.

"Come on!"

She gestured them forward, and the four of them raced through the doorway. She slid the bookcase back into place, just as a loud shout sounded above them.

"Son of a bitch!"

He knew they were gone.

They turned, racing across the room.

"What is this place?" Ashleigh asked, pausing to lean against the wall. She took a moment, dragging in a deep breath, trying to gather her energy and stared at the room around them. There were dozens of boxes piled on the shelves surrounding them. Each box had their names on them. One was labeled, *photographs*. Another labeled, *hair fibers*. Another labeled, *blood vials*, *fingerprints*.

"I think it's some sort of trophy room," Sydney said, gesturing her forward. "Every maniac has one. Come on." She grabbed Ashleigh by the arm, pulling her forward.

Together, they crossed the room, and she dragged the door open, revealing the tunnels on the other side. "See. I told you. Tunnels!"

"We never doubted you, Syd," Nikki said, as they hurried through the door. "Man, he wasn't lying, was he? He really did build this place from the ground up. I mean, he thought of everything. Even an escape plan!"

"Yes. We know. He's super smart, Nikki," Sydney said, rolling her eyes. "He has to be. He never would have been able to plan all of this if he wasn't, but please, don't give this man any props, Nikki."

"I'm not! I'm just saying..."

"Ash?"

Addison stopped, glancing over her shoulder, suddenly realizing Ashleigh was lagging behind. "Ash? Are you okay?"

Ashleigh shook her head, bracing her hand against the wall. "No. I don't think so. I... I'm wearing down, Addy. My body, the beating it's taken... I don't think I'm going to make it."

"The hell you aren't!" Addison cried, grabbing her by the arm and urging her forward. "Come on. You have to! Our lives depend on it!"

"What?"

"We made a pact. Either we all get out of here, or none of us do."

"You what?" Ashleigh stared at her in disbelief. "You can't make a pact like that!"

"We can, and we did," Nikki told her. "Now you best get your ass moving, because I am not going back to that bastard."

Ashleigh glanced at her friends and closed her eyes. She blew out a long breath, slowly nodding, and she shoved away from the wall. She trudged forward, and the four of them made their way through the tunnels.

"How much further do we have to go?" Addison asked a little while later, panting. "I'm not complaining, but I'm getting tired!"

"Not too much further," Sydney said, running her hand along the wall of the tunnel. "I just need to find... wait. I think I found it." She squatted down, staring through the metal grate at the running sewers underneath. "Look." she said, pointing. "The sewers."

"Now I'm really beginning to feel like a Ninja Turtle," Nikki muttered.

Ashleigh sputtered, a laugh escaping her mouth. "Nikki!"

"You two have a weird sense of humor," Sydney told them, gripping her fingers around the grate. "We're being chased by a psycho, and you two are laughing!"

"What can I say? It's a coping mechanism," Nikki told her. "So, are we going down there or what?"

"I'm trying," Sydney said, through gritted teeth, shaking her head as she tried to pull the grate free. "But it's stuck!"

"So, we're just stuck here?" Addison asked, nervously glancing over her shoulder.

"Hell no!" Nikki said, stepping up next to Sydney, and sitting next to her on the ground. "A little brute force should do the trick, don't you think?" she asked, giving Sydney a grin. "Wanna give it a try?"

"Like at cheerleading camp?"

"Exactly. The only time, in the last ten years, you and I ever saw one another," Nikki said. "On three?"

"On three."

"One. Two. Three!"

They kicked their legs out, striking their feet against the grate. It didn't budge.

"Again!"

They kicked it again, and it shook.

"Again!"

On the third try, the grate finally broke free, falling downward and landing with a splash in the water below them.

"That's what I'm taking about!" Sydney quickly descended the ladder. She dropped down into the water, glancing up at her friends. "Come on! It's not much further!"

"Ash, you should go first," Addison said, pointing to the ladder.

Ashleigh glanced at her, slowly nodding, knowing that she was worried about her. Hell, she was worried about herself. She was afraid that at any moment, she was going to cripple over from the pain she was in.

She quickly descended the ladder, dropping down into the water next to Sydney. Addison followed close behind, followed by Nikki.

"Eww! This is disgusting!" Nikki cried, wrinkling her nose in disgust. "This is one thing I never wanted to see." She glanced around at the muddy waters around them, shuddering. "Our sewers."

"Oh, will you stop complaining? It's our only way out of this place," Sydney told her, as they waded forward.

Thunk!

The sound of another door slamming shut sounded nearby, and they glanced at one another. He was getting closer. They had to hurry.

"Hey, Syd?"

"What is it, Addy?" Sydney glanced in her direction.

"Is that what I think it is?" Addison asked, pointing forward. They all looked in the direction she pointed, squinting in the darkness, just making out the ladder that was leaning against the wall just a few hundred feet from them.

Sydney smiled. "Yes. Indeed, it is."

"Oh my God!" Ashleigh glanced at her friends. "We're going to make it! We're going to get out of here!"

"Damn right we are," Sydney said, giving Ashleigh a small smile. They neared the ladder and she gripped the metal rungs, pulling herself out of the water. She made her way up the ladder, and when she neared the top, she grabbed the handle to the door lying just above her. She tossed it open, stepping out into the warm, California night. "Come on!"

"Ash. You first," Nikki said, nodding upward. "You should go first."

"No. You two should. It makes sense for me to go last."

"No. You're going first," Addison told her, giving her a look. "There's no sense in arguing with us."

They also didn't have the time for it, Ashleigh thought as she reached up. She wrapped her fingers around the metal rung, pulling herself out of the water. She reached a hand up, then another. Her arms shook, her legs shook, and she clenched her fingers around the ladder. "I don't think I can do this," she whispered, looking up at Sydney. "I'm too weak."

"Yes, you can. I know you can," Sydney said, extending a hand out. "You're strong, Ash. One of the strongest people I've ever known, and I know, that you can do this."

Ashleigh gazed up at her, staring at her extended hand, and she slowly nodded. She reached another hand up, then another, and she reached out, grabbing Sydney's hand.

"I got you," Sydney said, wrapping her fingers around Ashleigh's hand. She pulled her up, and out of the sewer. They both tumbled to the ground, and Ashleigh blew out a long breath, staring up at the sky above her as the wind whipped through the air. God, she was hurting. Every muscle... every tendon felt like it was on fire, but damn! She'd made it. She'd made it out!

"Oh my God. I can't believe we made it!" Addison cried, climbing out behind her, and tumbling to the ground next to her. "Oh. Look at that. The stars... the moon... and man, does the fresh air feel good! Nikki, come on. You've got to see this!"

"Hang on! I'm coming!"

Nikki grabbed the rung of the ladder and started up. She reached her hand forward, then another, and a hand suddenly wrapped around her ankle.

"Ah! Guys!"

"Nikki!"

Sydney and Addison lunged forward, peering down into the sewer. Their eyes widening, when they saw the man who'd held them hostage for the last six months, dragging Nikki back into the sewer.

"Nikki!"

"Let go of me, you bastard!" Nikki shouted, kicking her leg out.

"Nikki! You have to fight him!" Sydney shouted.

"You can't let him take you!"

"I know that!" Nikki shouted, as she tried to dislodge his grip from her ankle, but he was holding on to her so tight. Then she suddenly screamed, as he gave her a hard yank. Her hands slipped from the rungs of the ladder, and her body tumbled downward, back into the sewer.

"Nikki!"

Nikki hit the water with a splash, sputtering, gagging as the muddy water filled her mouth. She turned her head and scrambled backward, as the clown trudged toward her. His shoes splashed loudly in the water, and she caught a glimpse of a knife clutched in his hand.

No!

Her back slammed back against the wall, and she looked to her left, to her right. Crap! She had no way of escaping him!

"Please," she whispered. "Just let us go!"

"You've been with me long enough to know that that is not an option," the clown said as he boxed her in. He grabbed her by the back of the neck, pulling her to her feet.

"No!" Nikki swung her fists forward, trying to fight him off, but the clown just laughed. He grabbed her wrists, slamming her back against the wall. She winced, as her head bounced off the hard surface, dots swimming before her eyes. "Please..."

"Girls, you might as well come back down here," the clown said, as he jerked Nikki forward, pressing the blade of the knife to her throat. "Unless of course, you want me to slit her throat."

"No!"

"Don't do it!"

"Nikki!"

"Don't even think about it," Nikki gasped out, blinking, as she looked up at her friends. Her vision was wavering, but she could still make out Addison and Sydney, as they peered down into the sewer. "Don't come back down here. You have to go. Save yourselves."

"You have until the count of three," the clown said, pressing the blade of the knife tighter against Nikki's throat. "One."

"Syd, we have to go back down there," Addison said, glancing over at Sydney. "We can't leave her behind."

"But Addy!"

"Two."

"We promised," Addison said, softly. "We promised one another that we would only go, if we could all get out."

"Three."

"Hold on!"

"Addy! No!"

"Addy." Sydney grabbed Addison's arm, stopping her before she disappeared down into the sewer. She nodded to Ashleigh, who was sitting on the ground just behind them. "We can't let her go back down there. She can't endure anymore of what he put her through."

"Then she can go get help, but I can't leave Nikki."

"Neither can I," Ashleigh said as she pushed herself to her feet, wavering as she clutched a hand to her throbbing ribs. "We have to go back. We're in this together, remember?"

"Ash..."

"Addy! No!"

Nikki stared up the ladder in horror, as Addison started making her way down the ladder. Sydney close behind. *No! They couldn't possibly be...*

The clown laughed. "Oh, you four are so predictable."

"Predictable my ass!"

Suddenly feeling bold, and not caring if he killed her, Nikki swung her arm back, hard, slamming her elbow into his midsection. She would not allow her friends to endure more endless torture, again, because of her. No way! She would rather die than let any of them ever go through that again.

"Agh!"

The clown gasped in surprise, staggering backward. The knife slid in his grasp, and Nikki winced as it nicked her throat. She lifted a hand, feeling blood trickle from the wound, and swung her head toward the ladder.

"Addy! Syd! Get your asses back up there... now!"

Addison and Sydney stared down at her, confused. Then they saw the clown, as he stumbled in the muddy waters, realization suddenly showing in their eyes. They turned, scampering back up the ladder and out of view.

Blowing out a sigh of relief that they were out of harm's way, Nikki glanced over her shoulder, just as the clown rose to his feet. She turned and raced for the ladder.

"No!"

He reached for her, and she ducked, swerving around him as he lunged for her. His feet slid in the water, and he stumbled, falling into the muddy waters with a hard splash.

Yes! This was her chance!

She lunged forward, her fingers gripping the rungs of the ladder.

"Stop!"

"Not a chance, asshole!" Nikki shouted, as she raced up the ladder.

"I said stop!"

"No!"

Click.

The sound echoed in her ears, and Nikki froze. She turned, glancing back down at him, fear washing over her when she saw the gun pointed at her. *Where the hell had that come from?*

"What are you going to do? Shoot me?"

"If I have to. Get down here. Now."

Nikki stared at him, then up above her. It was just a few more steps. She could make it, couldn't she?

He cocked the trigger, and she raced up the ladder.

Bang! Bang!

The sound of the gunshot filled her ears, and she swung to the side, but she wasn't fast enough. The bullet pierced through her leg, and she yelped, struggling to keep her balance as her foot slid on the rung of the ladder.

"I told you." He strode forward. "You're mine. All of you are. Until the day you die." He started up after her.

"Like hell I am!" Nikki shouted, blinking past the pain, and racing up the ladder.

"No!"

"Nikki!"

Addison and Sydney reached down. They grabbed her by the arms, pulling her up and out of the sewer.

"We got you!"

"No, you don't!" Nikki shouted, glancing below her, as he raced up the ladder after her. "He's coming!" she cried, as he grabbed a hold of her ankle. "And he's got me. Again!"

"And we're not letting him take you!" Sydney shouted, gritting her teeth, as she tried not to lose her grip on Nikki. "God. He's strong."

"I know!" Addison cried. "I don't know how much longer I can hold on!"

"You have to!"

"We have to," Ashleigh said, appearing next to them.

"Ash! You're okay!"

"Ah. Okay is stretching it," Ashleigh said, as she reached forward, wrapping her hand around Nikki's arm. "But I sure as hell am not letting this madman drag Nikki back down there. Now let's do this!"

They nodded, and they all gritted their teeth, pulling with all their might, as they pulled Nikki out of the sewer.

"No!"

"Get off of me, you asshole!" Nikki shouted, kicking her leg out and catching him in the eye. He swore, his grip loosening, as he lost his balance and fell backward down into the sewer.

"Ah!"

"Serves you right, asshole!" Nikki shouted, as she stared down at him. "Rot in hell, you bastard!"

"I'm going to find you!" their captor shouted as he stared up at them. "I will find you. This is far from over!"

"That's where you're wrong!" Sydney shouted. "Because you will never lay a hand on us ever again. You're going to jail, asshole! And I promise you, you will never, ever see the light of day ever again." She slammed the lid shut, clasping the lock, and turned to her friends. "Come on. Let's get out of here."

"Can we? Please?" Nikki asked, wincing, as she staggered to her feet. "The bastard shot me."

"He what?"

Addison and Sydney swung around, their eyes widening, when they saw the blood gushing from Nikki's leg. "We didn't hear anything!"

"It was blocked out by the sound of the water in the sewer," Nikki said, wincing. "But I'm okay. I think."

"You think? My God, just look at us!" Addison cried, throwing Nikki's arm over her shoulders, as she stared at her friends. Their clothes were torn, they were drenched in sewer water, bruises marred their faces, and they looked completely exhausted. "We look like we survived a freaking horror movie!"

"In some ways, I think we have," Ashleigh said, as she rose to her feet. She stumbled, and Sydney hurried forward, throwing Ashleigh's arm around her shoulders. "Here. Let me help you."

Together, they made their way across the lawn. They walked, for what seemed like miles, when finally, Ashleigh pointed. "Look. I think I see a road, but it's so dark!"

"It's late, Ash. I highly doubt anyone's going to pass by any time soon," Nikki said, as they stumbled across the grass. "God, I'm tired."

"We're all tired, Nikki."

"Can we sit? Just for a moment?"

"We can't. What if he escapes the tunnels before someone finds us? We'll be right back where we started."

"Right."

"Look!"

Addison suddenly pointed, and they turned as headlights appeared in the distance. A second later, flashing blue and red lights lit up the night.

"Hey, girls. You lost or..." The officer rolled down the window, his eyes widening when he saw them. "Oh my God. It's you! We've been looking everywhere for you. We thought you were all dead!"

"Not dead. Just very beat up," Sydney told him, shivering as the cold breeze ripped through the air. "You might want to call for backup. The man who kidnapped us, he's back there." She jabbed a finger behind her, toward the manor.

"Already on it," the officer said as he stepped out. "And I'm calling for an ambulance. You girls need to get to a hospital. You look..."

"Terrible. Yes, we know," Addison said, as she hugged her friends close. "Then can we go home? Please?"

"Of course," the officer said, glancing at the four of them. He shook his head in disbelief, lifting the phone to his ear. "This is Officer Stillman. I found the missing girls and they're alive."

Chapter Three

Two Weeks later...

Man, this place is a madhouse! Ashleigh thought, as she stepped through the sliding glass doors of the busy, Los Angeles airport, scanning the crowd. She'd just talked to Addison. She'd said she was here, but where was she? There were so many people here!

She turned, pushing her way thought the crowd. "Excuse me! Excuse me! Exc—Oomph!"

She gasped, inhaling a sharp breath, as someone bumped into her. An elbow jabbed her in the ribs, and she wheezed, struggling for breath as pain coursed through her body. "Son of a..."

"I am so sorry! Are you okay?"

A hand touched her arm, and she jumped. She jerked her arm free, swinging around, staring into the eyes of a young, blonde-haired man wearing glasses.

"Uh, yeah. I'm fine. Thank you."

She backed away from the man, eyeing him warily. She did not like strangers. She didn't trust them, hell, who could blame her after everything she'd been through?

"Really, I am sorry. I really, really need to pay attention to where I am going," the man said, shaking his head, as he picked up the papers that had fallen to the ground. He gave her a small smile before turning and racing off.

Ashleigh stared after him, her breath coming out hard and fast.

Breathe, Ash. Breathe. You're okay.

She dragged in a deep breath, then another, trying to ease the panic rising inside of her.

It had been two weeks since she and her friends had escaped the manor. Two weeks full of doctor's appointments, interviews with the police, and appointments with her therapist. Nothing had helped, and nothing, was helping the anxiety she was feeling right now.

All she felt was fear, and it was eating at her like some sort of rapid virus. Each day it just got worse and each day, she had the fear that *he* would come for her. That *he* was watching her, and even worse, that *he* wasn't the only one out there like that. What if there were more out there like him? What if she wasn't safe anywhere?

"Ashleigh."

A hand touched her arm and she jumped. A scream ripped from her throat, and she spun around, staring into the light, green eyes of a young woman with dark, red hair. "Addy."

"Ashleigh, thank God I finally found you. I'm sorry if I scared you."

"No. No. You just startled me. I'm fine," Ashleigh said, shaking her head as her thumping heart started to relax inside her chest. She wrapped her arms around Addison, embracing her in a tight hug. "It's so good to see you. I've missed you!"

"I've missed you too. Are the others here yet?"

"No. Not yet." Ashleigh winced, holding a hand to her ribs. "They should be here soon."

"You okay?" Addison looked at her with concern, as she gripped the handle of the large, floral suitcase she was dragging behind her. She adjusted the white jacket she was wearing over her pink blouse, suddenly feeling guilty. She hadn't seen Ashleigh since they'd gotten separated inside the hospital two weeks ago, but not a day had gone by that she hadn't thought of her. Why hadn't she reached out sooner?

"Yeah, I'm okay. My ribs are still healing, though," Ashleigh said, wincing once more. "You know. Four broken ribs, they do take a little time to heal."

Addison grimaced. "God, Ash. I am so sorry. I should have reached out sooner..."

"No. No. Please don't think like that, Addy. We all had a lot going on."

Which was true, Addison thought, as she stared at her friend. She was looking better. The bruises on her face were nearly healed. She no longer had the black and blue, swollen eyes she'd had a couple weeks ago. But in her eyes, there was pain, fear, and something else Addison couldn't quite put her finger on. "How are you?"

"Me? I'm fine."

Addison raised a brow, and Ashleigh sighed. "Okay, I'm not fine. I'm, well... I'm dealing."

"Are you having nightmares?"

Ashleigh hesitated.

"I have them too, you know."

Ashleigh froze, staring at Addison in surprise. Not at the fact that she had nightmares, but the fact that she'd admitted it. They'd never talked about what each of them had gone through inside the manor.

"You do?"

Addison nodded. "Every night."

"Do you think it'll ever get better?" Ashleigh asked, shuddering, as she thought of the countless, sleepless nights she'd had since escaping the manor. He was always there in her dreams, grinning at her, mocking her, laughing at her. She shuddered again. "I see him every night," she whispered. "And that damned clown face..."

"It's so creepy!" Addison shuddered. "God! I used to love clowns. Now..."

"They're scary as fuck," Ashleigh said, nodding, knowing exactly what her friend was saying. "And the anxiety..."

"Anxiety?"

Ashleigh nodded. "It happens when I'm in public. I get this sense of fear, of panic, and the slightest touch sets me off. I scared this old lady the other day when she grabbed my arm to keep from falling. I tell you... complete meltdown! I don't know if I'll ever be able to trust anyone ever again. Well except you, Nikki, Syd, and of course, Billy." Billy was one of their oldest friends, and also a police detective for the LAPD.

"Ash, don't be so hard on yourself," Addison told her. "You've been through a lot, and you're still healing. You need to give yourself time."

"I know. It's just, I hate this! I want to feel like myself again, you know? Every time I look at myself in the mirror, I feel like I'm looking at a stranger. I don't even recognize myself anymore, Addy, and I can't help but wonder if there are others like him out there."

"I know. I've wondered the same thing," Addison whispered, glancing over her shoulder at the people around them. "What he did to us... what he put us through... do you think any of us will ever be able to recover?"

"I don't know," Ashleigh said, shaking her head, as she too scanned the crowd. "I mean he took six months of our lives, Addy. He took away our dreams... our hopes... I can't even think about being with a guy without thinking of him. He broke me, Addy. He ruined me."

"Oh, Ash." Addison reached out, squeezing her hand, her heart breaking for her friend. "I hate what he did to you. What he put you though, but he didn't ruin you. He could never. You're too strong for that. You went through hell in there, Ashleigh. More than any of us did. I mean what he did to you was... was..."

"Humiliating? Disgusting?"

"God ,no! I would never think that!"

"How can you not?" Ashleigh asked, averting her gaze. "You saw what he did to me, Addy. You saw the things he made me do."

"And it's because of you that we are all still alive," Addison said, gripping Ashleigh's hands in hers and meeting her gaze. "Ashleigh, you sacrificed yourself to keep us alive. It's because of you that I am standing, right here, in front of you."

"That's not true."

"Yes, it is! We owe you our lives, Ash! But right now, what we all need to focus on is healing, and putting that damn manor behind us. It's time to move forward. No matter how scary that may be."

"I couldn't have said it better myself."

The voice sounded from behind them, and they glanced behind them, as Sydney stepped off the escalator. She strode toward them, pulling her long, dark hair back into a ponytail. She had a black, leather duffel bag slung over her left shoulder, and she was wearing a brown, suede jacket over a white, lace blouse. Worn, denim jeans hugged her lean hips, and the heels of her boots clicked on the linoleum tile as she neared them.

"Sydney!"

"Oh, it is so good to see you guys!" Sydney cried, as she gave them each a hug. "I've missed you!"

"I see someone's developed a sentimental side," Addison muttered under her breath.

"Hey! I'm being serious! I really did miss you guys," Sydney said, swatting Addison in the shoulder, lightly. "I mean, I feel like it's been forever!"

"It's only been two weeks."

"A long two weeks!" Sydney cried. "And those shrinks. Did they really have to keep us apart? It was torture not being able to see you guys!"

"They were just trying to help, Syd," Ashleigh told her. "And I can't say it was the worst idea in the world."

"Seriously?"

"I kind of agree with her," Addison said, wringing her hands together nervously. "I mean, I get where they were coming from. We were a mess when we escaped the manor, and seeing one another, it could have set us all off. I don't know about you two, but I had some really, really rough nights after escaping."

Oh, she wasn't the only one, Ashleigh thought, as she gazed across the airport, thinking back to the nights after escaping the manor. The doctors had wanted to keep her there longer than the others. She couldn't say she blamed them, considering she'd had internal bleeding, four broken ribs, and a concussion. She hadn't wanted to. She hated hospitals, but she'd been in so much pain and doped up on so many different pain medications, she hadn't had the strength to argue with them. In the end, it was a good thing she'd stayed.

The nights following the escape had been hard. Every time she'd closed her eyes, he'd been there.

She'd woken up screaming, paranoid that he was coming for her. She'd thought that everyone who came into her room was a danger to her, and it had just gotten worse from there. Eventually, the doctors had had no choice but to sedate her, and she'd been advised to see a psychiatrist. Who had admitted her, concerned for her safety.

She sighed, staring across the airport. Her eyes stopped on a young woman, sitting in the corner of the airport, reading a magazine. An image of the four of them was plastered across the front cover. The words, *Home at Last...* written across the front in bright, yellow letters.

Ah, shit.

"Ash?"

She faintly heard her name being called.

"Ash?"

"Ash!"

"What?" she snapped, swinging her head around to look at Addison and Sydney.

"We called your name like five times!" Sydney cried. "Are you okay? Are you in pain? Do you need to sit?"

"No. No. I'm fine. It's just." Ashleigh sighed, playing with the ring on her finger. "It's that damned article."

"What article?"

"The article *that* reporter wrote." Ashleigh said, lifting the magazine that was lying on the table next to her, and showing it to them. "Just look at this picture of us. We look..."

"Horrible," Addison said, staring down at the cover as she took it from Ashleigh. "God, I hate this picture of us!" She stared down at the photo of them, huddled just inside the doors of the hospital. It'd been taken just hours after they'd been found. "We look so scared!"

"We were scared," Sydney said, snatching the magazine out of her hand and staring at the photo. "I heard about this, but I hadn't gotten a chance to actually see it for myself yet. How the hell did anyone manage to get this close to us? There were cops everywhere that night!"

"You'll have to ask Gloria Davis," Ashleigh said, narrowing her eyes as she thought of the local female reporter. "She's the one who wrote the article."

Sydney arched a brow at her, flipping through the pages, her eyes widening as she read through the article. "You're not serious? Listen to this." She cleared her throat. "Sydney, Addison, Nikki, and Ashleigh, victims of a strange man dressed like a clown, were found alive, but just what secrets do each of them hold? And how much of the truth are they hiding? Especially when each has a different version of the story to tell." She raised her head, staring at her friends in bewilderment. "Are you kidding me?"

"It gets worse," Ashleigh said, nodding to the magazine. "It goes on to outline the timeline of us being kidnapped, why she believes we were kidnapped, and at one point, she even blames us for what happened."

"That conniving, little... if I ever see her..."

"You're going to behave yourself," Addison said, taking the magazine from her and tossing it over her shoulder. "We do not need to give this woman any more ammunition than she already has. She did enough damage when she came to visit us. I mean, she promised to help us. She promised to find the person responsible. That she wouldn't rest until he was caught and behind bars, but she lied. She only wanted the story."

"We should sue her ass," Sydney said, still seething. "She said it was off the record!"

"Except we have no way of proving she promised that," Ashleigh told her. "It would just be our word against hers, and she's a public figure. We have to let it go."

Sydney scowled. "I still don't like it."

"You don't have to like it," Addison told her. "You just have to accept it for what it is. Especially since she has a book coming out later this year."

"She what?" Sydney's eyes widened in shock. "About what? The man who kidnapped us was never caught!"

"I guess it focuses mainly on the investigation," Ashleigh told her. "Apparently, she was a big help to Billy in trying to find us."

"Big help my ass," Sydney muttered under her breath. "I can't believe Billy even agreed to work with her!"

"Oh, he's just as pissed at her as we are," Addison said, grimacing. "When he saw the article, he was so livid I had a hard time calming him down." She smiled. "Do you know he stayed with me after I was released from the hospital? He wouldn't leave my side. Practically moved in with me."

"That does not surprise me," Sydney said, sharing a look with Ashleigh. They all knew Billy and Addison were close. Like super close, and often they all had wondered when the two would stop denying they had feelings for one another. "He was worried about you."

"Sure he was," Addison muttered, wringing her hands together. "That's why he let those cops grill us after we were found. God, they were so mean! All those questions... I felt like I was being interrogated!"

"They were just trying to do their job, Addy."

"I know, but Billy knows us!"

"And he had to be careful," Sydney told her. "He was in a rough spot already with his connection to us. He told me his boss did not like him being on the case, and that he was being watched for any sort of favoritism he showed toward us. Just one mistake on his part and he'd be thrown off the case and from my understanding the other detectives are not as thorough as Billy is. Hell, everyone was set to give up looking for us, but not Billy. He did everything in his power to find us. Even..."

"Even getting help from Gloria Davis," Ashleigh said. "We may not like the fact that he agreed to work with her, but he did it, out of love for us. We could never, ever be mad at him for that.

"Yes, I know, but..."

"But nothing. He did everything he could to find us and when we were found he was there for us," Ashleigh said, thinking back to the night they'd escaped the manor. When the news had broke that they'd been found, things had gotten chaotic. Cops had flooded the scene, reporters had been there, yelling questions at them, shoving cameras in their faces, and then there had been Billy. He'd been one of the first on the scene, and the look on his face when he'd seen them... well, it was the first time Ashleigh had ever seen him cry. He'd been barking orders at the other cops, yelling at the reporters, and then he'd had another officer whisk them off to the hospital. He would have done it himself, but he'd been needed at the crime scene.

"I know, but he could have told them to be nice!" Addison cried. "And, boy did he get a piece of my mind about it."

"Addy!" Sydney and Ashleigh laughed, shaking their heads. "When are you going to admit you have feelings for Billy?"

"I don't... we... we're just friends...I..." Addison stammered, glancing at her watch. "Hey, shouldn't Nikki be here by now?" she asked, quickly changing the subject.

Ashleigh rolled her eyes. "You are not getting out of that, that easily," she said, glancing down at her own watch. "She should be here soon. You know Nikki. She runs on her own schedule."

"And has no regard for anyone else," Sydney muttered under her breath.

Ashleigh sighed, ignoring Sydney's snide comment. She didn't mean it, but to be honest, Ashleigh was worried about Nikki. She'd barely heard from her since they'd escaped the manor. Billy had even been worried. Apparently, after she'd been released from the hospital, she'd disappeared.

Ding!

The elevator chimed, and Ashleigh cringed. She hated that sound. Being inside the manor, that very noise had signaled the start of a new day. A day full of torture, of pain, of...

She shook herself free of the thoughts, watching as people flooded out from the elevator. A smile crossing her lips when she saw a young woman with wavy, dark, brown hair, wearing a tiger print dress step out from the elevator. She slid her sunglasses from her face, plopping them on top of her head as she turned to scan the crowd.

"Nikki! Over here!"

"There you guys are!"

Nikki hurried across the room toward them, shaking her head. "Sorry I'm late! My Uber got lost. I think he's new here," she said, rolling her eyes.

"Dang, girl! You look amazing!" Addison cried, as she stared at Nikki. "Like... *wrrrao*!"

Nikki grinned, twirling. "I know, right? I feel amazing!"

"Nikki. Where have you been?" Sydney asked, crossing her arms in front of her. "None of us have heard from you in almost a week! You even had Billy worried."

"I needed to get away," Nikki said. "After we escaped the manor and dealing with the reporters, the cops... I needed a break. I went to Santa Clara for a few days."

"But you were supposed to stay in town!"

"And keep thinking about the damned manor?" Nikki snapped, her eyes flashing. "No thank you! I needed to get away. To refresh, and a few days at the spa was exactly what I needed."

"But..."

"Syd, let it go," Ashleigh said, sending her a glare. "We all have our ways of dealing. Don't ruin this by being bitchy."

"I'm not! I just think she should have let us know."

"All that matters is that we're alive, and together," Ashleigh told her.

"Exactly," Nikki said, gripping the handle of her black suitcase. "So, are we really doing this?"

"I think we have to," Ashleigh said, glancing around, nervously. "He's still out there," she whispered. "The cops never found him."

"I still don't understand how he cleared the manor out so fast," Sydney said, shaking her head in astonishment. "What was it? An hour after that cop found us when they stormed the manor? There was nothing there! No fingerprints. No pictures. No trophies. Nothing! It was like he vanished into thin air."

"And I bet none too happy that we escaped," Addison added.

They all shuddered, knowing exactly what she meant. He was out there, somewhere, and if he came for them, none of them would even know it. They had never seen his face.

"Which is why we need to go our desperate ways," Ashleigh finally said. "Just in case."

"I mean, I get why we're doing it," Nikki said. "But why are you staying in LA?" she asked, looking over at Ashleigh. "I don't like the idea of you staying here, Ash."

"Neither do I." Sydney said.

"Me neither!" Addison added. "I worry about you."

"Well, you guys need to stop," Ashleigh told them. "I am fine."

"Ash..."

Ashleigh held up a hand, stopping Addison's protest. "I am fine, and I am doing the best I can to move on with my life. Like you said it's going to take some time, but that maniac took six months of my life. That's six months of classes, six months of laughter, of crying, of living my life to the fullest, and I will be damned if he takes any more from me. I worked my ass off to get into UCLA. It has one of the best medical schools in the country, and I will be damned if he takes any more from me."

"But Ash..."

"Besides that, I just installed a new security system," Ashleigh continued, interrupting their protest. "And you see those two men over there?" She pointed to the two dark-haired men standing in the corner, flipping through their phones. "They're cops Billy assigned to watch over me until things blow over. I'm safe."

"Ash, I don't care if there's a hundred cops watching you or just one," Sydney told her. "If that psychopath wants you, he will find a way to get you. He was obsessed with you! Who knows what he'll do if..."

"Let's not even think like that," Ashleigh told her. "We have lives to live. Nikki! You're off to FSU. They have one of the best basketball programs in the country!"

"Not to mention all the boys," Nikki said, sighing, as she fanned herself. "I can just picture it now. Sitting on the beach, watching them surf, sweat glistening on their skin and only wearing..."

"Okay! Okay! We get it!" Addison cried, shaking her head. "But I get to go see the world!"

"You're finally going to get out and travel?" Ashleigh asked.

Addison smiled. "Yes. It's been a lifelong dream of mine, and after what happened, I decided now is the perfect time. It's not like I know what I'm going to do with my life anyways."

"And you, Syd?" Nikki looked over at Sydney. "Where are you going?"

"North Carolina," Sydney said, picking her bag off the floor and hefting it over her shoulder. "I applied to their psychology department last year and I found out I just got in."

"You're going to be a shrink?"

Sydney shrugged. "I haven't decided what I'm going to do with it yet, but I have options. Like all of us do."

"Damn right we do!"

"Now boarding flight 403 for Charlotte, North Carolina."

The intercom blared overhead, and Sydney sighed, gripping the handle of her duffel bag tightly as she glanced at her friends. "Well, that's me." She turned, then stopped, turning to look back at them. "We'll see one another again, right?"

"Of course!

"And it won't be like the last time?" Sydney asked, reminding them of the last time they'd gone their separate ways. It was almost ten years to the day. "It took us ten years to find one another again... and a psycho."

"We know, Syd," Nikki whispered, as the intercom sounded again.

"Now boarding flight 272, for Tallahassee, Florida."

"That's me." She stopped, glancing back at her friends. "Can we promise each other something?" she asked, turning to look at each of her friends in turn.

"Promise what?" Addison asked.

"That we won't lose touch," Sydney said.

"And when this is all over, and that bastard is behind bars, we meet right back here," Nikki said. "In this exact spot."

"And that we will always be friends," Addison added. "No matter where we are."

"I like that," Ashleigh nodded. "To being friends... always."

"To being friends!" Sydney held up her pinky. "Pinky swear?"

"Seriously?" Nikki raised a brow at her. "Sydney! We haven't pinky sworn since we were in the second grade!"

"Humor me, will you?"

Nikki sighed but extended her pinky. The four of them linked their pinkies together.

"To being friends," Sydney said. "During the good times. The bad times, and of course, the ugly times."

"And that this isn't goodbye," Addison added. "It's a see you later, because we're linked together. What that madman put us through, it bonded us and we will always be there for one another." She glanced around at her friends. "Do you swear to always be there for one another?"

"I swear!"

They uttered the words in unison, and again, the intercom sounded.

"Now boarding flight 109, for Phoenix, Arizona."

"Well, that's me," Addison stopped, gripping her bag. She glanced over her shoulder at them. "Video chat tonight?"

"Absolutely!"

"And Ash. Please watch yourself," Sydney said, sending her a look. "We all care about you."

"Yes, I know, and I will. Now please, will you go!" Ashleigh cried, shooing them away. "I do not want you missing your flights. Bye! I love you!"

"And we love you!"

They turned, disappearing through the crowd, and Ashleigh wrapped her arms around herself, watching as they went off in separate directions. She sniffed, wiping a tear from her cheek. God, she was going to miss them.

She turned, making her way through the airport, and she suddenly stopped. She turned, glancing around her. She had the strangest feeling. Like someone was watching her.

She shook her head. She was just being paranoid. She turned, making her way toward the doors, and her phone beeped. She glanced down. It was Billy.

Sorry, Ash. The department pulled the guys I had watching you. We just can't afford it. Please, if anything weird happens, let me know right away.

She sighed, scrolling through her phone and ordering an Uber. She should have known his protection wouldn't last long. She knew they were understaffed, and the last thing she wanted was to make things harder for Billy.

She walked through the doors, stepping out into the warm, California day, and her phone beeped. Her Uber was here.

"Wow! That was fast," she said, as she slid into the back seat.

"You're in LA. We move at the speed of light, plus the airport is the easiest place to get a ride-share." The young, dark-haired man said, turning in his seat, and his eyes suddenly widened. "Whoa. It's you!"

"You mean the girl who was missing for six months? Yup, that's me."

"Sorry, I didn't mean to stare. It's just, you're all over the news!"

"Yeah. I know. It gets a little tiresome," Ashleigh murmured. "So, can you take me to UCLA?"

"Oh! Of course!" He turned his attention back to the road. "You're going back to class?"

"Starting tomorrow."

"That's a little fast, isn't it?"

"I need to get back to my life. I can't hide forever."

"I suppose that's true. I hope everything works out for you, Ashleigh."

"Thank you."

They hit the freeway, and Ashleigh turned to look out the window, suddenly not being able to shake the feeling she was being watched. As much as she'd tried to put on a brave face for her friends, the truth of the matter was, she was scared. She was scared of being alone. She was scared of moving on, but more than that, she was scared that he was going to come for her.

And if he did, would she be able to protect herself this time?

They had no idea what was to come.

He watched them from the other side of the airport, silently chuckling as they stood there, trying to look all tough... but he knew better. All four of them were scared shitless.

For years, he had done his homework on them. He had followed them, gotten to know every little detail about them, and when he'd been ready to take them, he'd known just how each one of them ticked. Now, he knew even more, and because of his time with them in the manor, he knew what scared each of them. He just needed to start with one.

Ashleigh.

He stared across the room at her, his blood pumping as he stared at his beautiful sex doll. Of all his dolls, she had been his favorite. The things he'd done to her... the torment she had endured at his hands... the way she'd pleased him... it hadn't been enough. He wanted more. He needed more. He needed her to be his again, and she would be. Soon. All of them would, and where one fell, the rest would surely follow.

But first, he had a few loose ends to tie up.

He lifted his phone, scrolling through the social media app before stopping on a picture of two young girls.

"You will do just nicely," he said, chuckling, as a grin spread over his lips. "You're perfect for what I have planned, and soon, this damned city will know just who The Clown really is."

Chapter Four

"Go Tigers!"

"And to an undefeated season!"

They clinked their glasses together, throwing the shots back, and Ryan Eisenhower shook his head as the tequila burned the back of his throat. He raised a brow, glancing over at Roman Butler, one of the wide receivers for the football team, who was sitting across from him.

"Undefeated? Rome, it's preseason! Don't jinx us!"

Rome grinned, showing his perfectly white teeth. "Ryan! You know I don't believe in jinxes. Plus, this is the first preseason we've ever had. You know what that means?"

"What's that?"

"More football for us!"

"Yeah!"

Hoots wet up around the table, and Ryan shook his head, tossing back another shot. He grinned, as he looked over at

Rome. Rome was one of his oldest friends, and never failed to crack him up. His optimism was off the hook, and on the field, he never held back. He talked smack constantly. It got the whole team fired up. Even him.

But as he stared around at his teammates, Ryan couldn't deny that this year felt different. He'd been the starting quarterback for the Tigers for two years now, and even though he'd loved every squad, this team, this group of guys... it just felt right. Like maybe, this could be their year, and just maybe, they could finally bring home that trophy that had been eluding the school for the last twenty years. Lord knew, the city could use some good karma.

"You tell him, Rome!" Devante Harris came up behind Ryan, grabbing him by the shoulders and giving him a shake. "We kicked ass this preseason!" He grinned at Ryan. "And with Ry-Ice under center, we know we always have a chance at that trophy!"

"Hell yeah!"

"Would you stop calling me that?" Ryan asked grumpily, shoving Devante off of him. "I hate that damned nickname."

Devante chuckled, his long dreads swaying loosely. "Oh, Ryan, give it up. You're stuck with the name."

And boy, did he know it, Ryan thought, as he took another shot, thinking back to his sophomore year. He'd only been the backup quarterback back then, envious that all the other guys were getting their shot, when the starting quarterback, Matt Carver, had gone down with an ACL tear. He'd been thrown into the game with barely any practice, and somehow, had led the team to victory. After that, with Matt being out indefinitely, he'd been named the starter and he'd been the starter ever since.

"I don't even understand how I got that damned nickname in the first place."

"Seriously?" Jacob Reynolds, one of the other wide receivers for the team grinned at him, his green eyes gleaming with mischief. He tossed back another shot, flipping his long, blonde hair as he turned to wink at the redhead sitting in his lap. "Wanna hear the story of how Ryan got his nickname, babe?"

The girl smiled at him, running her finger down the center of his chest. "I'll listen to anything you want, baby," she purred.

Jacob grinned, while everyone else rolled their eyes.

Fucking player, Ryan thought, inwardly groaning. He loved Jacob, but man, was he a player. He had a different girl every night.

"So, it was sophomore year," Jacob said, as he poured himself a drink, bringing the cup to his lips. "It was, what? Ryan's third game as a starter?"

"Fourth," Devante told him, holding up four fingers. "You know, if you're going to tell the story, shouldn't you be able to tell it correctly?"

Hoots went up around the table.

"Anyways," Jacob said, glaring at Devante. "It was the fourth quarter. We were down thirty-one to twenty-eight, and there was what? Forty-two seconds left on the clock?"

"Something like that."

"Anyways, the ball snapped, and there are all these guys breaking through the line, heading for Ryan. He didn't even blink. He swerved around all of them and threw a forty-yard pass right to the end zone. Steven Ross, a senior here at the time caught it, and scored the winning touchdown. I tell you, cool as ice! He didn't even break a sweat!"

"A hell of a throw!" Devante shouted. "And that was just the beginning. Ryan here, is a star. He's broken just about every passing record at this school. Most passing yards, most passing touchdowns, the pros are going to be lucky to have him next year."

"Damn, Dev. Maybe you should be my PR rep," Ryan muttered, as he took a sip of his drink.

"Only if you pay me, really, really well," Devante told him with a wink.

Hoots went up around the table.

"You know, he had the chance to declare for the draft this year," Rome said, throwing his arm around a young woman who was standing near him.

"I never did understand why he chose to stay," Levi, one of the other wide receivers for the team put in. He muttered something Italian under his breath to a young woman walking by that no one paid any attention to, before continuing. "I mean, it's the dream! To go to the draft. To be selected. To have the chance to be the best. We all dream about it. Why'd you decide to stay?"

Ryan smiled, shrugging, as he took another sip from his drink. "What can I say? I just couldn't tear myself from all of you boneheads yet."

"Boneheads?"

"Who you calling a bonehead?"

"He's lying," Jacob said, staring across the table at him, again.

"It's because he's scared."

Marcus Dillon, one of the pass rushers for the Tigers walked up. He leaned over, snagging a drink from the table, and brought it to his lips. "I mean, what if he finds out he's not any good?"

"Uh-oh."

"Here we go."

Ryan just smiled, glancing over at the six-foot-nine, two-hundred-and-fifty-pound linebacker. "You sound jealous, Marcus."

"Why would I be jealous?"

"Well, because I'll most likely be going in the first round, and you... well, you'll be lucky if you go in the sixth round at the earliest."

Marcus's dark eyes flashed. "Lies! You know damn well I'll be going in the first round. I am the best defensive player in the class!"

Bullshit, Ryan thought, though he didn't say the words. There was no sense in getting Marcus more riled up then he already was. Lord knew, when Marcus got worked up, nothing good ever happened. The man had a temper, was self-centered, cocky, and they all knew there were better choices the pros could go with. Players, who hadn't violated the drug policy, and players, who didn't have a couple restraining orders against them.

He just shrugged. "Guess we'll just have to wait and see. One thing I do know is that we're stuck together for one more year, and I really want to win a championship!"

"Yeah!"

"Me too!"

"Let's do this!"

"Ryan."

Jacob stared at him from the other side of the table. "You still have something to explain."

"Oh. Right. You want to know why I stayed." Ryan leaned forward, tracing the tip of his finger around the rim of the cup. "The truth is, I stayed, because I thought it was important to work on the mechanics a little longer. Every pro quarterback I have talked to in the league, has advised me to wait. That the transition from college to the pros isn't always the easiest, or the smoothest. Plus," he grinned, glancing at the men around him. "If we win the championship this year, I'd be projected to go as the overall number one pick. Now, what could be better than that?"

"Right on!"

"Let's do it!"

"Let's win a championship!"

They clinked their glasses together, and then, silence suddenly descended over the house. Next to him, Marcus let out a long whistle.

"Whooee! Look at who just walked through the door."

"Who?"

Ryan swiveled in his chair, his eyes widening when he caught sight of the young blonde as she made her way through the crowd.

"Holy shit."

"Is that..."

"Ashleigh Carlson," Ryan said, nodding, as he glanced around the table. They all knew who she was. It was hard not to, considering her face was plastered all over the news.

"What is she doing here?"

"It's an open party, Rome. She's invited, just like everyone else."

"Yeah, but..."

But it was the first time anyone had seen her since she'd been kidnapped, Ryan thought, knowing exactly what Rome was trying to say.

"You know, I heard she was used as some sort of sex slave," Marcus said, his dark eyes gleaming as he took another sip from his drink. "I bet she's into all kinds of kinky stuff."

"Don't even think about it, Marcus." Ryan sent him a warning look. "She is not one of those girls you get to use then toss to the side. She deserves better than that. Especially after all she's been through, and I promise you. If you lay one hand on her, I will toss you across this room so fast, you won't be able to move for a week."

"You threatening me, Ryan?"

"Not at all. Let's just call it a friendly warning," Ryan said, flashing him a smile.

"You sound like her fucking bodyguard."

"Yeah, Ryan. Why do you care so much?"

Ryan glanced at Levi, then at the rest of his teammates who were staring at him in confusion. He shrugged, tossing back the last of his drink and setting the cup on the table. He twirled it around in his hands. "I don't. Not really. I just think she's been through enough is all."

"You're getting soft, Ryan."

He sent Devante a look. "I absolutely am not getting soft."

"He has been different ever since he dumped Kenzie," Levi muttered.

"Did he dump her? I thought she dumped him?"

"Oh my God. Will you guys stop!" Ryan reached into the bowl laying in front of him and tossed a handful of chips their way. "You sound like a bunch of gossiping old grannies!"

"We do not!"

"You absolutely do," Ryan informed them. "And I will say it again. I have not changed. I am still the same Ryan you have known for the last three years."

"Ah, Ryan, I hate to burst your bubble, but you have definitely changed," Jacob chuckled, ducking, as a fistful of chips came flying his way. "We all have. None of us are the same people we were when we first came here. Well except... Ah crud."

"What?"

"Looks like Kenzie just made her presence known," Jacob said, nodding to the petite blonde making her way through the crowd. "And she's making a beeline for Ashleigh."

"Please. Kenzie is harmless," Ryan said, waving his hand dismissively. "I mean, yeah, she might be..."

"Crazy?"

"Delusional?

"Narcissistic?"

"I was going to say, set in her own ways," Ryan told them. "Besides, she and Ashleigh grew up together. I'm sure they have some catching up to do." He glanced across the room, and froze, when he noticed the spot Marcus had been standing in just moments before, now empty.

"Ah, guys? Does anyone know where..."

"Where Marcus went?" Rome nodded toward the center of the room. "I'll give you two guesses, but my guess is you're only going to need one."

The bastard, Ryan picked up the drink on the table, and downed it. He stared across the room at Marcus as he made his way toward Ashleigh.

It looked like things were about to get interesting around here, and not in a good way.

This damned city was getting scarier and scarier by the moment, M.J. Hockenson thought, as she flipped through the television. Every, single channel was covering the story on the Dollhouse.

She stopped, staring at the image of the four women as it filled the screen, feeling sick to her stomach at what they had gone through. She'd had classes with them. She knew them!

The thought that this could happen to people she knew... it was more surreal than she could have ever imagined.

Ring! Ring!

Her phone jingled next to her, and she screamed. She jumped, glancing down, as Tracey Gilmore's face flashed across the screen.

"Good God, Tracey. You nearly gave me a heart attack!" M.J. cried, holding the phone to her ear. "I was just watching the coverage on the dollhouse investigation. Can you believe that's what they're calling it? Hell, I could come up with something better than that!"

"You know how cops are, M.J. They are not very creative," Tracey said into the phone. "But, you know, if you were here instead of in that boring house of yours, you wouldn't be thinking about that. I thought you said you were coming."

"To the party? Hell no!" M.J. cried, as she rose from the couch and walked toward the kitchen. She switched the call to speaker, ruffling through the cupboards, before pulling a bag of popcorn out. "You do realize that man is still out here, right?"

"The clown? Oh please! I'm sure he's long gone by now."

"I wouldn't be so sure of that. He spent a lot of time stalking those girls before making his move, and I bet you, he's still in this city. Just waiting to make his next move." She placed the popcorn in the microwave and pressed the button.

"You're being paranoid."

"No. I'm doing everything I can to stay alive," M.J said, leaning against the counter. "How's the party?"

"Boring. There hasn't been a single fight! No one's gotten completely drunk, and... oh my God."

"What? What is it?"

"You will never believe who just walked through the doors."

"If you tell me Justin..."

"No! Ashleigh. Ashleigh's here, M.J!"

"What?" the microwave beeped behind her, and M.J grabbed the bag. She yelped, the heat burning her, as the bag slipped from her fingers and fell to the floor. "You are making that up!"

"No! Look!"

Tracey switched the call to video, and M.J stared at Ashleigh, as she made her way through the crowded house. "Oh my God. I can't believe she's there! If I were her, I'd be locking myself inside my house, determined to never come out, ever again."

"So, does that mean you'll come now?"

"I..."

"Oh come on. Live a little!"

"Tracey..." the phone beeped, and M.J glanced down as another call came in. "Hey, Tracey, I'm going to have to call you back. Aimee's calling."

"Why am I not surprised." Tracey rolled her eyes. "Just ignore it, M.J. Your sister is never going to learn to stand on her own two feet if you keep bailing her out."

"She's my sister! I can't just turn my back on her."

"I didn't say turn your back on her. I'm just saying..."

"I can't listen to this right now. I'll call you back in a bit. Bye, Tracey!"

"M.J..."

"Aimee?" M.J. switched lines. "Everything ok?"

"No," Aimee said, her voice shaking. "M.J. I... I was in an accident. My car, it's totaled pretty badly, and I hurt my ankle. I think it's broken. Can you... can you come and get me?"

"Did you call the police?"

"Yes. They're here now, and they're towing the car. I... I don't want to go to the hospital. M.J, please..."

M.J sighed. "Ok. Fine. Where are you?"

"Over on Redwood Lane. You know, over by that old farmhouse?"

"Yeah. I know where it is. Hang tight. I'll be there soon."

M.J. hung up and grabbed her keys off the counter. She headed for the door, locking it behind her and made her way across the lawn. She pushed the button, the lights of the gray SUV flashing in the darkness and slid inside.

She dropped the keys into the cup holder next to her, followed by her phone, and pressed the button. The ignition roared to life and she reached for her seatbelt. It clicked into place, and she turned on the headlights, stopping, when she saw Aimee's car sitting in the driveway in front of her, undamaged.

What the...

"Hello, M.J."

She jumped, a scream ripping from her throat, as she swung her head around. She gasped, her eyes widening in horror when she saw the man sitting in her back seat. He leaned forward, his pale, white face glowing in the darkness, the locks from his green and blue wig falling over his forehead, as a sinister grin crossed his bright, red lips. It was the clown.

"What... what do you want?" M.J asked, as she reached for her seatbelt. She pressed the button, swearing silently when it stuck. She gave it another tug. Still stuck.

"Isn't it obvious, M.J?" The clown asked, raising his knife and running a gloved finger along the blade. "I'm here to kill you." He lunged forward.

M.J screamed. She dodged to the left, the knife whizzing past her ear, and striking the wheel. The horn blared loudly in the silence of the night, as she struggled to get her seatbelt loose. It finally came loose, and she reached for the door.

A hand wrapped around her throat, jerking her back. She gasped, wincing, as her head hit the back of the seat hard.

"I've been looking for someone like you, for a very, very long time," the clown said, as he jerked the knife free from the wheel, tracing it along the side of her face. "Someone with your name... someone who can help me make all of them remember."

"Rem... remember what?" M.J asked. She glanced to her right and reached for the book lying on the seat next to her.

"Oh, you don't need to worry about that. You won't be alive to know about it."

"I beg to differ," M.J said, grabbing the book and swinging it back. It hit the clown, hard, in the head. He startled, jerking back, the knife lowering and M.J took advantage of the moment. She shoved the door open, jumping out of the car and racing across the lawn.

"Get back here!"

She glanced over her shoulder, as the clown raced after her, and she slid to a stop in front of the door. She reached for it, turning the knob.

It was locked.

Shit.

Her keys. They were...

She froze, glancing back toward the car. Crap! She'd left them in the car!

She turned, and screamed, as the clown raced forward. She ducked, dodging the knife. It struck the window behind her, the glass shattering, and she swerved around him. She grabbed the pot of daffodils sitting by the door, tossing it at the clown. "Leave me alone!"

She turned, racing around the corner of the house, sliding to a stop when she saw her sister, Aimee, tied to the tree a few feet away. "Aimee!" She raced forward, ripping the tape from her mouth.

"M.J!" Aimee gasped out. "I am so sorry! He ambushed me when I got home. He made me call you!"

"It's okay. Just, let's get you down from here." M.J quickly undid the knot, the rope falling free. "Come on! We need to get to the back door. We need to get to the spare key and call the police."

"Don't you have your phone?"

M.J shook her head. "No. I left it in the car. Come on. I don't..."

"M.J, look out!"

She swung around, just as the clown raced forward, lunging toward her. The knife struck forward, and she stumbled back, falling to the ground. She scrambled back, staring up at him.

"Leave us alone, you freak!"

Rocks suddenly flew in the air, striking the clown.

"Agh!"

The clown stumbled back, shielding his face with his hands, and M.J spun around, staring at Aimee as she slung rocks at the clown. She jumped to her feet, grabbing Aimee by the arm, and dragging her across the lawn. "Aimee! You just saved my life!"

"What else was I going to do?" Aimee asked, as they raced across the lawn. They passed the pool and rounded the corner. They slid to a stop, and M.J peered around the corner as Aimee raced for the pot of daffodils lying near the door "Hurry! Get the key!"

"I'm trying," Aimee said, as she dug in the pot. "I... I... I got it!" she cried, as her fingers wrapped around the key. She pulled it out of the pot and stuck it in the lock. It clicked, and she blew out a sigh of relief as she shoved the door open. "Come on!"

They raced into the house, slamming the door shut behind them, and M.J sprinted across the room. She grabbed the tablet sitting on the table.

"911, what's your emergency?"

"Please. We need help. He's going to kill us!"

"Who's going to kill you?"

"I don't know. Some man... Please. Help us. He's going to kill us! He... he's dressed like a clown. Aimee, watch out!" she screamed, the tablet slipping and falling from her hands as the clown appeared behind Aimee.

Aimee turned, and she gasped, as the knife struck forward. It struck her through the midsection, and she gasped, falling to her knees.

"Why?" she asked, staring up at him, then down at the blood rushing out of her body.

"Because, you were chosen," the clown said, as he jerked her to her feet, and slit the knife across her throat. "And the message."

He tossed her to the side, glancing at M.J. "One down. One more to go."

"No! Aimee!" M.J stared at Aimee's lifeless body, then at the clown. He started toward her, and she turned, racing across the room. She grabbed a chair, tossing it at him, turning, and disappearing into the kitchen.

She rounded the island, grabbing the knife out of the block. She held it tightly in her hands, closing her eyes, tears rolling down her cheeks. *Please. Please. Just leave me alone!*

"M.J..."

Her eyes jerked open. She stared at the empty doorway, slowly rounding the island. She peered out into the living room, looking to her right, then looking to her left. No one was there.

Where the hell did he go?

She gripped the knife tighter in her hands, backing up a step, and froze, when she collided with a hard body. *No.*

She glanced behind her, a scream ripping from her throat when she found herself staring into the dark, cold eyes of the clown.

"Found ya," the clown said, a smile spreading across his red lips, as he raised his knife.

"No!"

M.J dodged the blade and raised the knife she was holding. She struck it forward.

"Now, now, M.J, is that any way to treat your guest?" the clown asked, capturing her wrist in his hand, and slamming it hard against the wall.

M.J screamed. She doubled over in pain, falling to the floor. The knife fell to the floor, sliding underneath the refrigerator, and she scrambled back. "You're not a guest. You're a monster!" she cried, as she held her throbbing wrist to her chest.

The clown laughed, shaking his head. "Oh, M.J, the things you still don't know."

He strode toward her, and M.J scrambled backward. Her back slammed back against the wall, and she froze, staring up at him as he dangled the knife in his hand.

"Looks like you ran out of room, M.J," the clown said, laughing. He raised his knife. "Bye. Bye. M.J."

He struck the knife forward, and M.J brought up her knee, striking him hard in the groin. He screamed, and she rolled underneath him. She jumped to her feet, racing out of the kitchen, and around Aimee's body. She held a hand over her mouth, trying not to sob, and raced for the stairs.

"Ahh!"

She screamed, as a hand grabbed her hair, jerking her back.

"You think I came all the way over here to let you escape, M.J?" the clown asked, chuckling once more. "Oh, M.J, you're not getting away from me." He raised his knife, trailing it down the side of her cheek, then he raised it, thrusting it into her chest.

M.J gasped. She stumbled, falling to the ground, staring up at him. "Please. Don't..."

"What? Kill you?" the clown asked, as he yanked the knife from her chest. "Now, what kind of fun would that be?"

Chapter Five

This was such a bad idea, Ashleigh thought as she stepped from the car. She slammed the door shut, turning, and gazing across the lawn at the luxurious, wooden, stoned house. *A very, very, very bad idea.*

This was not how she had expected her day to end. She'd had a plan. She was going to go to campus, talk to her instructors and get everything settled before diving back into her classes tomorrow. Then she was going to go home, curl up on the couch with a pint of Chunky Monkey, and watch the latest chick flick.

She had not expected to find herself at Jacob Reynold's house.

Jacob Reynolds. She'd never met the guy personally, but most of the girls at the college were head over heels for him. Not that she could blame them. He was drop dead gorgeous and was also considered one of the best receivers to come up in years. He was even being compared to the likes of Jerry Rice. Now, that was saying something.

She started across the lawn, and her foot kicked a red cup lying in the grass. She lowered her eyes, gazing across the lawn at the cups and beer bottles scattered across the lawn. *College kids really did have a knack for littering,* she thought, as she strode past a young couple making out on a nearby bench. She passed a couple of girls, smoking under a tree, and a group of guys drinking as they chatted about. All of them stopped to stare at her as she passed.

"Don't mind me," Ashleigh muttered under her breath, ducking her head as she walked past. "I'm just trying to get my life *back*."

She hated the stares, hated the whispers, but unfortunately it was what she was going to have to deal with until something else happened in this damned city.

I shouldn't be here. I should leave, now, while I have the chance.

But she was already here. She might as well make the most of it.

She clutched the wooden banister, making her way up the staircase. Each step she took, she felt dread washing over her. What if something bad happened while she was here?

Don't think like that.

Right. Be positive.

She blew out a breath and shoved the french doors open. Immediately, laughter filled the air. Music blared from the speakers, the latest pop song filling her ears, as she stepped inside, staring at the dozens of people inside.

There were football players everywhere! A group of them were sitting at the table in the dining room, laughing, as they knocked back shots. They'd just finished their preseason, from what she understood.

She took another step forward, pushing her way through the crowd. Men and women were dancing throughout the room. Some were making out. Some were talking, and then, silence descended upon the house as everyone turned to stare at her.

Well, I guess I know who the talk of the party is going to be.

"Addy!"

She frowned, turning, spotting a petite, young blonde as she pushed her way through the crowd toward her.

"Ah, I'm not Addy, Kenzie," Ashleigh said, crossing her arms in front of her chest, as she regarded Mackenzie Sinclair. "You know who I am. We grew up next door to one another!"

"Right. Right. Of course." Kenzie waved a hand, as if it weren't important. "But, Ashleigh, what are you doing here? I haven't seen you in like... forever!"

"Well, that does tend to happen when you're kidnapped by a psycho and held hostage for half a year."

"Yes. I heard!" Kenzie held a hand to her chest. "I am so sorry about what you went through. How are you?"

How was she? Now that was a loaded question.

Ashleigh regarded Kenzie. It had been years since she and Kenzie had talked. They'd been best friends once, but then she'd chosen the popularity crowd over their friendship. When she'd left, it had hurt. She'd been the only one of their group left.

Everyone else had moved away... and suddenly it had just been her. Why was Kenzie talking to her now?

"I'm doing just fine."

"I don't know how you do it," Kenzie said, shaking her head. "I mean, if it were me, I would be hibernating in my house with no intention of ever coming out! What happened to you... it's horrible!"

"Well, you know what they say," Ashleigh said, turning and snagging a drink from a nearby table. "You can't hide forever. Eventually, you need to get over your crap and move on with your life. Or something along those lines." She brought the drink to her lips. "I just want to get back to normal."

"Then, you should totally hang out with me!" Kenzie cried, linking her arm through Ashleigh's, and leading her through the crowd. "You stick with me, okay, Ashleigh? You hang with me and mine, you'll fit in again in no time!"

"I don't know..."

"Come on! Say yes... please? I want to make up for lost time."

Kenzie looked at her, giving her a pout, and Ashleigh sighed. "Fine. I'll go with you."

"Yay!"

Kenzie grinned, pulling her through the crowd. "Hey! Guess who I found?"

"Ashleigh! Oh my God!" Tanya Gunderson stepped forward, embracing Ashleigh in a tight hug. "I can't believe you're here!"

"Yeah. Me neither," Ashleigh said, sidestepping Tanya and bringing the drink to her lips. She took a small sip, regarding the tall, black-haired girl. She didn't know her very well, and she definitely did not want any hugs from her. "Hello, Tanya. It's good to see you. It's been a while."

"Yes. It has." Tanya said, shoving her hair out of her eyes, and pulling the black strands back into a ponytail. "Too long!"

"How are you?" Molly, a dark brunette asked, staring at her with wide eyes.

"Molly! Don't ask her that!" Sharon, another brunette cried, elbowing Molly. "It's rude!"

"No, it's fine. I get it. Everyone wants to know about me," Ashleigh said, wincing, and really wishing she were anywhere but here.

"But tonight isn't about you, remember?" Kenzie said, narrowing her eyes on Ashleigh, a smile spreading across her lips as a song filled the air. "Oh my God! I love this song! Come on. Let's dance!"

"No. I don't..."

"Oh, come on, Ashleigh! You need to let loose. Dance a little!"

Ashleigh finished off her drink, regarding Kenzie over the rim. She then glanced at the people around her. No one was paying any attention to her, and this was a party. What could it hurt?

"Oh, what the hell?"

She picked up another drink and joined Kenzie on the dance floor. She and the girls danced in the middle of the room, grinding their hips, as they moved to the rhythm of the song. Soon, Ashleigh found herself laughing, and enjoying herself. Something she hadn't done in a very, long time.

"You look like you're having fun."

Ashleigh startled, spinning around, looking up into the dark, steely eyes of Marcus Dillon. "Marcus."

"You know, I've been watching you," Marcus said, ducking his head and whispering in her ear. "You wanna get out of here? Have a private party... with me?"

"Ah. I don't think so," Ashleigh said, backing up a step, regarding Marcus. She'd never liked him. She'd heard the stories of how he treated the girls he was with, and to be honest, he really freaked her out. She definitely did not want to be alone with him.

"Ash, you should totally go with him!" Kenzie cried, her eyes glistening. "I mean, you said you wanted to get back to normal, right? And you know what I say... the quickest way to get back to normal is to get under someone else!"

"What she said. Come on!" Marcus linked his fingers with hers, dragging her through the crowd.

"Wait. Marcus. No!" Ashleigh gasped, as he pulled her through the crowd. She tried to pull her arm free, but he tightened his grip around her hand, and Ashleigh swallowed, turning to look around her, but no one was paying any attention. She was on her own.

"Come on."

Marcus dragged her into the bedroom, slamming the door shut. He pressed her up against the wall, boxing her in with his large body.

"Please. Marcus, let me go," Ashleigh whispered, panic starting to rise inside of her.

"Oh, come on, doll. You can't deny this, can you?" Marcus asked, grinning down at her. "I know you want it."

Doll.

Ashleigh froze at the word, her breath coming out fast and hard. That's what the clown had called her.

"Marcus. No! Please!" She shoved her hands against his chest, but he didn't listen. He didn't budge. Then, suddenly, it wasn't Marcus at all. It was the clown.

His face appeared before her. His face all white. His green and blue hair dangling and that red smile of his...

"You know you want it."

His lips scooped down, capturing her mouth. She tried to yell. She tried to scream, and then he was shoving her to the floor. His hands clamped down on her shoulders, and the sound of a zipper echoed in her ears.

"No! Please! I don't..."

"You know you want it, doll."

The clown's voice echoed in her ears.

"Go ahead, doll. Get on your knees. You know the way I like it."

She gasped, a cry escaping her lips, as tears rolled down her cheeks. "Please. Don't make me do this."

"But it's who you are," Marcus's face, and the clown's face blended into one. "You were his sex slave for a reason, Ashleigh. You pleased him. You did as he asked, without question. I only wish a woman would do that for me."

Ashleigh stared at him in disbelief, her vision focusing on Marcus once more. "You, bastard! I am not a sex slave, and I sure as hell am not someone you get to mock because of what some madman did to me. I did what I did, to save myself, and to keep my friends alive. I will never apologize for that." She shoved him out of the way, rising to her feet. "Never touch me again!" She turned, shoving past him.

"You think you can tell me no?" Marcus grabbed her by the shoulders, swinging her around, and slamming her against the wall. "No one tells me no... ever! Oomph!"

Ashleigh screamed. Her eyes widening, as hands grabbed Marcus by the shoulders, pulling him away from her. She slid to the floor, her head spinning and she jumped as a loud crash filled her ears. She spun around, wincing as her head pounded, stifling a gasp when she saw Marcus's body laying amongst the broken table on the other side of the room.

"Dammitt, Marcus. I told you to stay away from her!"

"Ryan! No!"

Running feet sounded, as four men raced into the room, placing themselves in between the man and Marcus.

"He's not worth it, Man!"

"He's drunk!"

"No, he's a jackass," Ryan said, shoving away the hands holding him back. "And it's about time someone put him in his place." He spun on his heel, striding across the room, and squatting in front of Ashleigh. "Ashleigh? Are you okay?"

"I... I think so," Ashleigh whispered, holding a hand to her head. "Oh man. I have a headache."

"Tends to happen when you drink," Ryan said, reaching forward.

Ashleigh jumped, jerking back from him.

"Hey. It's okay. You just have a bruise. He didn't hit you, did he?"

Ashleigh shook her head. "No. Those are from... before."

"Ryan!"

Marcus staggered to his feet, his eyes filled with fury, as he strode toward them.

"Marcus! Stop!" Jacob stepped in Marcus's path, blocking his way. "Walk it off, now, or God help me I will throw you out of this house and make you walk your ass home."

Marcus glared at Jacob, then his eyes connected with Ryan's. "We are not done. Not by a long shot," he said, before turning and walking out of the room.

"Whatever, Marcus." Ryan ignored him, turning his attention back to Ashleigh. "Come on, let's get you off of that floor," he said, extending a hand to her. "As much as I love Jacob, he does tend to throw a lot of parties here. Lord knows what's imbedded in that carpet from his many one-night stands."

"Hey!" Jacob glared at Ryan. "That is not..." he sighed, bowing his head. "Okay. Okay. That's fair."

Ashleigh giggled.

Ryan startled at the sound. He lifted his head, smiling. "Hey. I got a laugh!"

"Just a regular comedian, aren't you, Ryan?" Jacob muttered. "Asshole."

Ashleigh laughed again. She placed her hand in his, letting him pull her to her feet. "Thank you, Ryan," she whispered.

He started, his eyes widening. "You know who I am?"

"Come on, Ryan. You're the starting quarterback for the Tigers!" Ashleigh cried. "I'd be a fool not to know who you are. Especially, since, you are considered as one of the best."

Ryan blushed. "Well, thank you, ma'am. I'm honored you think of me that way." He dropped his hand, backing up a step. "You sure you're okay?"

"Yeah. He didn't get a chance to do anything," Ashleigh said, shivering, as she ran her hands up and down her arms.

"Here." Ryan shrugged out of his jacket, draping it over her shoulders. "Better?"

Ashleigh nodded. She pulled the jacket tighter around herself, the smell of his aftershave surrounding her. It smelt woodsy. Something between pine and cedar. She sighed, breathing in the scent, before looking up at him.

Ryan Eisenhower was an attractive man. Tall, tanned skin, and light brown hair that curled around the edges. He'd been the starting quarterback at UCLA ever since she could remember, and she'd always had a bit of a crush on him. Now, he'd just come to her rescue.

She shuddered, thinking of what might have happened if he hadn't intervened.

"Ashleigh? Everything okay?"

Ashleigh smiled, shaking her head as she looked at him. "You've asked me that like three times now. I'm fine. I just... I shouldn't have come here."

"Why did you? If you don't mind me asking?"

"Because I'm sick of everyone seeing me as the girl who got kidnapped," Ashleigh told him. "I miss being, just Ashleigh, you know? I just... I want to feel normal again."

"Well, I'd say you've had enough for one night," Ryan murmured. "Come on. Let me give you a ride home."

"What? No, Ryan, I can't ask you to do that! This is your party. I can't pull you away from it."

"I was just about done here anyways. Really, it's no big deal," Ryan told her, flashing her a grin. He reached into his pockets and sighed. "Crap. My keys. Can you give me a couple minutes, Ash?"

"Of course."

Ryan smiled, giving her hand a squeeze. "I'll be right back."

Jacob hung back, glancing at her from where he was hovering in the doorway. He stuffed his hands in his pockets, shifting restlessly. "Sorry you had to deal with this, Ashleigh," he said, softly. "If there's anything you need..."

"You can go with Ryan, Jacob. I'm fine, really."

Jacob smiled, bashfully, nodding, and hurried after Ryan.

"You do know that no matter how hard you try, you'll never be normal again, right?"

Ashleigh jumped, swinging her head around to stare at Marcus as he appeared behind her. "Marcus, if you came back to start something..."

"Please. I'm over that." Marcus waved a hand in the air. "Besides, a wounded bird like you could never handle someone like me. Let's face it, Ashleigh. You're weak. You're vulnerable, and no matter how hard you try, you will always be his."

"I'm not his."

"Except, you are. The moment he kidnapped you, the moment he forced you to do all those things, you became his, and no matter how hard you try, you will never be free of him. You're his, Ashleigh, and in the end... you'll die alone."

Chapter Six

"Ryan!"

"What?" Ryan glanced over his shoulder, frowning at Jacob, as he weaved his way through the crowd toward the kitchen. "I thought you were going to stay with Ashleigh. She shouldn't be alone right now."

"I know, and I was going to. I swear, but I just couldn't. She just looks... so sad!" Jacob sighed, running a hand over his face. "Ryan, I feel bad. What nearly happened to her, under my roof..."

"Is not your fault," Ryan told him. "You are not responsible for what Marcus does. At some point, he has to take responsibility for his own actions."

"I don't see that happening anytime soon," Jacob muttered. "But, damn, Ryan! You threw him into a freaking table! It was awesome, but you do know he's not going to let this go, right? He's going to retaliate. He always does."

"I don't give a shit what he decides to do," Ryan told him, as he stepped behind the marbled island. "He had it coming to him, and if he does decide to come after me, I will be all too happy to knock him on his ass again." He rustled through the papers on the counter. "Dammitt. Where the hell are my keys?"

"Did you check your pockets?"

"Of course I checked my pockets!" Ryan snapped, glaring at Jacob. "You were right there!"

"Oh. Right." Jacob grinned, leaning against the counter and fiddling with the papers. He gazed across the room. "Ah, shit."

"What?"

"Satan spotted us. She's on her way over here."

Ryan inwardly groaned, not even needing to look to see who Jacob was talking about. Kenzie was the only one Jacob ever called Satan.

"Of course she is. She has impeccable timing," Ryan muttered, glancing at Jacob. "Any chance I can talk you into distracting her for me?"

"Oh, hell no!" Jacob cried, snagging a cup off the counter, and bringing it to his lips. "I'm not getting within two feet of that woman. See you later, Ry."

"Coward!" Ryan shouted after him.

Jacob smiled, flipping him the finger, before disappearing through the crowd.

Ryan laughed, rolling his eyes, before rustling through the cabinets. Dammit, where were his keys? They had to be here somewhere.

"Hey, Ryan."

Kenzie leaned against the counter, flashing him a bright smile, as she reached a manicured hand forward. She traced a finger down his arm. "I was hoping I'd run into you."

"Well, you were bound to run into me," Ryan said, removing her hand and continuing around the kitchen. "I mean, this is a party to celebrate the football team, and I am on the football team."

"Oh, come on, Ryan. Don't be like that. I miss you," Kenzie said, placing herself in front of him. "And I was hoping we could talk about things." She reached down, lacing her fingers with his.

"Kenzie, please, will you stop?" Ryan asked, jerking his hand away. "I need to find my keys."

"Why? Where are you going?" Kenzie narrowed her eyes on him. "And where is your jacket?"

"I gave it to Ashleigh."

"You what?" Kenzie's eyes flashed. "Why?"

"Because she's had a rough night, and I'm going to give her a ride home."

"But... but you're supposed to leave with me! That was the plan. We were supposed to bump into one another here, make up, and get back together!"

Ryan chuckled, shaking his head. "Kenzie, you had to know that wasn't going to happen. I told you. We're done."

"But we were good together!"

"No, we weren't," Ryan told her. "And you know that, too. Now, please, will you move? I need to find my keys."

Kenzie pouted, crossing her arms in front of her chest. "Yes. You said that. I just don't understand what happened. She and Marcus..."

"Wait. What?" Ryan whipped his head around. "You knew she was with Marcus?"

"Well, it was kind of my idea. She said she wanted to get back to normal, and she and Marcus had this crazy vibe! Really, I didn't see the harm."

"You didn't see the harm?" Ryan ran a hand over his face. "Kenzie, you know who Marcus is. What he's like. Hell, you know what Ashleigh's been through. You and she used to be friends! Did you think of any of that before letting him take off with her?"

Kenzie shuffled her feet. "I was just trying to help, Ryan."

"No. You wanted to get her out of the way, so you could be the center of attention. It's all you ever want. You forget I know you, Kenzie, and to be honest, I don't understand you. You're not at all the girl I used to know."

Kenzie scowled. "Don't be a jackass, Ryan."

"I'm not. I'm just telling you the truth. Something, apparently everyone else is afraid to do." Ryan sighed. "I'm not finding my keys. I guess I'll see if I can borrow Rome's car." He turned, making his way through the crowd.

"Oh, Ryan. Are these what you were looking for?"

He sighed, turning to glance over his shoulder at Kenzie, as she held up a set of keys in her hand.

"Really, Kenzie? You knew I was looking for those!" Ryan strode forward, snatching them from her fingers. "See, this is what I'm talking about, and this, is the reason we are no longer together."

"Oh, Ryan, come on. You know you want me," Kenzie said, pressing herself up against him. "You know I was the best you ever had."

"Go sober up, Kenzie," Ryan said, stepping away from her. "You're drunk, and you do stupid things when you're drunk." He turned away.

"Ryan?"

He glanced up as Ashleigh walked into the kitchen. "Hey, Ash. Sorry. I just found my keys. They were... hiding on me." He gave Kenzie a look.

"It's fine. I just... I thought maybe you'd changed your mind."

"No. Of course not. You ready?"

"More than you would ever know."

Ryan frowned, glancing at her, then behind her at Marcus, who was watching them from the other side of the room. "Ash, did something happen? Did Marcus do something?"

"Oh, I'm sure he did. It is Marcus," Kenzie said from behind him. She narrowed her eyes at Ashleigh. "You know, I really don't understand you, Ashleigh. Like, what did I ever do to you?"

Ashleigh glanced at Kenzie. "I'm sorry?"

"I mean, all these guys. Do you really need all of them? Marcus. Ryan. I know Sean broke up with you in the hospital and all, but do you really need to hog them all? Didn't you get enough attention when you were taken hostage?"

"Kenzie!"

Ashleigh sucked in a breath, staring at Kenzie. "You did not just say that!" She narrowed her eyes at Kenzie. "So much for making up for lost time, you, Kenzie, are still the heartless bitch who turned your back on me when you were the only friend I had left, and to think I thought you might have changed." She glanced at Ryan. "Let's get the hell out of here."

Ryan nodded, turning, and following her through the crowd toward the door.

"Ryan! Ashleigh! Wait!" Rome broke through the crowd, hurrying toward them. "You can't leave yet!"

"Rome, now's not really the time," Ryan said, glancing over at his teammate. "I need to get Ashleigh home."

"No. Not yet. There's something you need to see."

"Rome."

"I'm serious. Just, come here." He gestured them forward, and Ryan glanced at Ashleigh.

She shrugged. "I guess it's important?"

They followed Rome to the other side of the room, stopping amongst the crowd that had gathered around the TV.

"It's been a somber night here in Los Angeles," the anchorwoman was saying into the microphone. "As just a couple hours ago, two local college students were found slain to death inside their home, only leaving this behind." She held up a package of a clown mask. "Just who is this clown killer? And just when is he going to strike next?"

Chapter Seven

This was a goddamn, fucking nightmare.

Detective Billy Turner stepped inside the two story, Victorian house on Mulberry Lane, running a hand across his face as he stepped through the doorway. He paused, glancing around the room at the carnage before him, the scene making his stomach churn. *God damn. I knew something was going to happen.* He'd had a feeling in his gut for the last two weeks. Ever since the girls had been found, and boy, had he been right.

Just twenty minutes ago, they'd gotten the 911 call that had chilled everyone to the very core.

"Please, hurry. He's going to kill us. He... he's dressed like a clown."

The voice of the young woman who had called, echoed in his head. He clenched his eyes shut, knowing they'd gotten here as fast as they could, but it hadn't been in time. They were dead. Two young lives lost, because of one deranged psycho.

He snapped his eyes open, staring around the room at the blood that was splattered on the wall behind him. At the blood that was on the banister leading up the stairs, the broken window just to his left, and finally, the two women who lay motionless in the middle of the room. Blood pooled from their bodies as they lay there, with lifeless eyes staring at him.

"It looks like a scene right out of a horror movie, doesn't it?" A police officer asked as he passed him. "And he wore a clown mask. Do you think..."

"I'm not sure of anything anymore," Billy told the officer. "But one thing I do know is that two young women just lost their lives, for no reason, and I will find the person responsible for it." He may be one of the youngest detectives on the force, but he had already seen his share of dead bodies, and he always gave a hundred and ten percent to his investigations.

"Hey, Detective?"

"What is it?" he asked, glancing up as another officer approached.

"Ah, well there's someone here to see you," the officer said, shuffling his feet, and Billy inwardly chuckled. Why was it that all the officers at the precinct seemed nervous around him? Did he really have that bad of a reputation?

"Now?" Billy asked, arching an eyebrow at the officer. "Officer..." he glanced at the name on his uniform, hell, he didn't know who the kid was. "Officer Monroe," he finally said, turning and gesturing to the dead bodies behind him. "I am in the middle of a homicide investigation. Can't this wait?"

"Unfortunately, no. It can't," a young, blonde-haired man with a goatee interjected, as he crossed the room toward them.

Billy glanced at the man, then over to the officer. "You let him in here? Officer! This is a crime scene!"

"Uh. I'm gonna go." Officer Monroe ducked his head, turned, and raced off.

Billy sighed, shaking his head, as he turned toward the man. "Uh, sir, I'm not sure who you think you are, but you can't be here. This is an active crime scene."

"I'm well aware of that, Detective." The man told him with a smirk. "And I'm just as qualified to be here as you are." He held up his badge. "I'm Detective Andrew Stark. Your new partner."

"New partner?" Billy laughed. "Detective Stark, I think you've been misinformed. I didn't request a new partner, and besides, I work better alone."

"Yes. I've heard that," Detective Stark said, chuckling. "You have quite the reputation, Detective Turner. Despite how young you are."

"You don't look much older than me, Detective," Billy cut in.

Detective Stark chuckled, again. "Yes. You and I are a lot alike, Detective. We're both young, and eager to make our marks, but unfortunately, it was your captain who put in the request. Something about it being department policy."

Department policy, Billy scowled. He hated the damned policy. It was pointless. No one liked working with him. He was a workaholic and put everything he had into his investigations, which his partners never seemed to like. Besides that, he had a temper, and if things didn't get done right, everyone knew about it. He hated having to rely on other people, and he certainly didn't like having to be responsible for someone getting killed on the job. It's why he liked working alone. He only had himself to worry about.

"Were you told why my previous partner left?" he finally asked.

Detective Stark nodded. "Of course. It's one of the first things I was informed about when I agreed to take the job. As a member of the police force, we're all under a lot of scrutiny these days. A lot of people don't trust us, with all the police violence going on around the country, and your partner did not help matters. I heard he got a little too physical with one of the suspects. The boyfriend of one of the girls that went missing? Did I get that right?"

Billy nodded. "Yes. Sean. He was Ashleigh Carlson's boyfriend." Billy cringed, thinking back. "Detective Johnson wasn't a bad detective. He was just under a lot of stress. Plus, he has a daughter the same age as Nikki, Sydney, Ashleigh, and Addison. He just snapped and went after the kid. I tried to pull him back, but he turned on me." Billy pointed to his shoulder. "The bullet went clean and through. He was asked to resign immediately."

"And now you're stuck with me. What am I? Your third partner this year?"

"Something like that," Billy muttered. He sighed. "Alright, Detective Stark..."

"Andrew. We're going to be spending a lot of time together, we might as well be on a first-name basis."

"Alright, Andrew, since we are apparently stuck together, follow me. It's time you met Sully."

"Sully?"

"Our medical examiner, he's old as a dinosaur, but he knows his shit." He spun on his heel, making his way across the room to where the two girls lay. "Hey, Sully."

"Hey, Billy." An older man with thin, white hair and a beard covering his jaw looked up from where he was examining the bodies. "Wish it were under better circumstances. Who's this?"

"Andrew Stark," the man said, nodding to him. "Detective Turner's new partner."

Sullivan Wilcox cracked a grin, shaking his head. "The boy's like the black plague, Detective Stark. He's lost three partners over the last six months, for one reason or another. Good luck to you."

"I don't scare easily."

"Then it's a good thing you're here."

"Can we get back to the investigation," Billy cut in, sending a warning look to Sully. He hated that everyone thought he was cursed or something. It wasn't his fault his partners couldn't stomach the job. "And quit talking about me?"

Sully laughed, shaking his head once more. "Of course, but did you gentlemen see the mask yet?"

Billy shook his head. "I heard about it, but I haven't gotten a chance to look at it yet. I've only been here for like five minutes."

"When the police got here, the victims were each wearing a clown mask," Sully told them. "You're not going to believe it."

Billy arched a brow at him, his gaze going to the plastic bags that were on the ground next to the bodies, his eyes widening when he saw it. "Holy shit. That..."

"Looks just like the face the four girls described when they escaped." Sully nodded. "Eerie, isn't it?"

"Um. Can someone clue me in here?" Andrew asked, glancing from one man to the other. "What's up with the clown mask?"

"Well, you know the story of Ashleigh, Addison, Sydney, and Nikki, right?" Billy asked, glancing over at Andrew.

Andrew nodded. "Of course."

"Well, their captor, was dressed like a clown, and that clown mask." He pointed to the mask. "Is exactly how they described it."

"So, what? You think that this is that same person?"

"I don't believe in coincidences," Billy told him. "Plus, we were never able to catch their captor. The girls. They never saw his real face."

"But you can't go around assuming this is related to the girls, Billy," Sully told him. "This is LA. This could very well be a copycat. You need to be careful. If your captain..."

He didn't have to say it, Billy thought. He already knew. If his captain knew he wasn't being objective, he'd pull him off the case. He could not make this personal. His very career depended on it.

"I know, Sully," he said, sighing, trying to reign in his emotions, but he knew this was connected to the girls. He knew it deep down in his gut, that the madman who had kidnapped them and tortured them was back, and now, he was killing people. Just what did he want? What was his end game? And how many people were going to die because of it? "Is there anything else I should know?" he finally asked.

"Well... we did find this." Sully held up another plastic bag, showing him the manuscript inside. "Recognize this?"

Billy took the bag from him, staring at the typed letters across the page, his eyes widening. "Of course I recognize it. It's Gloria Davis's..."

"Billy!"

A soft, feminine voice split through the air, and he inwardly groaned. She was here, of course she was here. Wherever there was a crime, Gloria Davis was one of the first on the scene.

"Billy!"

Again, the shout sounded, and he sighed. He turned, just as the petite, redhead broke free from the officer struggling to hold her back and raced across the room toward him.

"Gloria!"

Billy intercepted her, just before she could reach the bodies, grabbing her by the arm and pulling her back. "Jesus! What the hell do you think you're doing? You know this is a crime scene. You can't be here!"

"Screw that!" Gloria cried, jerking free from his hold and trying to peer around him. "Is it true? Were two girls murdered? And were they both wearing a clown mask?"

"That's confidential information," Andrew said, stepping up next to Billy and crossing his arms across his chest. "And like

Detective Turner said, this is an active crime scene. You cannot be in here."

"Who the hell are you? Do you even know who I am?"

"I'm pretty sure I don't care."

"Billy!" Gloria swung toward him. "Come on. Give me something. You owe me!"

"I owe you shit!" Billy snapped, his temper snapping. "Gloria, I trusted you. I allowed you to help me with the investigation, and then you went right ahead, and did what you always do. You took the girls tragedy and used it to your advantage. You destroyed their reputations. Their lives."

"Someone was going to write…"

"The book is pure speculation, Gloria!"

"And yet, it's sold over a million copies." Her gaze trailed down to the plastic bag Billy was still holding. "Wait. Is that my manuscript?"

"Indeed, it is," Billy said, holding it up. "Which means you are our prime suspect, Gloria."

"Wait. What?" Gloria's eyes widened. "But Billy! I didn't kill anyone!"

"I don't know that, and right now, you are our only lead," Billy said, holding up the handcuffs. "So, do you want to do this the easy way or the hard way?"

Gloria sighed. "Okay. Fine. I'll go." She glanced over at her cameraman, narrowing her eyes on him. "Jasper! Shut that damn thing off!"

"But I thought…"

"Not this," Gloria said, cutting him off.

He quickly lowered the camera, and she turned to Billy. "Okay. Let's get this over with."

"A wise choice." Billy glanced over at Andrew. "Meet you back at the station?"

"Of course. I'm just going to touch base with Sully quickly, then I'll be on my way. I'll see you in a bit." He turned, heading back toward Sully.

Billy nodded. "See you in a bit."

"Who is that?" Gloria asked again, as Billy lead her away. "I don't like him."

"You don't like anyone, Gloria," Billy said, as he lifted his phone to his ear. He needed to get a hold of Ashleigh. He didn't want her to hear about this on the television, because if he was right, and this was connected to the murders, she was in danger. Again.

Chapter Eight

This couldn't be happening. Not now. Not again.

Ashleigh rung her hands together in her lap, staring out the window of Ryan's Camaro as the city passed them by, her thoughts running rampant. He was back. Oh God, he was back. What was she going to do? Could she handle this? God. She didn't want to go through this again. She couldn't.

"You doing okay?" Ryan asked, glancing over at her.

Ashleigh felt a laugh bubble up inside her throat. "Ryan, how on earth could I be okay? I mean, it was only two weeks ago I escaped that madman. Now someone dressed like him is going around killing people! No. I'm not okay. I'm pissed. I'm scared, and dammitt, I am freaking out!"

"Ash. Breathe. You don't know if it's him," Ryan said, reaching over and squeezing her hand. "It could be some fan. Some copycat..."

"Or it could be him, only now he's killing people," Ashleigh whispered. She pulled her hand out from under his, wrapping her arms around herself. "I can't do this, Ryan. Not again. I barely survived my encounter with him the first time. I don't know if I can survive a second. Hell, I can't even get into a damned car without having to search the backseat first!"

"I know, Ash."

Ryan said the words quietly, but Ashleigh still winced. She hated that everyone knew what had happened to her. Would she ever be able to move past it? Would the world let her? Was there even a chance she could live a normal life again?

"You'll never be normal, Ashleigh. You're his. You'll always be his, and in the end... you'll die alone."

Marcus's words echoed in her head, and a small gasp escaped her lips. Was he right? Was there some truth to the words he'd said?

"Ash?"

"I'm okay."

"No. You're not. Something happened back at the party, didn't it? Marcus. Did he say something to you?"

"I... I shouldn't..." Ashleigh fiddled with the seatbelt, not wanting to put Ryan in an awkward spot. Marcus was his teammate. He had to see him every day. She did not want to get in between that.

"Ash, you can tell me. I promise. I'm not like Marcus."

He was nothing like Marcus, Ashleigh thought. Ryan was kind, nice, and something about him made her feel safe. Marcus, on the other hand... he gave her the creeps.

"Ryan..."

"You can tell me."

Ashleigh swallowed, debating.

"He... he said that I'll never be normal," she finally said. "That no matter what, I'll always be stuck in that manor, and in the end, I'll die alone."

"What!"

Ryan braked at the stoplight, swinging to look at her. "He said what!"

"He's right, Ryan."

"No, he's not. He's a selfish asshole who needs to get his ass kicked. Again."

"Ryan, please don't!" Ashleigh cried. "I don't want to cause problems for you or the football team."

"You don't need to worry about that," Ryan told her. He stared ahead, gripping the wheel tightly in his hands. He closed his eyes, blowing out a long breath. "Ashleigh, please don't listen to him. He doesn't know what he's talking about."

"But he's right, Ryan. No matter what I do, all I think about is that damned manor. I can't get it out of my head, and I'm alone! My friends, they're gone. My family, they live an hour away. I have no one."

"That isn't true. Your friends. Your family, they might not be here, but they're still here for you, Ash. No matter how far away they may live." He squeezed her hand. "Look, I don't know you, Ash, and obviously, you don't know me, but you went through hell inside that manor and you survived! It takes someone of great strength to survive something like that, and from where I'm standing, you're one hell of a woman."

Ashleigh shook her head. "No. I'm not."

"Ash."

"What?" She glanced over at him.

"I mean it, okay? Every damned word, and if you ever need someone to talk to, well, I'm usually pretty easy to talk to."

Ashleigh smiled. "I appreciate that." She nodded. "The light's green."

"Oh. Whoops!" Ryan laughed, flashing her a grin. "That's right. I'm driving, aren't I?" He floored the accelerator.

Ashleigh gasped, gripping the door, a laugh escaping her lips. "You forgot you were driving?" She rolled her eyes, pointing. "Take the next right, and I'm the first house on the left."

"Aye, aye, Captain."

She laughed again, shaking her head, as she watched him expertly navigate the vehicle.

His hands were sure on the wheel, his eyes focused on the road, and she suddenly recalled all the times she'd seen him play. He'd always had this confidence to him, this swagger, and she'd always been in awe of him. Of the way he handled himself, and it was strange to her, meeting the man beyond the football uniform. He was so much different than she'd imagined.

He pulled into the driveway, and Ashleigh shook herself free from her thoughts. She shoved the door open, hurrying toward the house.

"Ash! Wait!"

"What?" Ashleigh glanced over her shoulder, as she pulled her keys out.

"I just... I want you to be careful," Ryan said, shuffling his feet, suddenly feeling awkward. "It's dark out, and we live in Los Angeles. The people here are unpredictable." He frowned, glancing around the quiet street. "Aren't there supposed to be police officers watching you?"

"Billy had to pull them. The department's short-staffed, and they just don't have the extra manpower right now."

"Wait. After what happened, they don't have the manpower to protect *you*?" Ryan stared at her in dismay. "Are you kidding me? That should be their top priority!"

"They have other priorities, too, Ryan. It's not like I can do anything about it, besides, I don't want to make things more difficult for Billy than they already are." She stuck the key in the lock and shoved open the door.

She shouldn't have to think about that, Ryan thought, stuffing his hands in his pockets, once again thinking about Ashleigh and all she'd been through. Where did she get her strength? Her resolve? Her will?

As if sensing his eyes on her, Ashleigh glanced over her shoulder at him. "You wanna come in?"

Ryan smiled, shaking his head. This woman, he just couldn't get a read on her. One moment she was shying away from him, then the next moment she was inviting him inside her home. "Are you sure that's okay?"

"I wouldn't have invited you in if it wasn't, Ryan," Ashleigh told him as she flipped on the foyer lights and stepped inside. "It's the least I can do for you giving me a ride home."

"It really wasn't that big of a deal," Ryan said, stepping in behind her and closing the door. He eyed the three locks and the security system, as she punched in the code to disarm it.

Several moments later, he followed her through the house, walking past the white couch and loveseat that lay in the small living room. A small, oval shaped, glass coffee table sat in the middle of the room on light, thin gray carpet. A fireplace sat in the corner with a small, flat-screened TV on top of it, and pictures were scattered along the beige-colored walls. Some had flowers, others of various animals, and different landscapes. "Nice place."

"I'm barely here," Ashleigh said, shrugging, as she walked through the doorway and into the kitchen. "I'm always at school or working. It's just kind of where I sleep."

"I get that. Life gets busy, doesn't it?" Ryan leaned against the counter, fingering the pictures scattered across the countertop. "Your sisters?"

Ashleigh nodded. "Yes. That's Callie." She pointed to the young girl with long, dark hair and glasses. "She's a senior in high school, and that's Sadie." She pointed to a younger girl, with curly, chestnut colored hair. "She's a freshman." She tossed her keys onto the table and lifted the tablet laying on the counter. She pushed a button, enabling the security system. She then turned, ruffling through the cupboards. "Do you like tea? I'm going to make some for myself. Hopefully, it'll help me sleep."

"If it's not too much trouble."

"Of course not." Ashleigh reached up in the cupboard for the tea bags, and she winced, pressing a hand to her throbbing ribs. "Oh. Ouch."

"Here. Why don't you sit down," Ryan said, gently steering her out of the kitchen and toward the table. "I'll make the tea."

"What? No. Ryan, you're my guest..."

"Ash. Sit. You're obviously in pain."

"Ryan, I'm fine!" Ashleigh cried, grabbing the box from him. "I can make a batch of tea! I am not..."

She trailed off, her vision suddenly swimming.

"Whoa."

She grabbed the edge of the countertop, the box falling from her hands.

"Ash?"

She held up a hand, shaking her head, then suddenly all she saw was darkness.

"Ashleigh!"

Chapter Nine

"Billy."

The knock sounded on the door, and Billy turned, looking at Andrew as he walked into his office.

"Hey." Billy nodded to him, lifting the cup of coffee to his lips. It was after two a.m., and this was his sixth cup of coffee. He wasn't getting anywhere with this damned case. His chat with Gloria hadn't helped, not that he was surprised. Gloria Davis might be many things, but she was not a killer.

"Any luck getting a hold of Ashleigh?"

Billy shook his head. "No. I'm worried about her."

"I'm sure she's fine." Andrew leaned back against the desk, staring at the board.

"I worry about her," Billy said. "She went through a lot inside that manor, if I don't hear from her by morning, I'll stop by her place to check on her." He shook his head. "Man, I wish she'd listened to me when I told her to leave. The others left, but she... she's just so damned stubborn!"

He slammed his fist onto the desk, taking another sip of coffee, regarding the board. He'd put it together shortly after the girls had been found. A picture of Ashleigh, Addison, Sydney, and Nikki sat in the middle of the board. An arrow went from their pictures to the manor, and another arrow went from their pictures to an image of a clown mask.

"It must have been a relief when you found them," Andrew said, taking a sip from his own coffee.

"You have no idea," Billy said, closing his eyes as he thought back. "Getting the call that they'd been found was the best call I have ever gotten. They'd been missing for six months! No one thought they were still alive. Not my fellow officers. Not the feds, but I never once gave up hope."

"You knew them well?"

Billy nodded. "We grew up on the same street in Sarasota Bay. We did everything together, and they're like sisters to me. In fact, Addison and I are best friends." He smiled, thinking of all the times she'd come into the station and brought him lunch, or told him to stop obsessing over a case and to go home. She'd always taken care of him, and it killed him that he wouldn't be seeing her for a while.

"And you were still allowed on the case?"

Billy winced. "The captain did not want me anywhere near it, but I begged, pleaded with him that I knew the girls better than anyone. Then when the lead detective botched some evidence left in Ashleigh's car, he didn't really have a choice."

"The hair particles?"

Billy nodded. "There was a piece of hair left in the car. It was bagged properly, sent to the lab, and then poof! It went missing. The last person seen with it was Detective Walburn. He was let go immediately."

Andrew shook his head. "It could have helped us find them sooner."

"I don't know," Billy murmured. "This guy is smart. He doesn't make mistakes. I mean, he took all four girls without anyone seeing anything! Ashleigh, in her car, even though there are cameras everywhere around the restaurant. Sydney, at home. Addison, after dance, and Nikki, after basketball practice."

"Their parents must have been relieved."

Billy clenched his fist. "You'd be surprised." He picked up a photo on the desk, pinning it to the board. "Meet Wesley Jenkins, Nikki's father. Eight years ago, Nikki came home and found him standing over his wife's body with a bloody knife in his hand. She'd been stabbed ten times, and her throat slashed. He's in prison for life." He placed a photo of the crime scene on the board.

"Jesus."

"And then there's Jim and Stacey Anderson, Sydney's parents. A year after Wes was sentenced, they both died in a horrific car crash. Their car lost control, and they crashed into the bridge. The car exploded."

"Good God!"

"Then there's Addison." Billy placed another photo on the board, this time, under Addison's photo. "It wasn't long after

Sydney's parents got into that car accident, that Addison's parents decided to take a family vacation. They packed their bags and headed to Phoenix. Halfway there, they stopped at a gas station, in the middle of an armed robbery. They were both killed. The police found Addison in the car several hours later. It was a hot day, nearly ninety degrees outside. They were lucky they got to her when they did. She could have died."

"God damn!" Andrew ran a hand over his beard. "And Ashleigh?"

"Her father, Neil, died while serving in the military when she was thirteen years old. Callie was nine, and Sadie was six."

"Why do I get the feeling there's more to this story?"

"Because there is," Billy said. "Mary abandoned her children when Ashleigh was sixteen. Left in the middle of the night, only leaving behind a note that said, *I'm sorry.* Ashleigh practically raised her two sisters."

"Social services never found out?"

Billy shook his head. "No. Ashleigh was careful. She worked two jobs, kept her grades up, and was able to get the bills paid. She even made sure Callie and Sadie never missed a day of school. Social services never had a clue. Plus, my father checked in on them every now and then." He pressed is lips together, hatred filling him as he thought of his father, Charles Turner. "But I haven't been able to locate Mary. I've been trying for months, ever since Ashleigh was kidnapped, but it's like she disappeared into thin air." He tapped his finger against the board. "And of course, there's the Miller massacre."

"The what?"

"It happened ten years ago," Billy said, as he reached for a file. "I told you we all lived on the same street. On Sand Cherry Lane. That's where we met Meredith and Amelia Miller. They grew up with us. We played together. We went to school together, and then, one day they went missing. The same day their father and three brothers were found stabbed to death, their faces beaten beyond recognition, the only survivor being their mother, Lindsay Miller. She was beaten so badly, she lost vision in one eye, and the left side of her face was paralyzed. She has no memory of that day, and it took her a long time to recover. When she did, she left Sarasota Bay and moved to New York with her brother."

"And the girls?"

"After what happened, their parents feared for their lives. Nikki's family moved to Houston. Sydney's family moved to Montana. Addison and I, somehow, both ended up in Jersey."

"And Ashleigh?"

"Her family stayed in Sarasota Bay. I never understood why."

"And the killer?"

"Never found."

"And the girls just happened to end up in the same city? At the same college? And you... you just happened to become a detective in the same city?" Andrew arched a brow at him. "That's pretty ironic."

"I thought so too, especially when they were all kidnapped at the same time. I brought my suspicions to the captain, but he told me we couldn't go off conspiracy theories. That we needed proof."

"Detective?"

He glanced up, as an officer poked his head into the room. "Yeah."

"Here's the file you asked for on the victims."

Billy crossed to the door, taking the file. "Thanks." He turned, flipping through the file as he walked. Then he stopped, lifting his head to look over at Andrew. "You're not going to believe this.

"What?"

"The girls, MJ and Aimee." He walked to the board, putting up the photos. "Aimee... her name is really Amelia, and MJ, her name is actually Meredith Jo."

"You mean like the Miller girls?"

"Exactly, but that's not the only thing that's strange about this case. Earlier, when I talked to Sully, he said there was something familiar about this case. He did some searching through his old files, and guess what he found."

"I have no idea. Tell me."

"That the murder weapon used to kill the girls, is the exact replica of the knife Wesley Jenkins used to kill his wife eight years ago." He slapped the file closed. "Go home, Detective, get some rest. We'll reconvene in a few hours when the prison opens up because good ole Wes and I are going to have a long, overdue talk."

"You can't possibly think he's involved in this."

"No. Wes might be many things, but he would never do anything to hurt his daughter." Billy tapped the file against his hand. "But he always did say that he'd been set up. I never believed him, until now."

"Why didn't you believe him back then?"

"There was no evidence to back him up. I thought he was just spouting conspiracy theories, but now, I'm not so sure." Billy paused, thinking. "This killer, whoever he is, is fixated on the past. On what happened in Sarasota Bay. Wes is just a piece to the puzzle, and just maybe, he can help me put the pieces together."

"You think he'll talk?"

Billy shrugged. "I have no idea, but we have to figure out who this madman is. If he is indeed the same man who kidnapped the girls, he always does things with a purpose. He always has a plan, and my guess is that he already has his next target picked out. Which means more bodies are going to drop and the girls are going to end up in danger once more."

Chapter Ten

Tick. Tock. Tick. Tock.

The rhythmic sound of the clock filled her ears, and Ashleigh groaned. She threw an arm over her eyes, her head thumping madly, desperately trying to fall back to sleep. *The sun's not even up yet!*

Tick. Tock. Tick. Tock.

She snapped her eyes open, rolling onto her back, and stared up at the ceiling. Yesterday was a blur. So much had happened! From saying goodbye to her friends, to the party with Marcus, Kenzie, and Ryan...

Ryan!

She shot up in her bed, suddenly remembering last night. Oh, God. She'd passed out on him, hadn't she? She hoped she hadn't scared him.

But he had to have brought her up here, she thought, as she stared around her room, then down her body, realizing she was still wearing the same clothes she'd had on yesterday.

Tick. Took. Tick. Tock.

She ran a hand through her mangled hair. God. What a mess. Two girls had lost their lives last night. Was it him? Was he really back? God, she just wanted one day. One freaking day to catch her breath, to hit pause... just for a moment. But that was the funny thing about life. Life didn't have a pause button.

Tick. Tock. Tick. Tock.

"Oh my God! Just shut up already!" She grabbed the clock from where it was sitting on top of the dresser and tossed it across the room. It hit the wall, shattering, and she lifted a hand to her mouth, as a sob escaped her lips. God! She hated that damned thing!

Every time she heard it, she was reminded of the clock inside the manor. The clock, that had started everything, and that had eventually, lead her to being held captive by a madman for six long months.

She pushed all thoughts of the manor aside and reached for her phone. She scrolled through the screen. Billy had called her... multiple times. So had Sydney, Addison, and Nikki. She couldn't deal with any of them right now. She'd call them later.

She tossed the phone onto the bed and stared around the bedroom. It looked nothing like she'd once had it. The pale yellow that had once covered the walls was now a shade of light gray. When she'd returned home, she hadn't been able to look at that color anymore. It had reminded her too much of the manor. She'd gotten new clothes, tossing anything that was a reminder of that place, and had made everything hers again.

She spun on her heel and walked across the room. She passed the small, circular table that had a small plant lying on it, stopping a second to look at the photos lying there. One of her two sisters, then another of her father wearing his army uniform, before disappearing into the adjoining bathroom.

She flipped on the light and stared at herself in the mirror. Her face was pale, her eyes wide with horror, but the bruises were almost gone. Finally. She traced a finger under her eyes, where dark circles lay, wishing she could get a night or two of decent sleep, but he still plagued her dreams.

She winced as her ribs pulsed with pain, and she reached into the cabinet for the bottle of pills she had laying there. She didn't like taking them. She didn't like relying on them, but she didn't have a choice. The pain was too unbearable.

She twisted off the cap and plopped the pills in her mouth. They washed down her throat with ease, then she turned toward the shower.

Several moments later, she stepped under the hot spray, the feel of the hot water raining down on her feeling like heaven. She sighed, closing her eyes, suddenly thankful she could take a shower without someone watching her every move. Without being yelled at, scolded, and even worse, him joining her.

She shuddered, wrapping her arms around herself, trying to push the memories aside. Instead, she focused on the task at hand.

A little while later she stepped out of the shower and got dressed. Wearing a light blue blouse and dark, blue, denim jeans she walked out of the bedroom. She continued down the hallway, disappearing inside the office a few doors down, and took a seat at the desk. She logged onto the computer, knowing there were a few bills she had to pay.

She watched the computer come to life, typing her password into the field.

Thump!

A loud noise suddenly echoed through the house, and she jumped. A scream bubbled up in her throat, and she quickly pushed it down, fear washing over her. Oh, God. Was someone in her house?

Suddenly frantic, her heartbeat racing a million miles an hour, she reached for the tablet sitting on the desk next to her. She had several hidden around the house, just for this reason. She opened the app to her security system, flipping through the camera. Nothing seemed out of the ordinary, but what had been that noise?

"Son of a..."

The voice sounded from downstairs. There was definitely someone here.

She reached underneath the desk, her hand wrapping around the baseball bat she'd hidden there. She gripped it in her hands, rose to her feet, and made her way down the stairs. She gingerly walked across the living room, peering through the doorway and inside the kitchen.

"Ryan?"

"Jesus!" Ryan jumped, the pan he was holding falling from his hand and crashing to the ground as he swung around to look at her. "Holy Christ! Ash, you just scared the crap out of me!"

"I scared you? You scared me!" Ashleigh cried, lowering the bat. "I didn't know you were here. I thought someone had broken in." She stared down at the bat, then at Ryan. "I almost maimed you with a bat, Ryan!"

"I see that," Ryan said, chuckling as he rounded the counter. He took the bat from her. "I'm just going to put this in the corner, okay? I really don't want the entire school, or my teammates coming after you for taking out the starting quarterback before the first game of the season."

"Oh my God." Ashleigh's eyes widened. "I didn't even think about that. They'd all kill me!"

Ryan smiled. "I'd never let them do that."

Ashleigh smiled, shyly, her eyes trailing to the pan that was still lying on the ground. "Ryan, what are you doing here? Don't get me wrong, I'm glad it's you and not some intruder, but I thought you'd be gone by now."

Ryan shrugged. "I was worried about you," he said, returning to the kitchen and picking the pan up off the floor. He set it in the sink, rinsing water over it before drying it. "You scared me last night when you passed out on me. It didn't feel right leaving you."

"I was wondering about that," Ashleigh whispered, ducking her head. "I'm sorry, I didn't mean to scare you. I... I have to take better care of myself. I didn't eat much yesterday, and with my sore ribs, my body just couldn't take anymore. It just kind of gave out on me."

"You've been through a trauma, Ash. It'll take a little time to adjust," Ryan said, as he opened the refrigerator and pulled out the carton of eggs. "But I'm glad you're okay. That's what really matters."

"So, you slept on the couch?" Ashleigh asked, glancing over her shoulder at the rumpled blanket, wincing. "Oh, Ryan. That thing is so uncomfortable! You really should have gone home."

"That would have been a problem, considering your security system."

"Oh!" Ashleigh laughed, shaking her head. "Right!"

"I figured if I opened the door, I'd wake up the whole neighborhood, and I certainly wasn't going to wake you up."

Ashleigh smiled again, reaching for the tablet and disabling the alarm. She sighed, watching as the cameras flicked off, then on again. "Agh. This damn security system. I don't know why I pay for it. It always seems to…"

Ring!

The sound of the doorbell suddenly split through the air, interrupting her. She jumped, the tablet slipping from her hands and falling to the floor, as she swung around to stare at the door. *Oh, God. Oh, God. That noise!*

"Ashleigh?"

She vaguely heard Ryan calling to her, but she didn't respond. She couldn't, her gaze was solely focused on the door. She hated that sound. It reminded her too much of the manor, and the sound put her in a state of panic. Who the hell had rung it? No one ever rang it! She made sure of it.

She dropped to the ground and grabbed the tablet. She flipped through the cameras, but they weren't working. All it showed her was a black screen. Oh, God. Oh, God.

"Ash! Ashleigh!"

Ryan dropped to the floor in front of her, taking her hands in his. "Breathe."

"I... I... can't..."

"Yes. You can."

She shook her head. "No. I..."

"Ash, look at me."

She shook her head.

"Ash."

Finally, she lifted her head, staring up into his kind, brown eyes. She dragged in a deep breath, then another, her breathing slowly returning to normal.

"You're okay," Ryan whispered, gently squeezing her hands. "It's just the doorbell."

"I know, but the sound..." Ashleigh shook her head. "I put a note up specifically telling people not to ring it. It reminds me too much of that place. It's the way he started every morning, by blaring a similar noise throughout the manor." She dragged in another breath. "And I can't see who's at the door. The cameras aren't working."

"You want me to answer the door?"

Bang! Bang!

A fist slammed against the door, followed by a masculine voice.

"Ashleigh, open up! It's Billy. I know you're in there. Don't you dare make me knock this damned door down!"

"No, I got it. It's just Billy," Ashleigh said, rising to her feet. "I'm okay. Really."

Ryan gave her a look, but rose to his feet and backed away, giving her space. "If you say so."

Ashleigh pulled open the door, staring at Billy standing in the doorway. "Dammitt, Billy. What have I told you about ringing the doorbell?"

"Oh shit. I forgot." Billy ran a hand across his face.

"You forgot?" Ashleigh stared at him, pointing to the note. "There's a note next to the doorbell, Billy!"

"I know, I'm sorry. I didn't get much sleep last night and I wasn't thinking. I didn't scare you, did I?"

"Scare her? You gave her a freaking panic attack," Ryan said from the doorway. "Jackass."

"I..." Billy trailed off, his gaze swinging to Ryan. "Who the hell are you?"

"The name's Ryan."

"You got a last name, Ryan?"

"Guys! Stop!" Ashleigh placed herself in between the two men, glaring at one, then the other. "Good God! I do not need this right now. I have enough crap going on without you two fighting over who's the more macho of the two. Billy, Ryan is a friend, who helped me out last night, and who stayed just to make sure I was okay. And Ryan, this is Billy, a good friend of mine. A friend who is supposed to call before he comes over."

"I did call. I called twenty goddamn times," Billy said, his eyes flashing. "You didn't pick up."

"Oh. Right." Suddenly, she remembered the missed calls.

"I was worried about you, Ash," Billy said, wrapping an arm around her and pulling her close. "Especially, since you were the only one who ignored my advice and decided to stay in LA."

"You know why I can't leave, Billy."

"Yes, I do." He glanced over at Ryan. "You really stayed last night?"

Ryan nodded.

"I appreciate you looking out for her." He strode forward, extending a hand. "I'm Billy. Detective Billy Turner. Sorry. I didn't mean to freak out on you. It's been a long night."

"I can only imagine. Sorry I called you a jackass." Ryan shook his offered hand. "I'm Ryan Eisenhower."

Billy raised a brow. "Now I understand why you look so familiar." He glanced over at Ashleigh, winking at her.

"Don't you dare."

"Am I missing something?" Ryan asked, glancing between the two.

"No."

"Yes."

He raised a brow. "Well, that clears things up." He turned, disappearing into the kitchen. "I was about to make breakfast. Do you have time to eat, Billy?

"Unfortunately, no," Billy said, glancing at his watch. "I'm meeting my new partner over at the prison to talk to an inmate."

"Everything ok?" Ashleigh asked, looking over at him with concern.

"Yeah. Everything's fine."

"I heard about the murders. Is it true? Was there really a clown mask?"

Billy hesitated.

"Billy, if you know something, you have to tell me."

"I can't, Ash. Not yet." He leaned forward, brushing a kiss against her cheek. "I gotta go, but we'll talk later, ok?"

Ashleigh nodded, watching as he disappeared through the door. "He's hiding something."

"I'm sure he'll tell you when he can," Ryan said from the stove. "How do you like your eggs?"

"Scrambled is fine." Ashleigh took a seat at the table, watching him cook, and a few minutes later he was setting a plate of scrambled eggs, toast, and some fruit in front of her. "Aren't you going to eat?" she asked, as he set a glass of orange juice next to the plate.

Ryan shook his head. "No. I have to hit the weight room before class this morning. That is best on an empty stomach."

"I can only imagine." Ashleigh stared down at the plate, then over at him. "I can't believe the great, Ry-Ice made me breakfast."

Ryan winced. "Please don't call me that. I hate that nickname."

Ashleigh laughed, stabbing her fork in the food. She brought it to her lips and let out a moan. "Oh. That is good."

"Gee. Don't sound so surprised. I am good at other things, other than playing football."

"No. It's not that," Ashleigh whispered. "It's just, inside the manor, we didn't get much to eat. He pretty much just gave us scraps. Since escaping, I've developed a newfound love for food."

Ryan reached over, squeezing her hand. "Any time you need me to cook, just say the word. I just have one, teeny, tiny favor."

"What's that?"

"Can I use your shower? I still smell like last night's party, and I really don't want to go to campus smelling like booze."

Ashleigh laughed. "Of course, you can use my shower."

"Woo! That's a relief. I'm just gonna grab my bag out of the car."

"You keep an extra bag of clothes in your car?"

"Hell yes! Especially, when Jacob throws his parties." Ryan flashed her a grin. "Give me a little bit and I'll give you a ride. It's your first day back, right?"

Ashleigh nodded. "First day back at class. First day back at work. It's going to be a long day."

"Think you're ready?"

"I can't hide forever, Ryan."

"Yes, I know, but..." Ryan shook his head. "You know what, never mind. I'll just be a bit."

"You know, you don't have to give me a ride, Ryan."

"We're going to the same place, Ash. It's not like it's an inconvenience. I mean... what's the worst that can happen?" he asked, flashing her another grin, as he made his way toward the door. "That you might actually like me?"

That wasn't the problem, Ashleigh thought, as he disappeared through the door. The problem was, there was a killer out there. Probably the same killer who had kidnapped her, and she did not want Ryan getting caught up in her mess. It was too dangerous, and if something happened to him, because of her, she would never forgive herself.

Chapter Eleven

"Well, good morning, Sunshine," Andrew said with a grin, looking up from where he was leaning against his car in front of the prison as Billy walked up. "You look refreshed." He chuckled, taking in Billy's unshaven face, ruffled hair, and wrinkled clothes. "Rough morning?"

"Rough morning. Rough week. Rough month... hell, it's been a rough six months, but who's counting anymore?"

"You get a hold of Ashleigh?"

"No. She wouldn't answer her damned phone, so I swung by her house this morning." Billy sighed, shaking his head. "I forgot about the damned bell."

"Bell?"

"The doorbell. It reminds her of the manor. God, she was so scared! And because of me and my stupidity, she had a panic attack." He slammed his hand down on the hood of the car. "Dammitt!"

"Whoa. Hey. Easy on the car!" Andrew cried, cracking a grin. "And you, need to give yourself a break. You're only human, Billy."

Billy chuckled. "Am I? I feel more like a zombie these days." He sighed. "I just feel like I have no control, Andrew. There's a madman running around, killing people. My friends are struggling. I mean I can't even have officers trailing Ashleigh, because we're shorthanded. It's just wrong!"

"What does Ashleigh say?"

Billy shrugged. "She keeps saying it is what it is, but..."

"But you still worry." Andrew nodded. "I get it, but you also need to remember that Ashleigh is strong. She has to be, to have gone through what she has."

"I know she is. I'm just grateful she wasn't alone this morning."

"What do you mean?"

"There was a guy there. Ryan. She said he's a friend, but..."

"But you don't like him?"

"Well, he did call me a jackass."

Andrew threw back his head and laughed. "Well, were you?"

"Me? A jackass?" Billy quipped, raising a brow at Andrew. "No. Never."

Andrew laughed again, pushing away from the car and slapping Billy on the back. "Glad to know you still have your sense of humor, Partner."

"It comes and it goes," Billy told him, as they made their way toward the prison. "But in all fairness, I can't hold it against him. I was a jackass this morning. Both to him and Ashleigh."

"But you don't like him?" Andrew asked, again.

Billy shrugged. "I don't really know him and to be honest, right now I don't think I trust anyone."

"Can't say I blame you. What we do, trust does not come easy." He paused in front of the doors. "So. You ready?"

"For this?" Billy shook his head. "Never."

He hated coming to prison. Seeing the inmates, remembering the crimes they'd committed, it reminded him of how messed up this world was. How much it had changed. It was not a reminder he needed, but this visit was different. Wes, he was different. He'd known him. He'd been a big part of his life, but it had been years since he'd seen him. He'd been just a kid back then, and he'd said things he should have never said. Things he regretted saying now, because Wes just might be innocent, and he hadn't believed him.

He followed Andrew through the door, stopping, and leaning against the desk. "Hi, Trudy."

"Billy!" A huge grin spread across the older, black woman's face as she looked up. Her dark hair was pulled back into a bun, her small, plump body sitting on the stool behind the counter as she scrolled through the computer. "It's been a while."

"Yes, it has."

"Did you bring me my donuts?"

Billy smacked himself in the head. "I knew I was forgetting something! Sorry, Trudy. I didn't have time to stop this morning."

"With what you have going on, I'm not surprised," Trudy said. "I'll forgive you this time, Detective, but the next time, you'd better bring double!"

"What's this thing about donuts?" Andrew asked, looking from one to the other.

Billy laughed. "Well, it kind of started when I was a rookie."

"And a cute one you were," Trudy teased.

"Trudy!"

"But you were! All young, and wide-eyed. You were in awe of the place, and nice! Not everyone there was nice."

"Which was true," Billy said, glancing over at Andrew. "I was new to the precinct, and no one wanted to be partnered with the rookie. Most of the officers hated me on site. Considering my father was a well-known sheriff back in my hometown."

"They knew your father?"

"A couple of the guys did. Thought I expected to jump the line, but that's not the way I roll."

"Having met you, that doesn't surprise me. You seem like someone who likes to make your own path."

"You would be right," Billy said, nodding a thank you to Andrew. Maybe he was going to be a better partner than the rest. "I believe that you get what you give. A virtue that's been instilled in me since I can remember, and to prove that I did whatever they asked. I did the coffee runs in the mornings. I cleaned the bathrooms. Any odd job the detectives and officers found for me to do, I did it without complaint. Then, I saw how they treated Trudy. She was the only female working there, and they were so rude to her! So, when I went on the morning coffee run, I got two donuts. Once for me and one for Trudy. We would sit in the breakroom for a few minutes, talk, eat our donuts, and it's how we became friends."

"And ever since, he always brings me donuts when he comes to visit," Trudy said.

Andrew smiled. "Awe. Who knew you were such a softie."

"I've changed a lot since then," Billy told him. "That was pre-murders and killers. Now, I'm..."

"Hardened," Trudy finished for him. "You have to be. Considering what we see every day." She slid the bucket toward him, and he placed his keys, wallet, and gun in before walking through the metal detector.

"Your turn, handsome," Trudy said, winking at Andrew. "I'm sorry. I didn't catch your name."

"Andrew. Detective Andrew Stark. I'm Billy's new partner."

"Really?" Trudy glanced at him, then back over at Billy. "How long is this one gonna last?"

"Trudy!"

"What? You have gone through three partners in the last year."

Billy growled. "And for some reason, you all keep wanting to remind me of that!" He walked through the metal detector, stalking down the hallway.

"Damn! She is a hoot!" Andrew cried, hurrying after Billy.

"Yeah. She definitely is," Billy muttered, as they followed another officer. They headed down the hallway, taking several turns before the officer pulled open the metal door and lead them into the visiting area. They took a seat at one of the tables, and after several moments he finally spoke. "I'm not cursed."

"I never said you were."

"You stick in this city long enough, you'll hear it from most of the officers at the station. They all think I'm cursed, and the truth is, sometimes I feel like I am. Sully and Trudy aren't lying. I have gone through three partners this year, for one reason or another. I... I'm not an easy person to work with, Andrew, and this year... well it's been tough. With what happened with the girls and all."

"I get it, Billy."

"No. I don't think you do," Billy said. "It's not just what happened to the girls. I'm a workaholic, Andrew. I put in long hours. I obsess over my cases. I even get invested in them, and I expect the same from my partner."

"Billy, I told you. We're a lot alike." Andrew said, leaning forward. "You're not the only person who's been put through the wringer. I went through some shit too when I was younger. It hardened me, and I put a hundred and ten percent into every one of my cases. I'm dedicated. I'm passionate, and one thing I promise you is that I am one partner you will not scare off."

Billy opened his mouth to respond, suddenly curious about his new partner and what he'd been through, but he didn't get the chance. Behind them, the door opened, and they both turned, as a man walked through the door.

Wes.

Billy blinked, as the man shuffled through the door, barely recognizing the man. *He looks old*, Billy thought, as he stared at the tall, thin man with long gray hair. He had a long, gray beard covering his jaw, and he was wearing an orange jumpsuit. Behind him, two officers followed close by, the rhythmic clanging of the shackles around Wes's ankles clattering with every step he took.

"Hello, Wes."

"Well, well, well, if it isn't ole Billy Turner. It's been a while," Wesley said, as he took a seat at the table across from them. He glanced at the officers. "Can we take these damned things off?" He asked, raising his handcuffed wrists.

"No."

Wes sighed, turning back to Billy. "The officers are tyrants here. Never giving an inch, I tell you. A little respect would be nice." He glared at the officer behind him.

"The officers don't owe you anything, Wes," Billy said, leveling a look at Wes. "Leave them alone. They're just trying to do their jobs."

"You're defending them?"

"Of course I'm defending them."

"But I'm innocent!"

"Yes. You've been saying that for years."

"And none of you believed me. Not once," Wes said, looking pained.

"We never had a reason to, Wes."

"Yeah. Yeah. Everyone thinks I'm the crazy, old man spouting conspiracy theories, but look at you!" Wes grinned. "All grown up. You look well. Tell me..." "

"Wes, this isn't a social visit," Billy cut in. "I have a double murder to solve, and I'm pretty sure it has something to do with you." Billy slid a photo across the table. "Two young girls were found murdered last night."

"And you think I had something to do with it?" Wes asked, staring at Billy, then he let out a loud laugh. "Oh, Billy, you haven't changed, have you?"

"What do you mean?"

"I know you're the one who talked Nikki into testifying."

"That was her decision."

"You poisoned her against me, put thoughts into her head. She's my daughter, Billy!"

"Yes, she is, and you let her down, Wes."

"But I didn't do it!"

"I think you might be right."

"Wait. What?" Wes blinked, staring at Billy in surprise. He lowered his gaze, staring at the photo then his gaze jerked back to Billy. "Billy, what do you mean you have a double homicide to solve? How did you get this photo? Are you a cop or something?"

"Detective, actually," Andrew cut in, finally speaking for the first time since Wes had entered the room.

Wes glanced at him, then back over at Billy. "You're a detective?"

"I am."

"But your father never wanted that for you, Billy."

"I stopped caring about what my father wanted a long time ago, Wes. When he walked out on me and Mom."

"Billy, you don't understand…"

"I think I understand plenty. He was a coward. He didn't even bother to show up to Mom's funeral."

"He wanted to, Billy, but it was better if he stayed away."

"Better for who?"

"Everyone."

Billy regarded him. "Wes. You're not making any sense. Come on. Talk to me. I need to know what happened that day."

"Why?"

"Because I think you might have been set up."

"By who?"

"That's what I'm trying to figure out," Billy said, laying another photo on the table. "You recognize this?"

Wes glanced at the picture. "Yes. It's the knife that was found eight years ago. The knife that put me away."

"And this?"

Billy pointed to the other photo on the table, and Wes followed his finger, staring at the image. "It's the same knife." He raised his head to stare at Billy. "Billy, what does that mean?"

"One of three things," Billy said, leaning back. "One. You found some way to escape the prison last night and killed two young girls."

"You can't possibly think…"

Billy held up a hand. "Two. There's a copycat out there, or three. The real killer is still out there and framed you for the murder." He leaned forward. "And my gut, is telling me that theory number three is the one that makes the most sense."

"And you need me to, what?"

"Tell us about that night," Andrew said.

"But I already told you what happened that night."

"Yes, but I was just a kid back then, Wes. I wasn't thinking straight. I was only thinking about Nikki and didn't care what you said. Now. I need you to tell me again, Wes, because this time I'm thinking like a cop, not a seventeen-year-old boy."

Wes regarded him warily. "You promise I can trust you?" He turned to Andrew. "Both of you?"

"Of course."

He glanced from one to the other. He stopped, staring at Andrew. "You know, you look awfully familiar. Have we met before?"

Andrew smiled, shaking his head. "No, I can't say that we have, Wes. Considering I was born and raised in southern Florida."

"Oh. I could have sworn..."

"Wes."

"Right. You want to hear about that night." He took a moment, gathering his thoughts, then he finally spoke. "Okay, but this is the last time I am ever talking about this."

"Of course."

"We understand."

"Okay then." Wes tapped his fingers on the tabletop. "So, it was late. It had to have been around nine p.m, and I'd just gotten home. It'd been a long day at the office. I remember the house was dark, which was weird since Caroline always had the lights on for me. I walked through the door, and there was this god-awful smell. I flipped on the lights, and that's when I saw her."

Wes sniffed, tears streaking down his cheeks. "I will never forget the way she looked, lying on that floor, blood oozing from her body, and her eyes…" He hiccupped. "So lifeless. There were stab marks all over her body, and a knife was sticking out of her chest. I remember screaming, running toward her. I slipped and fell in a pool of blood, and somehow ended up with the knife in my hand. I don't even remember pulling it out of her body, but that's how Nikki found me. The look on her face…" He shook his head. "She really thought I'd killed her. I tried to explain, but she wouldn't listen. The next thing I knew, the cops were in the house, and I was being arrested."

"Do you have any idea who might have done it? If you were indeed framed?"

"I was a prosecutor, Billy. There's dozens of people who had it out for me."

"But do you think you know who did it?"

"Of course not."

Billy regarded Wes. "You're not telling me the truth, are you, Wes? What aren't you telling me?"

Wes chuckled. "Man. You are just like him."

"Who?"

"Your father. He had that same knack, being able to see through the bullshit."

"Wes."

"I want to tell you, Billy. I really do, but I can't."

"Why the hell not?"

"Because we all agreed."

"Who?"

"The nine of us. The night of the Miller massacre."

"Wait." Andrew held up a hand. This has to do with the Millers?"

"Everything has to do with it," Wes said. "It's why…"

He trailed off, the lights suddenly cutting out in the building.

"It's why, what?" Billy asked. He leaned forward. "Wes? Come on. Talk to me. Wes?"

Silence sounded, and he swore, rising to his feet. "Wes. So help me…"

The lights flicked back on, and he froze, staring at the empty chair Wes had been sitting in just moments ago.

"Ah, Andrew…"

"I'm already on it," Andrew said, jumping to his feet and racing toward the door. "Put this place on lockdown!" he shouted. "An inmate has escaped! I repeat. An inmate has escaped!"

Shit. He'd said too much.

Wesley stared across the table at the two detectives, about to bare his soul, when the lights suddenly went out. He raised his head, staring at the lights above him, and a noise sounded nearby.

Thump. Thump. Thump.

Footsteps.

Someone was coming.

He was coming.

He rose from the table, making his way across the room as quietly as he could, given the shackles he was wearing, and snuck through the door. He stumbled down the hallway, glancing behind him.

"Wes…"

The dark, raspy voice sounded behind him, and he glanced over his shoulder.

He was here.

He stumbled down the hallway, sneaked inside the cell, and slammed the door shut behind him. He slipped into the bed, pulling the sheet over his head. Praying he wouldn't see him. Praying the man who was after him, wouldn't find him. He didn't want to die. Not until he saw his daughter once again.

"Wes…"

The door to the cell opened, and he froze, drawing in a deep breath.

The sheet flew off of him, and the clown leaned down, a sinister smile crossing his bright, red lips. "I've been waiting for you, Wes."

"What do you want?"

"You." The clown said, raising his knife. "You have to pay, just like everyone else did."

"Haven't I paid enough?" Wes asked. "I'm in prison for a crime I didn't commit!"

"Oh, I know, Wes," the clown said, lowering his head to whisper in his ear. "And I know the person who did, and the person who framed you."

"You?"

"No. Not me," the clown said, leaning forward. "But I am the one who kidnapped your daughter."

"You bastard!"

Wes rose from the bed, but the clown grabbed him by the shoulders, slamming him back down on the bed.

"Please. Leave my daughter alone. She has nothing to do with this."

"Except, she has everything to do with this, Wes," the clown said. "She and her friends started this whole mess, and now, they have to pay for their sins. And yours, too." He raised the knife, striking it downward. The knife struck him in the throat, and Wesley gasped. He raised his hand to his throat, then let out a yelp as the clown grabbed him by the collar of his shirt and dragged him out of the cell.

"No. Please. Don't do this! I want to see my daughter again!"

"You should have thought about that before you and your posse devised your little plan," the clown said, as he dragged him down the hall. "If you had, none of this would be happening."

Chapter Twelve

She could do this.

Ashleigh stared out the window, as Ryan pulled into the parking lot of UCLA, staring off into the distance. *It looked so normal,* she thought, as she watched the students walk toward the college. She used to be one of them. Before...

I can do this. I can do this. I can do this.

She closed her eyes, once again chanting the words to herself. "Ash. You okay?"

Ryan's voice sounded from next to her and she smiled. *Ash.* Most of her friends called her that. It shouldn't feel different to hear him say the name, but for some reason, when he said it, it made her feel as if she'd known him forever. When in actuality, they'd really only known one another for less than twelve hours.

"Ash? You okay?"

Ryan asked the question again, and she laughed, silently. *How many times had he asked her that since she'd met him?*

"Yes. I'm fine."

Ryan stared at her. "No, you're not. What's wrong?"

Ashleigh sighed. "I don't know if I can do this, Ryan," she said, wringing her hands in her lap. "I'm scared. Everyone knows what happened to me, and what if I have a flashback to the manor? What if I have a panic attack? You saw how I reacted to the doorbell this morning. What if something happens?"

"You can't think like that, Ash."

"But after everything that's happened, people are going to have questions! Do I answer them? Do I ignore them? What do I do?"

"You do what you think is right," Ryan told her. "I can't tell you what to do, Ash. All I can do is tell you to do what you are comfortable with. You're back. You're starting to take your life back and establish some kind of normal. That is what's important."

"And what if I run into Marcus? Kenzie?"

"Ignore them. They don't deserve a second of your time." Ryan paused for a moment. "Do you have your phone on you?"

"Of course."

"Give it to me."

Ashleigh arched a brow at him. "You want my phone? Why?"

"Would you just give it to me?"

Ashleigh sighed, reaching down, and digging it out of her bag. "Fine. But you're not going to do anything weird with it, are you?"

Ryan belted out a laugh, shaking his head. "Of course not! Jeesh, woman. What do you think? That I'm some sort of weirdo?"

"Well, I did just meet you yesterday. I don't exactly know what you're like yet."

"I suppose that is true." Ryan tapped into her phone, then handed it back to her. "Here. I put my number in your phone, so if you need anything, you call me, okay?"

"Ryan, I can't ask you to drop everything for me!"

"Ash. I need you to promise me that you will call me if anything happens." Ryan turned to her, giving her a look. "No matter how small or big it might seem."

Ashleigh sighed, slowly nodding. "Okay. I'll call." She paused. "Hey, Ryan?"

"Yeah?"

"Why are you being so nice to me?" she asked. "Don't get me wrong, I'm grateful for everything you've done for me, but we never even talked before last night. I never thought you were this... sentimental."

"I'm not, normally," Ryan said, as he turned off the ignition. "I don't know. There's just something about you. I... I don't want anything happening to you."

Ashleigh smiled. "That's sweet."

Ryan winced. "Please don't say that in front of the football team. They apparently think I've gone soft."

"And that's a bad thing?"

Ryan shrugged. "Not necessarily, but I am the leader of the team. It comes with certain... expectations."

Ashleigh glanced at him. "Okay. I promise not to call you a softie in front of all your friends."

Ryan smiled. "Thank you."

They exited the vehicle and started down the sidewalk toward the main building of the campus. Ryan placed a hand on the small of her back, leading her through the crowd and Ashleigh jumped at the contact.

"Sorry." Ryan quickly lowered his hand.

"No. It's okay. I'm just not used to being touched, without..."

"You don't have to explain, Ash." He gave her a small smile, and Ashleigh inwardly grimaced. She hated that he knew what had happened to her. Why she flinched at the slightest bit of contact. It made her feel vulnerable. Transparent.

"Oh my God! Did you hear what happened last night?"

"The murders? Oh my God! Yes. It's horrible!"

"No. Not that. Did you hear about Ashleigh and Ryan? Apparently, they left the party together."

"No way!"

"Yes. I heard it from Kenzie, and boy, is she pissed!"

"Great. I'm the center of attention... again," Ashleigh murmured, ducking her head.

"Sorry, that's my bad. It follows me wherever I go," Ryan said, cringing. "It'll die down, I promise."

"Ryan!" One of the girls looked over at him as they passed by. "Is it true? Are you and Kenzie officially over? Are you and... oh hey, Ashleigh." The girl stopped, blushing when she saw Ashleigh standing next to him.

"Don't you people have anything better to do than gossip about me?" Ryan asked, narrowing his eyes on the girl, then at the group behind her. "Good God, we're not in high school. Leave us alone!"

He leveled a look at them, and the group turned, scampering away.

Ashleigh laughed. "Boy, you know how to clear a crowd."

"It kind of comes with the territory." Ryan glanced at her. "You okay?"

"I'm fine, Ryan. Really, you have got to stop asking me that."

"You're sure?"

"Ryan!"

"Okay. Okay. I'll stop." Ryan raised his hands in surrender. They stopped in front of the doors and he gave her a wink. "I'll see you later, okay?" He paused, pulling her in for a quick hug. "Text me later, okay? Just so I know you're okay. Oh, and don't forget to text your friends back." He stepped back, turning, and disappearing through the crowd.

Ashleigh stared after him, surprised at the hug, but more surprised that she hadn't jumped at the contact. Maybe she was starting to get used to him?

She turned, walked through the door of the building and pulled her phone out of her bag. She had a dozen texts from her friends.

Sydney: Ashleigh, where are you? I haven't heard from you all night. I'm getting worried!

Addison: Ash, Jesus Christ! Will you answer your texts? I'm worried about you!

Nikki: Is it true? Was there a murder in LA? Ashleigh, please, respond to me!

She laughed, shaking her head, as she typed into the phone.

Girls, chill, I'm fine. I went to a party last night and passed out. I've barely had time to even look at my phone.

Addison: A party?

Nikki: What party?

Sydney: Are you insane?

Yes, a party, and I met a guy.

Sydney: A Guy?

Addison: What guy?

Nikki: Girl, we need details!

It's Ryan.

Nikki: Ryan? Like Ryan, the football player?

Addison: Like, the one you've had a crush on for like... forever?

Sydney: Tell us everything!

Ashleigh shook her head, disappearing into the lecture hall and taking a seat toward the front. She tapped into the phone.

Later. I have to get to class. Bye!

Boo!

She laughed, setting her phone on the table, and reached into her bag. Her phone beeped, and she frowned, glancing at the screen.

Miss me, doll?

The text popped up on the screen, followed by a couple of clown emojis and she froze. She felt the blood drain from her face.

No. No! No! No!

She knew who it was from. She didn't even have to ask. It was him. It was the clown.

She picked up the phone, typing into the device with shaking hands.

What do you want?

Bubbles appeared across the screen, followed by another text.

To give you a present.

The text splashed across the screen, followed by a video invite. Drawing in a deep breath, she pressed accept.

"Hello, Ashleigh."

An image of the clown filled the screen, and she swallowed, as she stared into his familiar, dark eyes.

"I told you I wasn't done with you and look who I found."

The camera zoomed out, focusing on a dark-haired girl standing with her friends just outside the Sarasota Bay high school.

Callie.

"She looks happy, doesn't she?" the clown asked, and she closed her eyes, cringing at the familiar voice that haunted her dreams. She would never forget that voice.

"Answer me, Ashleigh."

"Y-yes," she stammered. "Yes, she does."

"Good, Doll. Now, go somewhere where we can be alone."

"Of...of course," Ashleigh gasped out, hating the words that came out of her mouth. She was no longer stuck in the manor, but he was still pulling the strings. If she didn't do what he asked, would he hurt her sister? It was not a risk she was willing to take.

She quickly gathered up her things, racing out of the room and down the hallway. She disappeared into the bathroom, checking the stalls to be sure they were empty, before jamming the doorstopper underneath the door. "Okay. We're alone."

"Very good." The clown smiled, his face filling the screen. "Man, do I miss you."

"Please. What do you want?" Ashleigh asked, hating the pleading sound that came from her voice. "What do you want from me?"

"Oh, Ashleigh, haven't you learned? I want you."

"Well, you can't have me!" Ashleigh snapped, suddenly tired of his damned games. "Not now. Not ever again."

The clown laughed. "Oh, Ashleigh. Haven't you learned by now that I always get what I want? I wanted the four of you and guess what? I got you."

A whimper escaped her lips.

"But I need more, Ashleigh, and what I want, is you. You're like a drug I can't get out of my system. The way you pleased me, I want more. I need more, and I will have you again. That's a promise."

Ashleigh shuddered at his words. "I'll never let that happen."

The clown laughed. "Well, listen to you, trying to be all tough."

"I am tough.'

"No! You're not. You're weak! Broken. I broke you!"

"I'm not broken," Ashleigh said, swallowing past the fear. "I'm strong."

"Oh, really?" The clown smiled. "That quarterback sure is an influence on you, isn't he?"

Ashleigh froze. *How did he know about Ryan?*

The clown chuckled. "Surprised, Ashleigh? I don't know why. I know everything about you, which is why I'm here. Right now." He gazed across the lawn. "Your sister sure is pretty. Callie, right? Maybe I should..."

"You lay a hand on her, I'll..."

"You'll what? Kill me?" the clown laughed. "You don't have the stomach for that, Ashleigh. I, on the other hand, do. In fact, I killed two girls last night."

"So, it was you," Ashleigh whispered. "Why? They were innocent!"

"No one is innocent, Ashleigh, don't you know that? Everyone has a part to play because everyone needs to remember what happened in Sarasota Bay. They all forgot, but they will remember and by the time I'm done, there will be a nice pile of bodies all because of you, Ashleigh."

"No! Please!" Ashleigh swallowed. "Please, don't kill anyone else." She bit her lip, then spoke into the phone. "I mean, you want me, right?"

"I do."

"Then why don't you grow a pair of balls and come get me!" Ashleigh shouted. "I'm done being your little puppet. You want me, come and get me!"

"With pleasure."

The stall door behind her suddenly swung open, and she swung around, just as someone dressed like the clown raced out of the stall. She screamed, the phone falling to the ground, and she ducked as he charged toward her. The knife missed her, and she turned, racing toward the door.

She wrapped her hand around the handle, pulling it open.

It stuck.

She swore, her eyes going to the doorstopper jammed underneath the door, and glanced over her shoulder, just as the clown raced toward her again. He lunged for her, and she ducked again. She dropped to the floor, sliding between his legs. "Hey, asshole!" she shouted, as she jumped to her feet.

He swung toward her.

"Take this!" She kicked her leg out, striking him in the middle of the chest. He stumbled, falling backward into the stall behind him, his head striking the toilet with a hard thunk.

"You're not dealing with the same girl you dealt with six months ago, ass clown," she shouted, glancing toward her phone. "I'm a different person now." She picked up her bag, kicking the doorstopper free from the door, and turned, racing out of the bathroom. She rounded the corner, and gasped, as she smacked into a hard body.

"Ashleigh!" Billy wrapped his hands around her shoulders. "What's wrong? Why aren't you in class?"

"He called me!" Ashleigh cried, her whole body shaking. "And he attacked me in the bathroom. He's dressed just like him! Billy.... he... he's coming for me."

Billy stared at her, then glanced toward the bathroom. "Stay here," he said, before disappearing around the corner.

"No! Billy!"

Ashleigh leaned against the wall, wrapping her arms around herself. Oh God. What if something happened to him? She couldn't bare it if something happened to Billy.

Several moments later, Billy reappeared, dragging a young man behind him.

"Hey! Let go of me!" A young dark-haired man was shouting, as he struggled against Billy's grip. "It was a prank! See! It's fake!"

"So, you think all of this is funny?" Billy asked as he dragged the kid toward the doors. "Four young women were kidnapped, by someone wearing that same, exact outfit you are wearing right now. Two young women were murdered, with that exact knife you're holding in your hand, right now. Did you, do it? Did you kill them?"

"What? No!"

"Did you kidnap those young women?"

"Of course not! I'm new in town! I didn't do anything!"

"Either way, you're coming with me."

Ashleigh stared at the kid, as he and Billy disappeared through the doors. She didn't even know him. Why would someone she didn't even know, want to hurt her? Scare her?

"Ashleigh?"

Ashleigh glanced up as a young man walked up. "Yes?"

"I'm Detective Andrew Stark, Billy's partner. Is It okay if I give you a ride to the station?"

Ashleigh nodded. "Yeah. Sure. That's fine. Thank you."

"Is there anyone you want to call?"

He held her phone out to her, and Ashleigh took it, for a moment thinking about Ryan. He'd told her to call, but she shouldn't. The clown already knew about him. She did not want to put him in danger.

"No," she finally said, slipping her phone into her bag and following the detective down the hallway. "I don't want anyone else to get involved in this. Too many people have been hurt already." She paused, glancing at the detective. "He called me," she whispered. "He's the one who killed those girls, and he said more are going to be dying. That he wasn't done, not until everyone remembered what happened in Sarasota Bay."

Chapter Thirteen

She was ignoring him.

Ryan sighed, tucking his phone into the pocket of his bag, as he made his way across campus later that afternoon. He should be grateful she wasn't calling him. He needed to focus on practice, not on Ashleigh. But dammitt, he couldn't stop thinking about her!

"Ry!"

"What?" He glanced up, as Jacob joined him. "What's up?"

"What's up? You completely disappeared on me last night! I thought you were coming back after you dropped Ashleigh off."

"I never said that. Plus, Ashleigh needed me. She had a bit of a rough night."

"I know. I was there!"

"Kenzie really went off the rails after you left last night," Rome said, as he hurried up to them. "You should have seen it!

She got w*aaay* drunk and got into a huge fight with one of the other cheerleaders."

"Complete cat fight!" Devante added as he fell into step with them. "It was... well... not what I was expecting."

"Guys, do you really think I care about what Kenzie does?" Ryan asked, glancing at them. "We're broken up!"

"You're kidding, right?" Devante raised a brow at him. "She's psychotic, Ryan!"

"You do know she has your wedding all figured out, right?" Micah, one of the cornerbacks for the team asked, as he walked past. "She showed her book to Bethany."

"I bet she even has the names of your children picked out," Christopher, a safety for the team, chimed in.

"See. What did I say?" Devante asked. "Psychotic."

"Come on, guys. She's not *that* bad."

They all gave him a look, before entering the building, and Ryan sighed, running a hand across his face. This day was getting longer and longer the more it passed.

He disappeared into the locker room, changing into his pads and uniform, before heading out to the field with the rest of his teammates.

"Alright boys, huddle up!"

The loud, booming voice split through the air, followed by the shrill sound of a whistle. They all hurried across the field, huddling around the six-foot-seven, black man as he gestured them forward.

"Afternoon, Tigers!"

"Afternoon, Coach!"

Coach, Ahmed Fitzgerald glanced at the men standing around him and tipped his hat to them. "Congratulations, boys. You made it through the first preseason." He clapped his hands together. "And, undefeated."

"We're not going to stop there, Coach!" Roman shouted. "We're going undefeated this year!"

Ryan sighed, as the rest of the team hooted. *Rome, you just poked the bear.*

"Undefeated? Did you just say undefeated?" Coach Fitz strode forward, stopping directly in front of Rome. "Rome, do you know how many teams go undefeated?"

"Ah. No."

"Do you know how many teams win the championship, that go undefeated?"

"Ah. No."

"Because it's extremely rare to go undefeated," Coach Fitz said. "Each and every year, every team puts their very best football on the field. You know why? Because each one of those teams has one goal. To bring home a championship, so, I do not want to hear anything about going undefeated, do you hear me? I want a damned championship!"

"Yes, Coach."

"Now, let's get to work!" Coach Fitz shouted, clapping his hands together. "And let's warm up!"

They scattered across the field, going through their warmups, and soon, they were split up into their respective groups. The offense on one side of the field, the defense on the other, and Ryan found himself throwing to his receivers.

"Set, hut!"

He stepped back, stepping over the blocks the coaches had placed on the ground, and threw a tight spiral through the air. It landed right in Jacob's hands.

"Hey, look at that! Jacob actually caught the ball today!" Ryan shouted as Jacob jogged back toward him. "What was it? Three dropped passes you had in our game the other night?"

"Ha ha. Very funny, Ryan."

Ryan shrugged. "If the shoe fits." He caught the ball Jacob threw his way, glancing up as Marcus walked by.

"Better watch yourself out there today, Ryan," Marcus said, as he walked past. "I still owe you for this nasty shiner you gave me last night."

"Can you just let it go, Marcus?" Ryan asked in exasperation. "We're on the same team. We have to work together. Can't we find some way to get along?"

Marcus didn't answer. He walked past him, bumping him in the shoulder, and headed off across the field.

"Jackass," Ryan muttered under his breath. "I should have done more than just give you a nasty shiner."

"Ryan, I'd watch my back if I were you," Devante told him, as he walked up. "He's been talking all day about destroying you."

"I'll keep my eyes peeled," Ryan told him. "But my offensive line had better hold up during our scrimmage today."

The whistle blew, and they stopped, glancing to where the coach was gesturing them toward the middle of the field. They all knew what that meant. It was scrimmage time.

Ryan drew in the offense, waving them in and huddling up. "Okay, guys, Marcus is on the warpath, and we need to show coach we've got this. This is my last year, and I really, really want to win a championship. So, let's do this!"

"You got it, Ryan!"

They clapped their hands together and broke free from the huddle. Ryan fastened the chin strip on his helmet, taking his spot behind the offensive line. "Set, hut!"

He took three steps back, going through his reads as he scanned the field. Jacob was running down the right side of the field, with the cornerback, Samuel, pressed up against him. Rome was running down the left side of the field, with Micah, hot on his heels. Two of the linebackers had Levi boxed in, and Jackson, their tight end was cutting up the middle, the safeties coming down to cover him. Then, he saw Devante, as he broke free across the middle of the field. He threw the ball, and Devante caught it with ease.

"Yes!" Coach pumped his fist in the air. "Now, that's what I'm talking about, boys!"

The next play was a pass down the left sideline to Rome, which he dropped. Another play was a handoff to Devante, which he was able to get five yards out of, and another was a pass downfield to Jacob. He caught it with ease and raced down the field. Unfortunately, he was tackled ten yards short of the end zone.

"Agh!"

Marcus let out a shout, and shook his head, pacing down the ten-yard line. "Come on!"

"He's getting worse," Levi said, as he glanced over at Marcus. "I don't like this, Ryan."

"Practice is almost over. We got this." Ryan took his place behind the offensive line once more. "Set hut!"

He stepped back, once again going through his reads. Much like before, there wasn't much separation between the receivers and the defenders, then he saw Jacob break free racing toward the end zone. He drew his arm back, but before he could get the throw off, arms wrapped around his waist, driving him to the ground.

Oomph!

"Told you I was going to get you, Ryan," Marcus said, grinning, as he stared down at him. "All day, baby. All fucking day!"

"Dammitt, Marcus, would you get off of me?" Ryan shoved Marcus off of him, wincing, as he rubbed his shoulder. "I know coach allows us to tackle in practice, but damn, did you have to hit me so hard? You could have taken me out!"

"Oh, please. You're not made of glass, Ryan, plus I owe you for last night."

"What are you? Ten? Get over it! You were a jackass last night, and I did the right thing knocking you on your ass. It's about time someone did." He dragged himself to his feet, walking across the field and pulled his helmet off. He took the bottle of water offered to him, taking a quick swig.

"Oh please. You couldn't take me again if you even tried."

Ryan raised a brow at him. "Marcus, the last thing I want to do is fight with you. We're teammates. We're supposed to be working together, but why do you have to make it so hard? You act like you're the star of the team when in reality, none of us are better than the other. We're a team. We win together. We lose together. It's why it's called a team sport."

"You do know..."

"That you're the best defensive player to come forth in years?" Ryan asked, chuckling. "Yes. I've heard you say that about a million times, but I also know you have a temper. It's the reason we lost the state championship game last year. Because you couldn't control that temper of yours."

"Ryan..."

"You did not just blame me for that game, again." Marcus strode forward, fury in his eyes as he ripped off his helmet and tossed it to the ground. "You know that call was bullshit!"

"You almost put that kid in the hospital!" Ryan shouted. "But it wouldn't be the first time now, would it?"

"You asshole." Marcus's eyes flashed. "You know nothing about..."

"About the kid you put in a wheelchair because of your temper?" Ryan asked. "Yes, I know all about that, and I also know about how your father swept it all under the rug. It must be nice having a rich Daddy to clean up your messes."

"Fuck you!"

"No. Fuck you!" Ryan shouted, swinging around, and gasped as arms wrapped around him, driving him into the ground.

"You know nothing about me, and nothing about what happened back then!" Marcus shouted as he tackled him to the ground. He raised his fist, striking Ryan in the face. "And I do not let anyone clean up my messes. I take care of myself!"

"And what a fine job you've done," Ryan taunted, dodging the fist that came his way, and wrapping his hands around Marcus's shoulders. He flipped him over, striking his fist forward, and punching Marcus in the face. "Four restraining orders. Two assault charges. You're an embarrassment to this team!"

"Ryan!"

"Marcus!"

Running feet sounded behind them, hands grabbing each of them and pulling them apart.

"Jesus Christ! Are we really doing this again?" Devante asked as he struggled to hold Ryan back.

"Please tell me this isn't still about last night," Jacob said, as he and two other guys fought to hold Marcus back.

"No, it has nothing to do with last night. It has to do with Marcus being an asshole and not taking any responsibility for his actions," Ryan said, jerking free from Devante's hold. "I'm good."

"Oh, I'm sure you are," Marcus said, turning, and spitting blood into the ground. "Good ole Ryan. Always the savior, aren't you? Always the good guy. Too bad your mother isn't around to see the guy you've turned into. I mean, it was your fault she died, wasn't it?"

"You asshole!" Ryan lunged forward.

"Ryan! No!" Rome stepped in front of him, blocking his path "He's not worth it!"

"I beg to differ," Ryan said, seething, clenching his hands into fists as he stared at Marcus. "He's intentionally goading me, and it's working."

"Just let it go."

Marcus laughed. "Oh, yes, Ryan, let go of the fact that you killed your own mother. Excellent advice. We all know you're the one who caused the accident. Does Ashleigh know? Think she'd look at you the same way if she knew what happened?"

"Leave Ashleigh out of this. She has nothing to do with this."

Marcus shrugged. "I know you have a thing for her, and we all know that you always lose the people you care about. Ashleigh, well, she's probably next. After all, she is being targeted by a killer. I'd be surprised if she lasts the week."

"You son of a bitch!"

Ryan broke free from Rome, diving forward and tackling Marcus to the ground. He raised his arm, striking him in the face, again and again.

"Ryan! Stop!"

Hands struggled to pull him back, and he glared at the men behind him. "Back off."

"No, Ryan, you need to cool off! This isn't helping anybody."

"Are you kidding me?" Ryan glared at Jacob. "This jackass has gotten away with far too much, for far too long. Did you know he told Ashleigh she'd die alone last night? Who does that?"

Marcus smiled, turning and spitting blood. "A realist."

"You..."

A shrill whistle sounded, interrupting them.

"Ryan! Marcus! What the hell is going on here?" Coach Fitz rushed up, as Ryan was dragged to his feet, stepping between the two. "Why on earth, are my two star players fighting with one another?"

"It's about a girl," Chris said, rolling his eyes.

"A girl?" Coach spun around, staring at them. "You're fighting over a girl? I'm trying to win a championship here!"

"Not just any girl, Coach," Ryan told him. "It's Ashleigh Carlson."

"Ashleigh..." His eyes suddenly widened. "Wait. Isn't that..."

Ryan nodded.

Coach swung toward Marcus. "You did something to her?"

Marcus grinned. "More than a little something."

Coach glanced at Ryan.

"Tell me you got a good punch in?"

Ryan laughed. Man, he loved his Coach! "More than one."

"He also got in a dig about Ryan's mother," Rome muttered under his breath.

Coach turned to Marcus. "Seriously? You brought that crap up again, Marcus?" He sighed, turning to Ryan. "Ry, I'm glad you're looking after Ashleigh. Lord knows she needs all the support she can get, and Marcus, should have never brought up your mother." He laid a hand on Ryan's shoulder. "But, next time there's a fight, you'll both be suspended from the game. Got it?"

Ryan nodded. "Got it."

"Good. Now, go clean up."

"Hey, Ryan."

Ryan sighed, turning to Marcus. "What is it now, Marcus?"

"I wasn't talking about last night," Marcus told him, grinning.

"What are you talking about?"

"Ashleigh. I wasn't talking about last night. My buddy and I, well, we gave her a little scare today. I bet she won't be coming back to class any time soon."

Ryan swung to the coach. "I'm going to kill him."

"No, you will not," the coach said, grabbing Marcus by the arm and pulling him across the field. "You are going to go check on Ashleigh, and I am going to deal with Marcus." He shoved Marcus forward. "Come with me, and you are going to tell me everything you know. If you don't, I'll call every coach I know, and tell them just how much of a prick you really are. Good luck getting someone to draft you then."

"Wait. You can't do that!"

"Oh, just watch me."

They disappeared from sight, and Ryan turned, racing off across the lawn.

"Ryan, wait! We're coming with you!"

Jacob, Levi, and Rome hurried after him, but Ryan barely even noticed. All he could think about was Ashleigh. Dammit, she had promised to call him! Why hadn't she? More importantly, when he found her, what kind of shape was she going to be in?

Chapter Fourteen

"So, let me get this straight...." Billy leaned back in his chair, gazing at the young man sitting across from him. "You, and your buddy, Marcus, decided it would be fun to dress up as the clown and scare Ashleigh?"

"Actually, it was Marcus and Kenzie's idea," Johnny Carson said, fidgeting in his seat as he avoided Billy's eyes. "They thought it would be fun to scare her."

"You know, I really don't understand you people," Billy said, shaking his head.

"What do you mean?"

"This generation... it's like you feed off of each other's pain. Do you have any idea what they went through in there?"

"No, Sir."

"Well, let me explain it to you," Billy said. "They were each tortured. Electrocution. Suffocation. Drowning. Rape. Does any of that sound humane to you?"

"No, Sir."

"Then stop being a fucking moron! People's lives are in danger, and this stunt is just pissing me off. I don't care who put you up to it, you are responsible for your own actions. Not Kenzie. Not Marcus. So grow the fuck up and stop wasting my damned time!" Billy sighed, running a hand through his hair. "Get out of here. Now. Before I find some reason to throw your ass in jail, and before you leave, you better apologize to Ashleigh."

The kid didn't need to be told twice. He jumped to his feet and raced out of the room.

Billy sighed, closing his eyes and pinching the bridge of his nose. This was a goddamn, fucking nightmare.

"You good?"

He snapped his eyes open, staring at Andrew as he poked his head into the room. "I'll live. What's up?"

"Kenzie and Marcus are here."

"Fantastic. Put them each in a separate room. I'll be in, in a minute." He rose to his feet, walking out of the room and down the hallway. He poked his head into his office. "Ash?"

"Hey, Billy." Ashleigh looked up from where she was sitting at his desk. "He say anything?"

"Sounds like it was just a prank set up by Kenzie and Marcus. They're both here now."

"You're questioning them?"

"I kind of have to, Ash. If they were involved in this stunt, who knows what else they were involved in? I highly doubt they were involved in killing those girls last night, or in your abduction, but I don't want to leave any stones unturned. I'd be a terrible detective if I didn't follow through on this."

"I know. I just... I don't like this. I mean, I know Kenzie. We were best friends once. How she could..."

"That was a long time ago, Ash. We really don't know her anymore." Billy placed a hand on her arm. "Do you want me to get you anything? A water? Soda?"

Ashleigh shook her head. "No. I'm good."

"Okay. Well, I'll be back in a bit to check on you."

"Thanks, Billy."

"Of course. Are you sure you don't to call anyone? Maybe, Ryan?"

Ashleigh shook her head. "No. I don't want him involved, Billy. Too many people are already dead or injuredbecause of me. I don't want anyone else getting hurt."

"Speaking of that, we weren't able to trace the number that called you, but I was able to get a hold of the Sarasota Bay police. They're putting a police detail on your sisters for a couple of days."

"Thanks, Billy."

"Of course. They're like family to me, too, you know."

"Yes. I know." Ashleigh tapped her fingers against the desk, staring at the board on the other side of the room. "I've been staring at your board for the last hour."

"Oh, jeesh. I'm sorry, Ash. I should have covered it up."

"No. That's not what I meant." Ashleigh paused, staring at it again. "It's just... when he called me, he said something about

Sarasota Bay. Do you think he was talking about what happened to the Millers?"

"It's the only thing that makes sense."

"I don't remember that time very well," Ashleigh admitted. "I was what? Thirteen?"

"Yes. I believe so."

"We were friends with those girls, weren't we?"

Billy nodded. "Yes. We all grew up together, on the same block. You really don't remember?"

Ashleigh shook her head.

"It's probably for the best. I wish I could forget it. I mean, I don't know a lot about what happened, but I do remember looking at some of the crime scene photos my dad had. It was bloody and gruesome, and…"

"And Mer and Aimee were never found. I know." She rose to her feet, stopping in front of the board. "And what about Wes?"

"We still haven't been able to find him."

"I have to tell Nikki. She has a right to know."

"I already did, Ash," Billy told her. He paused a moment. "Ash. Whoever this person is, he's obsessed with what happened back then, and he knows you're connected to the murders. I'm pretty sure it's the reason you were kidnapped in the first place, and now, he's killing people. I want you to be careful, okay? Whatever his endgame is, it can't be good."

"I promise, Billy. I'll be careful."

"Good." Billy pulled her to his side, giving her a hug. "Because, I don't know what I would do if something happened to you, kid."

Ashleigh rolled her eyes. "I hate it when you call me that."

"I call all of you that," Billy said, pressing a kiss to her cheek, as Andrew motioned to him from the doorway. He nodded. "I gotta go. Duty calls." He turned, disappearing out of the room to join Andrew in the hallway.

"She doing okay?" Andrew asked, as they walked down the hallway together.

Billy nodded. "Yeah. I think so. She's pretty tough, but eventually, she's going to break. I just hope she doesn't push away the person who's there for her when she finally does." He paused outside of the interrogation room. "So, which one you want?"

Andrew smiled. "You know what, I'll take Marcus. I heard he's a real prick, and I actually can't wait to get face to face with him." He rubbed his hands together. "I'll let you have her highness."

"Great. Just what I always wanted. To be stuck in a room with Kenzie." Billy sighed, gathering his thoughts, before entering the room.

"Hello, Kenzie. It's been a while, and boy, do we have some catching up to do."

Ashleigh leaned back in the chair, rubbed her eyes, and stared around Billy's office, hating the fact that she was here... again. She hated being here. It reminded her of the last time she'd been here, right after she'd escaped the manor. It was a time she would really not like to revisit.

She picked up a file on Billy's desk, fingering through the pages, stopping when she flipped to the mugshot of Wesley Jenkins.

She remembered Nikki's father as a nice man. He'd always been there for Nikki and her mother. He'd been loving, supportive, and not a million miles away like her own father had been. When she and her friends had had sleepovers over at Nikki's, he'd always made his famous snickerdoodle cookies. A hit with all of them. How could a man like that, be capable of murder?

When she'd heard the news, she'd been in shock. She'd tried to reach out to Nikki, but she hadn't been able to reach her. Later, she'd learned that her parents had forbidden her from talking to her. Why? She'd never gotten an answer.

She sighed, flipping the folder closed, and rose to her feet. She crossed to the board sitting on the other side of the room, wrapping her arms around herself as she stared at it. Was it true? Was this really connected to the Millers? If so, who was doing all of this, and why, had he set his sights on her? She knew nothing about that day.

She stared at the board, at the images of Meredith and Amelia Miller. They'd grown up on the same street as her in the big, red house on the corner. Amelia had been her age, with long, red hair and a snow white complexion. Meredith had been a year younger than them. She'd had dark, brown hair, and much like her sister, pale, white skin. She just wished she could remember them better. What had they been like?

She turned back to Billy's desk, rifling through the files, finding the one on the Miller murders. Maybe if she saw it, she could get some clarity? And maybe, remember the girls who Billy said she had been friends with for the first thirteen years of her life.

Chapter Fifteen

"Hello, Kenzie, thanks for coming in." Billy took a seat across the table from her, sitting back and regarding her.

"I still don't understand why I'm here," Kenzie said, twirling a lock of hair around her finger. "I didn't do anything!"

"Now, that's not exactly true, is it?" Billy asked, sliding a package toward her. "You bought this, didn't you, Kenzie?" He asked, pointing to the clown mask that lay on the table.

Kenzie glanced at it, then away. "No. I didn't."

"Kenzie, you don't need to lie. I already pulled your credit card statement. I know you did."

Kenzie sighed. "Fine. I bought the damned mask. So what?"

"And did you and Marcus tell your friend Johnny to wear it, to scare Ashleigh?"

"It was Marcus's idea," Kenzie said, dropping her hands into her lap and staring across the table at him. "He brought up the idea to me at Jacob's party. He was pissed that she'd gotten away from him, and even more pissed that she had left with Ryan."

"Why?"

"He and Ryan have never gotten along," Kenzie said, rolling her eyes. "Ever since they both got to UCLA and joined the Tigers, Marcus has been jealous of him. He wanted to take Ryan down a notch. He thought if Ryan was distracted, it might take him off his game."

"Seems kind of childish."

"You obviously do not know Marcus."

"And you? Why did you go along with it?"

Kenzie shrugged. "I was drunk and pissed. Ryan and I... we'd dated for three years when he suddenly decided to end it one day. When we were at the party, it was supposed to be my chance to get him back, but she got in the way. She always gets in the way."

"What do you mean by that?"

"Oh, Billy, don't be naïve. You may be a year older than us, but we still grew up together! We were all friends. All of us, until everyone moved away. Well except for her." Kenzie scowled. "Do you have any idea what it was like being friends with her? Seeing everyone constantly console her? Acting as if she was special? She always got everything, and I... I got nothing!"

"And then you turned your back on her, and joined the popular crowd?"

Kenzie smiled. "Yes. I got my own life, my own friends, and finally, I was able to get what I wanted."

Billy stared at her, thinking that she was not the same person he had grown up with, but pushed the thought to the side. He slid a photo across the table. "Do you know these girls?"

Kenzie nodded. "Yes. That's M.J and Aimee. M.J. tried out for the cheerleading squad last year."

"Did you know either of them well?"

Kenzie shook her head. "No. We didn't exactly run in the same circles."

"What do you mean by that?"

"Well, they weren't exactly popular. I try not to associate with anyone who's underneath me."

Billy raised a brow but didn't respond. "And last night? Where were you?"

"You know I was at the party. I bet twenty different people could vouch for me."

"So, you didn't sneak out and kill those girls? And you didn't kidnap Ashleigh and her friends six months ago?"

"What? No!" Kenzie's eyes widened. "I might be selfish, but I'm not a psycho! Plus, I thought it was a man who did those things?"

"We're not ruling out the possibility that two people could've been involved," Billy told her, taking the photo and tucking it back into the file. "What we do know, is that whoever is behind this, is obsessed with what happened ten years ago at the Miller household, and you, are connected to that time whether you like it or not, Kenzie." He rose to his feet. "Don't leave town. We might have more questions, but for now, you are free to go."

He opened the door, and strode down the hallway, stopping to stare through the glass window as Andrew interviewed Marcus

"You just can't help yourself, can you?"

Ashleigh glanced up from the file she was sifting through, staring at Kenzie as she stood in the doorway. "I'm sorry?"

"You. You always stir up trouble everywhere you go! They're accusing me of murder, Ashleigh!"

"That's not my fault," Ashleigh told her, anger starting to bubble up inside of her. "You started this, Kenzie, when you bought that damn mask and decided to trick Johnny into scaring me."

"It was a prank!"

"You know what happened to me, Kenzie. You know what I went through. How could you do that to me? We used to be friends!"

"Yeah. Like a lifetime ago," Kenzie said, rolling her eyes. "We haven't been friends in a long time. Not since..."

"The Millers, I know. That's actually what I'm reading about," Ashleigh said, holding up the file. "I don't remember much from that time, do you?"

"No. Not really." Kenzie took a step forward, peering over her shoulder. "Are you supposed to be reading that? Aren't those things confidential?"

"Probably, but it's Billy, plus he just left it lying around. I highly doubt he's going to arrest me." She glanced up at Kenzie. "What do you mean, I'm always stirring up trouble?"

Kenzie sighed. "That came out wrong. I just meant, you always seem to be surrounded by tragedy. I mean, your father was gone all the time. Obviously, that's not your fault, he was in the army, but then, he died!" She lifted a finger. "Then there was your mother, with her drinking and of course, her abandoning you." She lifted another finger. "Then, there were the Millers, and you, having to take care of your sisters."

"You make it sound like I intentionally made myself a victim."

"No. I know you didn't, and this is going to make me sound like a complete bitch, but being friends with you was exhausting! I felt like I was the one keeping you together, keeping you upright, and I just couldn't do it anymore. You just, you weren't the person I knew anymore. You weren't the strong, stubborn girl I knew. You were weak, whiney... a victim."

Ashleigh fiddled with the page. "I'm sorry. I didn't realize how much I leaned on you back then."

"No. I'm the one who should be sorry. I should have talked to you back then, not run away like a coward. And I really am sorry about what happened with Marcus, and today with the prank. I should have known better." Kenzie fiddled with a lock of her hair, thinking. "Ashleigh, have you ever felt... not like yourself?" she asked.

Ashleigh laughed, nodding. "Yes. All the time."

"I've felt that way, ever since the Millers. Like a part of me was missing."

"You know, I had the same feeling back then," Ashleigh said. "I chalked it up to growing up, maturing, but if you felt it too..."

"It can't be a coincidence."

A knock sounded on the door, and they both glanced up.

"Can we help you?" Ashleigh asked, staring at the young man standing in the doorway.

"Hi. Yeah, I'm Johnny. The prick who scared you in the bathroom," Johnny said, walking in. "I just wanted to say I'm sorry."

"Oh." Ashleigh stared at him, vaguely remembering him as Billy cuffed him and ushered him out of the campus building. "Yes. I remember. You scared the hell out of me!"

"I know. I'm sorry. Not my finest moment."

"Why'd you do it?" She glanced over at Kenzie. "Why did both of you do it?"

"Marcus."

They said the word in unison, and Ashleigh sighed. "It's always Marcus, isn't it?"

"He likes to make promises he can't keep, and make an idea sound better when in reality, it really isn't," Kenzie murmured. "He got to me at the party, when I was drunk and depressed. I was so sure Ryan and I were going to get back together. That we were soulmates, but we were never soulmates. We're too... different. Plus, he's different with you, Ash. He really seems to care about you and your safety. He was never that way with me."

"We're just friends."

"For now." Kenzie shook her head. "Anyways, I was drinking *way* too much, and he came up to me. He said he knew how

I felt, what it was like to feel betrayed and that he had a way to get back at you. I didn't really question it. I ordered the costume online and gave it to Johnny. The moment I handed it to Johnny, I immediately regretted it. I am so sorry, Ash."

"I wasn't manipulated quite as badly," Johnny told them. "I'm new here. Just got into town last night, and I really wanted to try out for the football team, but I missed tryouts. Marcus said, if I gave you a scare, and put on the clown costume that he would put in a good word with the coach. Little did I know that the costume was associated with a killer." Johnny shook his head. "I am so sorry, Ash. I trusted the wrong person."

"Yeah, you definitely did," Ashleigh said. "Marcus, well, he's..."

"An ass?" Kenzie provided.

"Yes. He's an ass."

They shared a laugh, and Ashleigh smiled, glancing at them both. "I forgive you. Both of you."

"Seriously?" Kenzie raised a brow.

"Life's too short to hold grudges," Ashleigh told them. "And you're right, Kenzie. I have been playing the victim card for far too long. I have to start fighting for myself. For my life, and I have got to stop being so damned afraid of this clown. I cannot let him control me anymore."

Kenzie smiled. "That's the Ashleigh I remember. I miss her."

Ashleigh laughed, shaking her head. "I think I've missed her too." She held up the file. "And now, I'm going to start educating myself. Knowledge is power, right? If I can remember any part of my childhood from ten years ago, maybe I can start to figure out who this person is, and what they're planning next."

"You want some company?"

Ashleigh raised a brow at Kenzie. "You want to help?"

"I'm not saying that we're going to be best friends," Kenzie said, as she took a seat next to her at the desk. "But we did grow up on the same street. We did hang out with the Millers. Maybe, there's something I remember that you don't?"

Ashleigh shrugged. "It's definitely worth a shot."

"I can help too," Johnny said. "I'm pretty good with puzzles."

"What the hell? Three heads are better than one, right?" Ashleigh asked as she spread out the papers in the file.

Chapter Sixteen

"You're not from around here, are you?" Marcus asked, staring across the table at Detective Stark. "You're new here, aren't you?"

"I'm going to be the one asking the questions here, Marcus," Andrew said, sitting back in his chair and eyeing the young man. "I see you have quite the rap sheet here. Twenty women have filed complaints against you, yet, none of them got to court. Why is that?"

Marcus smiled. "Maybe, I was just that good."

"And maybe, your dad has deep pockets. We found that each of the girls received a payment from your father. You know that's bribery, right? Your father could go to jail. He'd lose his job, and you. You would get kicked out of the school, off the team, and lose any chance of making it to the pros."

"Are you threatening me, Detective?" Marcus's eyes flashed. He jumped to his feet, clenching his hands into fists as he stared across the table at Andrew.

"Sit down, Marcus."

Marcus glared at him but sat back down.

"You also have quite the temper. I talked to your teammates. They said you have it out for Ryan. Why?"

"I'm not answering that." Marcus crossed his arms in front of his chest.

"Ok. Then answer this... why Ashleigh? Why did you target her at the party the last night? You could have chosen anyone, why her?"

Marcus shrugged. "I was bored and thought she might be into something freaky."

"And when she said no..."

Marcus's eyes flashed. "No one says no to me. That's why I devised the plan to scare her. To teach her a lesson, and when I saw her leave with Ryan, well it was perfect. He needed to be knocked down a peg, to remember his place in line."

"And you coerced Johnny into wearing the costume? Knowing he wanted a chance to be on the team?"

Marcus smiled. "Freshmen are easy to manipulate."

Andrew sighed, running a hand over his goatee. He reached down, picked up a package and set it on the table. "Do you recognize this?"

"It's the mask Kenzie bought. The one that Johnny wore to scare Ashleigh."

"It's also the same mask that was found on the murdered girls last night." Detective Stark said, sliding the photo across the table. "Tell me, Marcus. Do you know them?"

"Of course I do," Marcus said, grinning. "That's M.J, and that's Aimee. I fucked them both. In the same night."

Detective Stark sighed. The kid had no class, no dignity, and no respect. "Did you also know that this mask is a carbon copy of the one the man who kidnapped Ashleigh wore?"

"I did hear about that somewhere."

"And where were you, between twelve a.m and two a.m last night?"

"I was at the party, Detective. I'm sure a few people can vouch for me."

"And you didn't sneak out and murder them?"

"Detective, I don't need to kill to get what I want. I get what I want by taking it."

"And six months ago, did you help kidnap Ashleigh and her friends?"

"If I had, they would not have escaped from me."

The kid was an ass, Detective Stark thought, narrowing his eyes on him. *And he was really hard to read. He did not like it.*

He picked up the folder, rising to his feet. "We're going to be bringing your father in for questioning, and we'll also be holding you overnight. We're in the process of getting a warrant for your phone. If you made that call to Ashleigh this morning, we will find out."

He rounded the table, handcuffing Marcus's hands behind his back. "Congratulations, Marcus. You are officially our prime suspect."

He opened the door, passing Marcus off to the waiting officer. "So, what do you think?" he asked, as Marcus disappeared down the hall, glancing at Billy. "Think he did it?"

"He's definitely a prick," Billy said. "But my gut tells me he's not our guy. I mean, all of this is connected to the Millers. He was just a kid back then."

"He could still be the partner. You still think that's possible?"

"I mean, the man did manage to kidnap four women, in the exact same night. How would you explain that?"

"I can't," Andrew said. "But we'll know soon enough." He glanced down at his phone. "Looks like the judge just signed the warrant. I'm going to go talk to our tech guy and see about unlocking his phone. Something about this guy is off to me, Billy. I don't know why, but there just is."

Chapter Seventeen

"These are so gross!" Kenzie cried, staring at the photos laid on the table in front of them. "How does Billy even look at these things?"

"He loves solving mysteries," Ashleigh said, as she stared down at the photos herself, inwardly cringing, as she stared at the images of the Miller family.

From what they had gathered, ten years ago, some unnamed foe had broken into the Miller household, killing Fred, Max, Drew, and Alex Miller. The father and brothers of the girls.

She pointed a finger at the picture. "So, at nine p.m. that night, a call was placed to the police anonymously, saying there was a disturbance at the Miller house."

"And when they arrived, they found everyone dead, except for Lindsay Miller. The mother," Kenzie said, nodding. "She was always so nice."

"She was, wasn't she?" Ashleigh asked, smiling. "Whenever we came over to play with Mer and Aimee, she always had a plate of brownies ready for us, right out of the oven."

"She was always so easy to talk to," Kenzie said, softly. "I felt like I could talk to her about anything."

"You still have a tense relationship with your mom?"

Kenzie nodded. "She's always wanting me to be this perfect version of her. It only got worse after Dad left."

"I'm sorry, Kenz," Ashleigh sent her a tight smile, knowing they all had their tragic family stories.

"Anyways." Kenzie continued. "Who called in the tip?"

"It was anonymous. There's no way of knowing."

"Unless, we somehow get our hands on the recording," Johnny said from where he was leaning against the wall on the other side of the room. He tossed a ball he'd found on Billy's desk into the air. "I might be able to help with that. I have..." He glanced around the precinct, before lowering his voice. "Certain skills."

"Meaning, he's a hacker," Kenzie said, under her breath.

"Johnny, I can't ask you to do that. You could get yourself into trouble!"

Johnny shrugged. "It's nothing I haven't done before."

"I don't think you're going to be able to talk him out of it," Kenzie told her, eyeing Johnny. "He looks pretty determined."

She couldn't argue with that, Ashleigh thought, before turning back to the photos. "Anyways, the four men were each found stabbed to death, and their faces beaten almost beyond recognition. And Lindsay..." She pointed to the photo. "She was badly injured. Her arm was broken. Her ankle sprained, and she was stabbed eight times. She nearly died."

"But she didn't."

"And once she was released from the hospital, she left."

"And so did Syd, Nikki, Billy, and Addy."

Ashleigh nodded. "There's not much else to go on, is there?"

"There never was."

They looked up, as Billy entered the room. He leaned against the doorframe, staring at the three. "You three look awfully comfortable in here."

"We buried the hatchet," Ashleigh said.

Billy raised a brow. "That fast?"

"Some things you have to let go, Billy," Ashleigh told him. "Billy, where's the evidence from the crime scene?"

"There never was any. The only thing we had to go off was the knife found at the crime scene. A knife, that belonged to your father."

"My father?"

Billy nodded. "But at that time, your father was already dead, and the trail went cold. So the murder stayed unsolved."

"But Billy! My father would never hurt anyone!"

"Don't yell at me. I was just a kid back then," Billy said, holding his hands up in surrender. "I'm just telling you what the cops back then thought."

"You mean your father."

A look flashed across Billy's face, and he slowly nodded. "Yes. My father."

"Did they ever find Meredith and Aimee?"

Billy shook his head. "No. Their bodies were never found."

"It's so sad!" Kenzie cried. "And Lindsay... she lost everyone that day."

"Yes. It is, and that is why this should be left to the police. Not to you three, amateur detectives," Billy said, crossing to the desk and packing the papers back into the box. "This is highly confidential information. If my captain knew you were looking through this, I'd be suspended in a heartbeat. You do not want that happening, trust me."

"Sorry, Billy." Ashleigh rose to her feet. "I didn't realize. I was just trying to remember what I might be forgetting from back then."

"It's okay, Ash. I'm not mad. We just need to be careful. The captain already hates that I'm on this case. I don't need another reason for him to pull me off of it."

"I get it. I should get going anyways," Ashleigh said. "I have to get to work."

"You're still going back to work, after everything that's happened?" Billy asked, staring at her. "Ash. I don't know if that's a good idea."

"I have to go back to work, Billy. I need money, and last I knew, money did not grow on trees," Ashleigh said, picking her bag up, and draping it over her shoulder. "Plus, I need something to keep my mind off of everything that's happening."

"Ash, wait. I'll walk with you." Kenzie said, starting after her. "Oh, Billy. How'd things go with Marcus?"

"Oh, you know Marcus. You can never get a straight answer from him," Billy said. "Andrew's going through his phone now. Hopefully, we'll know something soon."

"Well, he didn't make that phone call this morning. I can tell you that," Andrew said, as he walked into the room. "Billy, take a look at this."

Billy took the phone from him, pressing play on the video that was on the screen. Immediately, an image of Marcus filled the screen.

"Hey, Babe, you coming?"

A feminine voice sounded in the background, and Marcus grinned, glancing over his shoulder as he pulled his shirt over his head. "Absolutely, Baby."

He rose, and behind him, was Kenzie laying in the bed.

Kenzie's mouth dropped open. "When the hell did this happen? I don't remember this!"

"Apparently, last night. Look, it's time-stamped," Andrew said, pointing. "At 1:23 am. We found his alibi for the murders, Billy."

"God! That's so gross! I can't believe he... I can't believe I..." Kenzie shook her head. "God! I'm going to kill him!"

"Like you said, a selfish prick," Billy said. "But, he didn't kill those girls."

"And neither did Kenzie, right?" Ashleigh asked.

Billy nodded. "Yes. Which means there's still a murderer out there, and we have no idea what he has planned next."

Chapter Eighteen

"Ashleigh! Oh my God!"

Stephanie Francis stared at Ashleigh with wide, green eyes, an hour later when she walked into the restaurant. "I can't believe you're here!"

"Me neither," Ashleigh said, as she stepped up next to the young, blonde woman, leaning over to punch in. "I feel like it's been ages since I've stepped inside this restaurant."

"You know I feel horrible about what happened, right?" Stephanie asked. "If I hadn't gone home early that night..."

"Then you might have been captured along with me," Ashleigh told her. "Don't blame yourself, Steph. It's not your fault. It's his and I'm guessing, if he hadn't captured me that night, he would have found some other way to do it. One thing I've learned about this psycho is that he is very determined to do what he wants, when he wants it, and no one will stand in his way."

She walked around the corner, disappearing into the back and passing the kitchen.

"Ashleigh!" Vinny Ricardo looked up from where he was placing a couple of plates in the window. "Oh my God! You're back!"

"Yes. I'm back and ready to get back to work," Ashleigh said, as she pulled her hair back into a ponytail, and smiled at the tall, dark haired man with tattoos covering his arms. Vinny had worked at the restaurant ever since she could remember. He was nice, sweet, and sometimes, got a little too protective over his female co-workers. Besides that, he was an amazing cook. "Didn't Franny tell you I was coming back today?"

"She did," Francesca Marinelli said, as she breezed past her. "But with the latest murders, we weren't sure if you were still coming in."

"I need something to take my mind off of it," Ashleigh said as she breezed past, smiling at the older woman. She was always full of energy, and the owner of the restaurant. She and her husband, Carlos had built it in Los Angeles almost fifty years ago. Even now, after his death, Francesca still had it bustling with business. Her three children even came by to help occasionally.

"Well, either way, we are glad to have you back."

"Yes! And look at the place!" Steph cried. "It is going to be a busy night!"

"Best news I've heard all day," Ashleigh said, as she set her personal belongings in the locker. She grabbed an apron, tying it around her waist, before picking up her order tablet, and walking back toward the dining room.

Francesca's was the most authentic Italian restaurant in LA. The walls were painted a dark purple, with pictures of Italy hanging around the room. Booths lined the perimeter of the room, next to large, bay windows. There were small, square-shaped tables positioned around the middle of the room, each table had a small candle laying on the table, along with a menu, wine list, and dessert book.

"Good evening." She walked up to the first table. "I'm Ashleigh, I'll be your server for the evening. How are we today?"

"It's been a day," the young woman said, shaking her head. She glanced up at Ashleigh, her eyes widening. "Oh my. You're that girl on the news!"

"One of them, yes, "Ashleigh said, sighing. "It seems, I can't get away from what happened to me."

"Oh, I'm sorry. I didn't mean..."

"It's ok. Really. I just would like to focus on work tonight. So, have you made a decision, or do you need more time?" she asked, nodding to the menus.

"Oh right!" The woman laughed, shaking her head. "I'm not sure. I'm undecided between the shrimp scampi and the blackened chicken Alfredo."

"You know, I was thinking about the shrimp scampi too," the dark-haired man sitting across from her said. "Tell you what. How about I get the shrimp scampi, you get the Alfredo, and we can share."

"That sounds perfect!" The woman beamed at the man across from her.

"And a bottle of Merlot to go with it," the man said, closing his menu and handing it to Ashleigh. "By the way, you, and the other girls. Your friends. You are all very brave, and a lot of people out there, are in awe of all of you. Just, the next time anyone says anything to you, or makes you feel uncomfortable, remember that."

"Thank you." Ashleigh gave him a small smile, before gathering up the menus and making her way across the room. She stopped at three more tables. A group of women ordered the ravioli. Another young couple, who looked to be on a date, one ordering the Turkey Caprese sandwich with a salad, the other ordering the Linguini. The last table, was a young woman sitting alone, working on her computer. She ordered the eggplant Parmigiana.

She zigzagged through the tables. "Hey, Vinny! Got some tickets for you!"

"You and the other six waitresses working," Vinny told her, grumpily. "Order up!"

She just rolled her eyes, taking the plates and handing them out at the table in the corner. "One Vegan ravioli, and one Spaghetti Carbonara. Is there anything else I can get for you?"

"No. Thank you. This looks lovely."

Ashleigh smiled, turning away, and making her way back across the room. The bell rang above the door, and she turned, as four football players walked into the restaurant.

Ryan. Crap. She hadn't responded to his texts, had she?

She watched, as he stepped into the restaurant, his eyes scanning the room before finally landing on her.

"Jesus Christ, Ash!" He hurried toward her, reaching out and resting his hands on her shoulders. "I've been trying to call you all afternoon! Marcus said he did something... are you okay?"

Ashleigh nodded. "Yeah. I'm okay. I'm sorry I didn't call you. I didn't mean to worry you," She stepped back, out of his reach.

Ryan dropped his arms, quirking an eyebrow at her. "You're sure?"

Ashleigh nodded. "Yes."

"What happened?"

Ashleigh swallowed. "He... he called me Ryan."

"Who called..." He stopped, his eyes widening. "You don't mean..."

Ashleigh nodded. "He's back, Ryan."

"Jesus." Ryan ran a hand along his jaw. "Ash, why didn't you call me? I told you to call me if anything happened. In fact, you promised me you would."

"Because I don't want to drag you into my mess!" Ashleigh snapped, brushing past him. "Look, Ryan, I appreciate what you've done for me. Really, I do, but you need to stay away from me. There's a madman out there, killing people because of me and I do not want you getting hurt because of me."

"Ash." Ryan reached out, grasping her hand in his. "Ash. Look at me."

She shook her head. She couldn't look at him, if she did, she'd cave. It was better this way.

"Ash."

Ryan cupped her chin in his hand, tilting her face up so she was looking into his eyes. "No matter how hard you try to push me away, I'm not going anywhere."

"Why do you even care?" Ashleigh whispered, a tear streaking down her cheek.

"I'm not even sure," Ryan said, chuckling as he wiped the tear away. "There's just something about you…"

Ashleigh smiled, reaching up and wrapping her hand around his wrist. She wanted to push him away. Everything inside of her was telling her to, but she also felt safe around him. "This isn't smart. If something happened to you…" She shook her head, stepping back and she suddenly gasped. "Ryan!" She touched a hand to his cheek. "What happened?" she whispered, staring at his bruised and battered face.

"Ah. Marcus and I got into it."

"Got into it?" Jacob walked up, chuckling. "Ryan! You kicked his ass!"

"Ryan, please tell me you weren't fighting over me," Ashleigh whispered. "I don't want to cause problems for you or the team."

"First of all, I didn't start it," Ryan informed her, wincing a little as he rotated his shoulder. "And it wasn't because of you. At least, not at first." He flashed her a grin. "And don't worry about me or the team. We'll be fine."

"But…"

"Ash. Please don't worry about it. You have enough to worry about," Ryan said, putting his arm around her and giving her a small hug. "Please."

Ashleigh glanced up at him. He was trying his best to give her his usual, heart stopping grin, but it wasn't quite reaching his eyes. "Ryan…"

"You know, I'm kind of hungry," Ryan said, glancing at Jacob. "You in the mood for some Italian?"

"Hell yeah!"

"There aren't any free tables," Ashleigh said, eyeing him. "There's room at the bar, though."

"Perfect! I could use a drink."

"Ryan…"

He hurried off, and Ashleigh sighed, glancing at Jacob. "Jacob. Is he ok?"

Jacob shrugged. "I think so. It's been a rough day, though. Marcus… he pushed some of Ryan's buttons today. Brought up some old things."

"What things?"

"It's not really my place to tell you," Jacob told her. "Don't worry. He'll tell you when he's ready." He turned and headed for the bar.

"There he is!"

Rome jumped up on the stool next to Ryan, punching him in the arm. "Marcus should be mindful of pissing you off from here on out! You're a force to be reckoned with, Ryan!"

"It was nothing, Rome," Ryan said, as the bartender set the beer in front of him. He lifted it to his lips, taking a sip, and winced again.

"Man! It was fucking awesome!" Levi cried as he bounced up to the bar. "You totally kicked his ass!"

"Levi Antonio!"

Francesca glanced up from where she was standing in the doorway just behind the bar, glaring at her son. "What did I tell you about using that sort of language in here?"

"Whoops." Levi ducked his head. "Sorry, Mom."

Ashleigh giggled, shaking her head. Through the last couple of years, she'd gotten to witness the relationship between Francesca and her son. It was always entertaining. She turned, disappearing into the kitchen. She reappeared a moment later, setting an ice pack on the table in front of Ryan. "Here. You look like you're hurting."

"Thanks." Ryan gave her another smile. "My shoulder's going to need it."

"You're a real prince, Ryan," Francesca said, walking up to the bar. She patted Ashleigh on the back. "Sticking up for our girl here."

"Your girl is capable of fighting her own battles," Ashleigh muttered under her breath.

"Now what fun is that?" Francesca asked, giving Ashleigh a smile. "Trust me, Carlos would have done a lot worse defending my honor."

"Speaking of..." Ryan lowered his beer. "What exactly did Marcus do?"

"Well, it wasn't just Marcus," Ashleigh told him. "It was Kenzie too. Though, to be fair, she was pretty wasted when Marcus came up with the plan."

"What plan?"

"To coerce a freshman into dressing up like the clown and scaring me."

"What!"

Four pairs of eyes swung toward her.

"Order up!"

Vinny shouted from the kitchen, and Ashleigh sighed. "Tell the bartender what you want," she said, glancing at the four. "It's on the house."

"Cool!"

"Nice!"

"Sweet!"

Ashleigh hurried away, stopping at the window to pick up the plates.

"So, since when have you been so friendly with the football players?" Vinny asked, giving her a look.

"Since now, apparently," Ashleigh said with a smile. It was funny how just last night she'd been all alone, and now, apparently, she had new friends.

"You and the quarterback look pretty close."

"He's been good to me," Ashleigh told him, stealing a glance back over at Ryan, as she turned away. "Don't be jealous, Vinny."

"I just don't want to see you hurt."

Ashleigh smiled. "Don't worry about me, Vinny. I'm stronger than I look." She turned on her heel making her way across the room and dropping the food off at their respective tables.

"Come again?" Ryan asked, staring at her as she returned to the bar. "Marcus and Kenzie, they..."

"Did a very, very bad thing," Kenzie said, as she walked up, sliding into the stool next to Jacob.

"Ah. There's Satan," Jacob muttered under his breath, as he took a swig from his beer. "I was wondering when you were going to show up."

"I am not Satan," Kenzie said, glaring at him. "And I feel horrible about what I did to Ashleigh. I can only plead that I was drunk, a bit mad, and jealous. Besides that, I really haven't been myself the last several years. I think it's time I figure out who I am again." She glanced over at Ryan. "I'm sorry, Ryan. For being such a bitch to you. You were right. We were never good together."

Ryan stared at her, his jaw dropping open.

Ashleigh giggled, and Kenzie rolled her eyes. "I know. I know. I never apologize. But then again, I never thought I'd sleep with Marcus either."

Jacob sputtered, spitting beer out across the counter. He let out a loud, belting laugh. "You and Marcus? Oh my! I... I..." he doubled over, laughing. "That does not surprise me at all!"

"Jackass," Kenzie muttered, giving him a look.

"I'm sorry, but I just don't believe you've changed," Jacob told her. "A leopard does not change their spots that fast, plus, I never really liked you."

"The feeling is definitely mutual," Kenzie said, before turning to Ashleigh. "Ash, I have something for you," she said, pulling her phone out. "Johnny just texted me. He got his hands on that recording."

"Already?" Ashleigh stared at her in surprise. "We just talked about this like an hour ago!"

"Apparently, it intrigued him."

"Am I missing something?" Ryan asked, looking between the two women. "When did you two become friends?"

"We were always friends, Ryan," Kenzie told him. "I mean, we did grow up together."

"And we were both there during the Miller massacre," Ashleigh added.

"The Miller…"

Ashleigh held her hand up, quickly filling him in on everything that had happened at the precinct.

"And, you now have this recording?" Levi asked, looking between the two girls. "Well, play it for goodness' sakes!"

Kenzie pressed play.

"Please! Please! Someone, help!" a feminine voice sounded over the phone, panicked. "There's been a murder… at the Millers. Everyone's dead!"

"Ma'am. Please, tell me where you are. I want to help you, but I need more information."

"Just send someone. Now!"

The line went dead, and they stared at one another.

"I know that voice," Ashleigh whispered.

"So do I," Kenzie whispered back, her voice shaking. "It's my mother."

"Kenzie!" Ashleigh stared at her. "You need to tell Billy. If your mother is involved, that means she might be in danger. She might be the killer's next target!"

"I know, and I will. But first, I need to talk to my mom. She's been keeping things from me, and I need to know what those things are."

"Okay, but please, be careful."

"I will."

She hurried out the door, and Ashleigh shook her head. "I don't like this. She shouldn't be going by herself. What if something happens?" She sighed, running a hand over her face. "Oh, screw this. I'm calling Billy."

She turned, lifting the phone to her ear, and the door to the restaurant opened. A tall, red-haired woman walked in, flanked by a couple of cameramen.

"Oh, you have got to be kidding me." She lowered the phone, and it slipped from her fingers falling to the floor. "Of all the luck..."

"What?"

The four men swiveled in their stools, looking toward the door.

"Wait. Isn't that..."

"Gloria Davis," Levi said, nodding, answering Jacob's unspoken question.

"The chick who wrote that article?" Rome asked, his eyes wide.

"The one and the same," Ryan said, taking another sip of his beer. He glanced at Ashleigh, then over at the woman standing at the door. "I just hope she's not going to cause any trouble. I'm not sure how much more Ashleigh can take."

Chapter Nineteen

"Mom?"

Kenzie walked into the house several minutes later, tossing her keys onto the granite countertop. Man, it had been a rough day! Now, she needed answers, the only problem was, she had to get them from her mother. That was going to take some work. They did not have the best relationship. They never had.

She turned, walking through the doorway and into the living room. She rounded the leather couch, glancing around the room.

"Mom?"

Silence echoed around her, and she sighed, her eyes landing on the coffee table that lay in the center of the room, atop the gray area rug that covered the wood flooring. She scowled, spotting the liquor bottles that were scattered across the surface of the table, and to the cigarettes in the ashtray.

Looks like she's at it again.

Her mother had been in and out of rehab for most of her life, she should probably know better by now. She was never going to change.

She disappeared back into the kitchen, rifling through the cupboard. Moments later, she returned with a garbage bag and some cleaner. Clearing off the coffee table, she dropped them into the bag and tied it shut. Then she wiped off the surface, before dropping the bag by the front door and returning the cleaning supplies to the kitchen.

It had been two years since she'd been back here. She wasn't exactly thrilled to be back. She crossed the living room, heading for the stairs.

"Mom? Are you home?" She started up the staircase, cringing, when she heard giggles coming from upstairs. *Oh, God. Mom has someone over.* She wrinkled her nose in disgust, returning to the living room and turning on the TV. She flicked through the channels, searching for something to watch, but every channel was covering the murders.

Great. Either I have to listen to my mom upstairs with some random guy or listen to the coverage of the murders.

Neither sounded like fun.

She growled, tossing the remote on the couch in frustration. God, this day! Could it just be over already? She leaned forward, dragging her hands through her hair as she thought of everything that had happened. Her talks with Ashleigh. The Millers...

She still didn't understand why this madman was so obsessed with a crime that had happened ten years ago. It was driving her crazy just thinking about it. What was the connection?

She sighed, rubbing her hands across her face. No matter how hard she tried, she just couldn't remember anything from that day. She vaguely remembered Meredith and Aimee, but other than that... nothing. What had happened? To them? To her? To her family?

Shortly after the tragedy at the Millers, her own family had fallen apart. Her parents had constantly fought. She remembered them yelling, screaming at one another, and finally them divorcing. It was shortly after the divorce that her mother had started drinking. It'd gotten so bad, that her father had eventually gotten custody of her. It was years later when she and her mother finally reconnected. Their relationship though... well it'd been rough. She'd always expected so much from her! For her to be this perfect person. She'd had a whole life planned out for her. Colleges for her to attend, business schools, it'd been exhausting.

And she'd gone along with it, Kenzie thought. She'd been so desperate to reconnect with her mother, that she'd let her mold her into a person she didn't even recognize anymore. She used to be kind. Someone you could depend on, and she hadn't been any of those things in a very long time.

She hated the way she'd treated Ashleigh. Back then, and even now. She'd once considered Ashleigh one of her closest friends and had felt awful for her when her mother had disappeared. She couldn't imagine being sixteen and having to raise your siblings. She'd wanted to help, but her mother had convinced her that if she wanted a future, she had to break ties with Ashleigh. That being friends with her, would only drag her down. Now she regretted that decision.

They'd been so close! Almost like sisters, but then she'd been kidnapped, and a question had been plaguing Kenzie for the last six months.

Why had they been kidnapped and not her? What made her different?

But then again, Billy had been there too. Did he know something he wasn't telling them? Did he remember something from that day?

She stared at the television screen, the thoughts running rabid, and slowly, a memory started to surface.

"Kenzie, you need to tell us what you know."

"But I don't know anything!" Thirteen-year-old Kenzie cried, wrapping her arms around herself, glancing to her parents, who were seated next to her, to the detective who was sitting across from her.

"Kenzie. I have four murders that I am trying to solve," the detective said, resting his hands on the table. "You and your friends were found at the crime scene. Your fingerprints are all over the house. If you know something, you need to tell me."

"Detective, watch your tone," Conrad Sinclair said, glaring at the detective. "My daughter has been nothing but cooperative with you. She's been through a trauma tonight, they all have, but if all you have is their fingerprints in that house, then you are grasping at straws. The kids have been friends with the Miller

girls for years. They spend a lot of time there, so naturally, their fingerprints are going to be found in the house." He stood up from his chair. "Now, if you don't have anything else, I'm taking my daughter home."

Kenzie started, her eyes widening at the memory. Where the hell had that come from? She reached for her phone, sending a quick text to Ashleigh. Oh my God! They'd been there? They'd found the bodies? What the hell happened that night? And why was she only remembering something about that night now?

Thump!

A loud crash sounded from upstairs, and she jumped. A small scream ripped from her throat, and she rose to her feet.

"Mom?"

She made her way toward the staircase, staring up into the dark hallway, then behind her, toward the dining room. Her eyes landed on the leather jacket lying across the back of the chair. She knew that jacket. It belonged to her father.

"Dad?"

She gripped the banister, slowly making her way up the stairs. What was her father doing here? He and her mother hadn't spoken in years!

"Mom? Dad?"

She flipped the switch at the top of the stairs, light flooding the dark hallway. She paused in front of her mother's bedroom, wrapping her hand around the knob. She twisted it, and it swung open.

"Mom? Dad..." She suddenly let out a scream, lifting a hand to her mouth. Tears spilled down her cheeks. *No!*

There was blood everywhere. It was patterned on the light, pink walls surrounding her. It was splattered across the mirror, which was now cracked, and her mother…

Kenzie stared at her, as she lay across the bedspread. She was wearing a white, lace nightgown, and her face was bloodied and bruised. She stared at her with her eyes wide open, a deep gash cut across her throat, blood pooling onto the bedspread, and down onto the carpet underneath.

"Oh, Mom." Kenzie closed her eyes, tears filling them. Her mother may have had her issues, but she certainly hadn't deserved to die, and especially, not like this.

She reached for her phone, and a loud crash sounded behind her. She jumped, spinning around, just as her father's body thumped to the floor from where it was laying across the broken window.

"Oh my God! Dad!"

Kenzie screamed. She stumbled back, falling back against the wall and sliding to the floor. A sob escaped her mouth, as she stared at her father lying on the floor on the other side of the room. He was wearing just a towel, and glass was embedded in his chest. His face was beaten and bloodied, the beard that covered his jaw coated in blood. His throat had been slit, and blood was pooling around him on the floor.

"Oh, Dad." Tears streaked down her cheeks, as she thought of the man who had been there for her. Who had fought for her. How could he just be gone?

Kenzie, you need to call the police.

The thought popped into her head, and she raised her phone, typing into it with shaking hands.

"Hello, Mackenzie."

She screamed, jumping to her feet, her heartbeat thumping inside her chest as the closet on the other side of the room creaked open. She squinted her eyes, trying to see who it was, and her breath suddenly gasped as he came into view. His notorious white face glowing in the soft light, his bright red lips, curling into an evil smile, and that wig of his falling loosely around his head.

It was the clown.

"Oh my God! It's you!" She stumbled backward, her back smacking against the wall, and she winced. "You! You kidnapped my friends! You killed those girls! You... you killed my mom and Dad!"

"Indeed, I have," the clown said, raising the knife in his hand and running a gloved finger along the sharp blade. "And how fun it has been."

"But why? What did they ever do to you?"

"They have sins to pay for, Mackenzie," the clown said, raising his eyes and looking directly at her. "You all do, and you all must pay for what you've done." He strode forward.

Kenzie stared at him, watching as he strode toward her and she turned, racing for the doorway.

"Nah. Uh. Uh. You're not getting away from me that easily." The clown grabbed her by the arm, jerking her back, and flinging her back against the wall.

Kenzie gasped, her body hitting the wall hard, and she cried out, as she crumpled to the ground. She raised her head, watching as he crouched down next to her.

"I finally have you, Kenzie," the clown said, as he traced the blade of the knife down the side of her face. "I couldn't get my hands on you six months ago, to join us in the manor, but now, you're mine!" He raised the knife in the air, stabbing it downward.

"I'll never be yours!" Kenzie shouted. She ducked, rolling to the side, and the knife sailed over her head and struck the wall behind her.

"No!"

"Take that, asshole!" Kenzie cried as she jumped to her feet, swerving around him as he lunged for her, and disappeared into the hallway.

"Get back here!"

He yelled after her, and Kenzie turned, racing down the hallway. *Crap!* Why hadn't she gone down the stairs? She should be racing for the front door!

Well, it's too late now, she thought, as she slid to a stop toward the end of the hallway. She pulled down the door to the attic, scampering up the steps before pulling the door shut behind her. She hurried across the room, ducking behind a pile of boxes, just as the door creaked open.

"Oh. Mackenzie..."

The door to the attic opened, the clown peering inside, and Kenzie clamped a hand over her mouth. She had to keep quiet. Her very life depended on it.

"I know you're in here," the clown said as he climbed the last of the steps. He paused, glancing around the room. "You can't run from me. I will find you." He grabbed an old Christmas decoration, tossing it across the room. It crashed against the wall and Macie jumped, watching as he tossed old family artifacts, Christmas decorations, and boxes across the room. He was getting closer.

"Oh, Mackenzie. Where are you?"

He said the name again, and she froze. No one ever called her that. It was always Kenzie, but for some reason, she remembered someone calling her that. Who was it? She wracked her brain, trying to remember, then she froze. Wait. Hadn't Ashleigh's Dad...

The shrill sound of her cell phone suddenly pierced through the air, interrupting her, and she jumped. She froze, fear washing over her, as she stared down at the phone in her hands. *Oh God! No!*

She quickly silenced it, peering through the boxes, at the clown from where he stood on the other side of the room. She watched as he stopped, turning to look in the direction she was hiding, and she grabbed the big teddy bear sitting next to her, hugging it to her chest. She closed her eyes, silently praying.

"Found ya."

She jumped, a scream ripping from her throat, as her eyes flung open. Boxes around her went flying, and the blade of the knife suddenly flew through the boxes.

It pierced through the bear, and she scrambled out from behind the boxes, racing across the room toward the window.

She slid to a stop, sliding it open, glancing over her shoulder, just as the clown ripped the bear free from the blade. He turned toward her.

Now, Kenzie!

She slid out the window, racing across the rooftop. She rounded the corner, stopping, gasping for breath as she peered around the corner. Where was he?

Then she saw him slide out the window and onto the rooftop.

Shit!

She turned, racing across the rooftop.

Thunk!

She jumped, just as a knife whizzed past her ear. It struck the side of the house, falling onto the rooftop next to her feet.

Throwing knives? He has fucking throwing knives?

She raised her head, glancing over her shoulder, watching as the clown grinned at her from the other end of the rooftop. He let out a loud, piercing laugh, jumping up and down on the roof. He withdrew a small knife from his sleeve and flung it in her direction.

Kenzie screamed. She dodged the knife, her foot slipping on the roof. She gasped, the knife whizzing past her just as she lost her balance and slid off the edge of the room.

"Ahh!"

She screamed, her body falling downward, and landing in the pool far below with a loud splash. She gasped, breaking the surface and wiping the water from her eyes, looking up at the now-empty rooftop.

Where the hell did he go?

She turned, swimming her way across the pool, and pulled herself out onto the grass. *Guess that's one way to get away from him,* she thought as she rung the water out of her shirt. She dragged herself to her feet, and raced across the grass, withdrawing her phone from her pocket. Thank God it was waterproof!

"Billy! It's me. Please, help me! He's here. He's going to kill..."

Shrink!

The sound of metal scraping against metal suddenly sounded in her ears, and she swung around. She gasped, the breath whooshing out of her, as she stumbled to the ground, staring at the knife that was now embedded in the center of her chest.

Oh no.

She turned, glancing over her shoulder, at the clown as he stood in the doorway of the house. She grasped the knife, pulling it from her chest. It slipped from her shaking fingers, falling in the grass and she reached a hand forward, dragging herself across the turf. She needed to get to her car. If she could just get to her car...

Shrink!

Again, the sound of metal whooshed through the air, and she screamed. Another wave of pain rushed through her, as the blade pierced her flesh, and through her left leg.

Shit!

She gripped the turf, her fingernails seeping into the dirt, as she dragged herself across the lawn. *Just a little further...*

Then a hand grabbed her by the back of the neck, jerking her back. She screamed, struggling against his grip, as the clown slammed her back to the ground. She groaned, staring up at him as he leered down at her

"I told you, you weren't escaping me," the clown said, as he towered above her, dangling the knife between his fingers. "You're mine, Kenzie. All of you are mine."

"But... why?" Kenzie asked, gasping for breath, as she stared up at him. His face was wavering in and out. She'd lost too much blood. There was no way she was going to make it.

"Because it's what you deserve," the clown said, raising his knife. "Bye, bye, Kenzie."

The knife plunged downward, striking her in the chest and the last thing she saw was the clown laughing as he stood over her.

Chapter Twenty

"Gloria."

Ashleigh lowered the phone from her ear, the device slipping from her fingers and falling to the ground, as she stared at the woman standing in the doorway of the restaurant. Anger seared through her, as she thought of everything this woman had done. The visits to the hospital, the article, her empty promises. Every, single thought making her madder by the second.

"What are you doing here?" she asked, trying to calm the anger coursing inside of her.

"Well, it is a restaurant," Gloria said, gesturing around at the people eating around them. "And last I knew, we do need to eat." She gestured to the cameraman standing behind her. "So, do you have a table for us?"

"Absolutely not," Steph said, walking up next to Ashleigh, and placing her hands on her hips. "You are not welcome here."

"Now, Steph, there's no need to be rude," Ashleigh said, laying a hand on Steph's arm. She looked like she was about ready to pounce, and she did not need that. She glanced around at the restaurant, where everyone had grown quiet, and sighed. She did not need this. Not today. She already had too much going on, this was just the cherry on top of the cake. "I mean, she was just doing her job."

"Right. Thank you for noticing that," Gloria said, smiling.

"What I don't understand," Ashleigh said, turning and aiming a look at Gloria, "is why lie? When we were in the hospital, you came and visited all of us. You seemed so... concerned for all of us. We believed you when you said you wanted to help us, and the next thing we knew, that damned article was written. Dammitt, Gloria, you blamed us for what happened! You said it was our fault we got kidnapped, and even worse, you said, and I quote 'although the four girls seem to be on the mend, the lasting scars will remain for decades. What happened to each of them, will take time to heal, but yet... the question remains. What really happened inside that manor? Especially, when all four girls, have different stories to tell.'"

"First of all, I did not lie," Gloria told her. "I did want to help you, I still do, but I can't help you when you won't be honest with me."

"We told you..."

"You all had a different version of what happened inside the manor," Gloria said, holding up a hand and interrupting her. "None of your stories matched. In fact, it was like you'd all been kidnapped by a different person."

"That's crazy!" Ashleigh cried. "We were all there, Gloria. We were in the same house, tortured by the same madman... you have no idea what we went through! What I..." She hiccupped, shaking her head.

"Ash, you don't owe her anything," Ryan said, rising to his feet and wrapping an arm around her shoulders. "She's already done enough damage with that article she wrote. The lies she told. She damaged your reputation, just to further he own career. Don't give her the satisfaction of seeing you crumble."

"How dare you judge me. You don't even know me," Gloria seethed, glaring at Ryan. "You have no idea what I have endured, or what I have sacrificed. I did everything in my power to find the girls, but the more I dug into their past, the more questions I had. There's more to this and I think it has something to do with what happened to the Millers."

"How the hell do you know about the Millers?" Ashleigh asked, swinging back to look at Gloria.

"I told you. I'm good at my job, Ashleigh," Gloria said. "And I have resources everywhere. I also know that you and your friends were the ones to find the bodies."

"What?" Ashleigh stared at her in dismay. "No. That's not true," she said, shaking her head. "We were at home."

"That's what your parents might have told you, but this photo suggests otherwise." Gloria reached into the brown bag that was hanging over her shoulder and withdrew a tablet. She tapped on the screen a few times, before handing it over. "Take a look for yourself."

Ashleigh took the tablet from her, glancing down at the picture on the screen. A gasp escaped her lips when she saw the black and white picture on the screen. Gloria was right, they had been there. This was proof of it.

She, Nikki, Addison, Kenzie, Billy, and Sydney were all standing right inside the police station of Sarasota Bay. They were huddled together, their parents standing behind them, and they looked scared. Really scared.

She swallowed, handing the tablet back to Gloria. "So, we were there. That doesn't mean…"

"Flip to the next photo."

Ashleigh gave her a look, but flipped to the next photo, her eyes widening when she found herself staring at the police report. Written right there, in neat handwriting, confirmed that they had been the ones to find the bodies.

"Then why were we told we were at home? Why don't I remember any of this?"

"A great question, and one, I aim to answer very soon," Gloria said, taking the tablet from her and sliding it back into her bag. "I've asked myself that question a million times. I mean, why lie? And I can only come to one conclusion."

"What?"

"That they're protecting one of you, or even all of you."

"What? You think that one of us killed the Millers? You think we conspired to kill them? We were friends with Amelia and Meredith! Why…"

Gloria shrugged. "Wouldn't be the first time a kid snapped."

"You are seriously deranged!" Ashleigh cried. "You and your lies and conspiracy theories! Haven't they gotten you into enough trouble already? I mean, do you regret anything you've done? The lives you've destroyed?"

"Of course not," Gloria said. "People had the right to know."

Ashleigh rolled her eyes. "Oh, that is such an excuse, Gloria. People did not need to know every, single detail about what happened inside the manor. They know everything that happened to me, because of you! Because you couldn't keep your damned promises! Do you know how much you are despised by all of us? It's sickening, how vicious you are."

"I'm not vicious, Ashleigh. I'm letting the public know what happened, so that they know to be careful out there. The man who kidnapped you is still out there. Someone, who I think is connected to the Millers, and who is now killing innocent people. Do you really want to be responsible for someone else going through what you did?"

Slap!

Ashleigh's hand struck forward, slapping Gloria across the face. Gloria stumbled back, a look of shock on her face, as a resounding gasp echoed through the restaurant.

"How dare you even think about blaming me for what that monster has done," Ashleigh said, as she lowered her hand. "I am not responsible for anything that he may, or may not do, but then again, you always have been good at blaming the victims, haven't you Gloria?" Ashleigh spun on her heel, striding away. "Don't ever show your face in here again, Gloria, or I'll have a restraining order filed against you."

"You... you hit me!" Gloria shouted, holding a hand to her cheek. "I have every right to sue your ass! Especially with all the witnesses in here!"

"I wouldn't suggest doing that," Ryan said, chuckling. "Trust me, they won't be siding with you, but what I do suggest is that you leave. Right now." He turned, hurrying after Ashleigh. "Ash!"

"I need to get out of here," Ashleigh said, shaking her head. "I need a moment to gather my thoughts. I mean, I hit her! I have never..." She shoved the back door open, and a scream suddenly escaped her lips. "Ryan!"

"Ash?" Ryan hurried after her, and slid to a stop, a gasp of disbelief escaping his lips. "Holy shit." He ran a hand over his face, staring at the body that was hanging on the fence next to the dumpster. Blood was dripping down from the large gash that was spread across their throat, a manuscript was clutched in their hands, and a clown mask was covering their face.

"It's him," Ashleigh whispered. "He killed someone else."

"I know," Ryan said, swallowing, as he wrapped an arm around her shoulder. He pulled her close.

"He's... he's going to keep killing, Ryan," Ashleigh whispered, burying her head in his shoulder. "Is Gloria right? Is..."

"No. Absolutely not," Ryan said, interrupting her. "This is not your fault. Come on." He steered her back toward the restaurant. "Let's get you back inside. We need to call Billy and get a hold of Kenzie."

Chapter Twenty - One

"You got here fast," Ryan said a little while later, as he stepped from the restaurant. He held a cup of coffee out to Billy, staring at the body that still hung on the fence, as he took a sip from his coffee.

"I've got a murder investigation and three dead bodies on my hands. It's not like I'm going anywhere," Billy said, taking the cup, and nodding a thank you to Ryan. "How's Ashleigh doing?"

"She's a bit shaken up."

"I can only imagine." Billy took a sip, shaking his head. "This whole thing is a fucking mess. My board in my office, I've got arrows everywhere. It doesn't make any sense."

"I thought this was connected to the Millers?"

Billy raised a brow in question.

"Ashleigh told me."

Billy chuckled. "She must be starting to trust you."

Ryan sighed. "Could have fooled me. She keeps trying to push me away."

"She's trying to protect you," Billy told him. "It's what she does when she thinks the people she cares about are in danger." He took another sip from his coffee. "Can I give you a little advice?"

"And if I say no?"

Billy laughed. "I'll give it to you anyways." He paused. "Ryan, I'm telling you this, because I think I might actually like you..."

"Oh, boy. You're going to give me the protective, big brother talk, aren't you?"

Billy laughed again. "No. I'm telling you, don't let her push you away. Keep coming back, no matter what. She'll never tell you this, but the people who stay with her through the thick and thin. That means more to her than anything."

"I wasn't planning on going anywhere."

"Good." Billy paused, cocking his head to the side. "And Ryan?"

"Yeah?"

"You hurt her, I'll hunt you down and kill you."

"Ah, there it is! The protective big brother. I knew it would come sooner or later." Ryan paused, a small smile spreading across his lips. "I have no plans to ever hurt her, Billy. I like her, plus, you do have a gun. I don't think I want to get on your bad side."

"Oh, trust me, you don't."

They stood there in silence for a moment, then Billy let out a breath. "But what Ashleigh told you is correct. It is connected to the Millers. This killer… he's focused on the past. What I don't get, is why he's waited so long. I mean, it's been ten years! And why kidnap the girls, then completely change his MO and start murdering people? It doesn't make any sense to me."

"You think maybe it's his way of staying in control?"

"Maybe. What I do know, is that I'm missing something. I'm just not sure what."

"Detective?"

The soft, feminine voice sounded behind them, and Billy turned, frowning when he saw a young woman with long, dark, brown hair step out from the coroner's van. "Where's Sully?"

"Taking a few personal days," the woman said, as she neared him. "He called me this morning and asked me to take over his cases." She extended a hand. "I'm Sophia Clausen. I've been studying under Sully for the last year or so, and I feel like I know you already, Detective. Sully is quite fond of you."

"I'm not exactly fond of *him* right now," Billy muttered, as he shook her hand. "Who the hell even has time to take a vacation right now?" He gave her a small smile. "It's nice to meet you, Sophia. Thank you for filling in."

"Of course, Detective. Now, if you don't mind, I have a job to do." She turned on her heel, walking toward the body.

"Well. She seems…"

"Random?" Billy asked, still watching the woman. "Yeah. I thought so too."

"I take it, she's not your normal medical examiner?"

"Nope."

"And this… Sully. Does he usually take time off?"

"Not in the twenty-five years that I've known him. Hell, I don't think he's even taken a sick day." Billy finished his coffee, crushing the Styrofoam cup in his hand. "I mean, why now? He didn't even take time off when..." he trailed off.

"When?"

"When the Millers were murdered," Billy whispered. "He was the medical examiner back in Sarasota Bay. It's where he started his career, and he was good friends with my father."

"You don't think..."

"That he could have been involved?" Billy asked. "I can't lie, the thought did cross my mind, but it's Sully! He was like an uncle to me, but every time I ask him about that day he always changes the subject. There's just no way..."

"Everyone has secrets, Billy," Ryan said. "And do we truly, ever know someone? It seems like there's a lot that happened back then, that you, Ashleigh, and your friends don't remember. Plus, Gloria's starting to dig into it. You do know that she's here, right?"

"She's a little hard to miss," Billy said, rubbing a hand across his jaw. "I feel bad for the poor officer who has to take her statement." He frowned, glancing at Ryan. "What do you mean she's digging into it?"

"She showed us the photo."

"What photo?"

"The photo of the six of you at the police station in Sarasota Bay. After you found the Millers."

"Tell me she did not show that to Ashleigh."

"Oh, she did."

"Christ!" Billy clenched his hand into a fist. "That woman has a knack for making my life more and more difficult. Ashleigh does not need this."

"You know, I really wish you would stop treating me like I'm going to break over every bit of information that comes out," Ashleigh said, walking up from behind them. "You should have told me about what happened, Billy. I had the right to know."

"Ash." Billy stared at her. "I was going to tell you, I swear, but..."

"But you had to play the big, protective older brother," Ashleigh said, crossing her arms in front of her chest. "And you need to stop."

"I just don't want you to get hurt again."

"Well, no one ever said life was easy," Ashleigh said, pulling Ryan's jacket tighter around her as she shivered in the cool night. "Have you heard from Kenzie yet?"

Billy shook his head. "No. Not yet. I've tried calling, but it goes straight to voicemail. Why did you think she might be in danger?"

"There was..." Ashleigh trailed off, her eyes widening, as the mask was removed from the body that still hung on the fence. "Oh my God. Billy..."

"It's Wes," Billy said, nodding. "I know." He lifted his phone to his ear. "Andrew, where the hell are you? I need you over here. We just found Wes..." He trailed off, as another call came through.

"Turner."

"Billy! It's me. Please, help me! He's here. He's going to kill..."

The line went dead, and Billy felt the blood drain from his face.

"Billy? What is it?" Ashleigh grabbed his arm. "I know that look. Something's wrong, isn't it?"

"It's Kenzie..."

"No!" Ashleigh held a hand to her mouth, shaking her head. "Dammitt! I knew she shouldn't have gone by herself."

"What are you talking about?"

"I'll tell you on the way."

"Whoa. Hold on a second." Billy held up a hand. "There is no way I am taking you with me."

"Well, I'm not staying here," Ashleigh told him, turning, and trudging off across the parking lot. "So, are you coming or not?"

"Ash..." Billy sighed, glancing over at Ryan. "You coming?"

"I don't think I really have a choice," Ryan said, following him. He slid into the back seat, glancing over at Ashleigh. "You're not the same woman I met yesterday. You're... you're different."

"You're right. I'm not," Ashleigh said, as she stared out the window. "You were right, Ryan."

"About what?"

"That I'm strong," Ashleigh said, softly. "When he called me this morning, he told me I was weak, and I kept hearing your voice in my head, telling me how strong I am. It made me realize, that I can't keep living my life in fear. I have to take my life back."

"And that means just running, blindly into danger?"

"I have to know what happened back then, Ryan," Ashleigh whispered. "It's eating at me."

"What you find out, you might not like."

"I know," Ashleigh whispered. "But he's hurting people because of something that happened back in Sarasota Bay. Something, that my friends and I did. I can't just be an innocent stander and watch. I need to know what happened."

"You're going to be putting yourself in danger."

"I'm already in danger, Ryan," Ashleigh whispered. "Sooner or later, he's going to come for me, and when he does, I need to be ready. It's the only hope I have in surviving all of this."

Chapter Twenty - Two

"Charlie!"

Sullivan Wilcox slammed his fist against the door of the old, log cabin just north of Los Angeles. "Dammitt! Open up. We need to talk!"

Silence sounded on the other side, and he sighed. *Damned bastard! Didn't he know what was going on?*

It'd been years since he'd seen his old friend, and he was worried. What if the killer...

He shook his head, trying to shove the thought away, and turned, walking around the house, peering into the windows.

"You got a reason for peeping in my windows, Trespasser?"

The voice sounded behind him, and Sully froze, as a man with a long, brown beard appeared in the reflection of the window. He was wearing a long-sleeved, flannel shirt over a white shirt and dark, blue, denim jeans. In his hands, he was clutching an axe, looking like he would not hesitate to use it in a second.

He slowly raised his hands in the air, turning. "Lower the axe, Char. It's just me."

"Sully?" Charles Turner lowered the axe, his eyes widening in surprise. "How the hell did you find me?"

"Your last postcard said you were up north, and that you'd bought a cabin. I also knew you wouldn't stray too far from your son, so it wasn't too hard to put the pieces together."

"How is Billy?"

"Still pissed at you. You know he's a cop now, right?"

Charles sighed, slowly nodding. "Yes, I know. I don't like it. I didn't want him involved in this life, but you know, he never did listen to me. So, eventually, I just stopped trying."

"You need to tell him the truth, Charles. He deserves to know what happened, and he needs to know that you didn't abandon him. Tell him, Char, before it's too late."

"I think it's already too late, Sully. Billy will never understand why I did what I did back then."

"Have you even tried?"

"Sully, did you come all this way to remind me of my failure as a father?" Charles asked, his eyes flashing with anger. "Or is there another reason you're here? I mean, it's been almost eight years!"

Sully sighed, shaking his head. *Damn, the man was just as stubborn as his son was.* "No, of course not. I would never do that. I know all you've ever done is try to protect him." He paused a moment. "Char, do you know what's going on?"

"Sully, I'm in the middle of nowhere. I have no phone, no radio, and no television. Of course I don't know what's going on." He cocked his head. "Whatever it is, it's bad, isn't it? You look worried. Scared, even."

"Damn right I'm scared! Dammitt, Charles, your son, the girls, they're in danger. He's... he's back."

"Who's back?"

"The clown killer."

Charles drew in a sharp breath. He hadn't heard the name in years, but now he understood why Sully was so scared.

"That's impossible," he said. "He's dead."

"Well, someone's dawned on the mask, Char. He kidnapped the girls, I think to see what they know. Then when they escaped, he changed his tactics. He's killed two girls and Wes, and I just heard over the radio about the Sinclair family. They're dead too, Char."

"Hot damn." Charles leaned back against the tree behind him and closed his eyes. He crossed his arms across his chest, breathing in the cool, northern air before opening his eyes. "Sully. I can't do this again. I can't face another clown. The last time, nearly destroyed me."

"I know, Char. I was there. We all were." Sully swallowed, thinking back to that day. It was exactly ten years ago today when a man known as the clown killer stalked the small town of Sarasota Bay. A killer, that they had created.

"Do you remember that day?" he asked, his voice coming out hoarse.

"Do I remember? Of course I remember!" Charles cried. "That day will forever be etched in my brain. The panic in Denise's voice, when she called me. The bodies... they were everywhere! Three young boys and their father, slain. Their faces beaten beyond recognition, and of course there was Lindsay." He shook his head. "God, I never thought she would make it."

"Neither did I," Sully whispered. "God, when I saw her in that hospital room..." He trailed off, shaking his head. "Her heart stopped twice in surgery. I thought for sure she was gone, but she's one hell of a woman. I'm just glad she left when she did."

"So am I. What she has to live with, knowing she lost her entire family and has no memory of it? It's gotta be horrifying."

"I can't even imagine going through that," Sully whispered. "God, Char. Did we make a mistake, doing what we did?"

"We were protecting the kids, Sully."

"I know, but Char, we framed an innocent man for murder!"

He said the words for the first time in nearly ten years, and Charles flinched. "I know, Sully," he said. "But we didn't have a choice. The kids, their fingerprints were everywhere and... and..."

"Billy was found, holding the murder weapon. I know, Char."

"We did what we had to do," Charles told him. "We had to protect them. They had their whole lives ahead of them, and Neil Carlson deserved what he got. He was not a good man, Sully."

"But did he deserve what we did to him?" Sully asked. "I know we all had our gripes with him, but we tortured him,

Char. We made him into a killer, and we are the reason he killed all those people. We are the reason he came after you."

"You think I don't know that, Sully?" Charles asked, his agitation mounting. "I almost died that day, Sully!" He lifted his shirt, pointing to the scars that still lay on his chest. "Eight stab wounds. I don't even remember how I was able to fight him off, but somehow, I was able to get a hold of my gun and I just kept shooting until he was dead. There is no way he's alive, Sully."

"Well, then, who the hell is wearing the mask, Char? He's killing our friends! He's cleaning house and it's only a matter of time before he comes after us."

No sooner had the words left his mouth, when the sound of tires crunching underneath loose gravel filled the air. He and Charles shared a look, their senses suddenly heightened, as they turned to stare at the silver SUV making its way up the drive.

"Expecting company?" Sully asked, raising a brow in question at Charles.

"Company? Sully, I nearly took you out with an axe! Of course I'm not expecting company!"

"Who else knows you're here?"

"No one." Charles picked up his axe. "And that's the way I like it. Come on. Let's go find out who's here."

They made their way across the lawn, and Charles paused. "Hey, Sully. You should take this," he said, withdrawing a small revolver from the small of his back and handing it to Sully. "Just in case."

"You're wielding an axe, and have a gun on you?" Sully asked, staring at him, but took the gun nonetheless.

"You can never be too careful," Charles informed him. "Which is why I also have weapons scattered out throughout the forest. Just in case."

"Seclusion has made you paranoid, Charles."

"No. Coming face to face with a murderous clown did that," Charles said. "The seclusion part... it's kept me safe, but I'm willing to bet that my time is about to run out."

They neared the SUV, both of them eyeing the vehicle warily, as the engine shut off. They each raised their weapons, as the door to the car swung open.

"Now, is this really the way you greet old friends, boys?"

The soft feminine voice floated through the air, and they both froze, glancing at one another before lowering their weapons.

"Mary?"

They uttered the name in unison, as the car door slammed closed. The tall, slender woman stepped into sight. She pulled her sunglasses off, plopping them on top of her long, wavy, blonde hair as she sent them a dashing smile. "It's been a long time, boys."

"Jesus, Mary. What the hell are you doing here?" Charles demanded, staring at the woman in disgust. "How the hell did you even find me?"

"Oh, I always knew where you were, Charles," Mary Carlson told him, as she strode forward. She stopped in front of him, trailing her fingers down his long beard. "I had to make sure you would stay in line. Hello, Sullivan."

"Hello, Mary," Sully narrowed his eyes on Ashleigh's mother. "You look well, considering..."

"Considering what?"

"That we're in this mess because of you!" Charles shouted, his temper snapping.

"Oh, Charles, you should really, really control that temper of yours."

"Why, you manipulative little..."

"Charles." Sully sent him a warning look, before turning back to Mary. "Mary, what are you doing here?" he asked, repeating Charles's question. "We told you we never wanted to see you, ever again."

"I know, but things have changed," Mary said, twirling a lock of her blonde hair around a red, manicured finger. "He's back."

"No. Not back," Charles spit out. "Neil's dead, Mary. You know that. You have the bloody video to prove it!"

"Don't you think I feel bad about what I did?" Mary shot back. "We were..."

"Friends?" Charles laughed. "Yeah, I thought so too. I would have done anything for you, Mary. Hell, I was in love with you, but you... you're incapable of feeling any sort of human emotion. If you were, you never would have blackmailed all of us."

"Charles, you have to understand..."

"No. I don't want to hear another word, Mary. Please, just go! You are not wanted here." He turned on his heel, striding back toward the house.

"Charles, please!" Mary hurried after him. "Don't leave me out here to fend for myself. He'll kill me!"

"That is not my problem," Charles said, seething, as he flung the door open and strode into the house. "You made your bed ten years ago when you alienated everyone who cared about you, Mary. God!" Charles ran a hand through his hair, swinging around to look at Mary. "Dammitt, I was there for you, Mary. We all were when Neil nearly..." He shook his head, not being able to utter the words.

"When he nearly killed me?" Mary asked. "Yes, I remember Charles." Her voice shook. "It wasn't the first time I came to you for help."

"And yet, you kept going back to him, even though I begged you not to," Charles said. "You knew I still loved you. Charlene even knew, hell, you were the first woman I ever loved."

"Like hell you did. You abandoned me, Charles."

"I was just a kid!" Charles snapped, swinging back to glare at her. "I wasn't ready to be a damned father!"

"And you think I was ready to be a mother?" Mary asked. "I was a senior in high school, Charles, and I was alone! And there was Neil. He was nice, kind, and..."

"Just ready to swoop in. You know damned well he always had a thing for you, Mary. We all did, and we tried to warn you that he was dangerous. That you couldn't trust him, but of course, you don't listen to anyone. You never have."

"I know. I messed up, Charles."

"I wanted to kill him when I saw you." Charles wrapped a hand around the handle of the refrigerator, dragging it open. He stared inside. "You were bloodied, bruised, and the kids..." He closed his eyes, remembering how they'd looked on his doorstep. "But I never in all of my life believed you would have manipulated me so badly. What we did to him..."

"Was a decision we all made," Sully said, closing the door behind him and joining them in the kitchen.

"Yes, but she goddamned videotaped everything we did!" Charles snapped, grabbing a couple cans of beer from the fridge. He tossed one to Sully, before handing one to Mary. "She told me the only way for this to work, was for Neil to believe he really did it. The things we did..." He shook his head, popping the tab on the can and taking a swig. "In all my years, I never imagined any of us capable of something like that."

"I didn't have a choice," Mary said. "You were all going to cave. Hell, Conrad was halfway to the police station after leaving the storage unit."

"Because his career was on the line!" Charles shouted. "All of ours were. Mine. Sully's. Wes's."

"It was my only way out, Charles. You know Neil. What he was capable of. It was the only chance I had to escape him."

"No. You took the easy way out," Sully said. "You could have come to us, Mary. We would have helped you, but you refused. You said you could handle it. That you would take care of Neil yourself."

"And he almost killed me."

"And that leaves us where we are now." Charles scowled. "I really wished Wes had gone to the cops. It would have been better than having to live with what we did for the last ten years."

"He did," Sully reminded him. "But then he was framed for the murder of his wife, remember?"

"Oh, yes. We never did figure out who framed him."

"I have my suspicions." Sully opened his beer, looking over at Mary, before taking a sip.

Mary just smiled, taking a sip from her own beer.

"Oh, you conniving little bitch." Charles stared at her. "You did it. You really framed him."

"He was going to tell the cops everything. We would have all gone to jail, and our kids would have gone through the rest of their childhood with a black cloud over their heads."

"As if you care about the kids," Sully muttered under his breath.

"I should have gone with my gut, and never listened to you," Charles said. "I should have trusted the process. Trusted my son. I know he's not a killer."

"Billy does has a mean streak in him, Charles. We've all seen it."

"Don't you dare talk about my son that way. You have no right. Not anymore," Charles said, glowering at Mary, before glancing over at Sully. "Sully's right. I need to make things right. It's time to tell Billy the truth. I'm going back to LA this night. I'm going to tell him everything."

"Are you crazy?" Mary stared at him. "Charles, you can't! We all agreed..."

"That was ten years ago, Mary," Sully said, as he took a seat at the small, square shaped table. "We're not those same people anymore, and we can't keep living with this guilt. We have to come clean."

"Either of you says a word, I'll release the videos."

"You're threatening us, again?" Sully laughed. "And you're the one who begged us to protect you. Why should we do that? You're manipulative, Mary. You never used to be that way, but Neil, he rubbed off on you. You're no better than he is."

"I'm nothing like him."

"Really?" Charles cocked a brow. "Then, why the hell did you abandon your children, Mary?" he asked. "You left in the middle of the night, leaving Ashleigh to raise her sisters. What kind of mother does that?"

"Because I couldn't look at them anymore!" Mary snapped. "Staring at them every day, staring into eyes so similar to their father's, I couldn't do it. Not after everything he put me through."

"So, instead of facing your fears head-on, you ran," Sully said. "Surprise, surprise, well, we aren't running, Mary. I'm going to go back with Charles. Ashleigh, she needs to know what's going on too."

"That's my daughter, Sully. I'll make the decisions on what she should and shouldn't know."

"Do you even care about what she went through inside the manor?" Charles asked. "She went through hell in there, Mary. The least we can do is give her some understanding as to why she's a target."

"They'll hate us for it, and we'll end up paying the same price Wes did," Mary said. "Our lives will be ruined."

"As far as I'm concerned, behind bars is exactly where you should be," Charles told her. "Plus, Billy already hates me. It's not like this will change anything."

"And it's not like I have much time left," Sully said. "I'm old, Mary, and have stage three lung cancer. I have nothing left to..."

Shink!

"Sully!"

Charles shouted, just as a blade sliced through Sully's throat. His body fell forward, his head hitting the surface of the table as blood oozed from his mouth.

"Hello, Charles. Hello, Mary."

The clown grinned, lifting his knife, the blood glistening off the blade in the low light. "Ready to play a game?"

Mary screamed, scrambling backward. The chair she'd been sitting in toppled to the ground, and Charles dove for his axe. He wrapped his hands around it, swinging around, and gasped when a knife slung through the air and hit him in the chest.

"Charles!"

"Mary! Run!" Charles shouted as he wavered on weak legs. He grabbed the knife, pulling it from his chest. Blood oozed from the wound, soaking his shirt, and he turned to the clown.

"So, what's it going to be, Charles?" the clown asked, cocking his head from one side, to the other. "You man enough?"

"Ahh!"

Charles sprinted across the room toward the clown, raising the knife in the air. He lunged, and three knives slung through the air. They hit him in the chest, and he stumbled back, falling back against the wall.

"Charles. Charles. Charles. It took me a long time to track you down," the clown said, as he walked toward him. He pulled a knife from his sleeve. He flung it across the air, the blade hit

Charles in the shoulder, pinning him to the wall behind him. He slung another knife in the air. The blade hitting his other shoulder.

"Please!" Mary cried from the other side of the room. "Leave him alone!"

"Don't you know by now, Mary?" the clown asked, glancing over his shoulder at her, as he stopped in front of Charles. He pulled the knife from his chest, slicing it across his throat. "You all have to pay for what you did."

"Charles! No!"

Charles slumped, and the clown grinned. "Your turn, Mary."

The clown strode toward her, and Mary stumbled back. She turned, glancing at Sully, then at Charles.

"Fuck you!" she shouted, spinning on her heel and racing for the door. "I haven't survived this long to be killed by some cowardly clown!"

She raced across the room, wrapping her hand around the doorknob and flinging it open. She stumbled out into the early morning, stumbling across the lawn.

"Help me! Please!"

She screamed, knowing damn well no one could hear her. She was in the middle of fucking nowhere!

Thunk!

The door behind her crashed open, and she glanced over her shoulder as the clown stepped out. Shit. He was right behind her!

She raced toward the driveway, pulling her phone from her pocket and raising it to her ear.

"You need to do it now!" She shouted. "Release the damned file!"

She disconnected the call, racing down the driveway toward her car. She typed into the phone, her hands shaking, glancing nervously over her shoulder.

"911. What's your emergency?"

"Help! He's going to kill me!"

"Ma'am, who's trying to kill you? Where are you?"

"I'm—"

Mary paused, raising her head, her breath catching as the clown rounded the hood of the car. He grinned, raising his bloody knife, and dragged it across the hood of the car.

"Ma'am?"

"It's the clown!" she shouted into the phone. "He's going to kill me!"

She turned, racing away from the clown and around the corner of the house. She stumbled, running down the steep hill, stopping to stare at the miles and miles of trees that stood before her.

Thump. Thump. Thump.

His footsteps sounded behind her, and she turned, disappearing through the trees.

Shrink!

The sound of a knife flung through the air, and she turned. She ducked, the knife flinging over her head and hitting the tree that lay just behind her.

Shit!

She turned, disappearing further into the trees. Her shoulder brushed a tree branch, her feet slipped on the damp grass, and she zigzagged further into the forest.

Behind her, feet crunched on the leaves, and her breath hitched. She turned, weaving through the trees, all the while glancing around her. Didn't Charles have a damned weapon hidden in here somewhere?

Then she saw it leaning against the tree just a few feet from her. The rifle.

She lunged for it, wrapping her hands around the weapon. She checked the chamber, breathing a sigh of relief when she saw it was fully loaded. She cocked the weapon, gripping it tightly in her hands.

"Oh, Mary…"

She cocked her head, listening. The footsteps, they were getting closer. What direction were they coming from? Her left? Her right?

"Oh, Mary."

Again, the voice sounded. It was coming from her left. It had to be. She was sure of it.

She lifted the rifle and pulled the trigger.

The sound of the gunshot echoed through the forest, and laughter filled the air around her.

"Oh, Mary. You are way, way off."

The voice sounded in her ear, and she jerked her head around, screaming, when she found herself face to face with the clown.

She raised the rifle, striking it toward him, but the clown just laughed. He wrapped his gloved fingers around it, tossing it behind him. "Not today, Mary. Today, it's your turn to die."

He raised the knife in his hand, striking it forward. Mary screamed, dodging the sharp blade and rolling underneath him. She raced through the trees, racing down the hill toward her car.

Just a few more steps, Mary. Just a few more steps.

She reached into her pocket, her fingers wrapping around her keys, and screamed when arms wrapped around her waist.

"No!"

She struggled to keep her balance but tumbled to the ground. She struck her elbow back, connecting with his sternum.

He swore, dodging another elbow blow, and grabbed her by the shoulders. He slammed her to the ground, pinning her down with his knee.

"Why are you doing this?" Mary asked, struggling for breath as his large body kneeled on her.

"You really have to ask?" the clown asked, as he leered down at her.

"I'm sorry!" Mary cried, tears streaking down her cheeks.

"For what? Making two men love you? Alienating your friends? Abandoning your daughters? Or covering everything up?"

"Everything!"

"You know what, Mary?" the clown asked, lowering his mouth next to her ear. "I don't believe you, but I do wonder one thing." He smiled. "Does Billy know?" he asked, just before he stabbed the knife through her heart.

Chapter Twenty - Three

"So, let me get this straight." Billy held up a hand, glancing over at Ashleigh. "While you were sitting in my office. While I was trying to deal with the whole Marcus situation, you and Kenzie took it upon yourselves to go searching for answers?" Billy clenched his fingers around the steering wheel. "Ash! Do you know how dangerous that is? You're going to get yourself killed!"

"I need to know what happened, Billy," Ashleigh said, crossing her arms in front of her chest and returning Billy's glare. "Lord knows I'll never get them from you."

"What are you talking about?"

"You don't talk to me, Billy. Every time I try to ask you about the case, you clam up, and I have to hear about things from people like Gloria Davis. I need to know what happened ten years ago, Billy. My safety may depend on it."

"I told you, you might not like what you find," Ryan said from next to her. "Sometimes, the truth can do more harm than good."

Ashleigh turned to him. "So, you think it's better to be left in the dark?"

"Sometimes, yes."

"I disagree," Ashleigh told him. "I don't care how messy the truth might be. It's better than not knowing anything at all."

"And to be left with the memories of it? Knowing you can't change what happened?" Ryan asked. "How is that better than not knowing?"

Ashleigh stared at him. "Ryan. Is something wrong?"

Ryan shrugged. "No. I'm fine."

"Are you sure? You seem…" Ashleigh trailed off, as the car pulled off the road and into the driveway. She stared ahead of her, her eyes landing on the blue and red flashing lights of the cop cars that sat in front of the large, two-story, brown house. She sucked in a breath.

Oh God. Am I brave enough for this?"

Ryan reached over, giving her hand a squeeze. She sent him a small smile of gratitude, and they all exited the vehicle.

"Billy."

Andrew hurried across the lawn toward them from where he'd been talking to a couple of officers, shaking his head. "Thank God you're here. It's bad. Really bad."

"How bad?"

"Two dead inside. Conrad and Denise Sinclair. They were stabbed, and Kenzie…"

"What about Kenzie?" Ashleigh asked, looking from Andrew to Billy. "What is it? What happened?"

"Ash..."

"Oh, God." Ashleigh stared at them, raising a hand to her mouth. "No." She shook her head. "No! No! No!" She turned and raced off across the lawn.

"Ashleigh! Wait!"

Ryan, Andrew, and Billy raced after her, but Ashleigh ignored them. She raced across the grass, past the officers, her eyes landing on the EMTs just down the hill. She slid to a stop, when she saw Kenzie's body lying on the ground as the EMT's worked on her. "No! Kenzie!"

"Ash!"

Ryan raced up behind her, and Ashleigh turned, falling into his arms. A sob escaped her lips, and she fell against his chest, tears streaming down her cheeks as sobs racked her body. "She's dead, Ryan! And it's all my fault!"

"No. No. Not at all," Ryan whispered, tightening his grip around her.

"I knew she shouldn't have gone alone. If I'd just—"

"We have a pulse!"

The words from the paramedic split through the air, interrupting her. Ashleigh spun around. "Wait. What?"

"She's alive, Ash," Billy said, stepping up next to her, a wave of relief washing over him. "Good God. I can't believe it! Like look at her. By all accounts, she should be dead."

"She's a fighter," Andrew put in.

"You have no idea," the paramedic said, shaking his head as he approached them. "We worked on her for twenty minutes before we finally got a pulse. She's not out of the woods yet, though. We don't know the extent of her injuries yet, and she's lost a lot of blood."

"Where are you taking her?" Billy asked.

"St. Mary's."

"We'll be over as soon as we finish up here." Billy tossed his keys to Ryan. "Take Ashleigh home, will you? It's going to be a long night. I'll pick up the car in the morning"."

"But I was planning on going to the hospital!" Ashleigh protested.

"She's going to be in surgery for hours, Ash. We probably won't know anything until the morning." Billy stopped, giving her shoulder a squeeze. "Go home, get some sleep. I'll call as soon as I know something."

"You promise?"

"I promise."

Ashleigh eyed him, wondering if she really trusted the words coming out of his mouth, before finally nodding. "Okay."

"Hey, Billy," Ryan dug his keys from his pocket, handing them to Billy. "So you're not stranded without a vehicle in the morning."

Billy stared at him, then down at the keys in his hand. "You're letting me drive your Camaro?"

Ryan shrugged. "Maybe I'm starting to like you too." He put an arm around Ashleigh, pulling her close. "We'll see you in the morning."

"Billy. Hold up a sec."

Billy glanced over at Andrew, as the car disappear from sight, grateful Ashleigh hadn't argued over going home. It was the last thing he needed to deal with right now.

"Billy?"

Andrew said his name again, and he pulled his gaze from the street to his partner. "Yeah?"

"There's something you need to see," Andrew said, walking to his car and leaning inside. He grabbed a folder, and returned to Billy. "I was working on this when you called me about Wes's body."

"Working on what?"

"Well, I was thinking about what you said about the parents. I mean, they, and the girls have all been the targets so far, right? And now, most of the parents are dead, right? So it got me thinking... what connects them?"

"You found something?"

Andrew nodded. "I was looking through their financial records..."

"Our accountant went through them already. He didn't find anything suspicious."

"Well, he missed something," Andrew told him, pointing at the page. "Because for the last ten years, they were all paying a Dr. Pollard a handsome sum of money. Including your father."

"Well, that makes sense," Billy said. "Because whatever happened ten years ago, I was a part of it." He cocked his head to the side. "Is this Dr. Eugene Pollard you're talking about?"

"Yes. Do you know him?"

"Not know him, but I've heard of him. There was an article about him online a few years back. Doesn't he specialize in memories, dreams, and the psyche?"

Andrew nodded. "Yes."

"But why would they be paying him?"

"My guess? They enlisted his services ten years ago," Gloria said from behind them.

Billy groaned. "Christ, Gloria! Do you have to be everywhere?"

"I'm just doing my job, Billy. I got another tip today. Another piece to this very, very messy puzzle of ours."

"From who?"

Gloria shrugged. "I have no idea. They want to remain anonymous, but what I do know, is that they want us to figure this damned thing out because they sent me another picture."

She held up her tablet, showing them the picture. "This was taken in Lindsay Miller's hospital room. She'd just come out of surgery, but see Charles, Mary, and Sully? It looks like they're arguing with Conrad. What do you think they're arguing about?"

Chapter Twenty - Four

Dammitt. Why hadn't he called yet?

Ashleigh stared at the coffeemaker, watching as the brown liquid dripped into the pot, and tapped her fingers against the countertop impatiently. She wanted to know about Kenzie. Was she still alive? Had she gotten out of surgery okay? It was killing her not knowing.

The coffeemaker beeped, signaling it was done, and she poured herself a cup. She wrapped her hands around the cup, the warmth chasing away the chill rushing through her.

She brought the mug to her lips, took a sip, and stared at the clock on the microwave.

Four a.m.

It was another sleepless night for her. It seemed to be a reoccurring theme these days.

She took another sip of the coffee, and a snore sounded from the living room. She smiled, leaning against the doorframe, watching Ryan as he slept on the couch. He mumbled something in his sleep, a lock of his brown hair falling across his forehead.

He looks so relaxed, she thought, something she didn't associate with Ryan Eisenhower. Sure, he smiled, made her laugh, but he was always super tense. Like he held the weight of the world on his shoulders.

She smiled, remembering when they'd gotten back to the house. She'd wanted to be alone, and had told him to go home, but he hadn't listened to her. Instead, he'd strode into the kitchen, made a pot of tea, and had told her that he wasn't going anywhere. Not until this madman was caught, and behind bars.

Ashleigh hadn't argued with him. What could she say? He was right. People she used to know, were dead, and she definitely was not going to complain about spending time with Ryan.

Ever since she'd started at UCLA, she'd had a bit of a crush on him. Who wouldn't? Starting quarterback for the Tigers. Good looks. Kind. He was the whole package. Although, she'd never envisioned meeting him like this.

She took another sip from her coffee, and a whimper suddenly sounded from Ryan's lips. She startled, turning, to see him toss and turn on the couch. His eyes snapped open, and he sat up on the couch, rubbing his hands across his face. "Fuck."

"I know that look," Ashleigh said, from where she was standing in the doorway. "Bad dream?"

Ryan startled, lifting his head to stare at her. "How long have you been standing there?"

"Just a few minutes."

"Well, that's embarrassing," Ryan said, rubbing his eyes. "I never wanted you to witness that."

"Witness what?"

"That I have nightmares, too. It makes me look weak, and I don't want you to see me that way." He rose to his feet, striding past her.

"Ryan." Ashleigh laid a hand on his arm as he passed. "I would never see you that way. Ever since I met you, you've been a rock, but you are human. What you've seen the last couple of days, it can't be easy."

"It's not that."

Ashleigh stared at him, vaguely remembering Jacob telling her Ryan had some of his own demons. "Do you want to talk about it? It might help."

Ryan grimaced. "I shouldn't. The last thing you need to deal with is my problems. Besides, it doesn't remotely compare to what you've been through."

"Ryan, don't do that."

"Do what?"

"Act like what you've been through doesn't matter. Come on. Talk to me."

Ryan stare at her a moment. "You're not going to take no for an answer, are you?"

Ashleigh smiled. "Probably not."

"You got any more coffee?"

Ashleigh laughed. "I just brewed a pot. There is plenty of coffee."

"Hold on a sec." Ryan disappeared into the kitchen. He returned a few moments later, cupping the mug in his hands. "It's my mom," he said, softly. "The way she died."

Ashleigh nodded, giving him his time.

"I hadn't thought about it in a long time until I saw the cop cars and the ambulance today," Ryan continued, bringing the mug to his lips and taking a sip. "I wasn't exactly the easiest kid in the world," he continued. "I was selfish, self-centered, and super competitive. I wanted things done when I wanted, had no patience, and was obsessed with being the best. I put everything I had into making myself the best football player I could." He smiled. "Growing up, I was fascinated with the sport. Obsessed even, and watching the likes of Bart Starr, Joe Montana, Jerry Rice, I told myself I wanted to be just like them one day."

"Your parents must have been very supportive."

Ryan smiled. "Oh, they were. My Dad worked with me on drills. My Mom made the meals to keep my body weight where I wanted it. I even set up nets in the back yard to work on my accuracy, but then came my senior year." He drank the rest of his coffee, setting it down on the coffee table, and leaned forward. He folded his hands in his lap, staring down at them. "It was the middle of the football season, and I hadn't gotten my license yet. It was the most important game of the season, and Mom was running late." He sighed, shaking his head. "God, I was so mad at her. Dad was already waiting for us at the field, and when Mom walked through the door, I just lost it. I yelled, screamed at her how this was the most important game of the season. That scouts were going to be there, and because of her, I was going to lose out on a scholarship. I was still yelling in the car. I just couldn't stop. She took her eyes off the road for a second. One second to yell at me, and that's when she veered into the intersection. A truck crashed into us, striking her side of the vehicle."

"Oh my God. Ryan..."

"She'd been so distracted by me, she hadn't put her seatbelt on," Ryan continued. "She crashed through the windshield. I was knocked unconscious for a few moments, but when I came to, I saw her laying on the ground, motionless. I screamed, and ran out of the car as fast as I could, but it was too late. There was blood everywhere. She was dead, I knew it the moment I saw her. She died because of me."

"Oh, Ryan, you can't think like that."

"She was running late because she forgot to pick up my uniform from dry cleaning," Ryan whispered, a tear streaking down his cheek. "If it weren't for me, she would have never veered into that intersection."

"Ryan."

"I carry that around with me every day," Ryan continued, staring down at his hands. "After that day, my father and I... our relationship was never the same. He couldn't look at me. I think he blamed me for her death, too. It was a few years later when he died in his sleep, but I think he really died of a broken heart."

"Oh, Ryan," Ashleigh reached her hand out, gripping his tightly. Her heart was breaking for the boy he'd been, and for the man who still carried that guilt around.

"It was a relief when I got to LA. It was a fresh start for me, but I definitely hit rock bottom. Far from the person I am today. I drank too much, smoked too much and I definitely slept with way too many girls. I was just lost, until I met Rome." Ryan smiled. "I was sitting on the steps, nearly passed out when he stumbled across me. He took me in, sobered me up, and listened to my sob story. Then he told me I needed to get over my shit. He told me that everyone goes through shit and that if I didn't straighten up I'd lose everything I'd worked so hard for. He was right. He's now one of my best friends, and after a little bit of therapy, I realized the guilt I was carrying, wasn't healthy for me. I eventually was able to live with what had happened and forgave myself, but every once in a while a nightmare or two still slip through the cracks."

"Like tonight."

"Yes. Like tonight," Ryan said, rising to his feet and yawning. "I just hope she's proud of the man I've become."

"I don't see why she wouldn't be," Ashleigh told him, as she followed him into the kitchen. "From that very first night I met you, you've been nothing but kind. Nothing at all like the kid you describe being once."

Ryan gave her a small smile. "Thanks, Ash." He paused, glancing at the laptop that lay open on the kitchen table. "Did you sleep at all?"

Ashleigh shook her head. "No. I was too wired. I just kept thinking about everything, so I started making a board similar to the one in Billy's office." She turned the laptop, showing him.

"You better not show that to Billy. He'll freak."

"He doesn't need to know everything, does he?" Ashleigh asked, rolling her eyes. "He's gone overboard with his overprotectiveness. So has Vinny."

"Vinny?"

Ashleigh nodded. "One of the cooks at the restaurant. He got super jealous over you and the guys coming into the restaurant the other day."

"What?" Ryan laughed, shaking his head. "Ash, these men in your life…"

"Are crazy. I know," Ashleigh said, as her phone vibrated from where it was laying on the table. Nikki's face popped up on the screen. "Oh! It's Nikki. I have to take this."

"Of course." Ryan gave her arm a squeeze. "I'm gonna grab another cup of coffee. Do you want one?"

"Yes, please."

Ryan took her mug and rounded the kitchen counter as she lifted the phone to her ear. "Hey, Nikki. How are you?" She asked, immediately concerned for her friend. She'd tried calling her earlier when Wes's body had been found, but she hadn't answered.

"Oh my God, Ash. I just got your message. Is my dad really…"

Ashleigh swallowed. "Yes." She whispered into the phone. "He's dead, Nikki. I am so sorry."

"I just… I can't believe it," Nikki whispered, her voice hoarse as if she were trying to hold back tears. "Even though my testimony put him away, he never stopped trying to get a hold of me. He always remembered my birthday, and he even reached out when we escaped the manor. But I never wanted to see him, now, I just have all those regrets.."

"I know you do, Nikki," Ashleigh whispered. "But you have to remember that he did still love you."

"I know. That's what makes this so hard!" Nikki cried. "God, Ash. I don't like this. I don't like all the people who are dying. People who are connected to us! And you! You're right in the middle of it."

"We're all in the middle of it," Ashleigh told her, smiling at Ryan as he set her mug in front of her, then went on to tell Nikki about everything that had happened. Including their theory that it was all connected to the Millers.

"You mean, we were there? We found the bodies?" Nikki screamed into the phone. "Ash!"

Ashleigh winced, holding the phone away from her ear, just as a text came through. She glanced at the notification that came across her phone. It was Johnny.

Turn on the TV. There's something you need to see.

She showed Ryan the text, and he nodded, heading for the living room. He flipped on the television, and Gloria Davis's figure filled the screen.

"Last evening, a disturbing 911 call brought officers here to a small, logged cabin in Bakersfield, California. Upon arriving at the scene, the police discovered three bodies." The images image flashed across the screen. "Former small-town sheriff, Charles Turner. Current medical examiner, Sullivan Wilcox, and Mary Carlson. Each were found wearing a clown mask, similar to..."

Ashleigh didn't hear the rest of what she said. All she could focus on was the picture of her mother on the screen. A gasp escaped her mouth, followed by a sob. "Oh my God! Mom!"

The phone clattered to the ground.

"Ash?"

"Ash?"

"Ash!"

Chapter Twenty - Five

Ashleigh stared at the television, shock filling her as she watched the images flash across the screen. Her mother was dead.

The realization hit her like a ton of bricks. A sob threatened to break loose, tears filled her eyes, and she felt her body start to shake.

"Ash."

She vaguely heard Ryan say her name, out of the corner of her eye watching as he picked up the phone from where it had fallen to the floor. He said something to Nikki, what, she wasn't sure. She felt like she was in a fog. She couldn't function. She couldn't move. Then suddenly he was right in front of her.

"Come on." He took her hand, leading her to the couch, but she couldn't move. She stared at him, her eyes glistening with tears. "I... I can't move," she whispered.

Without even thinking about it, Ryan scooped her up in his arms and carried her to the couch. "It's okay," he whispered, as he sat down, wrapping his arms around her. "I'm here. Whatever you need. I'm here."

"I just... I can't believe she's gone," Ashleigh whispered, hiccupping, as she laid her head against his chest. "I know I haven't seen her since I was sixteen. That she left me to take care of my sisters, but..."

"But she's still your mom. I know." Ryan whispered. "I know, baby."

Ashleigh froze. She opened her mouth to call him out on what he'd just called her, but she didn't get the chance.

"Even more disturbing is what we learned just a few short minutes ago," Gloria was saying into the camera. "As many of you may already know, ten years ago in the town of Sarasota Bay, four young men were found murdered, two young girls went missing, and a young woman was badly injured in a heinous attack. What many of us didn't know, was that the main suspect was in fact Neil Carlson. A man many of us thought had died while he'd been overseas. Now, we have found that not to be true."

"Wait. What?" Ashleigh stared at the television, her jaw dropping open. She glanced over at Ryan, but he just shook his head.

"Ten years ago, Neil Carlson's knife was found at the crime scene. He was arrested but was adamant that he was innocent. It was a year later when he was finally released, cleared of all charges, but Sheriff Turner still wasn't convinced he was innocent."

Gloria held up a folder in her hand. "Sheriff Turner went to extreme measures to get a confession from Mr. Carlson. Including kidnapping him, and taking him to an abandoned storage unit, then eventually, to an abandoned factory. There, Mr. Carlson endured hours of torture at the hands of Sheriff Turner. Methods that included electrocution, humiliation, seclusion, and waterboarding to name a few. It was weeks later when Mr. Carlson managed to escape, but the damage was done. He snapped, becoming deranged, erratic, and eventually becoming a man known as The Clown. He killed four people in Sarasota. Two police officers who'd arrested him, the public defender, and the judge who locked him up, but that's not the most disturbing part of all of this."

An image of her mother and Sully filled the screen, next to the picture of Billy's father.

"It has come to our knowledge, that with the help of Mary Carlson and Sullivan Wilcox, Charles covered up Carlson's crimes. Labeling them as unsolved murders, the case files were erased from the system, until today. The only question is, why would they cover it up? If not to protect someone? I have my theories, but until there's conclusive evidence of those theories, my lips will remain shut."

Someone shouted behind her, and she nodded. "Yes. One other thing we uncovered was that Charles himself was a target of Neil's as well. Stabbed eight times in the chest, he somehow managed to shoot Neil. Neil's body fell into the lake, just off the coast of Sarasota Bay, but his body was never recovered. So now the question is, is Neil Carlson still alive? And if he is, is he the same man who dawned the mask once again? Or is it someone else this time?"

"Oh my God." Ashleigh stared at the television. "That. That..."

Her phone buzzed, and she reached for it, from where it was sitting on the end table. "It's Billy. He's at the door."

"I'll get it." Ryan leaned forward, pressing a kiss to her cheek, before rising from the couch and heading for the door.

Ashleigh shuddered, suddenly feeling cold without his presence, pressing a hand to her cheek. Was he just being nice? Sweet?

"Hey, Billy." Ryan pulled the door open. "Look, it's really not a good time. Ashleigh..."

"You think I don't know that, Ryan?" Billy asked, shoving past him. "But she needs me right now. I know you think you know what Ashleigh needs, but I have known her a hell of a lot longer than you have."

"Billy!" Ashleigh stared at him in dismay. "That was rude!"

"I don't care," Billy told her. "Pack a bag, Ash. You're coming with me."

"Whoa. Hold on a second." Ashleigh held up a hand. "I don't care who you think you are, but you do not get to barge in here and tell me what to do."

"Ash, I'm trying to keep you safe! And the only person you're safe with is me."

"So, you think I have something to do with this?" Ryan asked from the doorway.

"I think it's awfully convenient that you showed up in her life as soon as the murders started happening."

Ryan stiffened. He glanced at Ashleigh. "Do you feel that way, too?" he asked.

"Of course not!" Ashleigh brushed past Billy, reaching out and taking Ryan's hand. "I feel safe with you, Ryan. I could never, ever think that." She raised a hand, touching his cheek, hating the pain and torment that was in his eyes. It was the same look she'd seen in his eyes when he'd told her about his mother. "Please, don't listen to Billy. He's just lashing out because he is in pain."

"The hell I am!" Billy snapped, his eyes flashing. "Ash. You're coming with me. I am not taking no for an answer."

"No. You need to leave," Ashleigh told him. "Before I call the cops and have you arrested. Now please, just go."

"Ash."

"Now, Billy."

Billy stared at her a moment, then he let out a long breath. "Fine. I'll go, but this conversation is not over." He dug Ryan's keys out of his pocket, slamming them onto the coffee table. "Here are your keys."

"Yours are in the kitchen."

Billy gave him a look before disappearing into the kitchen. He returned, looking from Ashleigh to Ryan. "Look. I didn't mean..."

"Just go, Billy. I don't want to see you right now."

Billy nodded, turning, and disappearing through the door.

The door slammed shut behind him, and Ryan dragged a hand through his hair. "Christ. I need a drink." He spun on his heel, heading for the kitchen.

"Ryan."

"I just... I need a moment, Ash," Ryan said, reaching into the cupboard above him, grabbing the bottle of vodka. He twisted off the cap, took a swig, and shook his head. "You know, every time I think I'm making progress with him, he proves me wrong."

"I'm sorry." Ashleigh rung her hands together. "He's always been like this. Protective... over all of us. It was hard having boyfriends around him. He always scared them off."

"I'm not sure that makes me feel better." Ryan took another swig, and his eyes suddenly widened. "Oh my God. Ash, did I call you..."

Ashleigh smiled. "You remember?"

"That I called you, Baby?" Ryan flushed, rubbing the back of his neck. "It just kind of slipped out. I'm sorry. If it made you uncomfortable..."

"No. Not at all. In fact, I thought it was sweet." Ashleigh walked up to him, taking the bottle from him. She lifted it to her lips, taking a sip. "Because I wasn't lying when I told you that I feel safe around you, Ryan." She set the bottle down. "And, that kiss on the cheek. That was sweet too."

Ryan grimaced, running a hand across his jaw. "Damn. I didn't even realize..."

"You didn't mean to do it?"

"Uh. Yes. No... Christ." Ryan closed his eyes. "Yes, okay? I've been wanting to kiss you for quite some time now, but I'm so scared I'm going to hurt you. You've already been through so much..."

"Ryan, I already have one man in my life who treats me like I'm made of glass. Please, don't be the second," Ashleigh whispered. "Because, I really, really want you to kiss me."

Ryan stared down at her, then in one, swift motion he grabbed her by the hips and hoisted her up onto the counter. He pulled her close, and a minute later his lips were finding hers.

Ashleigh gasped as their lips collided. His lips claimed hers in a desperate, hungry kiss that had her earning for more. She wrapped her hands around his shoulders, as his hands settled on her hips. His tongue trailed across her lips, nibbling, suckling, before thrusting inside her mouth. His tongue swirled with hers, and she moaned at the contact. It'd been a long time since she'd felt like this. Wanted. Needed. Too soon, he pulled away, his breath coming out hard, as he pressed his forehead against hers.

"We shouldn't do this, Ash. You. You've been through a lot today. You're vulnerable. I don't want to take advantage of you."

"Ryan."

"Please, Ash. Can we just wait until the dust settles a bit? I don't want you to have any regrets."

"I could never..."

"Please?"

Ashleigh stared into his eyes, hating the turmoil that was in the brown depths. Billy's words had hurt him, she just wished there was a way she could take it away. "Okay," she whispered. "We can wait."

"Thank you." Ryan squeezed her hand. "I'm going to go jump in the shower. Are you going to be okay?"

Ashleigh nodded. "Yes. I'll be fine, Ryan. I promise. Go take your shower."

Ryan smiled, helping her off the counter. Their bodies brushed together, and he sighed, brushing a lock of hair behind her ear. "This is going to be pure torture."

Ashleigh giggled, turning and walking away. "You're the one who wants to wait."

And why the hell did he want that? Ryan thought to himself. God, he was such an idiot, but he didn't want to rush her. She deserved to take some time, because if they started something and she ended up regretting it. It might just shatter him.

He turned, heading for the doorway, stopping when Ashleigh's phone buzzed. He glanced back at her. "Please tell me that's not more bad news."

"No. It's just Johnny." Ashleigh scanned the text. "He says he has something for me. He wants me to meet up with him in a couple of hours."

"Where?"

"Why, at Campus, silly, "Ashleigh said, rolling her eyes. "It's Thursday, and I believe we both have class. And you, have practice."

"Ash, don't you want to stay home today?" Ryan asked. "A lot's gone down in the last few hours. It might be best..."

"No." Ashleigh shook her head. "No way. I am not letting you jeopardize your football career for me, and I, am not going to let some psycho keep me from my future. We are going, Ryan, and don't bother even trying to argue with me. It won't work."

"I wouldn't dream of it," Ryan muttered under his breath. He stopped next to her, wrapping an arm around her and pulling her close. "Okay. We'll go, but you have to promise me something."

"What's that?"

"That this time, when I text you, you will not ignore me."

"I wasn't..."

"Ash."

"Ok. Fine, I'll respond to every text you send, okay?" Ashleigh asked. "Will that satisfy you?"

Ryan smiled. "For now." He brushed a kiss against her cheek, then disappeared up the steps.

Chapter Twenty - Six

"You did what?" Andrew stared at Billy, his eyes going wide. "Billy, please tell me what you just told me, is some sort of sick joke. That you did not barge over to Ashleigh's place, just after she learned the truth about her father, her mother, and demand she leave with you?"

"I'm trying to keep her safe," Billy said, pacing around the office. "And that quarterback, he…"

"Has been nothing but good to her!" Andrew shouted. "And you practically accused him of being a part of all of this! God, Billy, what were you thinking?"

"That I need to protect my friend, and that I'm the only one who can do it."

"No." Andrew held up a hand. "That's not why you did it, Billy."

"Oh?" Billy raised a brow. "So tell me why I did it, oh insightful one."

"Because you like to be in control!" Andrew shouted. "You like being the only guy in the girls' lives. You like that they come to you, and you can't stand it when they turn to someone other than you!"

"No, that's..."

"You have issues, Billy. Like huge issues, and you need to get help. Very soon." Andrew swiped a hand across his face. "Billy, this is bad. Really bad! The captain's been on a warpath ever since that file was released to the media. How do you think he's going to react when he hears about this? You're putting this entire case in jeopardy. Just like your father..."

"Don't you dare compare me to my father."

Andrew threw his hands up in the air. "I'm going for a walk. I can't deal with you right now." He threw open the door, strode out of the room, glaring at his fellow officers as they stared at him.

"Turner! Stark!"

The captain's voice rang out through the precinct, and Andrew blew out a breath. He sent Billy a glare, before heading for the captain's office. Billy following close behind.

"You called, Cap?" Billy asked, nervously, as they stepped inside the office.

"Close the door."

Andrew shut the door, eyeing the captain. This couldn't be good.

Captain Benjamin Vargas turned from where he was standing, looking out the large window overlooking the city. He blew out a deep breath, before speaking. "I just got off the phone with Ashleigh Carlson."

"Shit."

"Shit is right," Captain Vargas turned, laying his large hands on the desk, his dark, gray eyes staring intently at Billy. "Billy, I don't know what the hell to think right now. Like, what were you thinking?"

"I was concerned about my friend, Captain."

"She doesn't need you to be a friend right now, Billy. She needs you to act like a goddamn, fucking detective! That's what I need you to do. Christ!" He closed his eyes, inhaling a sharp breath. "Stark. Where were you when all of this happened?"

"I was finishing up at the Hospital, Sir."

The captain nodded. "Ok. I can accept that." He twisted a corner of his mustache, thinking. "Ashleigh wants you off the case, Billy, and I can't say I blame her."

"Captain..."

The captain held up a hand. "You're spiraling, Billy. You haven't had a day off since the girls went missing, and you're running yourself ragged."

"I can't take a day off, Cap. Not with some murderous, psycho roaming the streets."

"Which is why I told Ashleigh I couldn't take you off the case. You're my best detective, Billy. Even if I do have my reservations. Your father's involvement in this..."

"Makes it messy. I know."

Captain Vargas stared at him, then at Andrew. "I'm not taking you off the case, but I am making a change. Effective immediately, Andrew will be taking point."

"But Cap!"

"Take it or leave it, Turner, but if you choose to leave it, I warn you. I will take both your gun and your badge."

Billy sighed. "I guess I don't have much of a choice."

"You're also to keep your distance from Ashleigh, and when this is all over, you are to take a leave of absence, and," he paused. "You're going to go see Abigail."

"The shrink?"

"Yes. The shrink." Captain Vargas leveled Billy with a look. "You're as involved in this, as the girls are, Billy. There's no way this doesn't have some effect on you. Now, tell me exactly where we are with the investigation."

Between the two of them, they quickly filled him in on everything that had transpired.

"I don't think it was just Mary, Charles, and Sully who were involved in framing Neil for murder," Andrew said after they were done. "I think the other families were in on it too."

"I agree," Billy said, nodding. "I'd like to get access to the deaths of Addison and Sydney's parents. I think there's a connection."

"I can make a few calls. See if I can get them to you faster." Captain Vargas paused. "Any news on the Sinclair girl?"

"She made it out of surgery successfully," Billy told him. "But she lost a lot of blood. She's in a coma, and the doctors don't know if, or when she might wake up."

"Well, let's hope she makes it through. She may be the only one who can ID him," Vargas said. "So the next step is this doctor?"

"Yes," Andrew and Billy said in unison,

"Money doesn't lie, boys," Vargas told them. "This doctor, he is definitely a part of this puzzle. I need you to figure out what, and, solve this damned thing before it's too late."

"It's already too late, Cap," Billy told him, as they headed for the door. "And the sad thing is, all of this could have been prevented ten years ago."

Chapter Twenty - Seven

Finding Johnny is like finding a freaking needle in a haystack, Ashleigh thought in frustration later that afternoon, as she walked through the halls of the UCLA campus.

"I'll meet you at the entrance."

That had been the text she'd gotten this morning, followed by...

"Change of plans! Meet me by the cafeteria at noon."

So that's where she'd gone at noon. She'd been waiting several minutes when she'd gotten another text.

"Sorry! That's not going to work either. Meet me by the practice field at three."

Ashleigh sighed, pushing through the double doors and making her way across the lawn toward the practice field. Her phone dinged, and she glanced down, a smile spreading across her lips. It was Ryan.

"Hey, Ash. Just checking in. How's your day going?"

She blushed, thinking about the moment they'd had this morning in her kitchen. She'd been bummed when he'd said he'd wanted to wait, but she also understood. He was worried about hurting her, and she was still worried about him getting too close to her. She liked him, but what if she let him get close, and he died because of her? She would never forgive herself for that.

She pushed the thought away, tapping in a quick response.

"Same as earlier. Everyone was surprisingly quiet and nice today. Stop worrying!"

"It's what I do. What are you doing now?"

"Waiting for Johnny."

"He going to show up this time?"

"I sure hope do!" She grinned, glancing up, catching sight of him as he walked toward the training facility. *"I see you."*

He startled, glancing around, and then he spotted her sitting in the bleachers. He grinned, waving to her, before disappearing inside the building.

"Hey, Ash."

Someone slid into the seat in front of her, and Ashleigh glanced up. "Vinny! Oh my God. I've missed you!" She wrapped her arms around him and gave him a hug. "I feel like it's been forever since I've seen you!"

"I know," Vinny said, sighing. "I'm sorry I haven't reached out. I heard about what happened at the restaurant with your friend's Dad."

"You didn't see it?"

"Vinny shook his head. "No. Franny sent me home just before the body was found. I'd just finished up a twelve-hour shift and was exhausted. I passed out as soon as I got home." He leaned forward. "I've been worried about you. You doing ok?"

Ashleigh sighed. "Ok? I'm not sure, but I'm not freaking out, so that's a plus." She frowned. "Vinny. What are you doing here? I don't think I've ever seen you on campus."

"I'm taking some advice you gave me a little while ago?"

"What advice was that?"

"Well, you told me a while ago, after I told you about my time in Haiti, that I should think about starting up my own construction business."

"I remember. You said it was one of the most rewarding things you've ever done."

"And it was. I just finished signing up for some business classes. I start next week."

"Vinny, that's amazing!" Ashleigh cried. "I'm so happy for you!"

Vinny shrugged. "We'll see how it goes." He flashed her a grin, glancing at his watch. "I gotta run to an appointment, are you working tonight?"

Ashleigh nodded. "Yes."

He glanced off toward the football field. "And the quarterback? How are things going there?"

"Vinny!"

"Just looking out for my girl," Vinny said, flashing her a smile, before striding away.

His girl?

Ashleigh frowned at the words, watching as he disappeared from sight. She glanced down at her phone, sighing. *Where the hell was Johnny?*

"Don't worry. I didn't bail on you again."

She glanced up, as Johnny slid into the seat next to her.

"I was beginning to think you were never going to show up," she said, glancing across the field as the football team emerged from the building. They were dressed in their dark blue and yellow uniforms. They were wearing pads today, and they were laughing as they talked. Each of them held their dark blue helmets, with the UCLA letters written across the side in bold, white letters.

"No. No. I was. I just had to be careful. I'm pretty sure I'm being followed."

"What?" Ashleigh started, jerking her head up. She glanced around them, scanning the open field and the trees in the distance. "You don't think..."

"Don't worry. I'm pretty sure I lost them," Johnny told her, trying to comfort her, but the uncertainty in his eyes wasn't lost on her. He looked just as worried as she did. "But I wanted to give you this." He withdrew a yellow envelope from his bag and handed it to her.

"What is it?"

Johnny shrugged. "I never opened it, so I really have no idea. What I do know, is that it's from your mother."

"You knew my mother?" Ashleigh asked, staring down at the envelope she was holding in her hands. Her name was written on the front in bold, neat handwriting. She'd recognize the penmanship anywhere. This was definitely from her mother.

"I wouldn't say knew her," Johnny said, fidgeting, as he glanced around them. "About a year ago, there was a post on Facebook, asking for some help transferring some old photos. I had some free time and figured, why not. A little extra cash would be nice. Only, I soon found out, it wasn't for old photos. It was keeping this file safe, and when the time was right, I was to release a file to the media. I had no idea it was your mother who hired me until last night. She remained anonymous the whole time we communicated."

"She certainly did have her secrets, didn't she?"

"Everyone has secrets," Johnny said, as he rose to his feet. "It's only when they're discovered, that they have the power to hurt people. In this case, your family." He gave her a tight smile. "I gotta go, but if there's anything I can do, don't hesitate to reach out, okay?"

"Thank you, Johnny."

He gave her a small wave, making his way across the lawn and disappearing inside the main doors of campus.

Ashleigh sighed, leaning back, and gazed across the field. The football team was going through their drills. She watched, her eyes glued to Ryan, as he threw the ball long along the sideline. It floated through the air, landing in Jacob's hands.

"You really are the black angel of death, aren't you?" Someone said from behind you. "Kenzie was right about you. Death and tragedy follow you everywhere you go, and if it wasn't for you, Kenzie wouldn't be laying in a hospital bed right now."

Chapter Twenty - Eight

"Tigers on three!"

"One. Two. Three."

"Tigers!"

The team broke the huddle, and Jacob grinned at Ryan, nodding to where Ashleigh was sitting on the bench. "Your new girlfriend come to cheer you on today, Ry?"

Ryan swallowed, remembering the moment they'd had in the kitchen this morning. "I'm not sure what we are yet." He finally said.

Devante and Jacob shared a look.

"Oh. Did something happen?" Rome asked, glancing over at Ryan, batting his eyelashes at him.

"Oh! Will you cut it out!" Ryan smacked him lightly on the back of the head. "We're taking things slow."

"I suppose you kind of have to, don't you?" Jacob asked. "I mean, she has gone through a lot."

"That she has."

"You seem different with her though, Ryan," Devante murmured. "Happier, even."

"I think I like her. A lot," Ryan admitted. "But I want to do this right."

"You're a good man, Ryan. You'll do things the right way. You always do," Rome told him. "And then we'll get to tease you because we all know she'll have you wrapped around your finger."

"Oh? And you know this from experience?" Ryan asked, glancing at him, then to Jacob and Devante. "Last I knew, you three had a different girl every night!"

"Damn right!"

"We're football players!"

"It's not our fault women get their panties wet at just the sight of us," Rome added, grinning.

"Just you wait, Rome. One of these days you'll meet some woman who'll put a stop to your philandering ways."

"As if!"

"That'll be the day!"

Ryan shook his head, as they all took their spots at the line of scrimmage. He took his place under center, snapping his chin strap in place. "Set. Set. Hut. Hut!"

The center snapped the ball, and he gripped it in his hands as he dropped back. He gazed down the field, going through his reads, and from the corner of his eye, he saw one of the linebackers break free. He swerved, avoiding him and escaped the pocket, but he never let his eyes leave the field. It was a trick he'd learned a long time ago.

He watched as Jacob turned back, realizing his quarterback was in trouble. He raised his arm, throwing it across the field, over the defender's head, and right into Jacob's hands.

"Hell yes!" Coach punched his hand in the air. "That was fantastic, Ryan!"

"I'm not sure how you got out of that one, Ryan," the linebacker, Raymond said, panting as he grinned. "I thought I had you. Nice moves!"

"I surprise myself sometimes," Ryan told him, laughing. He took his position behind the center once more.

A handoff to Devante went for two yards. Another deep pass to Jacob got them to midfield. Then on first down, Rome cut left instead of right. Ryan threw the ball, and it sailed through the air, landing in the arms of the safety for an interception.

"Dammit, Rome! Did you not remember your route?" Ryan shouted as they jogged off the field. "You cut the wrong way!"

"Cool it, Ry," Coach said, leveling him a look. "Save it for the game next week."

Ryan growled, pulling off his helmet and taking a sip from the cup of water one of the volunteers handed to him. "Coach. I know this is practice, but we have to get this right!"

"I don't often agree with Ryan much, but on this. He's right."

The voice sounded behind him, and Ryan inwardly groaned. Of all the days...

He turned, staring at Marcus as he made his way across the field toward him.

"Hey, it's Marcus!"

"I didn't know he was back."

"Wasn't he in jail?"

"Your back?" Rome asked, his eyes wide as he stared at Marcus. "I thought you were..."

"In jail?" Marcus asked, laughing. "Nope. I've been cleared of all accusations. My father as well." He stopped in front of them, turning to the Coach. "Hey, Coach."

"Marcus. You're not supposed to be here." The Coach said, crossing his arms across his chest. "You're suspended."

"Which is bullshit."

"Not from where I'm standing," Coach told him. "You crossed the line one too many times, Marcus, and until the school board, including myself, are comfortable with you back on campus, you are to stay away. Feel free to go clean out your locker. You will not be a part of the team this season."

"What! That's bullshit! You people are sabotaging me and ruining my future!"

"You did that yourself, Marcus," Ryan said, as he strolled past him. "Don't blame your misfortunes on us. You dug your own grave when you chose to be an asshole." He smirked. "Hope you enjoyed your little sleepover behind bars. Can't say I feel bad for you."

Marcus blocked his path. "I didn't kill anyone, Ryan."

"I know. You were locked up when Kenzie was attacked last night, but that doesn't mean you're not a selfish prick." He glanced at the coach. "We done for the day?"

Coach nodded. "See you on Monday, Ryan."

"See you then."

Ryan headed across the field toward the training facility, pulling the jersey over his head, followed by his pads, glancing over his shoulder at Marcus. "Why are you following me?"

"We need to talk."

"I have nothing more to say to you, Marcus."

"But I have something…" Marcus trailed off, as the rest of the team ran in behind them. He scowled. "Don't you guys have somewhere else to be? I need to have a word with Ryan."

"Absolutely not." Jacob crossed his arms in front of his chest, not moving. "We know you already have it out for Ryan."

"And we all know, our best chance to win, is with Ryan behind center," Rome added, stopping next to Jacob.

Marcus scowled, as all the men stood there, refusing to move. He sighed, turning to Ryan. "Ryan. Something happened last night while I was…" He trailed off, interrupted when the lights inside the locker room suddenly went out.

"What the hell?"

"What happened to the lights?"

Clang. Clang. Clang.

The sound of metal scraping against metal sounded nearby, followed by the sound of a locker door slamming shut.

Ryan froze, raising a finger to his lips, as he glanced at his teammates. "Shh," he whispered. "Someone's in here."

"No shit. Really?" Rome whispered back, ducking down behind the lockers. "It's him, isn't it? The killer."

"Shh!"

"There's no way..."

The lights flickered on, and they all turned, to stare at the clown standing in the doorway.

"Oh shit."

"It's him!"

"Hell, I ain't scared of no clown," Devante, said, rising to his feet. He tossed his pads and helmet to the ground and flexed his muscles.

"Devante, don't you dare..."

He turned, racing down the aisle toward the clown.

"Devante, no!"

Ryan shouted, but it was too late. Devante lunged toward the clown and the knife appeared, slicing through Devante's arm.

Devante screamed, and the clown grabbed him by the arm. He dragged him to his feet, tossing him against the lockers.

"Devante!"

He crumbled to the floor, falling unconscious, and Ryan watched in horror as the clown strode forward. He dodged the football players who came after them, tossing them against the lockers. One after the other.

"Where is he?" the clown asked, as he tossed another body to the ground "Where is the boy?"

"Who's he looking for?" Ryan asked, glancing at Marcus.

"How the hell should I know?"

"Well, you are a deceitful bastard," Ryan said, gesturing to him, and disappearing around the corner. He ducked down, walking along the lockers, opposite of the clown, and turned, disappearing into the shower room.

They hurried inside, and he quietly closed the door, nearly jumped out of his skin when he saw someone hunkered down in one of the showers.

"Jesus Christ! You scared the shit out of me!" he cried, staring at the slender, dark-haired man. "What are you doing in here?"

"He... he's going to kill me..." the man stammered, his voice trembling with fear. "I thought I saw him following me. It's why I kept changing the time to meet Ashleigh, but after I gave her the file, I saw him again. That face! God!"

"Oh. You're Johnny." Ryan whispered, suddenly putting it all together. He cocked his head to the side. "He did say he was looking for someone, but why you? You have no connection toon to what happened in Sarasota Bay."

"Actually, I kind of do," Johnny said. "Ashleigh's mom hired me about a year ago. If anything were to happen to her, I was to release the files to the media. Plus, there's the file I gave Ashleigh."

"What's in it?"

"I don't know, but you should have seen his face. He's so pissed! He's going to kill me."

"Not if I have anything to say about it."

"Don't be an idiot, Ryan," Marcus said from behind them. He turned, peering out the window into the locker room. "You really think you can take this bastard on? He's killed eight people already. He won't hesitate to kill you, or me for that matter. We should give him what he wants so we can get out of here alive."

"We are not sacrificing Johnny to save our own asses," Ryan said between gritted teeth. He extended a hand to Johnny. "Come on. We're going to get out of this... together."

"But, how?" Johnny asked as Ryan pulled him to his feet. "He has us trapped! And... he has a knife!"

"By fighting back," Ryan said, turning and striding across the room. He reached above him, his hand wrapping around the loose shower rod. It'd needed to be replaced for the last two years, but right now, he was grateful it hadn't.

It pulled from the wall after a couple of tugs. He gripped it in his hand, glancing behind him at Marcus and Johnny. "This clown might have a knife, but I know there are weapons we can use throughout the locker room. Marcus, what do you think? You wanna kick this clown's ass?"

"Hell yeah," Marcus said, cracking his knuckles. "I've been itching for a good fight ever since you knocked me into that damned table."

Ryan rolled his eyes. "Come on. Follow me." He wrapped his hand around the doorknob, slowly pushing it open. He peered out into the dark locker room, looking left, then right. "It's clear," he said, gesturing them forward. "Come on."

They stepped into the locker room, and he nodded toward the lockers. "You guys should look through the lockers," he told them. "There might be a weapon you can use in there."

Marcus and Johnny inched forward, ruffling through the lockers. As they did, Ryan peered around the edge of the locker, staring into the dark locker room.

Where the hell did he go? he wondered, then suddenly gasped, as a shoelace wrapped around his neck. He let out a shout, the pipe falling from his hand and crashing to the ground with a loud clang as he was jerked back, struggling to gasp for air.

"Ryan!"

Marcus and Johnny turned at the sudden racket.

"Run!" Ryan managed to gasp out. "Get out of here, now!"

They ran.

"You're meddling in things that are beyond your understanding, Ryan," the clown whispered in his ear, pulling the shoestring tighter around his throat. "And you can't save them. They all deserve to die."

Ryan gasped, struggling to drag in breaths. Dots swam before his eyes, and he felt his body slack. *No. You have to fight. Do not let him win!*

He gasped, as he was suddenly tossed to the side. His body slammed against the lockers, and he crumbled to the ground.

"Johnny! Marcus!" he tried to shout, but no words sounded. He tried to get to his feet, but his body wouldn't move. All he could do was watch as the clown raced after them. He grabbed Marcus from behind, tossing him against the lockers. His body hit the lockers with a loud clang, his body crumbling to the ground next to several of his teammates.

"Johnny! Watch out!"

He finally managed to get his voice back, dragging himself to his feet. He grabbed a hold of the locker next to him, steadying himself, and reached for the pipe laying on the ground. He turned, half limping, half sprinting as the clown closed in on Johnny. He lunged forward, striking the pipe forward, but the clown spun around, grabbing the pipe from him. He jerked him forward, striking his leg out. His large foot caught Ryan in the stomach and he gasped, stumbling backward. He fell back against the lockers, glancing up, just as the pipe swung toward him. He ducked, dodging the weapon and he lunged to the side. A second later he felt something strike him in the temple.

"No!"

Ryan let out a shout, staring up at the clown as he dropped the pipe. His vision wavered, and he watched helplessly as the clown caught up to Johnny just before he reached the entrance. He grabbed him by the back of the neck, jerking him back, and struck the knife through his chest.

"No! Johnny!"

Chapter Twenty - Nine

"Tracey."

Ashleigh glanced over her shoulder, sliding the folder into her bag, staring at the young woman as she stopped next to the bleachers. Behind her, two other women stood, glaring at her with just as much hatred as Tracey was.

"I mean, why did you even have to come here?" Tracey continued. "There was a small school just a few miles from where you grew up. You could have gone there. Now, because of you, people are getting hurt. People are dying, all because you had to move to LA."

"You're not serious." Ashleigh slung her bag over her shoulder, climbing down from the bleachers, her temper snapping. "I am not to blame for any of this, Tracey. That damned psycho is."

"But you should have never come here!"

"UCLA has been my number one choice for several years now, and after all I've been through, I deserved the chance to give myself the resources to go after my dream. Did I consider going to a school closer to home? Of course I did. It's why I took that year after graduating off, but in the end, I decided it was time to start a new chapter in my life. Not that I have to explain myself to you."

She hopped down from the bleachers, striding past them. She did not need this shit. Not now.

"Oh, you had better explain yourself," Tracey said, grabbing her by the arm and spinning her around. "Because of you, my best friend is in a coma!"

"And I am truly sorry about that," Ashleigh whispered, swallowing. Between all that had happened, she hadn't heard about Kenzie. Finding out she was in a coma, this way. It just added to the pile of shit that had happened the last couple of days. "She was my friend, too, Tracey."

"She was never your friend!" The long-haired, brunette behind Tracey cried.

"Yes, she was," Ashleigh said, her eyes drifting past the girls to where the football team was still practicing. She watched them for a moment before turning back to the girls in front of her. "Kenzie and I grew up together," she finally said.

"That doesn't mean you know her!" The blonde woman standing next to the brunette cried.

"I beg to differ," Ashleigh said, crossing her arms in front of her chest. "I mean, do you even know what Kenzie went through? Her mother was a drunk who demanded nothing but perfection from Kenzie. Her parents constantly fought, and their divorce was hard on Kenzie."

"Her mom didn't drink!"

"Her mom loved her!"

Ashleigh smiled. "That may be the story Kenzie told you, but it's definitely not the truth."

"Why would she lie?"

"Because she didn't want you to see the real Kenzie," Ashleigh told them. "She wanted you to see the person she wanted you to see. The popular girl. The cheerleader. The girl who went for what she wanted without hesitation when in reality, she was really hiding the pain she was feeling."

"How do you know this?"

"Because it's what we all did," Ashleigh said, for the first time, truly admitting it. "We might not all remember what happened that day, but what happened in Sarasota Bay... it changed us. We grew apart. Some of us grew up, some of us got mean, and in the end, it ended up hurting us way more than it should have."

Across the field, she saw the football team wrapping up practice and she sighed. "Look, I got to get going, but you're right. I am partially responsible for what happened to Kenzie. I knew she was going home that night to talk to her mom. I tried to talk her out of it, but she wouldn't listen. If I had just called Billy..."

"Ash, Kenzie had her own ways of doing things. There's no way any of us could have anticipated what happened." Tracey sighed, dragging a hand through her hair. "God, I am so sorry, Ashleigh. I should have never said those things. I'm just. I'm scared," she whispered. "I've lost two friends. M.J, she was one of my best friends, as was Kenzie. I don't want to lose anyone else."

"Tracey!"

The girls behind her stared at her in dismay.

"Why are you apologizing to her?" the brunette asked.

"She's the enemy!" the blonde added.

"No. She's not. She's a victim in all of this, just like we are," Tracey told them. "We're all going through this and we have to do it together, not by tearing one another apart."

"But..."

"Bianca. Abigail. Just go! Or I swear, I'll cut you both from the squad."

The girls looked at one another, then turned, storming off.

"Why is she the captain?"

"Can you believe this?"

"Uh, thank you?" Ashleigh watched them walk away, turning to look at Tracey in shock.

"I owed you that," Tracey told her. "I was a total bitch, and rude. I am so sorry."

"I'm sorry too."

"You have nothing to apologize for, Ashleigh. You..."

She trailed off, interrupted by the sound of a loud crash behind them. They both spun around, just as the door to the training facility swung open.

"Help!"

"Call the police!"

"He's in there!"

The football players stumbled out of the training facility, their eyes filled with horror. Some were limping, others bruised and obviously hurting.

"Jacob!"

Ashleigh raced across the lawn, sliding to a stop in front of him, staring at the men around her. "What the hell happened?"

"The clown," Jacob said, glancing over his shoulder back toward the building. "He cut the lights and just tossed us to the side like we weighed nothing. He... he kept saying he needed to find someone me."

"Who?"

Jacob shook his head. "I don't know, but Devante..."

"What about Devante?"

He gestured behind them, and Ashleigh turned, gasping when she saw him holding a hand over the large gash in his arm, as blood seeped through his fingers.

"Oh my God! He was stabbed?" Ashleigh cried, swinging her head back toward Jacob.

Jacob nodded.

"Good God." The Coach ran up, staring at the carnage around him. "I'm calling the police."

"Jacob." Ashleigh scanned the crowd, sudden fear washing over her. "Where is Ryan?"

Jacob shook his head. "I don't know. I lost him inside."

What? No. No. No. No.

Her heart lurched, and she pushed down the panic rising inside of her. She turned to Tracey. "Tracey, can you hold onto this for me?" she asked, holding her bag out to Tracey.

"What? Why?"

"Because I'm going inside."

"What? Ashleigh, no!" Tracey grabbed her arm, stopping her. "You can't! I mean, just look around us!" she cried, pointing to the football players who were lying on the ground, panting, bloodied and bruised. "He took out a group of football players! Men who are big, strong, and fit. He'll kill you!"

"I have to go in, Tracey. If something happened to Ryan…"

"No. Absolutely not," Jacob cut in. "There is no way I'm letting you go in there. Ryan would kill me."

"I'm not going to just stand here, waiting to see if he's alive or dead," Ashleigh told him. "And it's not your decision. It's mine."

She turned, shoving past both Tracey and Jacob, racing toward the building.

"Ashleigh, no!"

"Ashleigh!"

The coach shouted at her, as did half of the football team, but Ashleigh ignored them. She zigzagged around them, as they tried to grab her, dragging the door open and stepping inside.

"Ryan?"

She stepped forward, making her way through the dark locker room. Her foot kicked something in the darkness, and she glanced down, spotting the metal pipe as it rolled across the floor. She reached down, gripping it in her hands, and continued down the row of lockers.

"Ryan?"

She whispered his name again, fear washing over her. What if he'd been kidnapped? Or worse… what if he was…

The lights suddenly flashed on above her, and she let out a scream, when she spotted him lying on the ground, motionless.

"Ryan!"

She raced across the room, falling to her knees next to him. "Oh my God. Ryan! Please. Please. Wake up." she cried, shaking him.

"Ugh," Ryan groaned, wincing, as he creaked his eyes open. He blinked, his eyes widening when he saw her. "Ashleigh!" he sat up quickly, glancing around the room, looking frantic. "What are you doing in here? The killer…"

"I know. I heard," Ashleigh said, interrupting him. "He's gone. There's no one else in here, Ryan."

"That's because he got what he came in here for," Ryan said, wincing, as he touched the side of his head.

"What do you mean?" Ashleigh asked, concern filling her as she stared at him. He was hurt, because of her. It was what she'd been afraid of. Was Tracey right? Was she the angel of death?

"He was after Johnny."

"Johnny? But why?"

"Because he's connected," Ryan said, pointing ahead of him.

Ashleigh turned, and she screamed, when she saw Johnny's body lying in a pool of blood just a few feet from the door.

"No! Johnny!"

Chapter Thirty

"Good afternoon, detectives." A tall thin man, with salt and pepper colored hair nodded to them, as he gestured them inside his office. "How can I be of assistance to you?" he asked, as he took a seat behind his desk, folding his hands in front of him. "I can't say I was expecting you."

"Are you serious?" Andrew stared at Dr. Eric Pollard, immediately disliking the polished man sitting in front of him. All the way from the way his hair was slicked back, to the light blue, long sleeve shirt he wore, his pressed black slacks, and the expensive watch on his wrist. "Have you not heard what's been going on?"

"Of course I'm aware of what's been going on," Dr Pollard said, picking up a stack of papers and fingering through them. "It's horrible, but what does it have to do with me?"

"What does it have to do with you?" Billy stared at him in dismay. "Dr. Pollard, I'm not sure if you've developed amnesia all of a sudden, or think we're morons, but we are well aware of your connection to Sarasota Bay."

"Sarasota Bay?"

"Yes. Sarasota Bay." Andrew strode forward, placing a photo on the desk. "Where you first started your practice."

"Ah, yes. That's right. Sarasota Bay. What a nice little town. That is, until those tragic murders." He shook his head. "What a tragedy."

"So, you do remember what happened."

"Yes. I vaguely remember it."

"And do you remember the clients you took up?" Billy asked, striding forward and setting another photo in front of him. It was the photo of the six of them, right inside the police station. The same photo Gloria had shown Ashleigh.

"I'm sorry, I…"

"Oh, cut the bullshit!" Andrew shouted, his patience snapping. "I know you recognize them, especially since one of those clients is my partner."

"Detective…"

"We have your bank statements, Dr. Pollard," Billy informed him. "We know their parents were paying you handsomely. Tell me, what exactly is it that you do here?" He wandered around the room, stopping in front of the framed photo of his PHD.

"Detectives, if you want any information about my patients, you're going to need to get a warrant."

"You didn't answer my partner's question," Andrew said. "What do you do here?"

"We specialize in the brain," Dr. Pollard said. "We help patients remember things; they have a hard time remembering. We also help patients analyze their dreams, and in some cases, even help them forget."

"Isn't that all a little... dangerous?" Andrew asked, stopping in front of a picture of the human brain. "I mean, the brain is a very complex part of the human anatomy. There's a lot we don't know about it."

"My team and I have dedicated years of research and clinical trials to our practice," Dr Pollard told them. "Everything we've done has been approved and backed by the FDA. Feel free to contact them. We have nothing to hide."

"Oh, we will. You can count on that," Billy told him. "You're really not going to give us anything?"

"I'm sorry, Detectives. My hands are tied."

"Even though I..."

"Yes, Detective."

Billy scowled. "Some help you are. There are people dying and your refusal to help could cost someone else their life."

"Billy." Andrew sent him a warning look. "Thank you, Doctor," he said, giving Dr. Pollard a curt nod. "We'll be in touch, and back with a warrant."

They exited the office, and Billy turned to Andrew. "What the hell was that? I wasn't done!"

"Yes, you were. We don't need you accused of harassing a possible suspect, Billy. Plus, we already got the information we needed. You saw his reaction when we showed him the photo."

Billy nodded. "Yes. He recognized us."

"And I'm willing to bet my last dollar, that he performed a procedure on all of you. That he's the reason, you can't remember that day ten years ago."

"You wouldn't be wrong, detective."

They turned, as they stepped inside the parking ramp, glancing behind them as a woman with curly, brown hair stepped through the doors, striding toward them.

"Excuse me?"

"I'm sorry?"

"You're correct in your assumptions, Detectives, the woman said, handing them a folder. "Ten years ago, Dr. Pollard did perform a procedure on the six children. Including you, Detective Turner."

"And you're just giving this to us?" Billy asked, taking the folder from her and flipping through the pages. He quirked a brow at her. "Betty, right? The receptionist?"

Betty nodded. "Yes. I've been working for Dr. Pollard for almost three years now."

"And you have access to these files, how?"

"DR. Pollard keeps exquisite records," Betty told him. "Including that day ten years ago. From what I read, your parents were adamant about keeping this quiet. So much, that they paid the doctor to keep this quiet. But I do need something in return, Detec—"

Thump!

She was suddenly interrupted, a scream escaping her lips, as a body flew through the air and landed on the ground in front of them.

"Eric!" Betty screamed again, staring down at the lifeless eyes of the doctor, her eyes going to the large slash across his throat. "He's here," she whispered, raising her head to stare at Billy and Andrew.

Thump!

"We know," Billy said. He turned, scanning the car garage around them, reaching for his gun. A giggle sounded nearby, and he withdrew his weapon, aiming it in front of him. His breath caught when he saw the clown standing on top of the car maybe a good thirty feet from them.

"Uh. Andrew." He nodded to his partner.

Andrew turned, withdrawing his weapon as he did.

"He's too far away..."

Another giggle came from the clown and they raised their weapons. Billy pulled the trigger, and the clown giggled, shaking a finger at him as he jumped from car to car.

"I can't get a shot off!" Andrew whispered. "He's moving too fast!"

The clown stopped, turning to look at them. He cocked his head to the side, raising his knife. He ran a gloved finger along the blade and giggled again.

"Why the hell does he keep giggling?" Andrew asked, irritatedly. He cocked the trigger, the bullet zinging through the air. The clown ducked, the bullet missing him and he reached into the pocket of his jacket.

"Betty!" Billy lunged forward, wrapping his arms around the woman, and diving to the ground. "Andrew! Get down!" he shouted, as the clown flung a circular object their way.

Andrew dropped to the ground, and smoke filled the air around them. Billy coughed, pulling his jacket over his mouth and nose. "They're smoke bombs!" he shouted, as the smoke clouded his vision. "I can't see anything!" He rose to his knees, trying to peer through the smoke.

"Ahh! Billy!"

He spun around, just as a rope swung through the air. It wrapped around Betty's throat, pulling her out of sight.

"Betty!"

He crouched down, making his way along the line of cars. A flash of white flew by. The clown. He raised his weapon, pulling the trigger.

The bullet hit the windshield of the car on the other side of the ramp.

"Shit!"

He aimed his gun. "Andrew? Can you see anything?"

Silence.

"Andrew?"

He made his way across the parking ramp. He held his gun in front of him, stopping when he saw Andrew's prone body lying on the floor.

"Andrew!"

He hurried over to him, pressing two fingers to his neck. He breathed out a sigh of relief. There was still a pulse.

"Andrew!" He shook him. "Wake up! I need you…"

Thump!

He jumped, just as another body flew through the air. It hit the windshield of the car in front of him, Betty's lifeless eyes staring back at him.

Shit!

He glanced over the hood of the car, staring at the clown, from where he was perched on top of the truck on the other side of the ramp. Billy raised his weapon.

The clown smiled, a wicked grin spreading across his lips. He pointed a gloved finger above him, and not a second later, the lights went out.

Shit!

Billy fumbled for his cellphone. He wrapped his hand around it, flicking on the flashlight, just as Andrew's body disappeared from sight.

"Andrew!"

He swung around, and jumped when he came face to face with the clown. He stumbled back, raising his weapon. He pulled the trigger once, twice, three times.

The clown stumbled back, the bullets hitting him in the center of the chest. He stopped, raising his head, another sinister grin spreading across his lips.

Billy rose to his feet. "What the hell? How the hell are you still standing?"

"Oh, Billy boy. Did you really think I didn't come here prepared?" The clown asked, lifting his shirt, and showing him the bulletproof vest underneath.

"I'm pretty sure I don't care," Billy said, raising his weapon. "Because I only need one shot." He pulled the trigger.

Click.

Shit.

"Sounds like you're out of bullets, Detective."

The voice sounded in his ear, and Billy turned, coming face to face with the clown once more. He raised the gun, striking it toward the clown. The clown grabbed his wrist, slamming his hand hard, against the window of the car.

Billy yelled, the glass to the window breaking. Blood spilled from his wrist, and the clown laughed, leaning close. "I've been waiting for this moment, for a very, very long time, Billy Boy."

He grabbed Billy by the back of the neck, slamming his head hard, against the side of the car.

Billy cried out, spots swimming before his eyes, as he slid to the ground. He stared up at the clown. "You're not going to get away with this," he said, trying to fight the unconsciousness that was swarming around him.

"Oh, I already have," the clown told him, raising his foot, and striking him hard in the side of the head.

He crumbled to the ground, falling unconscious, and the clown smiled as he stared down at him. "I finally got you, Detective. Now we can have some real fun together."

Chapter Thirty - One

"So, you saw the man in the clown costume?"

Ryan nodded, holding the icepack against his head, as he sat on the back of the ambulance getting examined. "Yes. That's correct," he said, answering the officer's question, wincing.

"And you decided it would be what? Heroic to go after him?" the officer asked as he wrote into his pad.

"No. I was trying to get the hell out of there!" Ryan snapped, lowering the icepack and glaring at the officer. "There was a madman in there, hurting my teammates. My friends! He wanted to kill Johnny. I tried to get him to safety, but I couldn't. I..."

"Officer, I think that's enough."

Captain Vargas walked up to the ambulance, clapping a hand on the officer's shoulder. "I got this one."

"But I..."

"I've got it from here, Officer."

The officer sighed, glancing from Ryan, back to his captain. He finally nodded, before turning and walking away.

"Sorry about that," Captain Vargas said, lowering his cap and shaking his head. "These young kids, I tell you. They can't wait to make a name for themselves, even in the wake of tragedy." He smiled. "Hi, Ashleigh."

"Hello, Captain." Ashleigh gave him a small smile from where she was sitting next to Ryan. "It's good to see you again."

"Wish it was under better circumstances," Captain Vargas said. He glanced over at Ryan. "You doing okay, Lad? That's some scary shit you went through in there."

Ryan nodded. "Yes, I'm okay. I'm just a little shaken." He gripped Ashleigh's hand, squeezing it. "I heard Marcus went missing. Have you been able to locate him yet?"

Captain Vargas shook his head. "Unfortunately, no. The last person to see him, was you. You don't remember seeing anything after he was thrown against the lockers?"

Ryan shook his head. "No. I was knocked unconscious myself."

Captain Vargas nodded. "I figured as much, but if you happen to remember anything, please don't hesitate to let me know." He shook his head. "It's just a shame. Another young life lost."

"Actually, he's not dead."

They all glanced up, as a young woman rounded the ambulance and joined them.

"Sophia, right?" Captain Vargas asked. "The coroner?"

"Coroner. Medical examiner. Whatever term you wanna use," Sophia said, as she slipped off her gloves. "And the boy isn't dead. There was a pulse when I got here to examine the body. The paramedics are working on him now."

A commotion sounded just behind them, and they all watched, as the paramedics rushed a gurney across the lawn toward the other ambulance.

"Come on! We gotta hurry. I don't know how much longer he's going to stay stabilized!"

They loaded him into the ambulance, and it raced off.

"He's alive?" Ashleigh asked, staring after the ambulance. "Oh my God. I thought he was..."

"Dead." Ryan nodded. "So did I."

"The kid must have a few guardian angels looking over him, that's for sure," Sophia said. "I'm sorry to run off, Captain, but there's another crime scene I need to get to."

"Where at?"

"Dr. Pollard's office."

The captain's eyes widened. He turned, lifting his phone to his ear. "Shit!"

"Captain?"

"Billy and Andrew went there to question the doctor," Captain Vargas said as he tapped into his phone. "Two more dead. God." He shook his head, glancing over at Sophia. "I'm going to follow you to the crime scene. I have a bad feeling about his."

"Captain? Is Billy..."

"Let's not jump to any conclusions yet, okay, Ash," Captain Vargas said, squeezing her shoulder. "I'm sure he's fine, but I'll call you as soon as I know something."

He walked off, and Ashleigh stared after him.

"Ash, don't do it."

"Do what?"

"Blame yourself for all of this. None of this was your fault."

"But it is, Ryan," Ashleigh whispered, slipping her hand free from his. She leaned forward, burying her face in her hands. "You could have been injured. Killed! And Billy…"

"Ash, I'm fine," Ryan told her, wrapping his arm around her and pulling her close. "And Billy can take care of himself."

"I just. I don't know what I would do if anything happened to you," Ashleigh whispered, lifting her head, and staring up at him. She lifted a hand, tracing the bruise on the side of his head, and leaned forward. She brushed her lips across hers.

"Ash…"

"I know. You want to wait," Ashleigh whispered. "But life's too short, Ryan, and I think I know what I need to do, now."

"What's that?"

"Go back to the place where it all started," Ashleigh told him. "I need to go back home to Sarasota Bay."

Chapter Thirty - Two

"You know, when I said I needed to go home, I didn't mean for you to come with me," Ashleigh said a few hours later, turning to look at Ryan as they drove down the interstate. "I meant that I'd go alone. I know I don't drive... not since..." She shook her head. "But I could have taken the train, or the bus, or..."

"If you think that I'm going to let you get on a bus or train when there's still a psycho clown out there, you have seriously lost your mind," Ryan informed her, as he flipped on his turn signal and merged. "I am not letting you do this alone. We don't even know where that bastard is! Plus, I did make you a promise."

"Which one?"

"That you're stuck with me until this damned thing is resolved."

"I know, but that was before..."

"Before I was nearly filleted by a psycho clown?" Ryan asked, glancing over at her. "Yes, that is true, but that doesn't mean I'm just going to split and run."

"You'd be better off doing just that," Ashleigh muttered under her breath.

Ryan shot her a look. "Ash."

She raised her hands in surrender. "Okay. Okay. I get it. You're not going anywhere." She smiled. "Not that I'm really complaining."

Ryan laughed. "Should I anticipate any more kisses from you?"

Ashleigh laughed, shaking her head. She turned, avoiding his gaze.

"Hey, don't be shy," Ryan said, taking her hand, and pressing a kiss to the back of her hand. "Plus, you're right. Life is short. We should make the best of it." He linked his fingers with hers. "No regrets?" He asked.

"No regrets," Ashleigh said, reaching into her bag and withdrawing the file Johnny'd given her earlier.

"Is that what I think it is?"

Ashleigh nodded. "I haven't had the chance to open it yet." She undid the clasp, opening the flap, reaching inside for the contents. "Oh my God. It's... it's about my dad," she whispered.

She flipped through the pages, stopping and staring at his mugshot. "I still can't believe he was a killer," she whispered. "The Dad I knew, could have never been capable of something like that. What they did to him... what they put him through..." She shook her head. "It's horrible!"

She reached into the envelope, her hand wrapping around a tape recorder. She stared at it, then over at Ryan.

"I think you'd probably better listen to it. Maybe, it'll help fill in some of the blanks."

Ashleigh nodded. She pressed play.

"Ashleigh. My dear, dear, Ashleigh," Mary Carlson's voice came over the speaker.

Ashleigh gasped, holding a hand to her mouth. It was the first time she'd heard her mother's voice, in almost seven years.

Mary sniffed. "Oh, Ashleigh. How I have been wanting to make this tape for so long... but I was scared to do it. Scared for you to learn the truth about what we did, but we didn't have a choice. We had to protect you." She paused, a rustling noise sounding in the background. "I don't have a lot of time. He's going to be back soon, and if I don't say this now, I never will."

She paused, before continuing. "Ashleigh, if you're listening to this, then two things have come to pass. The first being that I am most likely dead. A very sad concept, as I really did enjoy life, and two. That you have met Johnny."

There was another pause, and Ashleigh swallowed, waiting for her mother to continue.

"Ashleigh, what you need to know, amongst all the information you are hearing right now, is that your father was not a good man. He was mean, manipulative, and had dirt on everyone. Dirt that he threatened to use on several occasions. He wasn't always like that. He used to be nice. Kind, and I tried my hardest to preserve your memory of him. To remember the good in him. Which is why I went to such extreme measures.

We all did, but I won't tell you about that here. It's too risky. Instead, the truth lies in my journals back at the house. They're hidden in a secret place. In a place you know well. I trust that you will find them. Those journals will answer everything."

The tape ended, and Ashleigh frowned. *There should be more, shouldn't there?*

She opened the tape recorder, glancing down at the tape. *Side A...*

She took the tape and flipped it over. *Of course there was a side B.*

She pressed play.

"And for the next part of my message to you," Mary said, her voice once again sounding from the recorder. "Look, Ash, I know you hate me for what I did to you seven years ago. I don't blame you. You should hate me. I left you, to raise your two sisters when you were only a kid yourself. I just... I couldn't stay. Seeing you. Your sisters. It just reminded me of him..."

"So much for an apology," Ashleigh muttered.

"I will never apologize for what I did, Ashleigh," her mother said as if reading her thoughts "And you will understand that, too, very soon."

The tape ended, and Ashleigh scowled. "She didn't answer anything. I have more questions than ever now!"

"Let's just get to Sarasota Bay," Ryan said, giving her hand another squeeze. "Let's get those journals, and just maybe, start to piece this damned thing together."

"Yes. I know, you're right," Ashleigh whispered. She picked up her phone, closing her eyes. "I'm worried about Billy," she said. "They still haven't found him yet, and I hate to think that the last time I saw him…"

"He knows you care about him, Ash," Ryan told her. "No matter what you say, Billy would never hold it against you. He cares about you too much. He'll show up. I know he will."

Come on. Come on. Open your damned eyes!

Billy groaned, his head pounding as he creaked his eyes open. Where the hell was he?

He shook his head, the bleariness clearing from his eyes, staring down at his hands. They were tied together, as well as his feet. And he couldn't talk…

He lowered his head, his fingers gripping the duct tape that lay across his mouth, ripping it off.

"Fuck!"

He swore, his lips burning, and he blinked as his eyes watered from the sudden pain.

"Glad to see you conscious again, partner?"

He turned, staring at Andrew, from where he was sitting on the other side of the cell from him. His hands and feet were also bound.

"Andrew, what happened?"

"We got kidnapped by a fucking clown. That's what!" Andrew cried, wincing, and Billy stared at the blood trailing down his partner's face. He had a small gash on his left temple.

He blinked, thinking back. "Smoke bombs. He had smoke bombs, didn't he?"

Andrew nodded. "Yes, and he was fast. I don't think I've ever seen someone move like that."

"He must have gone through some sort of training. Special forces? Army?"

"Neil Carlson was in the army," Andrew murmured.

"You think he's one of Neil's old army buddies?"

Andrew shrugged. "The thought did cross my mind, but if it is, why wait so long?"

"Good point." Billy sighed, leaning back against the cell. He stared out the bars of the cell, staring around the small, gray room with no windows. There was a metal table in the middle of the room, with two metal chairs sitting on each side of it, and what looked like a polygraph sitting on top. Further across, he spotted a long window or mirror. "Are we…"

"Inside the manor?" Andrew asked. "Yes. I believe we are."

"But why? We…" He trailed off, his eyes widening. "Ah, shit. He's going to use us as bait, isn't he?"

"Pretty sure."

"God help us all."

Billy and Andrew stared at one another.

"That wasn't me," they said in unison.

"No, you fucking idiots. It was me."

They turned, staring into the far corner of the cell, their eyes locking on the young man who sat there.

"Marcus?"

"The bastard got to me too," Marcus said, his eyes narrowing. "Now our only hope lies with Ashleigh, and if she can figure this damned mess out before it's too late."

Chapter Thirty - Three

How the hell did we get ourselves into this mess?

Gloria Davis blinked, staring at the computer screen in front of her. The timeline she'd mapped out, looking more and more confusing the more she looked at it. How had it all come to this? Why would grown adults want to frame an innocent man for murder? And how did the kids fit into all of this?

She sighed, rubbing a hand over her face. God, she was tired. What she wouldn't give for a few nights of decent rest, but that wasn't going to happen until this madman was apprehended. Which meant, she needed to solve this very quickly.

She'd thought she'd been close six months ago. When the girls had been kidnapped she'd begged, pleaded for Billy to accept her help. She was good at this kind of stuff. She lived for it. The thrill of putting clues together. The excitement, of putting the pieces together. The sheer joy of bringing families back together, but she'd been wrong, and because of it, those girls had suffered far more than they should have.

She rubbed her eyes, hating what she'd done. She'd blamed them for what had happened, but she hadn't had a choice. Their kidnapper, he'd threatened her. He'd threatened her family. She'd had no choice but to write what he'd said, but now she was going to make this right. She opened up a new document, typing into the keyboard.

"Mrs. Davis?"

She screamed, spinning around, lifting a hand to her chest. A moment later relief rolled through her when she saw the short man with thin, brown hair standing in the doorway to her office.

"Jesus, Jasper! You scared the hell out of me!" she cried, breathing a sigh of relief when she recognized her cameraman.

"Sorry, Mrs. Davis. I was just bringing you this." Donny gave her a small smile, holding the cup of coffee out to her.

"Oh!" Gloria smiled, touched by his thoughtfulness. "Thank you." She took the cup from him, bringing it to her lips. "Oh. This is just perfect! Light on the foam, just the right amount of chocolate. You did good Jasper."

"Well, I sure hope so, Mrs. Davis. You only drilled it into me about a hundred times when you hired me."

Glottal smiled. That was true, she had. Just before the girls had been kidnapped, her previous cameraman had retired. She'd hired Jasper the day they'd gone missing, and he'd been a godsend.

"So, any luck cracking this thing wide open yet?" Jasper asked, nodding to the computer.

Gloria sighed, shaking her head. "Unfortunately, no, it's just all a tangled mess. And now with Billy, Andrew, and Marcus missing it's just getting even more tangled." She bit her lip, hoping Billy was okay. He might not like her very much, but she'd grown fond of him. He was a good man and a good detective. She just hoped he didn't end up being another body they found.

A beep sounded from her computer, and she frowned. Who was sending her an email at...

She glanced at the clock. *4 am.*

She clicked the notification, the email immediately popped up. It was from her anonymous source. The one who kept sending her photos.

Something I thought you should see...

She clicked on the attachment. Four pictures popped up on the screen. The first was of Neil, with three of his army buddies. There were two dark-haired men, dressed in their army uniforms, and next to Neil was a young woman, with dark, blonde hair. Her eyes went to Neil's arm where it was draped around her shoulders.

They look close, she thought, alarm bells going off in her head. She flipped to the next photo.

It was another picture of the woman. Again, she was with Neil, only this time she was very, very pregnant.

Had Neil had an affair? Was he the father of her baby? She jotted down a quick note on her pad, before continuing to the next photo.

This was a picture of Neil. He was obviously angry by the look on his face, as he stood in front of the mothers of the girls. It looked like they were arguing about something. But what?

She made another note, before continuing to the last photo. This one was of Mary Carlson. She was laughing into the camera, Billy's father, Charles had his arms wrapped around her and she was holding a baby. The date read...

Gloria froze. January 8th, 1998.

There was only one person who had that birthday.

Billy.

She rose from the desk, the chair tumbling to the floor. She gasped, staring at the four pictures. Two children? And what was the connection between...

She flipped through her notes. Mary and Charles. They'd gone to high school together, hadn't they?

She turned, heading for her bookcase. She pulled out the yearbook, flipping through the pages. She stopped on the picture at homecoming. Charles and Mary were dancing, and they both were wearing a crown. Homecoming king and queen?

She stared at the photo. Holy crap. How had she missed this? Had the two of them been having an affair? Was Billy... Ashleigh's brother? But wait a minute...

She flipped through the yearbook. Neil had gone to that same school, hadn't he?

She flipped through the pages. A photo of Neil, with Nikki's mother, Caroline. They were kissing. There was another of Addison's mother, Lisa. She and Neil were dancing, looking very much in love. There was another of Neil with Stacey,

Sydney's mother, and one of Neil with Kenzie's mother, Denise. Had Neil dated all of them? And what about Lindsay Miller? Had he dated her too? They'd all been childhood friends.

The thoughts filled her head.

"Jasper, come here. I need to show you something. I think…"

"Jasper can't talk right now."

The voice sounded from the doorway, and Gloria jumped. She swung around, a gasp escaped her mouth when she saw the clown standing in the doorway, holding a knife to Jasper's throat.

"You," she whispered, hugging the book to her chest. "You… you're the reason all of this is happening. You're trying to get revenge for him, aren't you? Are you… his son?"

"You're getting closer, Gloria. Only you're still very, very far off," the clown said. "But right now, I need your help."

He sliced the blade of the knife across Jasper's throat, and Gloria screamed. She stared at Jasper's bloodied body, as it tumbled to the ground, then back at the clown.

"Why would I ever help you?"

"Because, you did me a disservice, Gloria. That book you wrote," he lifted the manuscript in his hand. "You made it all about them. What about Neil? Or me? It should be all about me!"

"So, you want, what? Fame? Glory?" Gloria asked, slowly backing up a step. She reached a hand back, quietly opening the drawer to her desk, and reaching inside.

"No. I want the truth written for once," the clown said, striding toward her. "I want you to tell the real story. About what they did to Neil. About what they did to me. I want them all to suffer!"

"They're dead!" Gloria cried. "They can't suffer anymore. You killed them!"

"Oh, but the girls are still alive, and they all still have sins to pay for." He lunged forward.

Gloria spun around, lifting the canister in her hand. "I don't think so, asshole." She pressed the button, pepper spray spraying through the air.

"Ahh!"

He screamed, scrambling backward as he clawed at his eyes and Gloria spun around him. She grabbed her phone off the desk and sprinted out of the office.

She raced out into the dark hallway, hugging the yearbook to her chest, and slid to a stop in front of the elevator. She jabbed the button, tapping her foot impatiently. "Come on. Come on."

A crash sounded behind her, and she spun around. Her eyes widened when she saw the clown stumbling out of the office.

"Gloria!" he shouted, as he raced down the hallway. "I need you!"

"Fuck you, you psycho!" Gloria cried, turning and dragging the door open behind her. *Screw the elevator. I'm taking take the stairs.*

She raced through the door, it slammed shut with a loud bang behind her, and she trotted down the steps. She gripped the railing, turning, and racing down another flight of steps when she was suddenly jerked back. She gasped, dread washing over her as she lowered her gaze and stared at the heel of her shoe, which was now stuck in the stair.

Shit.

The door above her slammed shut with a loud bang, and she froze.

Oh, God. He was coming.

Thump. Thump. Thump.

His footsteps sounded on the stairs, and she reached for her shoe. *Please. Please. I paid a fortune for you!*

She wiggled it, but it remained stuck.

"Gloria..."

She jerked her head up, fear washing over her. She once again tried to wiggle the shoe free but to no avail. It looked like she was going shoeless.

Abandoning the shoe, she slipped out of the other and raced down the last of the steps. She slid to a stop in front of the door, wrapping her hand around the handle. She dragged it open, stumbling into the abandoned parking ramp. The door slammed shut behind her, the lights flickering overhead, as the sound of traffic sounded just below. She raced across the ramp, digging her keys from her pocket, sliding to a stop when she saw the clown sitting on the hood of her car.

"No!"

"I told you, Gloria. I need you," the clown said, jumping off the hood of the car and striding toward her. "You're so close to the truth. I mean, you were pretty close six months ago. You thought it was Billy."

Gloria shook her head. "No. Billy would never hurt the girls."

"Wouldn't he, though? I mean, he's the reason this whole mess started," the clown said, as he strode forward. "And Addison..."

"It's not Billy!"

She shouted the words, her voice echoing throughout the parking ramp, and she watched as he picked up his speed, racing toward her. She spun on her heel, racing across the concrete, back toward the door.

"Help!" she screamed, reaching for the phone she'd slipped in her back pocket. It slipped from her shaking fingers, falling to the ground and sliding underneath the car next to her.

Shit!

She dropped to her knees, frantically searching for her phone. *Please. Please. I need you. My whole life is on this phone!*

"Gloria..."

Her breath hitched, and she jumped to her feet. She raced across the parking lot, toward the door. She lunged for it.

Shink!

She screamed, her arm dropping limply as a blinding pain coursed through her body. She stumbled, bracing her hand against the door, looking at the knife that now stuck out of her shoulder.

"I told you, Gloria. I need you," the clown said, as he jumped down from the top of the car.

"Please. Don't do this," Gloria pleaded, as she reached for the knife. She wrapped her hand around the blade, pulling it from her shoulder. She winced, biting her lip to keep from crying out. "I have a family. Children."

"So did Neil Carlson," the clown said as he strode toward her. "Didn't do him any good now, did it?"

"Neil Carlson was a murderer."

The clown smiled. "So am I." He neared her, and Gloria gripped the knife in her hand, lunging for him. Then she gasped, stumbling, as a knife pierced through her abdomen.

"You're not killing me, Gloria," the clown whispered in her ear. "Not today, but I'm not killing you, either. You've got another book to write, and this time, it's going to be told from the perspective of the clown."

Chapter Thirty - Four

"Ash."

"Mmm."

"Ash. Wake up."

Ashleigh groaned, blinking, as she opened her eyes. She yawned, turning and looking over at Ryan. "Are we there?"

Ryan shook his head. "No. Not yet. I had to stop for gas, but I didn't want you to wake up and find me gone."

Ashleigh laughed, sitting up in her seat. "What? Afraid I'll have another meltdown?"

"It's been days since you've had one, but I didn't want to take my chances," Ryan told her. "Do you need anything?"

"A water would be nice. And maybe a snickers bar?"

"You got it." Ryan leaned forward, brushing a kiss across her cheek, before exiting the vehicle.

Ashleigh locked the doors behind him, watching as he went through the motions of filling the car up. She smiled as she watched him, amazed at how much had changed since they'd met. Was she really ready for this? Was she ready for them to be... more?

The thought both excited her and scared her.

She pushed the thoughts aside and reached for her phone. She scrolled through her texts. There was one from Nikki. She wanted to make sure she was okay, and if she needed to talk.

Ashleigh smiled, not surprised that she'd been the first person to reach out. Nikki knew firsthand what it was like for your father to be accused of murder. Only in Ashleigh's case, the accusations were completely true.

She scrolled further down. Sydney and Addison had also texted her. So had Francesca, Steph, and Vinny. She typed in a response to all of them, thanking them and letting them know she was okay. Then she saw a video someone had sent her. She clicked on the link.

"Tonight, our body count has officially hit the double digits," the anchorwoman was saying into the camera. "Upon arriving at the crime scene of Gloria Davis's workplace, authorities discovered the dead body of a local cameraman, Jasper Vickerman, who has been working with Mrs. Davis for the last six months. As for Mrs. Davis, she has yet to be found. It is believed that she is more than likely, another victim of the clown killer, much like missing detectives Billy Turner and Andrew Stark, as well as a missing college student, Marcus Dillon. We hope to have more information on this situation very soon. In the meantime, please keep yourselves safe."

A knock sounded on the window, and Ashleigh jumped. She jerked her head up, staring at Ryan as he peered in through the driver's side window.

"Sorry," Ryan said, as he slid back behind the wheel and handed her a bag. "I didn't mean to startle you."

"No. It's okay," Ashleigh whispered, her hand shaking, as she twisted the top off the water bottle.

"Ash. What's wrong?"

"Billy and Andrew have officially been reported missing," Ashleigh whispered, taking a small sip of water. "As have Marcus, and Gloria Davis is now missing too."

"Jesus." Ryan ran a hand over his face, pulling a bottle of soda out of the bag he'd handed her. He twisted off the top taking a sip, before glancing at her. "You want to head back?"

Ashleigh shook her head. "No, I need to be here. I need to find those journals and I get this feeling that they're going to give me all the answers to my questions."

"Okay. Then, I guess we continue on."

Ashleigh nodded, glancing back over at Ryan. "Ryan, you're not missing anything important today, are you? Like... practice?"

Ryan smiled, shaking his head. "No, not at all. It's Friday, and we have Fridays off. I just need to be back Monday for practice." He glanced over at her. "Are you coming to the game next week?"

Ashleigh fidgeted with her seatbelt. "I hadn't thought about it," she whispered. "I want to, but that's a lot of people to be around. I don't know..."

"Hey, I get it," Ryan said, reaching over and squeezing her hand. "You've been through a lot, Ash, but it would really mean a lot if you were there."

Ashleigh smiled, heat rising to her cheeks as he stared at her. How was it, that she, this ordinary girl, could be so important to this football player? To this man?

"And I would love nothing more than to be there," Ashleigh told him, pulling the snickers bar out of the bag and unwrapping it. "But I'm just not sure I'm ready to be around that many people just yet." She took a bite of the candy bar, sighing. Oh, that was good.

"Oh, I'm pretty sure you can handle anything you set your mind to," Ryan said, sending her a wink. "I mean, you are the same girl who went running into that locker room just a few hours ago, aren't you?"

Ashleigh winced. "Oh, God. I did do that, didn't I?" She shook her head. "I don't know what I was thinking. Everyone was yelling at me, and I thought Jacob was going to tackle me."

"I wouldn't have blamed him if he had," Ryan told her. "I was so scared when I saw you in that locker room. Please, please, don't ever do that again."

"I'll try not to."

They shared a look, and then Ryan nodded behind her. "Looks like someone's headed our way."

"What?" Ashleigh spun around, staring at the young, brown-haired woman with short, curly hair walking toward them. "I don't know who she is," she whispered, glancing back at Ryan.

"You want me to floor it? Get us out of here?"

"Ryan!" Ashleigh laughed, punching him playfully in the shoulder. "That's rude!"

"Hey. I'm just giving you the option," Ryan told her with a grin. "Anything for my girl."

His girl.

Ashleigh smiled, the words filling her with warmth, and turned, rolling her window down as the woman crouched down.

"Oh my God, Ashleigh? Is that you?"

"I... uh..."

"Oh! You don't remember me, do you?" The woman laughed. "I'm so sorry! It's me. Terri. We went to school together."

Ashleigh shook her head. "I'm sorry. I don't remember."

"I shouldn't be surprised," Terri said. "Back then, you and your friends... well you weren't the same after what happened with the Millers."

"What do you mean?" Ashleigh asked, immediately curious at what the other woman knew.

"It was like you all changed overnight," Terri said. "You were all quiet, withdrawn, depressed even. I mean, I don't blame you. What happened was terrible! Those poor girls... you know, they never did find them." She shook her head. "I feel so bad for their mother. Losing her children like that..." She shook her head again. "I heard about you and your friends too, Ashleigh. I mean, you were kidnapped!"

"Okay. I think that might be enough going down memory lane," Ryan interrupted, ducking his head down to look at Terri. "We really should be going. It's been a long couple of days."

"Oh, of course. I'm sorry." Terri stared at him. "Wait a minute. Are you... Ryan Eisenhower?"

"The one and the same," Ryan said, flashing her a grin.

"Oh my! Ashleigh, how lucky are you?" Terri cried, staring at her, then back at Ryan. "You know, I always did have a crush on you. So handsome." She gave him a smile, flipping her hair. "You know... you and I could duck away for a few minutes. Maybe make a few memories of our own, if you know what I mean?"

Ryan laughed. "Thanks for the offer, but I have other priorities to attend to," he said, revving the engine. "Bye, Terri." He shifted the car into gear and peeled out of the parking lot.

"Oh my god! Did you see her?" Ashleigh asked, lifting a hand to her mouth and laughing. "She was totally undressing you with her eyes!"

"Yeah, I saw," Ryan muttered. "I swear, as soon as a female learns who I am, that's all they can think about. It's depressing."

"What do you mean?"

"All they see are damned dollar signs," Ryan muttered under his breath. "Like there's more to me than that."

"There sure is," Ashleigh said, giving him a smile. "So, every female?" she asked, turning to look at him, as they headed down the road again.

"Well, I shouldn't say every female. I mean, you... you're different."

Ashleigh stared at him, the smile sliding from her lips. "What do you mean?"

"I mean, that you're not one to just throw yourself at me because I'll be a famous football player one of these days."

Ashleigh laughed. "Oh, God! No, I would never..." She shook her head. "I don't think I'd ever be that bold to throw myself at you. I'm too..."

"If you dare call yourself weak or vulnerable, I will pull this car over and show you how wrong you are."

Ashleigh laughed. "Okay. I'm not weak. I'm a strong, independent, fierce woman."

"Damn right you are," Ryan said, bringing her hand to his lips and pressing a kiss to the back of her hand. "And I wouldn't have you any other way."

Chapter Thirty - Five

She was quiet. Way too quiet.

Ryan pulled into the driveway of the small, yellow house, turning to look at Ashleigh.

"Ash. Is everything okay?"

Ashleigh wrung her hands in her lap nervously.

"Ash."

"Ryan, maybe we're making a mistake," she finally said, raising her head to look at him.

"A mistake about what?"

"Us."

Ryan stared at her, feeling as if she'd just taken his heart and squeezed it. "Ash. Don't do this."

"Ryan, I don't know if I will ever, fully trust someone again," Ashleigh told him. "What I went through inside the manor. I don't know if I'll ever be with you... intimately. You don't deserve that. You deserve someone who can be with you unconditionally. I just... I don't think I'm that person."

Ryan stared at her a moment, then he got out of the car. He rounded the hood of the car, opening her car door.

"Get out."

"Ryan."

"Get out of the car, Ashleigh."

Ashleigh stared at him, not sure what to say. She stepped out of the car, and Ryan closed the door behind her. He laid his hands on her shoulders, gently pushing her back against the car.

"You told me yesterday, to stop treating you like you're going to break," Ryan said, letting his hands slide down her body, to rest on her hips. "And we shared a very, very steamy kiss," he continued, as he inched his lips closer to hers.

"Yes. Yes, we did," Ashleigh whispered. "But you said you wanted to wait."

"We agreed just a few hours ago, that life's too short to wait, didn't we?"

Ashleigh swallowed. "Yes. We did."

"And the truth is, I never wanted to wait," Ryan whispered, leaning forward and resting his forehead against hers. "I was just scared."

"Scared that you're going to hurt me?"

Ryan shook his head. "I would never hurt you."

"Then what are you scared of?"

"That you'll break my heart. I'm falling for you, Ashleigh. I'm falling for you hard," he whispered. "And I would wait a million years for you if that's what it took."

Ashleigh gasped, staring up at him in surprise. He was falling for her? But they'd only known each other for a couple of days!

"I've never said that to a girl," Ryan whispered. "Please. Say something."

"Kiss me, Ryan. Now."

He didn't have to be asked twice. He dipped his head down, brushing his lips against hers and behind them, the front door slammed open.

"Who's there?"

Callie swung the door open, racing out, her hands clutching a bat.

"You're going to be in for a very big surprise buddy!"

Sadie raced out after her, holding a large frying pan in her hands.

Ashleigh lifted a hand, laughing. "Callie. Sadie. It's okay. It's just me."

"Ashleigh?" Callie lowered her bat, staring at her in surprise. "What are you doing here?"

"Here to check on you guys. I was worried about you."

"You were worried about us? We were worried about you!" Sadie cried. She rushed forward, engulfing Ashleigh in a tight hug. "Oh, how I have missed you!"

"I've missed you too, Sadie."

"And this? Who's this?" Callie asked, eyeing Ryan warily.

"That's Ryan. He's a friend," Ashleigh told her.

Ryan raised a brow at her.

Ashleigh sighed. "And the quarterback of the football team."

"Wait. Ryan?" Callie asked, her eyes going wide. "No way! Ashleigh, you..."

"You finish that sentence, and you will be getting coal in your stocking for the rest of your life, Missy," Ashleigh said, narrowing her eyes at Callie.

"You wouldn't do that!" Sadie cried. "You love us! Plus, it's not every day we get to meet the guy you've crushed on for years."

"Sadie!"

"Ah. So that's what Billy was referring to the other day," Ryan murmured. He winked at her, then turned to her sisters. "Well, I'm glad to know spunkiness runs in the family, and that you two come prepared." He grinned at Ashleigh. "As I recall, you almost took me out with a bat the other day."

"That was different!"

"Tomato, tamato." He waved away her words. "Now, are we going inside or what?"

"Yeah, about that," Callie shuffled her feet. "Someone broke in last night."

"What!" Ashleigh swung around to look at them. "How? The alarm..."

"Was dismantled. Someone got inside, Ash. It doesn't look like they took anything, but, I can't be sure. With everything that's going on with Mom, with Dad..."

"It could all be connected. I get it." Ashleigh hurried back to Ryan's car, taking her bag out and slinging it over her shoulder. "Come on, let's go see if anything's missing. Together."

Together, the four of them walked into the house, combing through the house. As they searched, Ashleigh realized how right Callie had been. Nothing seemed to be missing. They scoured through the kitchen, through the cupboards, even through some old photos, then Ashleigh found herself searching through some old family videos.

"Ah. Callie? Sadie? Didn't there used to be more videos in here?"

"Yeah! Mom and Dad had..." Sadie trailed off. "Oh, geez. I can't call him that anymore, can I? After what he..."

"You didn't know him, Sadie. You can call him whatever you want," Ashleigh told her. "He might be a murderer, but he was still our Dad."

"She's right," Ryan said, glancing over at the three sisters. "No matter what happened, or what he did, you will always remember the man he was... before the clown mask." He nodded toward the hallway. "I'm going to go check the attic."

"Not alone you aren't!" Ashleigh cried, staring at him in shock. "I mean, what if he followed us here? What if he's the one who broke in?"

"Then I guess I should be careful."

"You are so not funny!" Ashleigh told him, sending him a glare, as she walked to the closet. She pulled a flashlight out, striding past him. "You and I are going together. Don't you even try arguing with me."

"I would never dream of it," Ryan said, taking the flashlight from her. "But I'm going first."

"But..."

Ryan sent her a look, and Ashleigh pressed her lips together. "Fine."

Ryan grinned. "Thank you." He pressed a kiss to her lips before heading up the stairs.

"I totally saw you guys making out earlier," Callie whispered, grinning at her. "I approve, sis."

"And he is sooo fine!" Sadie added from behind them.

"Will you two shut up?" Ashleigh hissed.

"Never."

Ashleigh mumbled under her breath, following Ryan up the stairs. "You two are insufferable!"

"But you love us."

"That's debatable."

"There are journals hidden in the house. In a spot only you can find them. I trust that you will."

Her mother's words echoed in her ears, as they climbed the stairs toward the attic. She gripped the banister, staring at the photos on the walls. There were some of Callie and Sadie. There were some of her. There were even a few of their parents, and one of their dad sitting with a few of his army buddies.

It hurt her heart, thinking of them. How had everything gone so horribly wrong?

"You did what?"

Neil Carlson's voice penetrated through the house, and Ashleigh jumped, from where she was sitting in her room, playing with her dolls.

"I didn't have a choice, Neil. The kids... They're all so young. They can't have this holding over their heads."

"No. You saved one kid, Mary, and to protect him, you framed me!"

"And deservedly so," Mary told him. "Neil, you are a terrible person! You're blackmailing my friends. You cheated on me... several times! You had another child... that I didn't even know about!"

"You're one to talk. You're in love with another man!"

The memory came back to her, and Ashleigh gasped. She braced a hand against the wall, steadying herself.

"Ash?" Ryan glanced over at her, pulling down the door to the attic. "You okay?"

"I uh... I remember something," Ashleigh whispered. "Mom and Dad, they were having a fight. I don't remember them ever fighting."

"You were what? Thirteen?" Callie asked. "Ash. You were just a kid. There's probably a lot you don't remember from back then."

"But the way she talked to him..." Ashleigh shook her head. "It was so cold. So emotionless."

"What'd she say?"

"Something, about Dad cheating on her, and having another kid."

"What?"

Callie and Sadie stared at her, their eyes wide.

Ashleigh nodded. "And, apparently mom, was in love with another man."

"What?"

"There's more," Ashleigh whispered. "Apparently, Dad was blackmailing mom's friends. I can only assume she's talking about..."

"Your friend's parents." Ryan nodded. "Did they know each other before they became neighbors?"

Ashleigh nodded. "Yes. They were friends in..." She froze, her eyes widening. "In high school. Oh my God. I completely forgot about that. They grew up here in Sarasota Bay. They went to the same school. They were inseparable."

"And, apparently, had lots of secrets."

They followed Ryan into the attic, staring around at the boxes that were tossed around the room. Papers were strewn across the floor, pictures were broken, and Christmas decorations were shattered.

"Ugh. What a mess," Sadie muttered, kicking at an old stuffed animal.

"Someone was definitely up here," Callie added.

"It's been forever since I've been up here," Ashleigh said, reaching down and picking a stuffed elephant up off the ground. "Oh, Sadie look! It's Mr. Peanuts."

"Mr. Peanuts?" Ryan raised a brow, looking at the three women. "Who names an elephant Mr. Peanuts?"

"Because elephants love peanuts!" Sadie cried. "Or at least I thought they did."

"You loved this elephant!" Ashleigh cried. "You dragged it around everywhere, even, when you ended up in the hospital."

"Wait. Hospital?" Ryan glanced over his shoulder.

Sadie nodded. "I was born with a heart defect," she said. "My heart didn't develop right when I was younger. With mom gone, Ash had to work three jobs just to help pay the bill."

"She really stepped up when mom left," Callie added. "We owe everything to her. It's why we pushed her to move to LA. She deserved to do something for herself."

"Damn right she did," Ryan strolled across the attic, gazing around the room. "Ash, do you have any idea where your mother might have hidden those journals?"

"I'm not..." Ashleigh suddenly let out a scream.

"Ash?" Ryan hurried over to her. "What's wrong?"

"Look."

Ashleigh pointed, and they all turned, staring at the picture of the clown that was sitting, leaning against the wall.

"Holy crap." Ryan stared at the photo. "It looks just like him!"

"Mom drew it, didn't she?" Callie asked.

Ashleigh nodded. "Yes. Her initials are in the lower, left corner, see?" She pointed. "She used to come up here and draw for hours. Just like I..."

She trailed off, her eyes wandering to the piano in the middle of the room.

"Just like what?"

"Just like I used to come up here and play the piano." She made her way across the room, aware that everyone was watching her. She ran her fingers along the keys, then lifted the cover.

"No."

Tears pricked at her eyes. No. Not again.

"Ash. What's wrong?" Ryan hurried to her side. "Are you okay?"

Ashleigh shook her head. "No. He was here."

She lifted the note laying inside.

Hunting for answers, are we, my doll? Too little, too late. My terms, my rules, remember? But rest assured, when the time is right, you will learn everything. And when you do, you will be mine again. Because you are mine, until the day you die.

Chapter Thirty - Six

Ashleigh felt her breath catch. Her heart rate sped up, and she gasped, suddenly not being able to breathe. She needed to get out of here. Now.

The note slid from her fingers, and she turned, racing out of the attic.

"Ashleigh!"

She ignored the shout, racing out of the attic and through the house. She raced through the kitchen, sliding open the patio door, and stumbled outside. She gasped, dragging air into her lungs as she clutched the wooden railing, staring out across the lawn.

Oh, God. He'd been in here. He'd begin in her house. Near her sisters...

"Ashleigh?"

She held up a hand. "Please. I just need a moment."

"Ashleigh."

The soft, feminine voice sounded again, and Ashleigh froze. She lowered her gaze, staring at the older woman with dark gray hair standing just below the deck.

"Mrs. Miller?" Ashleigh stared at her in shock. "Oh my goodness. It's been..."

"A long time, hasn't it?" Lindsay Miller asked, giving her a lopsided smile. "I saw you pull up with that young lad of yours. I wanted to come say hi and give you this." She held up the pie in her hands. "I made too many for the picnic tomorrow. I hope you don't mind."

"No, of course not!" Ashleigh trotted down the steps and stopped in front of the older woman. She took the pie from her, staring at the woman in shock. "I didn't know you were back. I thought you'd left town for good."

"So did I," Lindsay said, giving her another half-smile. "After what happened, I didn't think I would ever step foot in this town ever again, but, it kind of called to me and I opened a shop downtown."

"Oh! I'm so glad to hear you're doing well," Ashleigh whispered, shuffling her feet, suddenly not sure what to say to the woman. What was there to say?

"More like surviving. Kind of like you," Lindsay said. "I heard you got into UCLA. I'm so happy for you, Ashleigh. It was always one of your top schools."

Ashleigh smiled. "Yes, it always was."

"What's your major?"

"I'm going for my medical degree."

"Oh my! That's right. You've been wanting to be a doctor ever since you watched Sadie go through all those surgeries."

"You knew about that?"

Lindsay smiled. "Of course. I may have been in New York, but I always kept in touch with this town, Ashleigh. I have a lot of friends here." She sighed. "Mer and Aimee would have been proud of you, you know."

Ashleigh smiled, nodding. "Yes. I know."

"Ashleigh?"

Ashleigh glanced up as Ryan appeared on the deck above them.

"And who is that?" Lindsay asked.

"This is Ryan, a friend from school. He's been helping me out the last couple of days," Ashleigh said, as Ryan descended the steps and joined them on the lawn. "Ryan, this is Lindsay Miller."

"A pleasure," Ryan said, extending a hand.

"Wow. What a gentleman," Lindsay said, taking his offered hand. "They don't make them like you anymore. I can certainly tell you that."

"What? Have manners?' Ryan asked, giving Lindsay a smile. "I was raised right."

"Indeed you were." Lindsay turned back to Ashleigh. "Ashleigh, I heard about what happened to you and your friends. I am so sorry for what you went through. If there is anything..."

"Oh no. Please don't think that," Ashleigh said, shaking her head. "I'm okay. Really. I'm just... recovering still."

"Mrs. Miller?" Callie and Sadie appeared above them, hurrying down the steps to join them.

"Hey, girls," Lindsay gave them both a smile. "It's good to see you both again."

"Again?" Ashleigh asked, giving her sisters a look.

"She came over the other day and asked for our help at the picnic," Callie told her, ignoring Ashleigh's glare. "You remember the annual Sarasota Bay picnic, don't you, Ashleigh?"

"Of course. The whole town gets together and enjoys a day full of food, games, and laughter," Ashleigh said, nodding. "But I didn't know you two were going to help." She also hadn't known that Lindsay Miller had moved back to Sarasota Bay. Something she was going to have a long chat with her sisters about.

"Well, that's the thing. We kind of can't," Callie said, wringing her hands together. "Because we're going to the football game."

"What football game?" Ashleigh asked, confused.

"*Your* football game," Sadie said, sending a look toward Ryan.

"Oh!" Ryan nodded, getting the hint. "Yes. Of course. We're all heading for LA tomorrow. Callie and Sadie wanted to spend some time with Ashleigh so they made plans to stay at her place for the week."

"Oh. I see. Well, I hope you all have fun." Lindsay glanced at Ashleigh, then over at Ryan. "You know, you two should come over for dinner tomorrow night. I don't get much company anymore, and, well it would be nice to catch up with you, Ashleigh."

"I'd like that," Ashleigh said, nodding. "You okay with that, Ryan?"

Ryan nodded. "Of course. What time should we be there?"

"Seven?" Lindsay asked.

"We can do seven."

"Great. I look forward to it." Lindsay turned, limping across the lawn, and Ashleigh grimaced. The poor woman.

She disappeared around the house, and Ashleigh turned, glaring at her sisters. "You two forgot to tell me she was back."

"Whoops."

"Did we?'

"Yes! I felt like I was ambushed!" Ashleigh cried. "I haven't seen her since before the massacre. I had a hard time keeping my composure. She looks so…" She shook her head, once again looking at her sisters. "And, just when did you two decide you were going to the football game?"

"Just now."

"It was the perfect excuse," Sadie said. "She's sooo creepy! I mean, she's always around and you should see her house. Meredith and Amelia's rooms are exactly the same. It's like she's waiting for them to come home when we all know they're dead."

"Sadie!" Ashleigh stared at her in shock. "That is so rude! That woman has been through hell. Show a little respect."

Sadie rolled her eyes. "Ash, I know what she's been through. We all do, but, coming back here years later? Even you have to admit it's weird."

"I just think, we should be helping her," Ashleigh whispered. "I mean, she lost everything."

"We do what we can," Callie told her. "But with school and work... there's just so much that we can do."

"I know. I just worry about her."

"Right now, I'm worried about you," Ryan said, looking over at Ashleigh. "Ash, are you okay? You ran out of the attic so fast, I thought there was going to be a trail of smoke left behind."

Ashleigh laughed, shaking her head. "I promise, there's no smoke. I'm just... I'm just so damned tired of this. It's like, no matter how close I am to figuring things out, he's one step ahead. It's so infuriating!"

Ryan stared at her for a moment, then he took her hand. "Come with me."

"What?"

"Come with me. I have an idea."

"Ryan, I can't just leave. We just got here!"

"And we'll still be here, when you get back," Callie told her. "Go with him, Ash. Maybe even, enjoy yourself a little?"

"I'm not sure I would ever use enjoy in the same sentence as this damned town," Ashleigh muttered. "Fine. Let's go. Just, promise me one thing?"

"What's that?"

"No clowns."

Chapter Thirty - Seven

"Ryan. I don't understand…"

Ashleigh turned to him twenty minutes later, quirking a brow in confusion, as stated across the street *Joe's Fitness Center*. It was one of two gyms in Sarasota Bay, and one of the longest-running businesses in the town. "Are you trying to tell me something?"

Ryan laughed, shaking his head. "God, no, you're perfect just the way you are."

Ashleigh blushed. "Then why…"

"Because, you need to let off some steam," Ryan told her, as they stepped out of the vehicle. "You need a way to let go of the anger. The pain. What you need, is to hit something." He opened the door for her.

"Ryan!" Ashleigh stared at him in dismay. "I'm not going to hit you!"

Ryan chuckled, pulling her close as they walked toward the entrance of the small, red brick building. "You're not. Now, come on. I promise it'll make you feel better."

I'm not sure if anything can make me feel better, Ashleigh thought, as they walked through the sliding glass doors, stopping in front of the receptionist.

"Good morning," Ryan said, flashing her a grin. "We're looking to get two passes for the day."

"Of course." The woman batted her eyelashes at Ryan, popping her gum, before typing into her keyboard. "It'll be forty bucks for the two passes. A daily pass gives you twenty-four-hour access to the gym, along with all the equipment. If there's anything you need, please, don't hesitate to ask."

"I think we're good." Ryan slid his credit card her way, wrapping his arm around Ashleigh. He pressed a kiss to her temple. "You good?"

Ashleigh nodded.

The receptionist narrowed her eyes at Ashleigh as if realizing she was there for the first time. She muttered something under her breath, before returning Ryan's credit card back to him. A moment later, she handed them each an access badge.

"Thank you."

They turned, making their way through the gym. They passed a room, which held various exercise machines. There was another room, where some woman was teaching a yoga class. Another room where a self-defense class was taking place. They turned, passing a pool and a weight room before Ryan finally turned into a private room.

He closed the door, and Ashleigh turned, staring at the punching bag that lay in the center of the room.

"Ryan, I don't know about this," she said, fidgeting. "I'm not sure hitting a bag is going to make me feel better."

"And has anything else helped?" Ryan asked as he stopped next to a rack that held various gloves. He picked up a pair of dark blue ones, handing them to her.

"Well…. no." Ashleigh took the gloves from him, slipping her hands inside them. She fastened the straps around her wrists. "I guess I hadn't thought of… this," she said, gesturing around the gym. "I've tried everything else, I guess."

"When you were in the hospital?"

Ashleigh nodded. "I woke up screaming most nights. The nightmares were unbearable, and the meltdowns…" She cringed at the memory. "The doctors didn't have many answers, so they sent me to a psychiatrist p, who ended up admitting me to the psych ward. She was concerned I might be a danger to myself."

"Oh, Ash." Ryan winced, the image of her dealing with all of that alone breaking his heart. "I'm so sorry you went through all that. I wish I'd known you back then. No one should have to go through that alone."

Ashleigh shrugged. "It is what it is. I got through it, but I still have nightmares. You really think this might help?"

Ryan shrugged. "Only one way to find out." He stepped behind the bag, holding it in place. "Go ahead. Hit it."

Ashleigh stared at him, then at the bag. She bit her, debating. After a moment, she raised her hands in the air, jabbing her left fist forward.

"Come on. I know you can hit it harder than that."

She hit it again, this time a little harder.

"Ash." Ryan let out a long breath, dragging his hand through his hair. "For this to work, you need to let go. You need to feel the fear, the pain, and really let it out."

"If I let it go, I'm afraid I'm going to fall apart. If I do that, I might not be able to stop."

"That's okay. It's just me here. You can take as long as you need."

Ashleigh stared at him, gazing into his kind, brown eyes. She drew in a deep breath, then closed her eyes.

"Hello, Ashleigh."

The voice of the clown, her captor filled her ears. She squeezed her eyes shut, fighting the urge to open them again. She had to do this. She had to.

His face appeared before her. His pale white face. Those red lips, as he smiled devilishly at her. That green and yellow wig and she swung her fist against the bag, hard. The sound of it hitting the bag echoed throughout the room.

She remembered waking up inside that dark, creepy manor. The photos that had hung on the walls. The weapons she had seen. The dolls that had been scattered around, laying on the shelves, inside cabinets. Then she remembered her friends. She remembered the fear in their eyes, and she remembered seeing them gagged, bound. Then she remembered the sound of the saw.

She punched her fist forward again, slamming it against the bag once more.

She remembered racing through that manor, trying to get to her friends in time. She remembered seeing those rooms. The pit. The bodies that had lay in the dirt and she remembered the moment she'd finally found them... and the clown. The way he'd laughed, and told her, that she was going to be his sex doll.

She remembered the months of torture she had endured. She remembered the way he had yelled at her, ridiculed her. The pain, the abuse she'd taken. She remembered the humiliation, the embarrassment and she slammed her fist into the bag again.

Images flashed through her mind. Memories of the gadgets he'd used, of the way he'd used to wake her, and how he'd used to watch her.

A cry escaped her lips, and she punched the bag again.

She remembered what she'd had to sacrifice, just to keep her friends safe. She remembered the weeks she'd spent in the hospital. The feelings of depression that had surfaced. The nightmares. The fear. She remembered the party. She remembered the words Marcus had said to her. Then she remembered Kenzie. She remembered Johnny. Billy...

Another cry escaped her lips, and she punched the bag again.

She thought of her mother. Of her father. Of all the lies. The secrets. The betrayal.

Then finally, she thought of her sisters. She thought of that moment when he'd been watching Callie. The video he had sent her. She thought about how he had been in their house. How he had beaten her to the journals, and how, he was always one step ahead.

She let out a scream, pummeling her fists against the bag. Tears streaked down her cheeks. Sobs sounded from her throat, and she slowly lowered her arms.

She was so tired.

She stumbled back, feeling as if all the energy were being zapped from her body. She leaned back against the wall, sliding to the floor as she wrapped her arms around herself.

"I... I can't..." she sobbed, as sobs racked her body.

"I got you." Ryan appeared next to her, wrapping his strong arms around her. "It's okay," he whispered, as he pulled her into his lap. "Let it all out. It's okay."

Ashleigh leaned her head against his shoulder, the sobs jerking her small frame. Tears ran down her cheeks, and she stayed like that for she didn't even know how long. Eventually, the tears subsided, and she lay there, spent. "I told you," she whispered against his chest. "I told you if I started, I might not be able to stop."

"And that's okay," Ryan told her. "You have so much emotion built up inside of you, it had to come out." He pressed a kiss to her temple. "You've had to be strong for so long, Ash, but you don't have to be around me. You can lean on me, I promise, I can take it."

Ashleigh was quiet for a moment. She ran a finger along his tear-stained t-shirt, thinking. "He humiliated me," she finally said.

"Ash…"

"He made me strip in front of my friends," she continued, as if not hearing him. "He made me walk around naked in front of them. He did things to me, made me do things… in front of them. I was so humiliated, and when we escaped, I… I withdrew from them. I said I was busy with doctor appointments, with the police, with the therapist, but the truth is I couldn't look at them."

"From my understanding, you sacrificed a lot, to keep them alive."

Ashleigh nodded. "I did. I did whatever he asked, so he wouldn't kill them."

Ryan squeezed her close. "That's what we do for the people we care about. We do whatever we can to protect them. Your friends know why you did, what you did. They would never think any less of you for it. I have to believe that."

"I know," Ashleigh whispered. "It's just, the memories…"

Were really raw, Ryan thought, guilt washing through him. "Ash, I'm sorry. I didn't mean to push you that hard. I just wanted you to have an outlet, a way to express all the emotions inside of you. If I made it worse…"

"No. No. Not at all." Ashleigh sat up, lifting a hand and stroking his cheek. "I needed this," she told him, her hand trailing down, and linking her fingers with his. "I needed a way to get it out, and even though I felt like part of me was breaking inside, I feel lighter. Like a weight has been lifted off my shoulders, but there is one little thing."

"What's that?"

"I'm starving now!" Ashleigh cried, just as her stomach let out a loud rumble.

Ryan threw his head back and laughed. "I think we can fix that," he said, as he climbed to his feet, and helped Ashleigh to her feet. "I just need to return these badges to the front desk. What are you in the mood for?"

"Let me think on it a moment," Ashleigh said, as they exited the room and continued down the hallway. It was eerie quiet and it looked as if all the classes had been completed for the day. She glanced outside, noticing the sun had already disappeared and nightfall was upon them. "I just need a moment to freshen up," she told him, nodding toward the restroom. "I'll meet you at the front desk in a few minutes."

Ryan nodded, giving her hand a squeeze. "I'll see you in a few."

He watched her disappear into the bathroom, then turned, making his way down the hallway toward the front desk.

"Hey, we're done for the day. I just wanted to return..." He trailed off, his blood suddenly running cold when he saw the young woman sitting behind the desk, unmoving.

"Ma'am?"

He rounded the desk, and froze when he saw her laying in the chair. Her eyes stared back at him blankly, and blood was dripping onto the floor, from her slit throat.

Shit.

He was here.

Ryan stumbled back, then he spun on his heel, racing through the gym.

"Ashleigh!"

Chapter Thirty - Eight

"Come on, Ash. Get a hold of yourself."

Ashleigh leaned forward, wrapping her fingers around the edge of the sink as she stared at herself in the mirror. She looked like crap. Her eyes were red, dark circles lay just underneath her eyes, and her hair was a mess.

She ran her fingers through the messy locks, trying to tame them, then turned on the water. She dampened a towel, trying to get rid of the mascara that had run down her cheeks, cringing. Ryan had seen her like this? God, she was a mess.

Thump!

The loud noise sounded behind her, and she jumped. She spun around, her eyes scanning the room, breathing a sigh of relief when she saw the four bathroom stalls behind her still empty.

"Breathe, Ash."

She let out a breath, closing her eyes. *One deep breath. Two deep breaths...*

Thump!

Again, the noise sounded, and she snapped her eyes open. *Ok, I'm done here,* she thought, hurrying out of the restroom. She was hearing things. She had to be.

She stepped out of the restroom and started down the hallway. *When did it get so dark in here?* She wondered as she made her way down the dark hallway. She trailed her fingers along the wall next to her, making her way toward the front desk. She turned the corner, and above her, the light flickered.

"Ashleigh..."

The dark, raspy voice echoed through the air, and she froze. She knew that voice.

"Ashleigh..."

Again, it sounded. She turned, glancing over her shoulder, just as the light at the end of the hallway flicked on and the clown stepped into view. He raised his knife, a sinister smile spreading across his lips, as he ran a gloved finger along the blade. "Hello, Ashleigh."

Ashleigh gasped, stumbling back. She backed into the wall behind her, fear snaking toward her as he started down the hallway. "What... what do you want," she stammered.

"Oh, that's easy," the clown said, chuckling. "I want you." He raced forward and Ashleigh turned, disappearing into the room behind her. She slammed the door shut, flipping the lock. She hurried forward, drawing the blinds closed, and crouched down against the wall. Her body shook, as he thumped the blade of his knife against the window.

"Go away!" she shouted, tears streaking down her cheeks. "Please. Just leave me alone!"

She scrambled across the empty room, hiding behind a punching bag, and the sound of glass breaking echoed throughout the room. She gasped, swinging around, watching as his arm snaked through the window of the door. The lock flipped, and the door swung open.

She slid to the floor, pressing a hand to her mouth. She peered around the bag, watching as he rounded the bags on the other side of the room. She rose to her feet, bracing her hands on the bag, and sprinted out of the room.

"Ryan!" she shouted, as she raced down the hallway. "Ryan! He's here!" She glanced over her shoulder, just as the clown barreled out of the room, racing after her. "Ryan!"

She rounded the corner, racing forward, and lunged for the door. She twisted the knob.

Locked.

Shit.

She glanced over her shoulder, the sound of his footsteps sounding closer. She turned, racing down the hallway, trying doors as she went. The knob twisted, and she raced inside, slamming the door shut behind her.

She drew in a couple of deep breaths, turning and stared at the locker room in front of her. *What?* She must have taken a wrong turn. She was nowhere near the front of the gym. How was she ever going to find Ryan?

She walked along the aisle of lockers, searching through the lockers. Maybe there was a weapon in here she could use?

She made her way further down the row, and a door slammed shut nearby. She jumped, glancing over her shoulder.

Thump. Thump. Thump.

He was in here.

She turned, and screamed when she found herself face to face with the clown.

"Found you." His hand snaked out, wrapping around her throat, and slammed her back against the locker. She winced, her head bouncing off the locker. "Please..."

"What? Don't do this?" the clown asked, running a finger down her cheek. "Or this?" His hand trailed down her body, circling her breasts, and stopped at the juncture of her thighs. "I told you I wasn't done with you, Doll," he whispered in her ear. "You're mine. You will always be mine, and I will have you again. You're the last piece of the puzzle, and before I kill you, I will have you again."

"Like Hell you will!" Ashleigh blinked, the dots fading from her vision. She stared at the knife, pressed against her throat, and swung her knee up hard.

"Agh!" He swore, stumbling back. The knife slid, nicking her, but she didn't even notice. She raced forward, slamming him back against the locker behind him. "You will never touch me, ever again!" she shouted, grabbing the door to the locker and slamming it against his head as he staggered backward. "Not as long as I'm still breathing." She turned, racing back through the locker room. She raced out the door, and screamed when she collided with a hard body.

"Ash. Ash. It's me!"

Ryan's familiar voice filled her ears, and Ashleigh threw herself in his arms. "Ryan! He's in there!" she cried, pointing behind her. "He tried to take me, but I wouldn't let him. I fought back!"

"Thank God!" Ryan pulled her close, relief rushing through him. "God, Ash, I was so scared!" He looked over her head into the locker room. "He's in there?"

Ashleigh nodded.

"Call the police," Ryan said, gripping her by the shoulders as he pulled away. "I'll be right back." He disappeared inside the locker room.

"Wait. Ryan! No!"

Ashleigh fumbled for her phone, putting it to her ear. She stared at the doorway, relief washing through her when she saw Ryan re-emerge.

"911. What's your emergency?"

She quickly talked into the phone, ending the call and walking up to Ryan. "What's wrong?" she asked. He was looking worried.

"He's gone."

"What?" Ashleigh stared at him. "Ryan. He was in there! I saw him. He was lying on the floor, unmoving. I did not imagine it!"

"I know you didn't," Ryan said, putting an arm around her shoulders and leading her toward the entrance. "He killed the receptionist."

"What? No!"

"Come on. We should wait for the police," Ryan said as they walked. He slid his keys out of his pocket, staring down at them, then stole a quick glance at Ashleigh. There was a small streak of blood on her neck, and he felt guilt prick at him.

This was his fault. He should have never brought her here, and because of him, she could have been kidnapped... again.

Chapter Thirty - Nine

"Ash?"

Ashleigh glanced up several hours later, from where she was curled up on the couch, wrapped up in her favorite blanket.

"What's up?" she asked, as Ryan walked in from the kitchen. It'd been a long night. It had taken the police two hours to get there after they'd called. Two hours! Ryan had been livid, she'd been agitated, and then it'd taken another hour before anyone had even talked to them.

"I made you some tea," Ryan said, setting the mug down on the coffee table in front of her. "I thought it might help."

"Thank you."

"The girls made some mac n cheese earlier. Do you want some? I know we didn't get a chance to eat earlier. If you want, I can heat some up for you."

Ashleigh shook her head. "No. That's okay. I'm really not that hungry."

"Oh. Ok." Ryan paused in the doorway, glancing her way. "Just, uh, let me know if you need anything."

Ashleigh stared at him, picking up the mug, and blew her breath across the hot beverage. Something was wrong. Ever since they'd left the gym, Ryan had been acting differently. He'd withdrawn from her, and she wasn't liking it.

"Ryan, what's wrong?"

"Nothing."

Ashleigh stared at him. Everything had been fine just a few hours ago. He'd been laughing, smiling. Now he wouldn't meet her eyes. He wouldn't even touch her. It was like ever since the clown...

She froze. "Oh my God. Ryan, please tell me you aren't blaming yourself for what happened tonight."

He avoided her gaze.

"Oh my God. You are! Ryan, you cannot blame yourself for this."

"The hell I can't!" Ryan snapped. He strode past her into the living room, pacing the room.

Ashleigh jumped, watching him. She'd never seen him like this. It was like he was a caged animal, just waiting to escape.

"Christ. I am so sorry, Ash," Ryan said, as he paced the room, well aware of her reaction when he'd raised his voice. It made him feel even worse.

"Ryan, please don't do this. You can't blame yourself. You could have never guessed that he would have attacked there of all places."

"That's just it. I should have known," Ryan said, stopping, and turning to look at her with pained eyes. "I knew he was here. I knew he'd been in this house, and I knew there was a possibility he could still be lurking around here. But I was so certain I could help you, I ignored it. Because of me, you could have been taken. I don't know what I'd do..."

"Oh, Ryan..." Ashleigh strolled across the room, taking his hands in hers. "Ryan, look at me."

He slowly raised his head, and Ashleigh's heart broke at the turmoil deep in his eyes. "I need you to listen to me," she said. "This is not your fault."

"You didn't even want to go..."

"You're right, I didn't. At first," Ashleigh told him. "But I'm glad I did. It helped me, Ryan. It truly did. I don't feel as weak, or vulnerable as I did. In fact, I think I feel stronger. All that fear, the humiliation, was weighing down on me. Letting all that go, it's what allowed me to fight him off today." She raised her hand, cupping his face in her hand. "This is not on you, Ryan. This man... this clown, he's made it clear that I'm next on his list. Which makes me think there's a real connection to all of this. Billy. Andrew. Gloria. Me. He needs all of us for something." She raised up on her tiptoes, brushing a kiss across his lips. "Oh, and if you're to blame for this, am I to blame for what happened on campus?"

"Of course not!" Ryan scowled at her. "I see what you did there."

"Reverse psychology. It really does work," Ashleigh returned to her tea. "Agh. It's cold."

Ryan laughed. "I'll make you some more. Come on."

He took the mug from her and disappeared into the kitchen. Ashleigh followed him, leaning against the marbled counter, watching as he moved around the kitchen.

"You know you don't have to coddle me, right?"

Ryan laughed, as he took the kettle from the stove, and poured the hot water in the mug. "I'm well aware. The last thing I see you as is weak. I really hope you know that and I didn't mean to get all mushy back there. It's just when I saw that woman..." he shook his head. "I ran back to you as fast as I could, and when I couldn't find you the worst images were flashing through my mind. Then I heard you scream." He dropped the tea bag into the mug, pushing it her way. "I freaked."

"You're allowed to freak, Ryan. This is not an easy situation to be in. I did warn you about that."

"Yes. I know." Ryan joined her at the counter, leaning against it. "It's just... so real now. I mean, I've only been in your life a few days. I've seen things I never thought I would, but you... you've been dealing with this for over six months now. It amazes me you're still standing."

"Sometimes, life doesn't give you a choice." Ashleigh raised the mug, taking a small sip. "I have got to figure this out," She traced her finger along the rim of the cup. "It's gotta be connected. My father. My mother. Billy. Gloria. Andrew. Marcus. I'm just not sure how."

"You said they were all friends in high school?"

Ashleigh nodded. "Yes." She exited the kitchen, disappearing into the living room and reappearing a moment later with a handful of books. "These are her yearbooks." She placed them on the countertop.

"Then, let's take a look. If they all went to school together, there's gotta be some sort of clue here, right?" Ryan took one of the yearbooks, flipping it open. "Ooh! Look at the hair!" he cried, as he flipped through the pages. "It's like... so high!"

"It was the 80s," Ashleigh said, rolling her eyes, laughing. "It was the era of the hair." She took the book from him, flipping through the pages, stopping on a picture of her mother wearing a light gray dress and a crown on top of her head. "This is her senior yearbook," she said, pointing. "This was the year she won homecoming queen."

"Who was the homecoming king?"

Ashleigh frowned. "You know, I actually don't know. She flipped through the pages, finally landing on the photo. "Oh my God. I never even realized..." She stared down at the photo of a young man, with his arms wrapped around her mother's waist. He was wearing a black suit, a crown on top of his head, as he smiled into the camera. "It's Billy's dad," she whispered. "I didn't even realize they were together. I mean, look at them. They look so happy!"

She flipped through the pages, finding several other photos of them together. Pictures of them laughing, kissing. She didn't remember her mother ever looking at her father this way.

"Ash, look at this." Ryan pointed to the photo of them at homecoming. "You see who's in the background?"

Ashleigh nodded. "Yes. It's my father."

"He doesn't look too happy, does he?"

"No. He doesn't."

Ryan stared down at the photo, then he flipped through the pages to the back.

"Ryan, what are you doing?"

"What's the most important part of a yearbook?" Ryan asked, glancing over at her.

"The back!" Ashleigh cried. "Where people sign it. You really think…"

Ryan shrugged. He took the mug from her, taking a sip of her tea.

"Hey! That's mine!"

Ryan just smiled at her, before glancing back down at the yearbook. "Ash, look at this."

Ashleigh scooted closer to him, staring at the scripture in the middle of the page.

"Congratulations, Mama! You did it. You graduated from this god awful place, and just think! In six months you're going to be a mom! I'm so happy for you. You're going to get everything you want. Love you!"

Lindsay

"She was pregnant?" Ashleigh stared down at the page, shock filling her.

"Wait. She's not talking about you?" Ryan asked.

Ashleigh shook her head. "No. She didn't have me, until she was in her twenties. Which means, my dad isn't the only one who had a child. My Mom did too, and from the looks of it, the father is Charles Turner. Billy and I have a sibling."

Ryan reached over, squeezing her hand. "That connects you and Billy."

Ashleigh nodded. Yes. "Now, we just need to connect the rest. She flipped through the yearbooks. "Look at this," she said, pointing to a picture of the cheerleading squad. All of them were there. Mary. Stacey. Caroline. Lindsay. Charlene, Lisa, and Denise.

"They're all there," Ryan said, staring down at the photo. "And look." He pointed. "Homecoming queen. Prom queen. Student council. Cheerleading captain. The list goes on and on. They were the "it" group it seems like."

"And look. In every single photo, my father is right there," Ashleigh said, pointing. "He's just looking at them, with this look in his eyes. It's so creepy!" She shuddered.

"Jealousy can be a deadly emotion," Ryan murmured, as he flipped through the pages. "Did they go to college together, too?"

Ashleigh nodded. "Yes. They all attended college together. Hold on." She hurried out of the kitchen, returning a moment later with a small box. She set it on the table, rifling through the contents before laying a photo on the table.

"This was taken their sophomore year in college," Ashleigh said, pointing to the photo of a group of women. "It was my mom's birthday and they went clubbing. Though, I don't know who these two women are," she said, pointing to a short-haired woman with ash, brown hair and then to another woman with long, reddish-brown hair.

"Hmm." Ryan tapped a finger underneath his chin. "The woman on the right. She kind of looks like Gloria, doesn't she?"

Ashleigh stared at the woman a moment, then she pulled her laptop across the table, typing into the field. "Guess it's a good thing Gloria has a Wiki page." She scanned the paragraph, her mouth dropping open when she turned to Ryan a few minutes later. "Gloria is the daughter of Johnathan and Shelby Myers. Shelby Myers, aka, Shelby Mitchell, attended Sarasota Bay college..." She turned the laptop, lifting the photograph she held to the picture on the screen. "It's a perfect match. Oh my God. She's connected to all of this, Ryan!"

"So, we just have two more to connect."

"Yes. Marcus and Detective Stark." Ashleigh tapped her fingers against the tabletop, before reaching for her phone. "Hey, Addy. It's me."

"Hey, Ash. What's up?"

"You worked in the administrative office at UCLA last year, didn't you?"

"Yes. Why?"

"I'm trying to get some information on Marcus. Do you know anything about his mom?"

Silence sounded from the other end of the phone.

"Addy?"

"You didn't hear this from me," Addison said, finally. "But she died about twenty years ago at a party in San Francisco."

Ashleigh froze. "How did she die?"

"I don't know. Randy Dillon, the dean, and Marcus's father never talked about it. I just happened to overhear it one day when he and Marcus were arguing one day."

"Okay. Thank you, Addy." Ashleigh hung up the phone, glancing back over at Ryan. "Did you hear that?"

"Every, last word." Ryan picked up a pen, took the photo out of the frame and flipped it over. He scribbled on the back. "So, this woman, is Marcus's mother?"

"I think so." Ashleigh did a quick search, nodding several moments later. "Yes, it's her. Look." She pointed to the photo of the same woman on Marcus's Facebook page as she held an infant in her arms. "See, it says: even though I never really knew you, I'll never forget you."

"So that connects him."

"Now we just have to connect Andrew." Ashleigh took the photo from Ryan, flipping it over and staring at the women. "They're all accounted for. Where does he fit in?" She started gathering up the yearbooks, piling them up and a photo slid out from one of the books, falling to the floor.

Ryan reached for it, setting it on the table and Ashleigh gasped. "Oh my God! Will you look at this? It's one of their Christmas cards!" She picked up the card, staring down at the photograph of the Millers. "They used to send one every year."

She stared at the family across the front of the card, tracing a finger over Lindsay's face. She'd been so pretty. Tall, elegant, and had long, dark hair that had run all the way down her back. Most days she'd had it braided, and next to her, was her husband, Fred. He was a tall man, with short, red hair. His beard was neatly trimmed as he stared into the camera. Their five children stood in front of them.

"This was taken just two years before the massacre happened. Aimee was eleven, and Mer was nine." She pointed to the two girls sitting in front on the grass. "And these are their three brothers." She pointed. "The oldest is Max." She stared down at the brown-haired teenager. "He was five years older than Aimee. Just eighteen years old when he died." She pointed to the boy in the middle. "This is Alex." He was a tall, lanky blonde. "He was three years older." Then she pointed to the dirty, blonde-haired boy. "And this is Drew. He was two years older."

"Wait. Drew?" Ryan arched a brow. "As in, Andrew?"

Ashleigh froze. She stared at him, then back down at the card. *Those eyes...*

All the Miller boys had had them. Deep blue, gray eyes. They'd gotten them from their father. "Oh my God. Could it be?" she asked, thinking back. "You know, when I first met him, I thought there was something familiar about him, but I thought I was imagining it. What if he's one of the brothers? What if one of them... survived?"

Chapter Forty

It was another sleepless night.

Ashleigh sighed, snapping her eyes open and staring up at the ceiling. She couldn't sleep... again, but this time it was for a completely different reason.

She couldn't stop thinking about what she and Ryan had uncovered earlier. She sighed, sitting up in the bed and rubbing her eyes. She had a brother out there, and what about the memory she'd had about her father? Her father had had an affair too. He had another child out there somewhere, but with who? Did they know?

The thoughts ran rapid and she rose to her feet, thinking about the other mystery they'd uncovered... or thought they'd uncovered. One of the Miller brothers was alive.

She reached for her phone.

"Are you awake?" she texted into the phone.

Bubbles appeared across the display, followed by three texts simultaneously.

"Yes."

She sent another text. *"Video chat?"*

"Absolutely!"

She made her way across the room, careful not to wake Ryan, who was fast asleep on the floor. She paused in the doorway, watching as he slept. He looks so peaceful.

Her phone buzzed, and she glanced down, as a group chat invitation popped up on the screen. She slid out of the room and pressed accept.

"Is anyone as sick of these sleepless nights as I am?" Nikki asked, yawning. "I've tried everything! Counting sheep music, That music, warm milk. Nothing helps! I am so exhausted, and it won't be long until basketball season is here. I need my sleep!"

"So do I," Addison said, rubbing her eyes. "Plus, this time change is really messing me up."

"Where are you even? "Sydney asked.

"Germany."

"Dang! You must be exhausted, girl!"

"We're all exhausted," Ashleigh said, cutting in. "But I think my nightmares are subsiding."

"Oh?" Nikki grinned at her. "Does that have something to do with a certain football player in your life?"

"Nikki!"

"What? Inquiring minds want to know," Nikki said, ignoring her protest. "Have you guys…"

"No!" Ashleigh cried. "We're taking things slow. I'm not sure if I'll be ready for that anytime soon." She paused. "But it's been nice, sweet even, and he's been there for me. Even tonight when the clown attacked."

"What?"

Three pairs of eyes swung toward her, and Ashleigh swallowed.

"When?"

"Where?"

"How?"

She quickly filled them in on what had happened. "And the police department here has not changed," she told them. "It's just as slow as ever."

"Obviously, considering what our parents got away with," Sydney muttered. "I can't believe they did that! I mean, framing a man for murder? Why?"

"To protect one of us," Addison whispered. "That's the only reason they would have done it. I have to believe that." She looked at Ashleigh. "Is Billy..."

"He's still missing," Ashleigh told her. "But I don't think he's in any danger, at least not yet. When the clown came after me today, he said I was the missing piece. That I'm the last one he needs."

"Last one for what?"

"For his revenge," Nikki said. "I can't believe you have a brother out there, Ash. I wonder what he's like."

"If he even knows about me."

"You think Charles is his Dad?"

Ashleigh shrugged. "I have no idea."

"And what about my dad?" Nikki asked. "Do you think…"

"Well, Billy did think he was being framed," Ashleigh told her. "And it seems, there's only one person who was manipulating everything back then."

"Who?"

"My mother." Ashleigh leaned forward, thinking. "Everything leads back to her. I think she was the one pulling the strings. I think she's the one who wanted to keep everything hidden because nothing came to the surface until she died."

"You think she had something to do with my Dad?"

Ashleigh shrugged. "I don't know, Nikki. All I know is that she had a lot of secrets."

"I think they all had secrets," Sydney said, as she wrote in her notepad. "And it all circles back to what happened in Sarasota Bay." She held up the pad. "I just wish we could remember that time in our life. Billy didn't say…"

"Billy and I had a bit of a fight," Ashleigh said, fidgeting. "He, um, was acting very protective. He was rude, wouldn't listen to me, and accused Ryan of being the killer."

"Ash! Why didn't you tell us?"

"I've kind of had a lot going on."

"What was the name of that doctor?" Sydney asked, still scribbling on the pad.

"Eric Pollard."

Sydney froze, her eyes widening. She dropped her pen. "You mean… Dr. Pollard?"

"Yes. Have you heard of him?"

"I remember my parents talking about him," Sydney said, thinking back. "They said he was some weird doctor who dabbled in the psyche. He specialized in dreams, memory loss..." she picked up her pen, scribbling again. "And I remember a pretty hefty payment going to his practice. I wonder..."

"You think we were his patients?" Addison asked, her eyes widening. "Why?"

"To help us forget," Nikki whispered. "Whatever happened ten years ago, in the Miller house, it was so bad, so gruesome, they wanted us to forget about it. And because of it, we are now in danger."

"Not you. Me," Ashleigh said, wrapping her arms around herself. She pulled the blanket from the couch, cocooning herself inside of it. "And he's not going to stop until he has me."

"Ash."

"Please. I don't want to talk about it anymore," Ashleigh said. "Can we just watch a movie?"

"Ash?

Ryan opened his eyes, squinting at the clock.

Three a.m.

He yawned, stretching his arms over his head. He rose to his knees, and froze when he saw the bed empty.

"Ash?"

He shot to his feet, racing out into the hallway. He stumbled, hurrying down the stairs, and slid to a stop when he saw the television on. The credits were rolling, and he blew out a sigh of relief when he saw Ashleigh asleep on the couch.

He quietly walked across the room, turning off the television, then he glanced at her phone. A smile crossed his lips when he saw three other women fast asleep on the device. He had to assume they were Nikki, Sydney, and Addison.

"Ash." He leaned down, gently shaking her.

"Mm."

"You fell asleep on the couch."

"Oh." Ashleigh opened her eyes. "Ryan. Is everything okay?"

"You mean, minus you giving me a freaking heart attack?" Ryan asked, smiling. "Yes. Everything's fine. I just didn't think you'd be comfortable on this couch. Come on. Let's get you back to bed."

He picked her up, turned and headed for the stairs.

"Wait. My phone..."

"Leave it," Ryan told her, as he started up the steps. "A few hours away from that device might do you a little good."

"But my friends..."

"Are already asleep," Ryan said, as he entered the bedroom. He placed her on the bed, drawing the covers over her.

"Ryan! You don't have to tuck me in."

"Humor me."

Ashleigh chuckled, rolling her eyes.

Ryan leaned down. "What were you guys watching?"

"The Princess Diaries," Ashleigh whispered, her eyes drifting closed. "When we got out of the manor, it was our go-to movie. It helps us fall asleep."

Ryan smiled, pressing a kiss to her forehead. "Sweet dreams, Ash." He turned away.

"Ryan?"

"Yeah?" He turned, looking back at her.

"Stay with me?"

He smiled. "I'm not going anywhere, Ash. Go back to sleep."

"No. I meant lay with me."

Ryan froze. "Ash, are you sure? I don't want to..."

"I wouldn't be asking if I weren't sure."

Ryan smiled, recalling those same words she'd said to him the first night they'd met. It felt like a lifetime ago now.

He rounded the bed, crawling under the beds, and wrapped his arms around her. "This okay?" he asked.

"Mhmm," Ashleigh murmured. "I always feel safe with you, Ryan."

Then she fell asleep, her even breathing filling the room. Ryan smiled, pressing a kiss to her cheek, knowing he was in trouble. This girl, she already had a hold on his heart, and he didn't want to ever let her go.

Chapter Forty - One

"*Ashleigh.*"

The voice of the clown filled her ears, and Ashleigh cringed. She clenched the thin sheet around her, squeezing her eyes shut.

"*Ashleigh.*"

The door rattled, the jingle of the key sounding in the lock, and a moment later the door swung open.

No. Please. Please go away!

She curled herself up in a ball, hoping, praying that he would think she was sleeping, and leave her alone. But that was wishful thinking, she thought, as the bed slumped. She knew he was in the bed with her. She knew what he wanted. It was the way every morning started.

"*I know you're awake,*" *he whispered in her ear.* "*Open your eyes, Doll. You know what I want.*"

"*Please. Go away.*"

"And, why would I ever do that?" the clown asked, his hands gripping her shoulders and slamming her down on the bed so she was staring up at him. "You're perfect, doll, and just what I need."

Ashleigh screamed, the sound ripping from her throat. She snapped her eyes open, struggling against the arms wrapped around her waist. "Let me go!"

"Ashleigh!"

"No!" Ashleigh squeezed her eyes shut, tears streaking down her cheeks. "I can't," she whispered. "I can't do it anymore! Please. Don't make me!"

"Ashleigh!"

Somehow, through her daze, she realized someone was saying her name. It was masculine, but it wasn't the clown. It was...

"Ryan?"

She blinked, staring up at her. The nightmare, the memory fading away, and stared up at Ryan. "What..."

"You had a nightmare," Ryan told her. "But he's not here, Ash. It's just me." He raised a hand, brushing a lock of hair away from her face.

"Ryan." Ashleigh pulled out of his embrace, backing away from him. "Please. Don't."

"Don't what?" Ryan stared at her, noticing the fear, the uncertainty in her eyes. "Ash, you know I would never..."

She didn't give him a chance to finish the sentence. She turned, disappearing into the bathroom and slamming the door shut. She clicked the lock in place, tears rolling down her cheeks.

He'd snuck into her dreams, this time when Ryan had been here.

She sunk to the floor, hugging her knees to her chest. She hadn't wanted him to see her like this. She didn't want him to see this weak, vulnerable, shell of a person.

"Ash. Please, open the door. Please. Talk to me. You know I would never hurt you."

Ashleigh bit back a sob, covering her hand over her mouth. "Yes. I know that."

"Please. Let me in."

"I... I can't."

Ryan sighed, leaning against the door. "Ok. I'll leave you alone," he whispered. "But I told you, you don't have to be strong when you're around me. You can lean on me, Ash. But if you're scared of me..."

Ashleigh unlocked the door, swinging it open. "Of course not." She raced forward, throwing herself in his arms.

Ryan wrapped his arms around her, pulling her close. "What is it, baby?" He whispered. "What's wrong?"

Ashleigh shook her head. "I'm too humiliated to tell you."

Ryan pulled back, tracing a finger down her cheek, and wiping away the tears. "You don't ever have to be embarrassed around me, Ash. I'm here for you. Whatever you need."

Ashleigh sniffed. She laid her head on his shoulder. "You're the first person who's been in the same bed with me since I escaped the manor," she whispered.

"You asked me to stay with you."

Ashleigh nodded. "Yes, I know, and I was okay until he entered my dreams. It felt so real! Like I was right back inside the manor. With him."

"I'm so sorry, Ash." Ryan hugged her closer.

"He used to crawl into my bed," she whispered. "I'd wake up to him watching me. He was always there... watching me, and if for some reason I didn't wake right away, he would push this button. It sounded like a doorbell. Only louder, and he..." She hiccupped, shaking her head. "I'm so sorry, Ryan. I didn't want you to know..."

"You have nothing to apologize for, Ash," Ryan told her, tipping her head up so he could look into her eyes. "What he did to you. To your friends. That isn't on any of you."

"I know. I just feel so out of control," she whispered. "I feel like I'm taking two steps forward, then three steps back. One moment I feel strong, in control of my life, and the next, I'm that person I was back in the manor. Weak. Helpless. I don't like being that person."

"Just give yourself time, Ash."

"I have."

"More time."

"But, Ryan, if we do this." She gestured between them. "Whatever this is between us, you're going to want sex eventually. I don't know if I can ever give that to you."

"Ash."

"I don't want you to give up everything for me, Ryan," Ashleigh said, her eyes glistening with tears. "You deserve to be happy and to be with someone who can give you everything you need. I'm not that person, Ryan."

"Ash, I need you to listen to me." Ryan placed his hands on her shoulders, stepping back a step. "You went through hell in that manor, and you are that strong woman you like so much. I know that because I've seen her. I admire her, but you can't keep the part of yourself you don't like as much locked up inside. You gotta let her out, but you lean on me when she does, okay? Because I'm not going anywhere."

"Ryan..."

"You're my girl, Ash," Ryan told her. "And I told you. I'll wait as long as you need me to, but I know what I want."

"What's that?"

"Why, for you to be my girlfriend, of course," Ryan said, flashing her a grin, before walking across the room to where his bag was laying.

Ashleigh stared at him. "Really?"

"I mean what I say," Ryan told her, as he dug in his bag. "But only if you want..."

Ashleigh crossed to him, framing his face with her hands. "Ryan Eisenhower. Where have you been my whole life?" She rose on her tiptoes, brushing a kiss across his lips. "And yes. I want the same thing, but it's going to take some time and lots of patience."

"All I've got is time, Darling," Ryan drawled. "Well, except for when it comes to football. The game's next week, which means I need to get out for a run. Is that okay?"

Ashleigh smiled, nodding. "Of course! You don't need my permission, Ryan. You still have a life."

"Well, right now, you're the most important thing to me," Ryan told her, stroking her cheek, before pulling away. "I'll be back in a bit. Lock up behind me."

He turned, disappearing out of the room, and Ashleigh sighed, leaning back against the wall.

"He's good for you, sis."

She jumped, a small shriek escaping her mouth when she saw Callie sitting there. "Callie!"

"Sorry," Callie said, grinning, obviously not the least bit sorry. "But it's nice to see you so happy, Ash. It's been a long time, and I like him." She leaned close. "And I know you do too."

Chapter Forty - Two

"It's nice to see you so happy, Ash. It's been a long time, and I like him. And I know you do too."

Callie's words echoed inside her head, and Ashleigh dragged the brush through her hair, thinking about what Callie had said.

She was happy, she thought, as she stared at herself in the mirror. Ryan made her happy. Happier than she'd ever been, and that scared her. With Sean, it'd been so casual, and he'd never made her feel the things Ryan made her feel.

She finished with her hair, applying a little bit of makeup, then she turned, walking into the bedroom and sifting through her clothes. She'd made a point to leave some here, for whenever she visited. After a few moments, she decided on a green blouse and a pair of jeans. Several moments later, she made her way down the stairs, not even realizing she was humming.

"She's humming," Sadie said, glancing over at Callie, from where she was sitting at the table, scrolling through her phone. "What's wrong with her?"

"Nothing's wrong with her. She's in love," Callie said, grinning from ear to ear.

"I am not in love," Ashleigh said, as she opened the stainless, steel refrigerator. She sifted through the items, pulling out some eggs, milk, and bread. "I'm just..."

"Happy?" Sadie asked.

Ashleigh shrugged. "I'm not sure what I am yet." She started cracking eggs into a bowl.

"Ash."

Ashleigh glanced at Callie.

"What?" Ashleigh asked. "Okay, he makes me happy," she conceded, as she whisked the eggs together. "Like really happy, but I'm so scared," she whispered, as she added some milk to the bowl, followed by a splash of vanilla and some sugar.

"Scared of what?"

"That I'm not ready. That he's going to get killed... because of me." Ashleigh stopped, staring into the bowl. "I've been through so much," she whispered. "What if I can't handle this?"

Silence descended in the room.

"We know, Ash," Callie finally said. She went to the refrigerator, pulled out a pack of strawberries, and started to slice them. "I hate what happened to you. When you went missing, it was really hard on both of us."

"We were so scared we'd never see you again," Sadie added. "We cried, begged, pleaded, even prayed that you would make it back to us. Then when we came to visit you in the hospital, it took everything I had not to break down."

"Both of us," Callie told her. "We didn't want to leave you. We wanted to stay, but the doctors said you needed to rest. Plus we had school..."

"I know, Callie," Ashleigh said, as she began cooking the French toast over the stove. "And I would never want you to miss class for me. Even if I was bruised and broken."

"We would do anything for you, Ash," Sadie told her. She walked into the kitchen, pulling plates out of the cupboard. "We owe you everything. I mean, you're the reason we turned into half-decent human beings."

"Half decent? You kicked me out a year after I graduated!"

"We did not kick you out," Callie told her, placing the freshly sliced strawberries in a bowl and walking them to the table. "But we knew that if you didn't leave then, you would never leave. We didn't want you to have regrets."

"I would never regret taking care of you guys."

"But you shouldn't have had to," Callie told her. "Mom..." she shook her head. "I just can't believe how many secrets she kept. Like, we have a brother out there!"

"Technically, we have two siblings out there."

"Right. Two." Sadie fidgeted with the silverware in her hand. "Sadie, you okay?"

Sadie sighed. "I just... I want you to give Ryan a chance."

"I am!"

"Right now you are," Callie said. "But you have this habit of pushing people away, Ash. Us. Your friends. Sean."

"Sean was a spineless coward."

"I know! I mean, who dumps their girlfriend in the hospital?" Sadie scowled. "I never liked him."

"But Ryan, we like," Callie told her.

"Plus, he is very fine," Sadie said, fanning herself.

"Sadie!" Ashleigh tossed the towel at her, and Sadie ducked. It sailed over her head, dropping on the table. The three of them looked at one another and they all smiled, before bursting into laughter. Behind them, the door opened, and they turned as Ryan stepped through the door.

Ashleigh stared at him as he walked through the door. He shook his head, sweat droplets dripping from his brown hair and she swallowed. Her gaze trailed down his tanned, muscular chest, outlining his very, visible abs, and stopped on the pair of shorts covering his hips.

"Um. Have a nice run?" She asked, quickly averting her eyes. P

"I did." Ryan stopped at the refrigerator, pulled a bottle of water out, staring around the kitchen. "You made breakfast?"

Ashleigh shrugged. "I always make breakfast in the mornings here, plus, I wanted to do something nice for you as a thank you. You've done a lot for me the last few days."

Ryan twisted off the cap, taking a sip. "I don't want you to thank me, Ash. I want you to trust me," he said, disappointment showing in his eyes.

"Ryan, that's not…"

"I'm going to go take a shower. I'll be back in a bit."

"Ryan…"

He disappeared up the stairs, and she glanced over at her sisters. "Did I do something wrong?" she asked.

"Do something wrong?" Callie stared at her.

"You're kidding, right?" Sadie stared at her, her mouth dropping open. "Ash! That man is crazy about you, and you wanted to... thank him?"

"I was being nice!"

"No. You're pushing him away... just like I said you would," Callie said, picking up her bag, and swinging it over her shoulder. "You need to tell him how you feel, Ash. You need to learn to trust him. He's not one of the bad ones. He's a really, good guy."

"I do trust him!"

"Does he know that?" Sadie asked. "You're holding yourself back, Ash, and it might just cost you your happiness and one hell of a guy." They headed for the door.

"Hey. Where are you going? There's breakfast!"

"For you and Ryan," Sadie told her with a wink. "We need to get to school."

They walked out, the door slamming shut behind them, and Ashleigh sighed. She closed her eyes, drawing in a deep breath as the shower shut off upstairs. They were right. She was holding back, but they could never understand why. No one could. She started up the steps.

"Ryan." She leaned against the doorway, watching as he pulled clothes from his bag.

"Ash." Ryan glanced over his shoulder, guilt obvious on his face. "I'm sorry."

Ashleigh pushed away from the wall, shaking her head. "Ryan. You have nothing to be sorry for."

"You were doing something nice, and I..." Ryan lowered his eyes. "I was rude. I know you trust me, it's just..."

"That I haven't completely let you in yet." Ashleigh reached down, taking his hand. "I'm just scared, Ryan," she whispered. "I'm so scared of losing you."

"You're not going to lose me, Ash."

"You have no way of knowing that," she whispered. "We could die, Ryan! But that's not the only reason I'm scared. I'm... I'm scared of my feelings for you, because... I..."

"How do you feel, Ash? Tell me, please. I'm dying here."

"I think I'm falling for you."

Ryan groaned, tightening his fingers around her hand and pulling her close. He tipped her head up. "Well, that makes things easy, because I know that I'm falling for you," he whispered, before dipping his head and brushing his lips across hers.

Ashleigh moaned, her hands rising up to grip his shoulders. She tipped her head up, returning his kiss. She met him lick for lick, thrust for thrust and she froze when his hands started to trail up her sides. "Ry..."

"Ash. Look at me."

She raised her head.

"It's just me, okay?" He whispered. "Only me, okay?"

Ashleigh nodded, her eyes locking with his. He picked her up, setting her on the bed and he leaned down, brushing a kiss across her lips, down her neck, lightly nibbling on her ear. She gasped, her fingers digging into the bedspread as her head dropped back. She closed her eyes, and as soon as she did, *he* appeared in front of her.

"Ash. Open your eyes."

She snapped her eyes open to find Ryan looking at her intently.

"Don't close your eyes. It's just me. Only me, okay?" He took her hand, linking their fingers. He kissed each finger, and Ashleigh nodded. "Only you."

Ryan smiled, his lips kissing up her arm. His other hand was stroking the left side of her body. His fingers trailed up, stroking each of her ribs, before cupping her breast through the fabric of her shirt.

She gasped as panic started to rise inside of her. "Ry..."

"Ash. Look at me."

She raised her head, her eyes locking with his. A calm seemed to wash over her as she stared into his eyes. His fingers lightly kneaded her breast, and she realized at that moment that she wasn't scared. That this... was exactly what she wanted. To be here, with him, like this.

"You doing okay?" he asked, shifting uncomfortably.

Ashley nodded. "Yes. Yes, I'm good." Her eyes trailed down, staring at the bulge in his jeans. "Ryan."

"Don't look there," Ryan said, tipping her chin back up. "Look at me instead."

"At you."

"That's right." He leaned forward, brushing another kiss across her lips. "Can I touch you, Ashleigh?" he asked.

She slowly nodded.

"Tell me."

"Yes," she whispered. "Yes. You can touch me."

Ryan slipped his hand under her shirt, trailing his fingers up her bare flesh. He traced each rib, just his touch sending a wave of desire through her and a moment later he was pulling her shirt over her head.

"I've wanted you for so long," Ryan whispered in her ear. "But this is about you. We won't do anything you don't want to do, okay? You just have to say the word, okay?"

"Okay."

The shirt fell to the floor, and Ryan laid her back on the bed. He trailed his fingers over her ribs again, pressing a kiss to each bruise, each scar. "Do they hurt still?" He asked, raising his head to look at her.

"Not so much hurt. More of a dull ache," Ashleigh whispered, arching her back as his lips continued their track up her body.

"Don't close your eyes."

Ashleigh smiled. "I'm not."

"Good." His hand cupped her breast, and she moaned, as he fondled her nipple through the fabric of her white, lace bra. "Ryan..."

"Yes, baby?"

"Don't stop."

Ryan smiled, leaning forward and brushing another kiss across her lips. He cupped her breast, gently kneading, before reaching behind her and unclasping her bra.

"You still good?" he asked, glancing down at her, raising a brow in question.

Ashleigh nodded. "Yes."

He ducked his head, pressing kisses along her abdomen, along her rib cage. His tongue glided over her skin, tracing each one of her ribs, stopping when he got to her breast. He raised his head, making sure her eyes were still open, before ducking his head and gently suckling on her nipple.

Ashleigh gasped, pleasure washing through her, as his tongue latched her nipple. He licked and sucked, with each motion pleasure washing through her. She moaned, clenching the sheet and her eyes drifted closed.

"Hello, Doll."

She screamed.

"Ashleigh! Ashleigh! Open your eyes. Look at me."

She opened her eyes again, her eyes locking with Ryan.

"You have to keep your eyes open," he told her. "He can't get to you, when I'm here, okay?"

She nodded.

"It's just you and me." He pressed a kiss to her cheek, to the side of her neck. "Just us." He pressed another kiss to her elbow, another to her shoulder, before suckling on the spot between her neck and shoulder. "Ohh..."

He pressed a kiss to each one of the scars, before finding her nipple again. He licked, suckling, while his fingers played with her other. Ashleigh gasped, squirming. "Ryan..." His name came out a gasp, and he smiled, raising his head to look at her.

"Eyes on me." Then he turned his attention to her other breast. As he did, his fingers trailed up and down her side.

"Ry.."

"Yes, love?"

"That tickles!" She gasped out.

Ryan chuckled, his hand trailing further, and further down. He lifted his head, staring into her eyes. "Can I?"

Ashleigh stared into his eyes, knowing what he was asking. It meant so much to her that he asked. She'd wanted this ever since she'd met him, but it had scared her. She didn't know if she'd ever be ready for this, but now, with him. It felt right.

"Ash?" Ryan propped up on an elbow. "You're beautiful," he said, pressing another kiss to her stomach. "I want to see all of you. Touch all of you. Kiss every part of your body, but if you're not ready..."

"No. I want this," Ashleigh whispered. "I just... I wasn't expecting..."

"What, love?"

Ashleigh smiled. "To feel, so... desirable."

"Oh, baby. You're more than desirable. You're a goddamned goddess, and I want to show you how deeply I want you." He trailed a finger across the waistband of her jeans, his eyes never once leaving hers. He dipped a finger inside, gently stoking her. His finger dipped further, tracing circles around her sensitive bud.

"Oh..." Ashleigh gasped.

He continued watching her, his fingers quickening their pace and Ashleigh gasped, as tension built up inside of her. "Oh. Ryan."

"Come for me, baby," Ryan whispered. "It's just me. Only me." He thrust a finger inside of her, as he continued to rub her, and she threw her head back. She thrust her hips back, gasping out his name, as she climaxed. "Ryan!"

"You still good, baby?"

Ashleigh nodded. "Yes. Yes. I'm good."

He smiled, slowly undressing her. P "God, you're beautiful," he whispered, pressing another kiss to her abdomen, another to one thigh, then to the other, before reaching the part of her that was aching for him.

"Oh my God. Ryan!" Ashleigh gasped, as his tongue flicked over her. He suckled gently, swirling his tongue, feasting on her, before thrusting deep inside her. "Ryan!" she screamed, gripping his hair, as he worked his tongue. She gasped, calling out his name as her muscles clenched and she came completely undone. "Ryan... I need. I want..."

"What do you want, baby?" Ryan asked. He raised his head, looking at her, before continuing to drive her crazy with his tongue. Ashleigh moaned. "I want... I want you inside of me."

Ryan raised his head, his eyes locking with hers. "Are you sure? I don't..."

"Ryan." Ashleigh raised her hand, stroking his cheek. "I want you. I have for a long time, even before I was kidnapped. It's always been you, Ryan, no matter how much I've tried to fight it."

Ryan stared at her, and Ashleigh saw the war raging inside of him. The indecision. She let her hand trail down, her fingers running down his chest. "It's always been you," she whispered, tracing his abs.

"Ash..."

Her fingers trailed lower, stopping at the bulge that lay just underneath the fabric of his jeans.

"Ash..."

She undid the button, pushing both his jeans and boxers down, staring at his erection, as it popped free.

"Oh..."

"Ash. Look at me."

She raised her head, staring into his eyes. The moment they locked, she cupped her hand around him, suddenly no longer afraid. She wanted this. She wanted to touch him. To please him, just as he had pleased her.

She stroked her hand along the length of him. She started slow, then gradually, she quickened her pace. His breath caught, and he groaned, gripping the bed as her other hand reached down, gripping his balls. She stroked one, then the other, all the while her hand riding up and down his cock.

"Oh, God. Ash..." Ryan groaned in her ear, gripping her by the hips. He picked her up in his arms, spinning around until he was laying on his back on the bed. He reached into his bag, grabbing the condom, before tossing the bag onto the ground. "This is all you," he told her, as he reached led the condom on. He ran up her sides, cupping her breasts, his eyes never once leaving hers. "We go whatever pace you want to go, okay?"

"But you…"

"Don't worry about me. This is about you." He cupped her cheek, stroking her face with his thumb, before brushing a lock of her hair behind her ear. "It's all about you."

Ashleigh swallowed, staring down at him before she gripped him in her hand and brought him toward her.

The moment he entered her, it was like something had been missing. She groaned, at the same time he did, rocking her hips back and forth.

"Oh, God. Ash."

He groaned, and Ashleigh quickened her pass. She bounced up and down, pleasure mounting inside of her with each movement. This… this was nothing like she thought it would be and she felt as if she might explode from the pleasure.

"I'm not sure I can hold back much longer," Ryan moaned, as she rode the length of him. He reached up, playing with her nipples, his hands trailing down to clench her hips. He gripped her butt, squeezing slightly, before circling her sensitive bud.

"Ryan…"

"Come for me, baby," he whispered, as he stroked her. His fingers quickened their pace and Ashleigh let out a scream.

"Ryan!"

She clenched around him, and Ryan called out her name, pleasure rocking him as they came at the same time.

"Ash. Oh my God. That was…"

"Amazing?" Ashleigh asked, collapsing next to him on the bed.

"Absolutely." Ryan wrapped his arms around her, pressing a kiss to her cheek. "You okay?"

Ashleigh nodded, smiling as she turned in his arms. "Yes. I'm good. I'm really, really good."

"Good," Ryan said, as he pressed another kiss to her lips before grabbing her hand. "Come on. Let's go get cleaned up, then, I want to eat this breakfast of yours you made, because I am starving!"

"You seem different."

Nikki stared at her through the phone several hours later, frowning, then she suddenly smiled. "Oh my God! You guys did it!"

"How the hell can you possibly know that?" Ashleigh asked, blushing, as she finished cleaning up the kitchen and putting the dishes away. "But yes. We did."

"Oh my God! Ashleigh!" Nikki squealed in excitement, bouncing up and down in her chair. "I am so happy for you! Tell me everything!"

"It was... really, really nice," Ashleigh said, sighing, as she stopped and leaned against the counter, smiling. "He was so sweet... and gentle. It's nothing like I've ever experienced, Nikki."

Nikki squealed again. "Oh, Ash, you deserve this. After everything you've gone through. You know... with him."

Ashleigh cringed, thinking about what Nikki was saying. "Yeah, I know," she whispered, taking the phone with her and climbing up the steps. She reached the attic, stepping inside. She walked across the room, stacking boxes as she went. She took a seat on the floor, pulling a box toward her, and opened the flap. "I'm going to be so glad when this whole thing is over."

"I get this feeling it's not going to be over any time soon," Nikki said. "Because, I get this feeling that this whole thing goes back further than any of us realize."

"So do I."

Ashleigh pulled out a pile of pictures, flipping through them. She smiled, looking at pictures from holidays, birthday parties, and cook outs.

"Nikki, look at this." She showed her the photos. "I don't even remember most of this. Do you?"

Nikki shook her head. "No. I don't. Hey. Is that Berkman Park?"

Ashleigh nodded. "Yes, I'd recognize that park anywhere. It was the only decent park in Sarasota Bay, and we went there every Saturday. We would spend hours there, playing in the sandbox, taking turns on that big slide, seeing how high each of us could go on the swings, and even racing one another on the monkey bars. It was our place."

"I can't believe you remember all of that."

Ashleigh frowned. "Me too. It just kind of came to me." She flipped through the pictures, then stopped. "Oh my God."

"What?"

"Look."

Ashleigh held up the photo, showing Nikki the picture of her mother and Charles Turner. They were both laughing into the camera, Charles's arms were wrapped around Mary and her very, very pregnant belly. "I was right. They did have a kid together."

She flipped the photo over, staring at the back.

"One of two of my precious joys with this man."

She gasped, flipping through the photos frantically. There were more photos of the two of them, then she stopped when she got to the photo at the bottom. It was of an infant. She stared down at the infant, taking in his scrunched-up face, his button-up nose, and the dark hair on top of his head. She flipped over the photo.

"Baby Billy. Born February 19th, 1998."

She gasped, holding a hand to her mouth. "Oh my God!"

"Ash?"

"Nikki, look! It's Billy! He's my half-brother!"

"Ash. Stop." Nikki leaned forward. "There is no way Billy is the killer. He's a cop! He's our best friend. He would never hurt us."

"I know that," Ashleigh whispered. "And I don't think he's the killer," she said, holding up the picture at the bottom of the pile. "I think he's the one everyone was trying to protect."

Chapter Forty - Three

"*Ashleigh. Are you going somewhere?*"

Mary Carlson glanced up from where she was sitting on the couch, nursing baby Sadie, nodding to Callie who was playing on the floor.

"*I'm going over to the Millers,*" *thirteen-year-old Ashleigh said, as she grabbed her coat from the closet, and headed for the door.*

"*Are their parents going to be there?*"

Ashleigh sighed. "*Yes, Mom.*"

"*And that boy?*"

"*Billy is my friend, Mom. So, yes.*"

"*Just be careful. I don't trust him.*"

"*You don't trust anyone,*" *Ashleigh said, rolling her eyes, turning and walking out the door.*

She walked down the driveway, pulling her jacket on as she walked.

"You good?" Sydney asked, meeting her at the end of the driveway.

"I'm good," Ashleigh said, as they walked down the street. Nikki joined them handing her a bag. "So, are we doing this?"

"Hell yes!" Kenzie ran up, joining them. "This is going to be so epic!"

"We're going to be in sooo much trouble if anyone finds out," Addison said nervously, as she caught up to them.

"Addy! Stop worrying!" Billy cried, shaking his head at her. "Live a little!"

They all laughed, walking down the street, and turning. They cut through the yard, ducking through the hole in the old, wooden fence, and stopped to look at the small, white House in front of them.

"Ole Miss Paulson." Billy reached into the bag, pulling out the can of spray paint. "Here's for giving me an F on that paper. A paper I worked hard on!" He walked forward, pressing the sprayer. Black paint sprayed out across the garage door.

Ashleigh laughed, pulling out the roll of toilet paper. "Nikki! Help me!"

They tossed the toilet paper roll over the trees, laughing as the toilet paper spread out over the tree branches, and across the yard. Behind them, Kenzie, Addison, and Sydney pulled out a carton of eggs. They tossed the eggs, the yolk crashing against the windows.

"Hey!"

A light went on inside, and they looked at one another.

"Run!"

They dropped the stuff in their hands, turning, and racing off, just before the front door swung open.

"Oh, you ungrateful little brats! I know who you are, and I will find you!"

They giggled, racing through the lawn and back toward the cul-de-sac where they all lived.

"That was epic!"

"Wait until we tell Mer and Aimee!"

"Where are they?"

"I thought they were coming too?"

They slid to a stop, turning and making their way up the driveway. They stopped in front of the large, red house with a black roof and awnings.

"It looks really dark," Addison said, nervously.

"Did they go somewhere?"

"No." Ashleigh shook her head. "We were all going to go to the park today, remember? It's Saturday. Our day. We always go to the park."

She stepped forward, rapping her knuckles against the door and the door swung open.

"I don't like this," Kenzie said, looking inside the dark house, then back at her friends. "I'm scared."

"Oh, don't be such a baby," Sydney said, rolling her eyes. "Come on."

She stepped inside, turning on the light near the door. Light flooded the hallway, and she scrunched her nose. "Eww. Something smells in here."

"Come on. Let's go." Nikki followed her inside the house, and she suddenly stopped. Her foot brushed against something and she lowered her eyes. "Mr. Miller?"

"Oh my God! Mr. Miller!" Ashleigh raced forward, falling next to him. "Mr. Miller. Wake up!" she cried, shaking him.

"Ash, I don't think he can," Billy said, nodding to his chest. "He's been stabbed."

"What?"

Addison peered over Billy's shoulder. She held a hand to her mouth. "Oh my God. I think I'm going to be sick," she whispered, staring at the blood oozing from Fred Miller's chest.

"There's blood everywhere," Kenzie added, pointing to the pool of blood next to him. A pool of blood they had all stepped in.

"I'm going to go find Mer and Aimee," Sydney said. She swallowed, stepping around the body, and disappeared into the kitchen.

"I'm coming with you!" Nikki cried, hurrying after her.

They disappeared inside the house, and Ashleigh rose to her feet. She walked down the hallway, stopping to fix a family portrait that was hanging crookedly before rounding the corner.

"Ah!"

"Ash!"

Everyone hurried after her and she pointed. "They're all dead!" she screamed, pointing to the bodies that were laying on the floor in the living room. That's when they saw them. Max, Alex, and Drew.

They raced forward, falling to the ground next to them. "Max. Please." Ashleigh pressed a finger to his throat, stroking his bruised and battered face. There was no pulse.

"Anything?" she asked, glancing over at her friends.

They all shook their heads.

"I'm... I'm calling my mom," Kenzie cried, sobbing. She took out her phone.

"Guys!"

They all turned as Nikki and Sydney hurried down the stairs.

"Did you find them?" Ashleigh asked, turning to look at them. Sydney shook her head. "I can't find them."

"It's liked they just vanished," Nikki added. She stared at them, then at the bodies on the ground. "Are they..."

"I think they're all dead," Ashleigh whispered. "Wait. Billy. No!"

"Ash!"

"Hmm."

"Ash!"

"What?"

Ashleigh blinked, staring at Ryan. "What's going on?"

"You fell asleep," Ryan said, as he crouched in front of her. "I heard noises when I got back from the store. You, okay?"

Ashleigh nodded, taking the hand he offered, letting him pull her to her feet. "Yes. I think so." She glanced behind her at the photos that were scattered across the floor. "I think I just had a memory."

"What kind of memory?"

"The day we found the Millers," Ashleigh whispered. "I think I know why they did, what they did," she whispered. "I think they were protecting Billy." She looked at Ryan. "He was holding the knife, Ryan."

"He…"

Ashleigh nodded. "And he's my brother. Well, half-brother." She shook her head. "I wonder if he's known all along. He's always been so protective of me, but…" She blew out a breath. "I don't think he's the one Lindsay was talking about in the yearbook. I think there's another out there, somewhere."

"And the hits just keep on coming, don't they?" Ryan asked as he led her out of the attic. "Come on. Let's get this new security system put up, then don't we have dinner with that Miller woman?"

"Yes, but not until later," Ashleigh said. "How long do you think it'll take to put up the security system?"

"Maybe an hour. Why?"

"Because, Eisenhower, there's something I want to show you," Ashleigh said, rising in her tiptoes and brushing a kiss across his cheek. "Come on. We've got work to do."

Chapter Forty - Four

It'd been years since she'd been here.

Ashleigh gripped Ryan's hand, as they made their way across the street, toward Berkman Park. She stopped, just inside the gates, a chill washing over her.

"You okay?" Ryan asked, squeezing her hand.

Ashleigh swallowed, nodding. "Yes. I just haven't been here in a long time."

"You came here a lot?"

Ashleigh nodded. "Every Saturday."

She walked across the lawn, past the playground, and stopped in front of the bench. She crouched down, running her hand along the surface. "A year after they went missing and they still hadn't been found, the town put together a memorial for them. I didn't go. It was too hard to, but from what I understand, they had some sort of slideshow put together for them.. There were candles, music, and they put in this bench." She traced the engraving. "From Sarasota to the grave…" She smiled. "It was a promise we all made to ourselves when we were younger. That we would stick together no matter what."

"Sounds like you're starting to remember more about them."

Ashleigh nodded. "I think it was the dream," she said. "Everything's starting to click. Like I can remember what they look like, I can remember their laugh, their smile. I can even remember playing with them. I remember birthday parties, playdates we used to have, and I remember how they were like sisters to me. I can't believe I forgot about them. They were two of my best friends," she whispered. "How could I just forget?"

"I'm starting to think that it wasn't that you forgot," Ryan said. "I think someone made you forget."

"Like that doctor."

Ryan arched a brow at her.

"Sydney mentioned something about him the other night."

"Ah. That makes sense, but did you know that he developed a surgery to help erase memories? In fact, he won an award for it."

Ashleigh stared at him. "Wait. Are you saying he operated on me? On us?"

"It would make sense, wouldn't it?" Ryan asked. "But there's more, Ash." He took her arm, sitting on the bench with her. "When I went on my run this morning, I made a call to my psych instructor. I told her about Dr. Pollard, and she said something that's stuck with me all day." He took her hand, linking his fingers with hers. "She said, that there is no way to ever completely erase a memory. Anything can trigger it, and I think that dream, that memory was that trigger."

Ashleigh stared at him. "Oh my God. My mom, our parents, they paid someone to take away our memories? They made us forget our friends?" She held a hand to her mouth. "This. This... is insane, Ryan! How could they do that to us?" Tears filled her eyes, streaking down her cheeks. "I didn't think I could hate her anymore than I already do, Ryan. She not only abandoned us... me... she took away two of the most important people in my life!"

A sob escaped her mouth, and Ryan scooted over, pulling her into his arms. "I know, but I think in her mind, she was trying to protect you, Ash."

"She didn't do this for me, Ryan. She did this to protect herself. To protect her secrets, and I am officially done pretending she cared even a little bit about us because she obviously didn't." She rose to her feet, shaking her head. "Come on. Let's go get something to eat. I'm starving."

"Ash."

She spun on her heel and strode away.

"Ash!"

"Ryan. I can't talk about this anymore," Ashleigh said, as she strolled through the gates and started down the sidewalk. "I am so mad at her right now! She has so many secrets. I mean I have two siblings! Well, three technically, if you count the child my father had. And she's dead! I can't yell at her. I can't tell her how much I hate her. There's nothing I can do!"

She stopped, turning to look at him. "She was my mom, Ryan. She was supposed to be there for me. But she wasn't, and I... I hate the fact that I have all this anger toward her, all this hatred. I can't help it."

"No matter what she did, she's still your mom, Ash," Ryan told her, stopping next to her. "I know she's done some unspeakable things, but she did love you. I have to believe that. Just like your father loved you."

Ashleigh laughed. "I'm having a hard time believing any of that. Come on. Let me show you my favorite restaurant here." She grabbed his hand, pulling him down the sidewalk. They passed several stores, and finally, she stopped at the door on the corner.

Lenny's Pizzeria.

She opened the door, heading inside.

"Oh my God. Ashleigh!"

An older man with short, white hair looked up from behind the counter. He grinned, rounding the counter and engulfing Ashleigh in a tight hug. "It's so good to see you!"

"Hi, Lenny." Ashleigh returned the older man's hug, gesturing to Ryan. "Lenny, this is Ryan. My... my boyfriend." She blushed. It was the first time she'd introduced him as that.

Ryan grinned, squeezing her shoulder, then taking the hand Lenny offered. "Hello, Lenny."

"Hello to you, young man," Lenny said, as he shook Ryan's hand. "A pleasure. A friend of Ashleigh's is always welcome here." He winked at Ashleigh. "I remember you and your group of friends coming in here all the time when you lived here.

You all would sit in that corner." He pointed. "And do your homework."

"It's also where I got my first job," Ashleigh told Ryan. "When Mom left, I needed something flexible in case Callie or Sadie needed me. Lenny here was the best boss I ever worked for."

"Aww, shucks, Ash. You're going to make this old man blush." He gestured to one of the booths. "Take a seat. You want the usual? Half pepperoni. Half cheese?"

Ashleigh glanced at Ryan. "That good for you?"

Ryan patted his stomach. "Ash. I love pizza. Any pizza is good enough for me."

Lenny stopped Ryan before he walked away. "That one's one fine lass," he told him. "I don't think I ever met anyone who works as hard as she does and has the compassion she does. Don't let her go."

Ryan smiled. "I don't plan to."

He slid into the seat across from Ashleigh, gazing around the restaurant. It was small, and not a lot of people were in today. The booths were a dark burgundy and sat just underneath the windows. Red topped circular tables were scattered throughout the room on top of the checkered floor, and just to their left, you could hear the bustle of the kitchen. A young girl was at the register, and a couple of elderly men were sitting at the bar, talking to Lenny.

"I know it's nothing like LA," Ashleigh said, placing her hands on the table. "But I always had a soft spot for Lenny and his pizza. He gets everything shipped straight from Italy, and every pizza is made from scratch. It really is delicious."

"I hope you're right," Ryan said, giving her a wink. "I mean, I did grow up in New York."

"What was it like living there?"

"Hectic, and very, very noisy," Ryan said, reaching for her hand and running his thumb over the back of her hand. "Everyone was always busy running somewhere. Traffic was insane, and honestly, I hated it. I hated it even more after my mom died." He swallowed. "But hey, let's not talk about that. I did hear from Levi, though."

"Oh! Levi!" Ashleigh lifted her head to look at him. "Is he okay?"

Ryan smiled, nodding. "Yes. He's okay. The knife didn't hit anything major. He had to have a few stitches, but he should be ready to go for the game next weekend."

"That's great. I hate that he was injured because of this madman," Ashleigh whispered. "Captain Vargas called me this morning."

Ryan raised a brow.

"They still can't find Billy. They even went to the manor except... well, it's gone."

"What? How does a building just disappear?"

"I don't know." Ashleigh shook her head, sniffling. "But Johnny. Captain Vargas said he didn't make it," she whispered, looking up at Ryan with teary eyes. "They lost him on the way to the hospital."

"Damn. Ash, I'm so sorry."

"Me too. He was a good guy."

"Yes. He was." Ryan squeezed her hand, looking up, as Lenny placed the pizza in front of them, along with a basket of breadsticks.

"Oh. That smells amazing!"

"Told you," Ashleigh said, giving him a grin, as she picked up a breadstick. She broke it in half, plopping it in her mouth.

"I suppose you did," Ryan said, as he picked up a slice of pizza. He took a bite, sighing, as the mixture of spices, pizza sauce, and cheese filled his senses. "Okay. New York doesn't have anything on Lenny's pizza. This is delicious!"

Ashleigh giggled.

Ryan glanced over at her. "I love that sound," he said, staring at her across the table. "Your laugh. It's so free, so light."

Ashleigh blushed. "I haven't had a reason to, you know. But you. You always have this way of making me smile or laugh. No matter how dire things may seem."

"Well, I guess I'll just have to continue being charming," Ryan said, flashing her another grin. They dug into the pizza and breadsticks, chatting. It felt so nice, so casual, and a little while later Ryan tossed a few bills on the table.

"Whew! I don't think I can eat anymore," he said, leaning back. "I'm stuffed. So, what's next on the agenda?"

"The cemetery," Ashleigh said, rising to her feet. She waved to Lenny, before following Ryan out of the restaurant. "But we need to make a stop first." She pressed the button, stopping at the light and waiting for the light to change. She tapped her foot, gazing around the street, and stopped when she found herself staring at a young, red-haired woman sitting on the bench across the street.

"Aimee?" She stared at her, tapping Ryan on the shoulder. "Ryan. Look."

"What?"

Ryan turned, frowning. "Ah, Ash. There's no one there."

"What?" Ashleigh turned, staring at the now empty bench. "Ryan, there was a woman there! I swear, and she looked just like Aimee."

"I believe you, Ash, but it's been ten years. Are you sure you remember what she looks like? Plus, we don't even know if she's alive."

"I know. But what if she is, Ryan? What if she's here? In this town?" The light changed, and they made their way across. "What if she's the one who was sending Gloria those pictures!"

"Let's cross one bridge at a time."

"Right. One thing at a time. There's no sense in jumping to conclusions." She turned, stepping through the doorway, the smell of flowers immediately surrounding her. She sighed, turning to gaze around the flower shop.

"Anything in particular you're looking for?" Ryan asked as they walked around the shop. He stopped, glancing down at a bouquet of roses, raising a brow at Ashleigh.

"Do not buy me roses," Ashleigh told him. "They're too traditional."

"And your favorite flower is..."

"Lilies," Ashleigh told him. "But not white."

Ryan smiled. "Duly noted."

"Do not…"

"I promise. I will not buy you flowers. At least not right now," Ryan told her.

Ashleigh eyed him, clearly not believing a word he said.

"Is there something I can help you find?" A young woman walked from the back of the store, then she stopped, her eyes widening. "Ashleigh?"

Ashleigh turned, freezing when she spotted the dark-haired woman. "Mallory?"

"Oh my God!" Mallory squealed, racing forward and pulling Ashleigh in for a hug. "I can't believe it's you! I heard about what happened to you. I'm so glad you're okay, alive, and here!"

"Mallory. I can't believe…" Ashleigh shook her head, tears spilling down her cheeks. "The last time I saw you was…"

"Mommy?"

A small voice sounded, and moments later a young girl peered around Mallory's legs.

"Oh my God. Is that…"

"Lily. Yes." Mallory picked up the young girl, plopping her on her hip. "Lily, this is an old friend of Mommy's. Her name is Ashleigh."

"Oh my God. She's gotten so big.' Ashleigh turned to Ryan. "Ryan, this is Mallory. She was a year behind me in school, and we didn't actually meet until we crossed paths in the hospital my senior year of high school. She was a pregnant teen and had some complications with her pregnancy. It was when Sadie was having one of her heart procedures. We were sitting together in the waiting room and we just started talking. Oh, Mallory, I'm so sorry I didn't reach out..."

"Don't you dare apologize. I know better than anyone what it's like to recover from tragedy." Mallory gave her a smile.

"A pleasure to meet you," Ryan said, extending a hand.

"Mallory, this is Ryan. My boyfriend."

Mallory smiled, taking his offered hand. "A pleasure." She pulled her hand away. "So, is there anything I can help you find?"

"I need six white roses," Ashleigh said. "I'm headed to the cemetery."

Mallory raised a brow. "Have you been there since..."

Ashleigh shook her head. "No. This will be my first time there."

Mallory nodded, turning and walking down the aisles. She plopped a bouquet of roses from their spot, making her way toward the cashier. She rang them up, taking Ashleigh's card. "It was great seeing you again, Ash. Make sure you stay in touch, okay? And remember, you do still have friends here."

"Thank you."

Ashleigh took the bouquet, turned, and walked out of the store. She started walking down the sidewalk and frowned. Where was Ryan?

She turned, scanning the street. He'd just been here, hadn't he?

She turned, heading back toward the shop, and the door swung open as Ryan hurried out. "Ryan! Where were you?"

"Sorry. I was looking for something," Ryan said, giving her a grin. "Come on. Let's go."

"You're acting strange."

"No. I'm not." Ryan pressed a kiss to her cheek, taking her hand. "Come on. We've only got a few hours left until we have to be at the Millers' house for dinner."

The Millers. Right.

Ashleigh cringed, remembering what Callie and Sadie had said about the place. It was going to be so awkward walking into that place, now that she remembered more about the Millers.

She pushed the thoughts aside, walking down the sidewalk, her thoughts running rapid, before turning and walking through the metal gates. They walked under the metal arch that read, *Sarasota Bay Cemetery.*

"Wow." Ryan paused just inside the gates, staring at the rolling hills of headstones that surrounded them. "For a small town, this is quite the cemetery."

"It may be small, but it's also been home to a lot of people for the last hundreds of years," Ashleigh said as they walked down the narrow road, turning up the hill and walking up the pebbled path, before stopping, the name, *Miller,* reading across the large headstone in front of them.

"I'm going to give you a minute," Ryan said, squeezing her hand, and nodding to the bench behind them. "I'll be over there if you need me."

Ashleigh nodded, watching as he walked away, then she knelt in front of the headstone. She grazed her hand over the surface, tears filling her eyes. "I'm so sorry I forgot about you guys," she whispered, pulling out a rose and laying it in front of the headstone. "You guys were like a second family to me. To all of us." She sniffed, wiping away the tears that streaked down her cheeks. She moved down the line, placing a rose in front of each of the headstones. First, Fred's, then in front of Alex's, Max's, and Drew's. She stopped when she got to the final graves.

Meredith Jane Miller

Amelia Sophia Miller

She dropped to her knees, placing a rose in front of each of the headstones. She traced the graving, tears streaking down her cheeks. "I am so sorry," she whispered. "Sorry I forgot about you. Sorry our parents went to such extreme measures to make us forget, and most of all, I am so sorry we didn't get there sooner. Maybe if we had, you would still be here."

It didn't matter that their bodies had never been found. Everyone believed they were dead, but she kept thinking about that woman from earlier. Was it possible that they were still alive? It was crazy to think that, right?"

She raised her head, looking at the sky above her. Then she stared across the graveyard, her eyes locking with the young redhead she'd seen earlier.

"Ash? You about ready?" Ryan asked, walking up.

"Ryan. Look."

Ryan glanced across the lawn, his eyes landing on the young redhead, who was staring at them. Then she turned, sprinting across the lawn. She slid to a stop in front of a silver sedan, glancing over her shoulder at them before getting in the car and speeding off.

"Is that the woman you saw earlier?"

Ashleigh nodded. "Yes. Do you think she followed us here?"

"I'm not sure," Ryan said, offering her his hand, and pulling her to her feet. "You really think she looks like..." He gestured to the headstone in front of them. "Amelia?"

"She looks just like her."

"If it is her, she obviously isn't ready to talk," Ryan said, taking her elbow and leading her back toward the entrance. "We have to give her time, Ash. She'll come to you when she's ready."

"I hope so," Ashleigh whispered. She glanced over her shoulder, back at the graves. "I'll be back," she whispered. "And I promise. I will never forget about any of you, ever again."

Chapter Forty - Five

A few hours later, Ashleigh stood in front of the long mirror just inside the bathroom, running a hand down the sundress she'd picked up in town earlier. It was light blue, with white flowers on it. It hugged her hips, her curves, but still covered her scars and bruises that were still healing.

She ruffled her hair, fluffing it a bit, before reaching into the drawer for her makeup bag. She applied the mascara and eyeliner, before stepping back. Happy with the look, she applied some foundation, a little blush, then reached for her purse that was hanging on the door behind her.

She hadn't been inside the Miller house in over ten years. While she was sure she was overdressed for the occasion, she wanted to look nice. Ms. Miller deserved that.

She walked out of the bathroom, grabbed her white sandals from the closet, and headed out of the room and down the stairs.

She trotted down the stairs, stopping when she saw Ryan standing at the bottom. Her breath caught, when she saw him standing there in a light, blue dress shirt, and dark, blue jeans. In his hands, he held a colorful bouquet of flowers.

"Ryan. What..."

"I kind of placed an order at that floral shop earlier."

Ashleigh stared at him. "Wait a minute. Is that why you didn't come out right away?"

Ryan smiled sheepishly. "Guilty."

Ashleigh shook her head, trotting down the last couple of steps, and taking the flowers from him. She stared at the colorful lilies laying in the bouquet. Some were blue, some were yellow, some were purple, and a few were orange. "Their lovely."

"And you are beautiful," Ryan told her.

Ashleigh blushed. "You don't look so bad yourself, Eisenhower."

"You about ready?"

Ashleigh nodded. "Yes. Let me just put these in some water."

She disappeared into the kitchen, riffling through the cupboards until she found a vase. She filled it with water, placing the flowers in it, before setting the vase in the middle of the table. "Ok. I'm ready," she said, as she stepped into her shoes. "At least as ready as I'll ever be."

"It'll be okay, Ash. Ms. Miller seemed really nice. It sounded like she misses you."

"She's always been a very, nice woman," Ashleigh said, as they made their way across the lawn, walking up the short driveway that lead up to the house. They climbed up the steps, up onto the white porch where lights were strung up on the railing. "She was like another mother to us. She was always there for us if we needed anything. She even taught us how to bake. Oh, the times we spent in that kitchen." She laughed, shaking her head. "It was mayhem!"

She stopped in front of the door, rapping her knuckles against the wood. Immediately it opened, an older man filling the doorway as he looked down at her.

"Uh. Hi." Ashleigh peered into the house, before turning her attention back to the dark-haired man filling the doorway. "I... we..."

"Ashleigh, it's okay," the man said, giving her a smile. "Lindsay said you were coming over for dinner. I'm Leo, her brother. I know you might not remember me, but I certainly remember you. I remember all of you. You were all quite the posse. You guys were inseparable."

Ashleigh smiled. "Yes. I suppose we were." She regarded the man, vaguely remembering him coming by every once in a while to see Aimee and Meredith. She remembered him chasing them around the lawn, even playing catch with them. She also remembered him sitting next to Lindsay at every dance recital or concert. "I think I do remember you," she whispered. "You came up from the city for their recitals and plays, didn't you?"

Leo nodded. "Indeed, I did. I wouldn't have missed it for the world. I really loved those rugrats." He swallowed. "I just wish they were still here."

"Me too," Ashleigh said, as she stepped past him into the house. "Leo, this is Ryan. My boyfriend."

"A pleasure," Ryan said, offering a hand.

"Oh no. The pleasure is all mine," Leo said, taking his offered hand. "I'd recognize you anywhere, Ryan. You're a hell of a football player. They say you're going to go first overall in the draft next year."

Ryan laughed. "That is the rumor, but you know how the draft works. It is not easily predictable. It all comes down to who gets that number one pick. That team might not even need a quarterback, plus, that kid at Alabama is pretty good too."

"A humble man. I like you, Ryan," Leo said, clapping a hand on his shoulder. "So, tell me, are the Tigers going to go all the way this year?"

They walked away, talking football, and Ashleigh turned, wandering down the hallway. She glanced back at the door, remembering the body of Fred Miller, as he'd lay there bleeding. Her gaze drifted to the living room, where the three bodies had laid. It was as if she were reliving that moment in her life all over again.

She swallowed, running a hand along the wall. It had been repainted. It was no longer beige, but a light gray now. Pictures hung on the walls. There was a picture of Fred and Lindsay on their wedding day. Fred and Lindsay were in the middle of a dance. Lindsay was beautiful, her long, dark hair long, and hanging down her shoulders. She was wearing a white, lace dress that trailed all the way down to her ankles. Fred was dressed in a black tux and black slacks.

She turned, continuing down the hallway. There was a picture of Meredith and Aimee, on the swing set. A picture of their three boys, all three of them holding a baseball in their mitts. A family picture of all of them together, at the park. Even a picture of the whole family in front of the Christmas tree.

She continued through the house, walking across the living room. The carpet had been replaced. It was a dark brown now, not the white she remembered. She gazed around, staring at the television they had watched the Thanksgiving parade on. Lindsay and Frank had always done Thanksgiving. It's been a tradition, where their families all got together. They'd been like one big family.

She ran a hand along the black, leather couch, glancing at the similar loveseat across the room, and the matching recliner. She remembered Lindsay crocheting in that same chair. She'd made blankets, sweaters, mittens.

She turned, walking past the fireplace, where she remembered sharing cocoa with her friends during their countless sleepovers. She continued on, heading up the winding staircase, stopping, to glance back down below her. She could hear Ryan and Leo talking and she turned, disappearing down the hallway. She ducked her head into the room on her left, her eyes widening.

Callie and Sadie had warned her, but she hadn't been prepared to see it.

The room looked exactly like it had ten years ago.

She stepped forward, running a hand across the white bedspread, glancing behind her at the posters of Taylor Swift. In the corner, lying on the bookcase amongst all the books, was a flute. The flute Amelia had played.

She walked to the bookcase, scanning her fingers over the romance books lining the shelves. Amelia had been a romantic. She'd always believed in happily ever after.

She walked further into the room, looking at the clothes still hung in the closet. Shoes still lined the floor. It was exactly the same.

She walked out of the room, and through the doorway across the hall. Meredith's room. There were tennis and softball decals hanging on the wall. Signed baseballs and bats lay in the glass cabinet on the other side of the room. On the nightstand, a couple of autobiographies lay in a stacked pile.

She took a seat on the red bedspread, picking up an autobiography of Serena Williams. She flipped through it, tears filling her eyes.

"You must think I'm crazy for keeping their rooms this way."

She glanced up as Lindsay paused in the doorway. "No. Not at all," she said. "It shows how much you loved them."

"I did. I loved all of them, I just couldn't force myself to pack up their belongings. It would just seem so final, when I don't believe they're really gone."

Ashleigh raised her head in surprise. "You think they're still alive?"

"A mother knows things, Ashleigh," Lindsay said, giving her arm a squeeze. "Come on, dinner's about ready and it looks like you could use a glass of wine. Being back here must be bringing up a lot of memories."

"Like you wouldn't believe." Ashleigh set the book down, glancing behind her at the room one last time before following Lindsay to the kitchen.

Lindsay pulled a bottle of wine from the cupboard, popped the cork, and poured two glasses. She held her glass up, gesturing to Ashleigh. "To old friends, to new friends, and to those we have lost."

Ashleigh smiled, clinking her glass with Lindsay's. "And to family. We were always like a close-knit family, weren't we?"

"Indeed, we were."

They both took a sip, glancing up as the men walked into the room.

"You doing okay?" Ryan whispered in her ear, as he poured himself a glass.

Ashleigh nodded. "Yes. I'm good."

"Wine, Leo?" Ryan asked, lifting the bottle.

"Why not? Everyone else seems to be drinking it," Leo said, grinning. "This is nice. Kind of like old times." He glanced over at Ryan. "Lindsay and Fred used to host dinner parties and Thanksgiving. It was like one big family."

"Sounds nice."

"It was. I can't tell you how nice it is to have company again," Lindsay said, just as the oven beeped. "Oh! The Lasagna's ready."

"Do you need any help with anything?" Ashleigh asked.

"Oh, goodness no! You're my guest, Ashleigh. I would never put you to work."

"You didn't. I offered."

Lindsay looked at her for a minute. "Well, I guess you could make the salad if you really wanted to."

"I would love to."

"Leo, can you set the table?"

"Of course." Leo walked out of the kitchen and into the dining room. He opened the china cabinet, taking out a stack of plates. "Ryan, can you grab the cloths from that drawer?" he asked, as he started setting the plates on the table.

"Of course." Ryan opened the drawer to the china cabinet, pausing when he saw Leo staring off toward the kitchen. "Everything okay, Leo?"

Leo shook his head. "I don't think anything will ever be okay. My sister, she's fragile and I worry about her. This place, it reminds her of everything she lost. I keep telling her to sell the damned house, but she won't."

"I can't imagine losing as much as she did," Ryan whispered. "Were you here when it happened?"

Leo shook his head. "No. I was back home in San Francisco. That's our home. It's where we grew up. Lindsay moved here just after college when she met Fred. She loved it here. Said it was quiet, peaceful, and far different from the bustling busyness of the city. I didn't go to college, instead I worked construction and eventually opened up my own construction business." He took the cloths from Ryan, folding them into a triangle, and set them next to the plates. "I was on a job when Aimee called me."

"Aimee called you?"

Leo nodded. "God, she was so scared. Said there was someone in the house, and then I heard all this yelling, then the screams... then nothing."

"Oh my God. Leo, were you on the phone when..."

Leo nodded. "I will never forget how I felt when I heard her scream. I tried calling Charles, the police, but I couldn't get through. There had been some major accident, and they were backlogged. By the time I got there, the police were there, and the kids were being taken to the police station. I lost most of my family that day."

Ryan nodded, not entirely sure what he could say. What was there to say?

"I was at the police station for a while. Longer than I expected," Leo continued, taking a seat at the table. "When I got to the hospital, and saw Lindsay..." He ran a hand over his face, shaking his head. "God. She was so beaten up. She'd fought back, but not without consequence. The doctors never thought she'd make it, but Lindsay has always been strong. She defied the odds, even if she doesn't have any memory of that night. When I had to break the news about her husband, the kids..." He shook his head. "It was the hardest thing I've ever had to do. When she was released from the hospital, I took her out of this damned town. I moved her in with me and made sure she saw a shrink. I drove her to every single one of her therapy sessions."

"And the killer was never found?"

Leo shook his head. "I kept tabs with the police here, and I knew about Neil's knife, but when news broke out about his death overseas, I knew it wasn't over. I was so scared that whoever had done this, would come back for Lindsay. But years went by, and no one ever came for her. Eventually, I started to let down my guard. I let her go to the coffee shop by herself. I even let her get her own apartment. Then the murders started happening, and she told me she was coming back here. I tried to talk her out of it, but she was determined to come back."

"Why did she come back?"

Leo shrugged. "Closure, maybe? I think on some level she thought if she came back, she might be able to remember that night. That she might be able to help, but she can't. That night is just gone."

Ryan sat in the chair next to him, thinking. "Leo, why did Aimee call you? She could have called Billy's dad. The police. Why you?"

"I asked her the same question, and she wouldn't answer me. Just said it wasn't safe."

Wasn't safe? Ryan thought about that. Why would a thirteen-year-old girl think it wasn't safe to call the police? To call Billy's Dad? Unless she knew something... something that someone didn't want her to know.

He opened his mouth, then closed it, as the women came into the dining room.

"Well. Look at her. Here we are doing all the work, and the men are just sitting around talking," Lindsay said, winking at Ashleigh.

Leo grumbled, rising to his feet, and taking the pan of lasagna from Lindsay. "You're lucky I love you, sis," he said, kissing her cheek.

"Let me take that from you, Ash," Ryan said, taking the salad from her. "You should both sit. Is there anything else we need from the kitchen?"

"There's garlic bread. I can grab it."

"No. Sit. I'll go get it." Ryan disappeared into the kitchen, returning with the garlic bread and another bottle of wine. "This looks delicious, Mrs. Miller."

"Oh please, call me Lindsay," Lindsay said, waving a hand. "We are a very informal family, Ryan."

"Okay, Lindsay." He took a sniff, his mouth suddenly watering. "This bread smells amazing. Did you make it from scratch?"

"Sure did," Lindsay said as the men joined them at the table. "It's my mom's secret recipe. I'll never make any other recipe."

Leo grunted from across the table.

Lindsay laughed, as she passed the salad. "You'll have to excuse my brother. He and our parents didn't get along."

"I wonder why," Leo muttered, as he heaped lasagna onto his plate. "They only remind me every time I saw them that I should settle down. Get married. Have a family. They never understood me, Linds. I never wanted that."

"They were old fashioned, Leo. You know that."

"And they constantly pressured me about going to college. They hated the fact that I dropped out of high school, but I had other dreams. I liked working with my hands and look at me now. I'm a successful businessman."

"They'd be proud of you, Leo," Lindsay said, squeezing his arm. "Just as I am." She turned to Ashleigh. "Ash, you remember my parents, don't you?"

Ashleigh nodded. "I do. They lived in Florida, right?"

"That's correct. They came up twice a year."

"Her parents weren't fond of California," Ashleigh told Ryan. "They said it was too... congested I think is the word they used. As soon as Lindsay and Leo moved out, they were gone."

"They were scared that California was going to drop right into the ocean," Leo said around a mouthful. "And when they came to visit, never failed to remind us that we were doing something wrong."

"Like what?" Ryan asked.

"Like how my children were raised," Lindsay said. "Or how Leo was in debt. Or how I shouldn't have dyed my hair. Little things. I had my issues with them too, but I was able to reconcile with them before they died. Leo, unfortunately, did not."

"I'm sorry to hear that they passed," Ashleigh said. "How long ago?"

"About five years ago. After the incident, they came by to check on me. Mom didn't want me getting my own place, but I put my foot down. Told her that I was not going to live my life in fear. That I had already lost so much, and that I would not lose any more. It seemed it was something they both needed to hear. I laid into them about Leo too. They didn't talk to me for a couple years, then a year before they both died we started talking on the phone. They flew up once a month, and we had lunch. It was nice, until they both died peacefully in their sleep, together."

"At least they were together when they died," Ashleigh said, pushing her food around the plate.

"Everything okay, dear?" Lindsay asked, glancing over at Ashleigh. "Is the food okay?"

"Oh, the food fantastic," Ashleigh said. "Just, hearing about your parents, it makes me think of my own."

Lindsay nodded. "Yes, I heard about what happened. I'm sorry you're going through all that, Ashleigh."

"I just keep thinking about my childhood," Ashleigh whispered. "My father. He was a nice man."

"He really wasn't, Ashleigh."

She raised her head, looking at Lindsay. "What?"

"Your father, he was a jealous son of a bitch, and when he got jealous, he got mean." Lindsay sat back in her chair, taking a sip of her wine. "I remember back in high school, he was always around. The six of us girls, we were close. We did everything together and your mom... well everyone wanted her, but she only had eyes for one man."

"Billy's father."

Lindsay raised a brow. "You know about that?"

"Just found out. I found a photo in the attic."

"Ahh. That makes sense. Well, when your mother and Charles started dating, Neil went crazy with jealousy. He stalked her. Sent her flowers. Love letters, then he set his sights on each of us. Neil... he had this way of getting whatever he wanted, and he wasn't afraid to get his hands dirty to do it."

"Like blackmail?" Ryan asked.

"Among other things. We weren't exactly stellar human beings when we were in high school. We were mean, stuck up, and thought we were better than everyone else. We got into our share of trouble, and we made some very bad decisions."

"So you each... dated my father?"

Lindsay nodded. "Among other things, and then our senior year Mary got pregnant." She shook her head. "When she passed out in the middle of cheer practice, it scared all of us. She didn't wake up until she was in the hospital. That's when she found out she was pregnant. When she told Charles, it did not go over well. He wanted nothing to do with the child, even threw money at her to get it taken care of."

"He wanted her to get an abortion?"

Lindsay nodded. "Mary even considered it. She was seventeen years old. She'd be giving birth just before graduation and she didn't think she'd be able to care for it. To give it what it needed, then when she heard the heartbeat, everything changed. She was going to keep the baby. She was so happy, but with pregnancy came the hormones. She was crying one day, freaking out, and that's when Neil swooped in. She confided in him, comforted her, and two months later they were married."

"Oh. Wow."

"We were all skeptical over it," Lindsay continued. "We didn't like Neil. We didn't trust him, but Mary defended them. Said he was there, when Charles refused to be. That Neil was sweet. Kind. That is, until the baby was born."

"What happened when the baby was born?"

"The birth was hard on Mary. She'd lost a lot of blood, and almost died on the table. She was in recovery for a few days, but when she woke, the baby was gone."

"Where'd it go?"

Lindsay fiddled with her cloth. "Neil gave it away."

"What? How? Where?"

"I told you. Neil had a way of getting what he wanted, and what he'd always wanted was Mary. He did not want a reminder of her and Charles. So, one night, he brought some papers to her, saying it was some sort of business proposal, but he needed her help financing it. She didn't bother to read it, just signed it. Only to find out several months later that the papers were giving up her rights as a parent. Charles had already signed his, and the baby was put up for adoption."

"Oh my God."

"Mary did everything she could to find him. She tried to fight, even hired a lawyer to get her rights back. Unfortunately, Neil was too powerful, and nothing she did worked. She lost her son because of him. After that, she threatened to leave him. Divorce him, but Neil wouldn't allow it. Said she was his now, and if she did anything against his wishes, he would make her pay. After that day, Mary was essentially a prisoner inside her own home. She did what he did without question. She bared the brunt of his wrath. He beat her if someone looked at her the wrong way. He forced himself on her. She eventually ran away, finding herself in the arms of Charles once more, and once again, she became pregnant."

"With Billy."

Lindsay nodded. "Yes. She was so scared. She didn't want to lose another child because of him. This time, Charles was there for her. He was all set to kill Neil for her, but we convinced him not to. Neil knew too many people. If he knew Mary and Charles had been sneaking behind his back, he'd surely kill him. So together, we got Mary a new identity and sent her off to Florida. That's where she had the baby, and when he was born, she gave him to Charles and Denise. Said it was the best thing for him. Then she went back to Neil. She made up some extravagant tale about how she'd been in an accident and had been recovering. The next thing we knew, she was pregnant with you, then Callie, and finally Sadie."

"So, she stayed with him."

"I don't think she had a choice. Once you were born, she wanted to protect you. Which is why she signed him up for the army."

"To get some space from him."

"Exactly, but before Callie was born, he was honorably discharged. He came home, and he was even worse than before. There was one night, she showed up bloodied and bruised on Charles's doorstep. He took her in, took care of her, but Neil found her there. He beat Charles so badly, he was in the hospital for weeks. Eventually your mom turned to drugs, and that's why Sadie was born with the heart defect."

"I can't believe I never saw what a monster he was," Ashleigh whispered.

"That's because she never wanted you to know. She wanted you to have good memories of your father, which is why she went to Dr. Pollard in the first place."

Ashleigh's eyes widened. "You know about Dr. Pollard?"

"We all did. His face was everywhere. On every billboard. On every magazine. Even on television. That's how Mary got the idea to plant good memories of your father in your brain. It was the first of two times she used the doctor. The other time..."

"Was after the massacre."

Lindsay nodded. "We tried to talk her out of it. Both times, but Mary was adamant that it was the right thing to do, and eventually, she convinced everyone to do it as well. Your mother, after everything she went through, wasn't the same person I grew up with. She... she turned out to be just like him. Conniving. Obsessed, and she had ways of getting what she wanted."

"This. This is crazy!" Ashleigh cried, staring at her with wide eyes.

"Except, there's more, Ashleigh." Lindsay poured herself another glass of wine, taking a long sip. "You have a half-sister out there."

Chapter Forty - Six

Ashleigh swallowed, slowly nodding. "Yes. I know."

Lindsay arched a brow. "You know?"

Ashleigh nodded. "Yes. When we were in the house, I had a memory come back. Of my parents arguing, and my mother said something about my father having another kid."

Lindsay nodded. "Yes. That's correct. It happened while he was in the army. A fellow female soldier and he had an affair, which resulted in a child. A child, that's just a couple years younger than you, actually. She came to visit your mother, when your father was arrested for the murders."

"What did she want?"

"To prove your father's innocence. She had proof that your father was with her at the time of the murders, but all your mother could think about was her revenge."

"And protecting Billy."

Lindsay smiled. "You know about that too?"

"I've done a lot of searching the last twenty-four hours," Ashleigh said, smiling at Ryan as he took her hand and gave it a light squeeze. "I am surprised that you know, though."

"Are you kidding? The women were yapping about everything in my hospital room. They thought I was sleeping, but I heard everything."

"And you didn't go to the police?"

"Why would I? Billy was like a son to me. I knew he wasn't capable of murder. There's not a mean bone in that boy's body."

"What happened with that woman and my mother?"

Lindsay smiled. "Oh, you know your mother. She, in no kind terms, told the woman to get out of this town, and if she ever came back, she'd ruin her."

"My mother was not a woman to mess with."

"Even more so back then," Lindsay said. "Your mother always had your interests at heart, Ashleigh. It's why she went to such great lengths to keep this all under wraps. We all did. Including myself." She swallowed. "I didn't leave town right away, Ashleigh, as much as Leo wanted me to. I still had funeral arrangements to make, but those were all put on hold the day your father escaped from Charles." She shook her head. "When Neil was cleared of all charges, Charles was furious. He was livid at the things Neil had done to him. To Mary, and even though legally Charles couldn't arrest him, he had to do something. Which is why he kidnapped Neil and brought him to an isolated location. He, Sully, and Mary all had a plan. That they would torture him, drive him insane, so that the only thing Neil could do was confess to the murders. Only when he escaped, it was worse than any of them could had imagined. The electroshock messed with his brain, and soon we had a killer on our hands."

"They told you?" Ryan asked.

"Sully confided in the rest of us. What they planned. It was taking a toll on him. Sully was a good man. Honorable, and he always tried to do the right thing. He knew Mary and Charles were taking it too far, but then while he was with us, he got a call from Charles. That Neil had escaped. The first person he visited was Mary, and, he went after you."

Ashleigh gasped.

"He nearly killed you," Lindsay whispered. "He was so set on his revenge, on what he'd turned into, he nearly strangled you to death. Mary saved you. She fought him, hitting him over the head with a frying pan. She had no idea how long he'd be unconscious, but she couldn't stay there. She was three months pregnant with Sadie, so she did the only thing she could. She asked if I'd watch you kids while she dealt with Neil."

"What happened?"

Lindsay shook her head. "By the time Mary got back to the house, your father was gone. Several hours later, several men and women were found dead inside their home. Stabbed. Then he came for Mary. He chased her all the way to the lake, where Charles met them. There was a big showdown. Charles was stabbed multiple times, and it was by sheer luck that he was able to get the shots off. Neil fell into the lake, and that's when the men showed up. They dragged Neil out of the lake, cleaned his wounds, and dressed him in his army uniform. Then they dumped him back in the lake, hoping the body would show up somewhere. Except, it never did."

"I can't believe you knew all this and didn't tell anyone."

"We made a pact," Lindsay said. "And if anyone broke it, or even considered going to the police Mary had no trouble putting us back in line. Just look at what happened to Wes."

"Wait. Are you saying..."

"That your mother framed Wes?" Lindsay nodded. "You bet she did."

"Oh my God. That's terrible! She ruined his family. She caused the rift between him and Nikki. She..." She trailed off, raising her head, as the lights flickered. She stared up at the chandelier, fear washing through her, as a loud, scraping noise sounded outside just seconds before the lights went out.

"He's here," she whispered, looking at the people at the table around her. "He's here, and my guess is that he knows that Lindsay helped cover up everything. He doesn't just want me. He wants her dead, too."

Chapter Forty - Seven

The doorknob rattled on the front door, and Ashleigh jumped to her feet. "We don't have a lot of time," she said. "Leo. You need to get Lindsay out of here now!"

"How?" Leo asked, glancing over his shoulder, nervously. "Ashleigh. He's killed dozens of people. What makes you think we can outrun him?"

"Because there's one thing he wants more than Lindsay," Ashleigh said. "Me."

"What?" Ryan swung toward her. "Ashleigh, no! You are not using yourself as bait."

"We don't have a choice, Ryan," Ashleigh told him. "I will not let anyone else die on my watch."

She turned, hurrying through the kitchen. She grabbed Leo's keys, and Lindsay's purse, shoving them into their hands. "Leo. Take Lindsay and wait by the door to the garage. When you hear me say the word, you are to get in your car and drive out of here as fast as you can." She returned to the kitchen, rummaging through the cupboards, before wrapping her hand around the handle of a heavy, iron frying pan. She returned to the dining room, handing it to Ryan. "Ryan, you're going to stand behind the cabinet in the corner. When I say the word, you're going to hit him as hard as you can over the head with it. Hopefully, it can give us some time."

"Linds, come on. We need to listen to her." Leo helped Lindsay out of her chair and lead her toward the door that led to the garage. They disappeared from sight, and Ashleigh looked at Ryan. "You ready for this?"

"Hell no!" Ryan cried, staring down at the frying pan in his hands. "Ash." He raised his head, looking at her. "What's the word?"

Ashleigh smiled. "Tiger."

"Leo! Lindsay! Did you hear that?"

Leo ducked his head around the corner. "Tiger. Got it."

He disappeared again, and Ashleigh gestured to Ryan. He hurried across the living room, ducking behind the cabinet, and Ashleigh hurried across the room to the recliner. She angled it, so it was facing the front door and took a seat.

Seconds went by. Minutes, then, suddenly, the front door slammed open. She jumped, as it bounced off the wall. Pictures rattled, dropping and shattering as they hit the ground. She gripped the sides of the chair, listening as his footsteps thumped down the hall. He rounded the corner, and she lifted her head. "Hello, Clowney."

He stopped, a grin spreading across his lips. "Well, well, look at what we have here." He strode forward, dropping down in front of her, and raised his knife. He ran a finger down the blade, reaching out and cupping her chin in his hand. "I've missed you, Doll."

Ashleigh jerked free from his grasp, rising to her feet and walking away from him. She stared across the room, then back at the clown. "I know why you're here," she said. "I know everything."

"So, you finally understand why I'm doing all of this."

"Understand? No." Ashleigh shook her head. "I will never understand why one person would want to inflict so much harm on everyone, but I do understand why you did what you did to us inside the manor." She swallowed. "You tortured each one of us, just like my father was tortured."

"Very good."

"And now you're here for Lindsay."

"The bitch as to die."

"Hasn't she been through enough already?" Ashleigh asked, turning and walking around the room. "She lost her whole family. She doesn't remember that night, and she barely survived. She'll forever walk with a limp. She'll never see out of her left eye again. Please, I'm begging you. Let her go."

"Oh, Ashleigh. You know I can't do that." The clown wandered around the living room, stopping with his back turned to the cabinet. "Because a..."

"Tiger can never change its stripes."

The clown raised a head, frowning. "Tiger? Isn't it..."

The door slammed shut in the kitchen, and the clown froze. "You little bitch. You think you can fool me!" He turned just as Ryan stepped out from behind the cabinet, swinging the frying pan and striking the clown over the head. He crumbled to the ground.

"Ryan! Come on. We have to go!" She grabbed his hand, turning and racing through the kitchen. They stepped through the door, just as the garage door slid open and Leo backed out at a neck-breaking speed. He glanced at Ashleigh, giving her a nod, before shifting the car into gear and racing down the road. They disappeared from sight, and she let out a breath. "They're gone. Come on. Let's get the hell out of here."

"I couldn't agree more."

They trotted down the steps, racing across the lawn, and a loud crash sounded behind them. They turned, glancing over their shoulders, as the clown crashed through the window. He landed on the ground in front of them, grinning at them.

"That was smart, Ashleigh," the clown said, as he rose to his feet. "Distracting me so they could get away. Your boyfriend, hitting me over the head with a frying pan. You got what you wanted. I can't get to Lindsay, but I can get you."

He lunged forward, raising his knife in the air.

"No!"

Ryan lunged forward, wrapping his arms around the clown and tackling him to the ground. "Ash! Run!"

"Ryan! Watch out!"

Ashleigh screamed as the clown jabbed the knife forward. Ryan dodged the blade and the clown took advantage. He flipped Ryan over, slamming him to the ground. Ryan groaned, his head hitting the turf with a loud thud.

"Heroic, aren't we, Quarterback?" the clown said, grinning. "Stupid though. You just signed your own death warrant." He raised the knife, and Ryan blinked. He shook his head, trying to clear his vision.

"Ryan! Move!"

His vision cleared, the knife coming toward him, and he jerked his knee up. He struck the clown in the groin, and the knife landed in the ground just inches from his head.

The clown yelped, writhing in pain, and Ryan grabbed him by the shoulders, tossing him off of him. He jumped to his feet, striding toward the clown. "Tell us where Billy is," he said, grabbing the clown by the back of the neck and dragging him to his feet.

The clown laughed. "Never."

Ryan slammed his fist into his face.

The clown's head jerked back, and he laughed, spitting blood.

"How about now?" Ryan asked.

"Nope."

Again, Ryan's fist slammed into his face. And again. And again. Still, the clown refused to answer.

"You think this is a game, asshole?" Ryan asked. "Tell us where they are, or I swear I'll kill you."

"You won't kill me. You need me. You'll never find them if I'm dead." The clown said, spitting more blood.

Ryan's fist punched forward, and the clown ducked. He lunged forward, smacking his head against Ryan's. Ryan gasped, stumbling back. He fell to his knees as the clown ripped the knife from the turf. He raised the knife.

"Get away from him!"

Ashleigh raced forward, jumping onto his back. She clawed at his eyes, and he yelped, swearing as he tried to dislodge her. He reached behind him, and Ashleigh screamed as he tossed her across the lawn. She gasped, her body hitting the ground with a loud thunk.

"Oh. Ow." She stumbled to her feet, as the clown withdrew an item from his pocket. He held it in his hand, pressing the button. He swung the whip, catching Ryan in the side of the head. Ashleigh screamed, watching as he crumbled to the ground. "Ryan!"

The clown turned, striding toward her. Ashleigh turned, racing across the lawn. She stumbled, falling, just as she reached the steps to the front porch of the Millers' house. She reached into the garden just to her left, grabbing a handful of dirt.

The clown came up on her, and she turned, tossing a handful of dirt in his face.

"Ahh!"

He screamed, clawing at his eyes, and Ashleigh raced up the steps of the porch, grabbing the flowerpot. She turned, just as he raced up after her.

"Not today, asshole," she said, raising the pot and bringing it down over his head.

He crumpled to the ground, and she turned, racing across the lawn.

"Ryan!" She dove forward, falling next to him. "Ryan! Wake up!"

"Ash?" Ryan groaned, staring up at her.

"Ryan! You have to get up!" Ashleigh cried, pulling his arm. "I knocked him out, but I'm not sure how much time we have." She glanced over her shoulder, back toward the house. A gasp escaped her lips when she saw the spot he'd been lying in just moments ago now empty. "Ryan. We have to go. Now!"

She dragged him to his feet, and they turned, racing across the lawn.

"Sadie! Callie!"

She stumbled up the steps of the deck, slamming her fist against the glass door.

Sadie looked up from the book she was reading, racing forward and sliding the door open. "Ash? Ryan? What the hell happened?"

"The clown. He's here!" Ashleigh cried as they raced inside the door. She slammed the door shut, staring across the lawn. She spotted movement on top of the roof of the Millers' house, and she blinked. Staring at the clown as he looked right at her, grinning, before disappearing from sight.

"Ash."

"What?" She turned, a gasp escaping her lips, when she saw blood oozing from Ryan's side. "Oh my God. Ryan!"

She fell next to him, rolling his shirt up, and staring at the stab wound. "Ryan! You've been stabbed!"

"Yeah. It hurts like a son of a bitch."

"Callie. Go get the first aid kit," Ashleigh said, as she grabbed a towel from the pile on the table, pressing it to the wound.

"I got it!" Callie raced into the room, handing it to her. Ashleigh took it, rifling through the supplies. "Sadie, hold this to the wound. I need to wash my hands."

"What are you going to do?" Sadie asked, her eyes full of worry.

"I'm going to wash my hands, then I'm going to give him some stitches."

"What?" Ryan winced, as he jerked his head up. "Ash..."

"I'm a med student, Ryan. One thing I know how to do is stitches." She returned, going through the process of cleaning the wound, then she grabbed the needle and thread.

"This is going to hurt. Like, a lot," she said, locking eyes with him, then she glanced at her sisters."And when I'm done, we are all getting out of this damned town."

Chapter Forty - Eight

One week later...

"Come on, Tigers! Protect your quarterback!"

Ashleigh cupped her hands over her mouth, screaming the words amongst the hundreds of fans in attendance. It was the first game of the season, and things were not looking good.

She winced, watching, as Ryan took another hit. The ball slipped out of his hands and everyone made a mad dash for the football as it spun on the ground.

"No!"

"Boo!"

The fans around her voiced their displeasure, and Ashleigh sighed, shaking her head. *This was not good.*

"They're not looking so good, sis," Sadie said from next to her, taking a bite from her hot dog.

No shit, Ashleigh thought, breathing a sigh of relief when Levi landed on the football. *Whoo! At least they still had possession of the ball. Even if they did lose like fifteen yards.*

"Your man is looking like a damned piñata out there!" Callie shouted around a mouthful of popcorn.

That was putting it mildly, Ashleigh thought, as she watched the offense huddle up. It was only the second quarter, and the Tigers were already down twenty-one to three. Ryan had been sacked six times, and no one was getting open. If things didn't turn around soon, it was going to be a very, long second half.

The team broke the huddle and she pressed her hands together, holding them to her lips. She closed her eyes, sending out a silent prayer. Things had been quiet for the last week, ever since they'd had their encounter with the clown. She shook her head, remembering trying to convince Ryan to take it easy while his wound had healed. Trying to get a football player to take it easy was no easy task.

After they'd left Sarasota Bay, the four of them had taken up residence in her small townhouse, and they'd all gotten into a nice routine, but Billy was still missing. It had been weighing on all of them. One thing she didn't mind though, was waking up next to Ryan every morning.

She caught him glancing in their direction, as he fastened the chin strap to his helmet. He sent her a wink, and Ashleigh blushed.

"He's good for you," Callie whispered in her ear. "And you two are sooo cute together!"

"They could tone down on the PDA though," Sadie put in. "Eww! Like, get a room!"

"Oh, shut up." Ashleigh elbowed her, grinning, not going to deny she was the happiest she'd ever been. "Let's focus on the game."

The ball snapped, and she held her breath as the linebackers rushed forward. They broke through, headed straight for Ryan. Ryan swerved, dodging one linebacker, then another before drawing his arm back and letting the ball rip.

It sailed through the air, seeming to hang in the air forever, before landing right into Jacob's hands.

"Yes!" she shouted as he raced down the sideline. "Go! Go! Go!"

He tucked the ball under his arm, swerving around one defender, breaking another tackle, then a collective gasp echoed through the stands as the safety came barreling out of nowhere. He lunged forward, wrapping his arms around Jacob and tackling him hard to the ground.

Jacob's head bounced off the ground, and a sickening snap could be heard, as his arm twisted awkwardly.

"Jacob!"

She screamed, watching as he lay there unmoving. "Oh no. That does not look good."

"You think he's okay?" Sadie asked as she looked on.

Ashleigh shook her head. "I don't know."

"I think I saw him move," Callie said, as the rest of the team raced toward Jacob. She saw Ryan drop down next to him before he was pushed aside by the medical team. Several moments passed, then finally, she saw Jacob sit up.

"Oh, thank God," she whispered, watching as he was helped to his feet, hugging his left arm to his chest. "But his arm..."

"Let's just wait and see what the doctors say," Callie said. "It might not be as bad as it looks."

They could only hope, Ashleigh thought, because the team was going to need him.

She watched him disappear into the locker room with the medical staff, turning her attention back to the game just as Ryan threw his second interception of the half.

"Dammitt!"

Ashleigh threw her hands up in frustration, watching as the clock ran down to zero. *Well, at least it's halftime.*

She watched as Ryan stomped off the field, throwing his helmet down in frustration. He glanced up at her again, and she sent him a small wave. He gave her a nod, before disappearing into the locker room.

"Poor Ryan. I think he's going to need some consoling after the game," Callie said, laughing. "Oh! I have to pee. I'll be back in a bit."

"Wait. I'm coming with you!" Sadie cried, hurrying after her.

"Be careful!" Ashleigh shouted as they disappeared from sight. She took a seat, scrolling through her phone. It seemed everyone was checking in on her.

Addison: Have fun at the game!

Nikki: Eat lots of food and stay loud!

Sydney: Any news yet? I'm getting worried.

Then there were her coworkers.

Steph: Girl. I need a girl's night. Drinks after work?

Vinny: Come ready to work. It's going to be madness tonight!

She responded to the texts, slipping the phone back into her pocket as the football teams came back onto the field. She rose to her feet, cheering with the rest of the crowd. The ball kicked off, and they were off again.

"Yeah!" she shouted, as the defense sacked the quarterback. "That's the way we want to start!" A tipped ball and an incomplete ended the series. A quick three and out. It was exactly what the team needed.

After a quick break, the offense took the field, and boy, did they look like a different team. Ashleigh yelled, jumping up and down, as Devante broke through the line, rushing for ten yards. "Yes!" She pumped her fist in the air, another shout escaping her throat as Ryan passed over the middle to a wide-open Rome. Another hand off to Devante went another three yards, and four plays later Ryan found Levi in the end zone for a touchdown.

"Touchdown, Tigers!"

"Yes!"

She screamed as the loudspeaker blared through the stadium, clapping her hands together as Ryan fist-pumped his teammates. They hurried back to the sideline, big grins on their faces as they celebrated together. Maybe things were finally turning around.

She turned, stopping, when she saw the spots next to her empty. Callie and Sadie weren't back yet?

A chill raced down her spine. She grabbed her phone, lifting it to her ear. "Callie, where are you? The third quarter just started."

"Hello, Ashleigh."

She froze. The familiar dark, raspy voice coming across the line. It was him.

"What did you do to them?"

"Oh, nothing, yet."

"Ashleigh!"

"Don't do it!"

She heard her sisters screaming in the background, and she clenched her fingers around the phone. "What do you want?"

"You know what I want."

Ashleigh blew out a breath, staring across the field at Ryan. He was going to be so pissed, but she didn't have a choice. People were counting on her. If she didn't go, people would die. She could not allow that to happen.

"Where do you want me to meet you?"

The clown laughed. "Oh, that's easy, Ashleigh. Meet me where it all started."

Chapter Forty - Nine

Twenty minutes later, Ashleigh. braked the car to a stop at the top of the hill, staring at the empty field before her.

"What the hell?"

She exited the vehicle, hoping Ryan wouldn't be too pissed that she'd stolen his vehicle. Wait, not stolen. Borrowed.

She made her way down the hill, staring across the empty field. Captain Vargas had warned her about this. He'd said the manor had disappeared, but it had to be here somewhere. He wouldn't have wanted her to meet her here if it wasn't.

She glanced around her, her eyes dropping to the escape door that lead to the sewer. It was how they'd escaped. She was definitely in the right spot.

She walked forward, lifting the door, and a loud rumble filled her ears. She turned, glancing over her shoulder as the ground suddenly shook. The ground gave away, and moments later she found herself watching as the manor rose from where it had been under the ground.

"You and your damned mind games," Ashleigh muttered under her breath, as she stared at the manor as it stood before her. She'd hoped she'd seen the last of it.

She drew her phone from her pocket, lifting it. No signal. Great. It looked like she was on her own.

She took a step forward, then another Until she reached the door. She reached a hand forward, her fingers wrapping around the circular, black handle and dragging it open. The moment the door opened, dust spewed around her, and she ducked her head, coughing, before flipping on the flashlight on her phone. She stepped inside, and almost immediately the panel in front of her slid open to reveal a television.

I'm feeling a sense of de ja vu here, Ashleigh thought as the television flicked on, the clown filling the screen.

"Hello, Ashleigh."

Ashleigh rolled her eyes. "Could you be any less predictable?"

The clown laughed. "What can I say? The first time was so much fun, I wanted to do it again."

"Just let them go. Please. You have what you want. You have me, so, please, just let them go."

"But then we wouldn't be able to play the game."

"I'm sick of your damned games!"

"And you, don't have a choice. Again."

The clown disappeared, six separate camera feeds filling the screen instead. She gasped, staring at the familiar faces as they filled the screen. They looked terrified, and they were bruised and bloody. Each of them bound to chairs in their respective rooms.

"Do we really have to do this again?" she asked, swallowing.

"Indeed, we do," the clown said, grinning as he filled the screen once more. "But, before you begin, get rid of your phone."

Behind her, the tile in the floor slid open, revealing the dark depths far below. Above her, another panel opened, and she watched as a rifle lowered, aiming toward her.

"Now, Ashleigh."

She sighed, tossing her phone through the panel.

"And the keys too."

She scowled, pulling them from her pocket and tossing them through the opening.

"Very good." The panel slid closed. "Now, go find your friends, Ashleigh, and then the fun can really begin."

The screen faded to black.

Fucking assclown.

Ashleigh turned, making her way down the hallway. She disappeared inside the doorway to her left. *The weapon room.* It was the same room she'd woken up when she'd first been brought here, only, this time she was not going to go through this damned place without some sort of weapon.

She scanned the room, her gaze going from weapon to weapon, before landing on the axe that lay inside the glass cabinet. She strode forward, pulling the handle.

Locked.

You didn't think it would be that easy, did you, Ash?

She glanced around the room, looking for something to break the glass with. Finding nothing, she knew she only had one option.

She turned, and struck her elbow out, slamming it through the glass.

She yelped, tears filling her eyes as the sharp glass cut through her flesh. Blood streaked down her arm, but she pushed past the pain, instead reaching for the axe. She pulled it free from the cabinet, clutching the weapon in her hands. Then she grabbed the lighter sitting on the shelf and slipped it into her back pocket. Just in case.

She turned, making her way back toward the door. She paused in the doorway, peering first left, then right. Finding the coast clear, she scampered toward the door laying just across the hall from her. She shoved it open, hurrying inside, and slammed it shut behind her. She blew out a breath, clutching the axe in her hands, and she froze when she saw the metal, rectangular table sitting in the middle of the room. It was the interrogation room.

She shoved her away from the door, passing the table, the large mirror that sat along the wall, and gasped when she saw the cells laying on the far side of the room.

"Ashleigh?"

She walked around the first cell, walking down the path between two other cells, before finding the owner of the voice.

"Marcus?"

Ashleigh stopped in front of the cell, staring at Marcus as he lay hunched in the corner. "Oh my God!" She quickly undid the chain, throwing the door open and racing inside. She leaned the axe against the wall, pulling the handkerchief from his mouth. "I am so sorry!" she cried, as she untied him. "Are you okay? Did he hurt you?"

"I'm fine," Marcus said, as he staggered to his feet. "Billy took the brunt of most of his anger."

"Oh, God."

"Guess you pissed him off real good."

Ashleigh winced, not liking that Billy had suffered for what she'd done.

"Marcus, you should get out of here," she said, picking up the axe and making her way back toward the door. "It's not safe here."

"If anyone should be getting out of here, it's you," Marcus said, as he followed her. "He's going to kill you, Ashleigh."

"I know, but I can't leave. He'll kill them. I can't let that happen."

"Then I'm going to help you."

Ashleigh raised a brow. "Why?"

Marcus shrugged. "I kind of owe you. Plus, we'll get everyone out of here quicker if we work together."

"Can't argue with that."

They exited the room and made their way out into the hallway. Above them, the lights flickered, and Ashleigh raised her head as a television lowered from above them. It flicked on, the image of two young girls running through a field filling the screen.

Aimee and Meredith.

She stared at the image, as it flashed across the screen. The sound of their laughter filled the air around her and behind her, a noise sounded. She spun around, just as Billy stumbled around the corner.

"Billy!"

She raced forward, sliding to a stop when she spotted a shadow just behind him. "Billy! Watch out!"

She screamed as the clown appeared behind him. He lunged forward, just as Billy turned, striking the knife through Billy's chest.

"No! Billy!"

She raced forward, watching as the clown disappeared through the open wall just behind Billy. His giggles filled the air as the wall closed behind him.

"Oh my God. Billy…"

Ashleigh fell to her knees next to him, staring at the blood oozing from his chest. "How did you even get out here?" she asked, as she pressed her hands to the wound. She had to try to stop the bleeding. He'd die if she didn't.

"I wanted to get to you… before he did," Billy gasped out. "I had to get to you. He's going to kill you, Ashleigh. He's going to kill all of us, and then he'll go after the others. I can't let that happen. I…I have to protect you. You're… you're like family to me."

"I know," Ashleigh whispered, gripping his hand. "And we are family, Billy. You're my brother."

Billy gasped in surprise, blinking. "I..." He blinked. "Ash. I need you to promise me something." He tightened his grip around her hand.

"Anything."

"If... if I don't make it out of here I need you to tell Addy..." He trailed off, his eyes drifting closed.

"Wait! Billy, no. Don't close your eyes!" She shook him. "Billy! Please, wake up!"

"I don't think he's going to be waking up any time soon, Ashleigh," Marcus said from behind her.

"He has to," Ashleigh whispered. "There's so much I have to tell him."

"You'll have plenty of time to talk. After all, it won't be long until you'll be joining him."

Click.

The sound echoed in her ears, and Ashleigh froze. She turned, staring at the gun Marcus had aimed at her. "Marcus." She raised her hands in the air, slowly rising to her feet. "Please. I need to help him. He'll die if I don't."

"He's already dead. You all are." He cocked the trigger.

"Please. Marcus, don't do this! We need one another if..." She froze, staring at him. "Wait a minute. You... you're working with him aren't you?"

"And she finally figures it out." Marcus grinned. "After all, he can't very well be in two places at once, can he?"

"But why?"

"For revenge."

Ashleigh stared at him. "For your mother?"

Marcus's eyes narrowed. "So, you know about that?"

"Addy told me. She said you and your father were arguing about her."

"The bitch should learn to keep her mouth shut," Marcus said, his eyes flashing. "Your mother and her friends, they were poison. They had this way of making you feel special and then tossing you away like you were nothing."

"That's what happened to your mother?"

"Of course it did. Your mother and her friends were nothing but predictable," Marcus said.

"Sounds like you have a lot of hatred inside of you, Marcus."

"I grew up without a mother. What the hell do you expect?"

"What happened, Marcus?"

"I was six months old," Marcus said. "And my mother was in her first year of college at the small college in Sarasota Bay. She and my dad had moved to the small town right after graduation. Just before she gave birth to me. It was there, that she met Mary and her friends. It started innocent enough. Just a group of girls hanging out, until the night they had a girls' night at Mary's house. When Stacy found my mother and Neil talking quietly upstairs."

"Oh no."

"Stacy told Mary and Mary immediately cornered my mom, demanding to know what she was talking to Neil about. That's when my mother told her the truth. That she had been the one to help smuggle her child out of the hospital."

Ashleigh gasped.

"Mary was livid. Betrayed. She tossed my mother out of the house, and they refused to have anything to do with her. My mother tried everything to make things right. Then, she tracked down the baby. She called Mary, told her to meet her at the Sarasota Bay bridge. When Mary and her friends got there, they found my mother already drunk. She was crying, sobbing. She apologized over and over again, telling them she had no choice. That she'd needed the money. She was standing on top of the bridge, and she lost her balance. She fell, her body splattering across the pavement."

"Oh, God! Marcus... how... how did you find out?"

"My father. He finally had the balls to tell me about it a month ago, and when the clown appeared, asking for my help I couldn't say no."

"When... when did he ask you for help?"

Marcus smiled. "Before you were kidnapped."

"So, you... you..."

"Helped kidnap you? Yes."

"And that night at the party?"

Marcus grinned again. "Just making sure you stayed exactly where we wanted you. Only. We didn't plan on Ryan."

"You're sick!"

"Nah. I just know how to go after what I want." He gestured the gun. "Now come on. Move that pretty, little ass of yours. I don't have all day."

"Oh, I know. The clown is waiting," Ashleigh said, as she started down the hallway, reaching her hand into her pocket.

She wrapped her hand around the lighter. "But you know something, Marcus?"

"What's that?"

"That I don't play by his rules anymore," she said, spinning around and flicking the lighter. He screamed as the flame hit his face, stumbling back, and Ashleigh dove for the axe she'd dropped. She swung around, striking the axe forward. The handle hit him in the head, and he crumpled to the ground in a heap. "Asshole."

"Ashleigh!"

The shout sounded nearby, and Ashleigh jumped to her feet. She raced down the hallway, sliding to a stop at the door toward the end of the hall, a wave of relief washing through her when she saw Callie and Sadie.

"Oh my God! You're alive... and together!"

"He tricked us," Sadie sobbed, as Ashleigh removed the gag from her mouth. "I'm so sorry, Ashleigh."

"You have nothing to be sorry about," Ashleigh told her, as she untied her. "This is all on him."

"He's going to kill you," Callie said, tears running down her cheeks. "I don't want to lose you, Ashleigh."

"You're not going to lose me, Callie," Ashleigh told her, gripping her shoulders. "But I am going to end this."

"You can't!"

"Yes, I can, because I know everything now." The rope fell to the ground, and she pulled Callie in for a hug. "But I need you to do something for me."

"What?"

"Go find Ryan, tell him where I am, and then go to the police."

"But..."

"No. I can't do this with you here. I need you to promise me. Both of you."

They nodded, turning and racing out into the hall. She stepped into the hall behind them, watching as they pushed open the door and disappeared. Then she picked up her axe and walked through the door at the end of the hall.

The pit.

She shoved the door open, the smell of manure instantly filling her senses. She crinkled her nose, staring down into the dark depths.

"Help! Help! Please. Someone help me!"

She gasped, staring at the hand sticking out of the dirt. She raised her head, looking at the dirt that was pouring from above and she hurried toward the door. She lunged forward, pressing the button lying next to the door. The contraption above the pit shut off and she hurried back toward the pit. She gripped the ladder, quickly descending it.

"I'm here!" she cried, jumping down into the pit. "Can you hear me?"

Crap. They'd better not be dead.

She dropped to her knees, digging through the dirt. It seemed like my mutes went by, dread filling her the further she dug when she suddenly saw a hand appear through the dirt. Breathing out a sigh of relief, she wrapped her fingers around their hand and pulled them free from the dirt.

"Andrew?" Her eyes widened in surprise. "What the hell are you doing in here?"

Andrew coughed, shaking his head. "Billy got us free, but the bastard came out of nowhere. He split us up." He coughed again. "You shouldn't be here."

"None of us should be here." Ashleigh rocked back on her heels, studying him. "Andrew, I think I know why he targeted you."

"I'm afraid I don't know what you're talking about, Ashleigh."

"Andrew, you don't have to keep it from me. I know you're one of the Miller boys."

"One of the..." Andrew coughed. "No, Ashleigh, I'm not. I..." He coughed again, struggling to breathe.

"Andrew?" Ashleigh laid a hand on his arm. "You need to breathe. You inhaled a lot of dirt. Who knows what kind of damage it's done to your body."

"I don't have time. I need to get us out of here."

"No. You need to stay here, while I take care of this," Ashleigh told him, as she climbed up the ladder after him.

"No. You can't..."

Whap. Whap.

Gunshots rippled through the air, and Ashleigh screamed as two bullets sailed over her head, striking Andrew in the chest. She spun around.

"Marcus!"

"He was already dead," Marcus said, aiming the gun toward her. "And you know what, screw what the clown said. It's your turn."

He pulled the trigger, and Ashleigh screamed. The gunshot rippled through the air, striking her in the shoulder. She gasped, stumbling back. Her foot slipped on the pavement, and she screamed as she fell backward, falling far below into the pit.

"A perfect ending, wouldn't you say?" Marcus asked, chuckling, just before he pressed the button next to the door. Dirt and manure spewed down from above, and then all she saw was darkness.

Chapter Fifty

Forty-two seconds.

This was what football players lived for. The thrill of the game. The anticipation of the next snap. The suspense. The unknown if they could make the miraculous comeback.

Ryan took his spot behind the center, the roar of the crowd filling his ears, and then silence descended over the stadium. He glanced around at the faces around them, seeing the nervousness in each of their faces. Were they going to be able to do it?

It'd been a shitty day, as far as the first game of the season had gone, but they'd gotten their asses back in gear this quarter. They'd been down twenty-four to ten at halftime. Now, they were just a field goal away from tying the game. The score was thirty-four to thirty-one, and there were forty-two seconds left on the clock.

The ball snapped, and he dropped back. He scanned the field, out of the corner of his eye seeing the defensive end dodging the tackle, heading right for him. He lunged forward, and Ryan swerved, just avoiding the tackle. His eyes went down-field, and he raised his arm, throwing a strike downfield.

Arms wrapped around him, dragging him to the ground. He winced, his body hitting the hard ground with a thud, and sat up, watching as the ball sailed through the air toward Levi. He jumped, grasping the ball in his hands. His feet landed in bounds, he hurtled over the defender and raced down the sideline. Moments later, he dove, landing in the end zone.

"Touchdown, Tigers!"

The clock was at zero.

"Tigers win!"

The intercom blared through the stadium. Cheers filled his ears, as everyone seemed to suddenly come onto the field.

"Ryan! Fuck! That was some throw!" his offensive lineman said, as he dragged him to his feet.

"And some catch!" Ryan shouted as he raced toward the end zone, engulfing Levi in a hug. "We did it, man! We fucking did it!"

"Fuck yeah we did!" Levi shouted, grinning from ear to ear. "Hell of a game!"

"Hell of a game is right!" Ryan shouted back, turning, and scanning the crowd. He withdrew his helmet, looking for Ashleigh and her sisters. His eyes zeroed in on the seats he'd seen them sitting in earlier. They were empty. Where were they?

He shoved through the crowd.

"Ryan!"

He turned, as Jacob pushed through the crowd, racing toward him.

"Holy shit! Ryan, that was awesome!" Jacob shouted, stopping next to him and punching him in the shoulder. "I'm so pissed I couldn't be out there!" He lifted his left arm, showing Ryan the sling. "I might miss most of the season."

"Yeah. I'm sorry about that. That really sucks, man." He scanned the crowd.

"Ryan, everything okay?"

"I'm not sure," Ryan said, turning back to Jacob. "I haven't seen Ashleigh yet. Or her sisters. Have you?"

Jacob shook his head. "No. Not since the first half."

"Jacob..."

"I'll see if I can find her. You get showered and changed."

Ryan nodded, heading for the locker room. Twenty minutes later, he was showered, changed, and reaching for his phone. He unlocked it, frowning.

No signal.

"Hey, Rome. Do you have a signal?"

Rome shook his head, looking up from his phone. "No. You?"

Ryan shook his head.

"That's weird, isn't it?"

"That we both don't have a signal, even though we have different cell phone carriers? Yeah. It's definitely weird."

He reached into the locker, searching his jacket pockets for his keys. What the...

He pulled it out, searching both pockets, then the top shelf of the locker, then the bottom. They were gone.

"What is up with these damned cell phones?" He could hear nearby.

"I can't make any calls," another said.

"Can't send any texts either."

"What the hell is going on?"

He slammed the locker shut. It seemed no one was getting any reception, and that, was a big, red flag to him. Something was going on.

"Ryan!"

The shout sounded as he exited the building. He stopped, scanning the crowd, his eyes landing on Sadie and Callie as they raced toward him.

"Sadie. Callie. Thank God!" A wave of relief washed through him, as he hurried toward them. "I was so worried when I didn't see you." He frowned, scanning the crowd once more. "Where's Ashleigh?"

"He's got her!"

"Who's got her?"

"The clown!" Callie cried, her eyes full of fear. "And he had us!"

"He tricked us," Sadie said, her voice shaking. "He snuck up on us. Said he was an old friend, and the next thing we knew... we were in the manor!"

"Wait. Hold on." Ryan held up a hand. "He captured you two?"

They nodded. "He used us as bait."

"And now she's inside, trying to save everyone!"

"Who's inside?"

"Ashleigh! She found us. She told us to find you... and to get the cops. Ryan! He's going to kill her!"

"Jesus." Ryan rubbed a hand across his face, staring down at the phone. "Shit. That must be why no one can get a signal. He's blocked it. He doesn't want any distractions, because he's got her right where he wants her."

"Ryan!"

"I know." Ryan stared down at the jacket in his arms, shaking his head. "She stole my damned keys."

"What?"

"Ashleigh. She stole my keys. She knew what she was doing. Hell, I admire her for it. She's facing her demons, just to save everyone."

He glanced up as the door opened behind him. "Levi!"

Levi grinned, hurrying over to him, then he quickly sobered. "What's wrong?"

"It's Ashleigh. She's in trouble," Ryan said. "I need your help."

"Of course. What do you need?"

"A ride," Ryan said, turning and starting for the parking lot.

"Okay. Sure, but to where? And why can't you take your car?" He glanced at the two girls trailing them. "And who the hell are they?"

"These are Ashleigh's sisters, Callie and Sadie," Ryan said as they neared Levi's SUV. "And I can't take my car. Ashleigh has it."

"Okay... so where is she?"

"At the manor."

"The *manor?*" Levi's eyes widened. "Ryan..."

"Levi, I don't have time for this," Ryan said, as they got into the car. "Ashleigh's in danger, and I have no way of getting into contact with her. Which is why I need you to take me there. To the manor."

"Ryan..."

"And once you drop me off, I need you to take Callie and Sadie to the police station. Ask for Captain Vargas and get him to the manor as soon as possible."

"Ryan, is that madman..."

Ryan nodded. "He's with her, inside the manor. It's his final showdown, and if we don't hurry, there will be more dead bodies in the morning. Now, can I count on you, Levi?"

"Damn straight you can."

Chapter Fifty - One

Was he gone?

Seconds went by... maybe even minutes, yet she couldn't make out his footsteps leaving. She held her breath, pressing her lips together, nearly gagging from the horrendous smell surrounding her.

"Damned bitch better be dead. I don't have time for this shit."

"What the hell did you do?"

The voice sounded from above and Ashleigh cringed. She'd recognize the voice anywhere.

"I..."

"I specifically told you to leave this up to me! That you were only supposed to lead Ashleigh to me. Now look what you've done. The detective... he's dead! And Ashleigh... where the hell is she?"

"Dead. I hope."

"What?"

Ashleigh lifted her hand, wiping the dirt from her face, peering through the muck to look above her.

"You stupid, stupid boy. She was mine!" The clown shouted, turning and pacing on the platform. "Mine!"

"What is it about her that…"

"Shut your damned mouth!" The clown shouted. "I had a plan and now look at what you've done. You've ruined it!" He stopped, turning to look at Marcus. "Well, I guess I don't need you anymore."

He strode toward the door, pressing another button on the door. Above them a panel opened, a large hook descending from the rafters.

"What's that for?"

"You," the clown said, just before he grabbed him by the shoulders and tossed him over the pit.

Marcus screamed, and Ashleigh gasped, muffling her scream as Marcus's neck caught on the hook, the sharp end plunging through his flesh.

"This is why I work better alone," the clown said, staring down into the pit. "Well. Guess I'm off to North Carolina." He turned, disappearing into the hallway, his footsteps sounding down the hall.

Sydney.

Ashleigh broke free from the dirt, coughing. Dirt spewed from her mouth, and she wiped the back of her hand across her mouth, rising to her feet. She had to stop him. She couldn't let him find Syd, or any of her friends.

"Help..."

The voice sounded above her, and she raised her head, staring up at Marcus. Blood was spewing from his mouth, and he was staring down at her as if begging her to help him.

She glanced up at Marcus, from where he was hanging from the large hook above the pit. The hook had lodged itself in the back of his neck, and blood was spewing from his mouth.

"You made your own bed, Marcus, when you agreed to join forces with a serial killer," Ashleigh said, as she crossed the pit, and climbed up the ladder "You deserved what you got."

She climbed out of the pit, striding toward the small, metal door, and raced through the doorway. The last time she'd been here... she'd been racing to stop a damned saw.

She trotted down the wooden steps, dragging the large door open, and slid to a stop when she saw Gloria sitting at the metal desk sitting in the corner.

"Oh my God. Gloria."

Ashleigh hurried across the room, stopping, and staring down at the shackles around her wrists. Her left one was shackled to the desk, while her right one was raised high in the air, enclosed in the shackle that hung from the chain above. "I am so sorry you got caught up in all of this."

"No. It's my fault, "Gloria said, shaking her head. "I should have never agreed to what he asked me to do."

"What are you talking about?"

"The article I wrote about you and your friends, it wasn't the article I intended to publish," Gloria said. "I had a different one written. One that didn't place blame on the four of you.

One, where I hailed you as an inspiration when you escaped the manor." She shook her head. "But the night before it was set to go to print, the clown paid me a visit in my home. He threatened my husband, my kids, if I didn't publish the one he'd written. I am so sorry, Ashleigh. I couldn't put my family in danger."

"Of course not!" Ashleigh. Ride. "Gloria, your family should come first. I could never blame you for doing what you could to protect them."

"I was going to make things right. Honestly, I was, then he kidnapped me. He... he wants me to write his story, Ashleigh, uh I don't know if I can. He's hurt so many people. He's killed..."

"I know. Trust me." Ashleigh turned away from her, scanning the room. There had to be some way to get the damned shackles off, right? She gazed around the room, stopping when she noticed the tile in the wall. It looked different from the others...

She strode forward, staring at it.

"You're the last piece to the puzzle, Ashleigh."

The clown's words echoed in her head, and she pressed her palm to the tile. A moment later it slid open to reveal the silver key hanging just inside.

"Damned bastard."

She grabbed the key, and a loud roar suddenly filled the air. She jerked her head around, just as the wall on the other side of the room opened. A large ball with spikes slid out from the wall, headed right for Gloria.

Shit.

"Holy shit! Is that..."

"Yes," Ashleigh said, as she raced back to Gloria. She inserted the key in the lock and turned it, breathing out a sigh of relief when she heard the click.

The shackle fell free, and she turned, glancing over her shoulder as the ball seemed to suddenly gain speed, heading right for them.

Shit.

"Hurry!"

"I'm working on it!"

She turned back to Gloria, sticking the key in the lock with shaking fingers. She swore, as she struggled to turn it, then the key slid in the lock. The resounding click filled her ears, and she wrapped her arms around Gloria. "Gloria, I'm sorry about this," she said, before diving for the ground.

Behind them, a loud crash sounded, and she swung around, staring at the desk that now lay broken in the corner.

"Holy crap! That could have been us!" Gloria cried, her eyes wide, as she stared at the mess, gulping.

"It's all part of his game," Ashleigh said, raising to her feet. "Come on. Let's get out of here."

She helped Gloria to her feet, and her eyes went to Gloria's left wrist. "Gloria. What happened to your wrist?" she asked, staring at it, as it lay limply against her chest.

"Pretty sure he broke it," Gloria said, hugging it to her chest. "When I refused to do what he asked, he got mean. Angry."

"We've got to get you out of here. You need a doctor. Like now."

"I'm not the only one who needs a doctor," Gloria said, staring at the blood staining the shoulder of her blouse, then at her banged up elbow. "Have you seen the detectives?"

Ashleigh nodded. "Yes. They're both dead."

"Oh my God! And Marcus?"

Ashleigh scowled. "He was an accomplice to the clown."

"Seriously?"

"Yes."

"The bastard! And your sisters? I think I saw them in here, didn't I?"

"You did, but I managed to get them out. They went to go get help."

"Good. That's good."

They walked through the doorway, trotting up the steps, and Ashleigh stopped in the doorway. She peered into the room, staring inside at the pit. It was quiet. Too quiet.

"Come on." She gestured to Gloria, quickly descending the ladder. "This way."

"I have to go through... that?"

"We both do," Ashleigh said. "Come on."

Gloria stared at her for a minute, then finally, she descended the ladder behind her. She winced, clutching her arm to her chest, and Ashleigh stopped to help her down. They walked across the pit, and up the other ladder.

They stepped up onto the pavement, and Ashleigh headed for the doorway. She peered out into the hallway. "It's clear," she said, and they hurried down the hallway. A moment later a shadow fell across the floor and Ashleigh froze. She turned, looking over her shoulder.

"So, I guess you're not dead," the clown said, as he rounded the corner. He grinned, flipping the knife he held in his hand, before flinging it through the air toward her.

Ashleigh ducked and it sailed over her head.

"Ashleigh…"

A gasp sounded behind her, and she swung around, just as the knife plunged into Gloria's abdomen.

"Gloria!"

Ashleigh screamed, racing toward Gloria. She fell next to her. "I'm so sorry! I didn't mean…"

"I know," Gloria gasped out, staring behind them at the clown as he strode toward them. "But you need to go!"

'What about you?"

"I'll be fine," Gloria gasped out. "But I'm not the one he wants. You are. Now… go!"

Ashleigh stared at her, then glanced back behind her as the clown got closer. Then she did the only thing she could. She ran.

Chapter Fifty - Two

"Ryan, I don't like this."

Levi braked the car to a stop, staring through the passenger window at the manor that lay just a few feet away. "Going in there... it's suicide!"

"I have to go in, Levi," Ryan said, wrapping his hand around the door handle. "Ashleigh's in there, and I can't let her do this alone. She needs me."

Levi sighed, dragging a hand over his face. "Okay. Well, if you're going to insist on doing this, at least take this." He reached into the glove box, wrapping his hand around the gun, and handed it to Ryan.

"Levi, why the hell do you have a gun?"

"I think the better question is, why don't you? We live in LA, Ryan. There's a crime in every corner of this damned city."

"You do have a point." He took the gun from Levi, nodding his thanks, before exiting the vehicle. He stopped, lowering his head to look at Levi.

"Don't leave them alone, Levi."

"Wasn't planning on it."

"And Callie. Sadie. Make sure you tell them everything."

"We will," Callie said, nodding.

"Go help our sister," Sadie added.

"I'll bring her back to you. I promise."

Ryan stepped back, watching as the taillights disappeared into the distance, then he turned and made his way toward the manor. He tucked the gun into the waistband of his jeans, stopping in front of the door. A shudder rippled through him, as he thought of the months Ashleigh and her friends had been held hostage here. Just what was waiting on the other side of the door for him?

He wrapped his hand around the handle, dragging it open, and stepped inside. The door slammed shut behind him, and he started down the hallway. He blinked, his eyes adjusting to the darkness, staring down the long hallway. *Good God.*

Thunk!

He jumped at the sound of the door slamming shut once more. He spun around, grabbing the gun and aiming it toward the door. Whoever was about to sneak up on him, was not going to like what awaited them.

"Wait. Don't shoot!"

The familiar voice sounded from the other end of the hallway, and Ryan frowned, lowering the gun.

"Jacob? What the hell are you doing here?"

"Levi left a note on my car before you guys left. He thought you might need backup."

"Backup? Jacob, this is dangerous! People have been hurt... killed, and you... you only have one good arm!"

"It's just as dangerous for you as it is for me," Jacob said as he neared him. "And I'm just as good with one arm as I am with two." He lifted the crowbar in his hand. "Especially with the help of this. Now come on, let's go get this motherfucker."

Ryan sighed, knowing by the look on Jacob's face that there was no use arguing with him. He gestured him forward, and they made their way down the hallway, peering into room after room.

"Damn. This is some fucked up shit," Jacob said, shaking his head. "I mean a torture room? A weapon room? An interrogation..."

"Ryan."

The voice sounded down the hallway, and they both stopped. They turned, staring down the hallway at the body lying on the floor. They raced forward.

"Billy! Oh my God!"

Ryan rushed forward, falling next to him, staring at the knife sticking out of his chest. "Jesus. How the hell are you still alive?"

"I've been asking myself the same thing," Billy gasped out. "Ryan, you need to find Ashleigh."

"I know. I'm working on it."

"No. You... you don't understand," Billy said. "This man, he's someone she knows. He's someone who knew Neil. Who thinks he's doing the right thing avenging him, and he's going to kill her. Please! You have to get to her before it's too late."

"I will. I promise, but I can't leave you alone." He glanced back at Jacob. "Jacob. I need you to stay with him."

"Oh, hell no. I am not leaving you alone in this manor."

"He'll die if you don't."

Jacob scowled. "I don't like this, Ryan."

"You don't have to like it. Just keep him alive," Ryan said, just as an ear-piercing scream split through the air.

Ashleigh.

Oh God. Oh God. He was behind her.

Ashleigh turned the corner, racing down the hallway, glancing over her shoulder. She could hear him! He was getting closer!

She turned, rounding another corner. Above her, a panel opened. To her right, a walk slid open. Good God. He could be anywhere!

"Ashleigh..."

She stumbled, fear washing through her. She fell against the wall, bracing her arm against it to keep from falling and she winced as pain pulsed from her shoulder. She pressed a hand to it, dots swimming before her eyes. She was losing too much blood. She was never going to make it out of here."

"Ashleigh..."

His voice sounded again, and she raced forward. She raced around the corner and screamed when she collided with a wall of hard muscle.

"Ash! Ash! It's me!"

"Ryan?"

She stared up at him, then she lunged forward, right into his arms.

"Oh, thank God, I found you," Ryan whispered, wrapping his arms tight around her. "I found Billy. I was so scared..."

"I'm okay, but he's behind me somewhere," Ashleigh said, glancing over her shoulder nervously. "I've been trying to lose him in this damned manor, but I keep going around in circles." She blew out a breath. "You shouldn't be in here Ryan."

"As if I would ever let you do this alone."

"Everyone in here is dead, Ryan. I do not want you to be next."

"Not everyone's dead, Ash. Billy... he's still alive."

"But I saw..."

"Jacob's with him. He's going to stay with him until the police get here. Levi and your sisters went to go get them."

"Levi. Jacob..." Ashleigh shook her head. "Wow."

"We've got your back. I promise, Ash."

Ashleigh smiled, reaching a hand up to stroke his cheek.

Thunk!

They both jumped, spinning around, just as Andrew tumbled out into the hallway.

"Andrew!" Ashleigh rushed forward. "Oh my God! I can't believe you're still alive!"

"Well, I do think I was a cat in a past life," Andrew said, smirking. "But I also know to always come prepared." He lifted his shirt, showing her the bulletproof vest. "Hurts like a bitch, though."

"Come on. Let's get you inside here." Ryan wrapped an arm around the man, helping him to his feet and into the room behind him. He leaned him against the wall, glancing behind him, his eyes widening when he saw the pit. "Holy shit."

"I went around in a fucking circle!" Ashleigh cried. "I was just here, but where is..."

"Ashleigh, watch out!"

She turned and screamed, as the clown jumped out from behind her. He grabbed her, tossing her across the room. Her body hit the wall, crumbling to the ground.

"Ashleigh!"

Andrew stumbled to his feet, charging toward the clown, but the clown caught him in midair. He tossed him to the ground, slamming the heel of his boot against his temple.

"Nighty, night." The clown turned toward Ryan.

"Son of a..." Ryan fumbled for his weapon, and a second later hands grabbed him from behind. He yelled, his body sailing through the air and falling downwards into the pit. He coughed, sputtering as the dirt filled his mouth, scrambling to his feet to stare up at the clown as he peered down into the pit.

"She's mine now," the clown said, tossing the ladder down. Then he withdrew a small gun from his pocket and pulled the trigger. The ladder on the other side shook, and he pulled the trigger again. It struck the bolt of the ladder, and it shook, falling into the pit. "And you won't be able to save her. Not now. Not ever."

Chapter Fifty - Three

"Jacob. That's your name, right?"

Jacob nodded, whipping the shirt over his head, and pressing it to Billy's wound. "Yes. That's right."

"You need to go help Ryan," Billy gasped, struggling for breath.

Jacob shook his head. "No way. I promised Ryan I'd stay here. I am not leaving you here to die."

"You and I both know I'm as good as dead. I haven't eaten in days. I haven't had anything to drink, and I've been stabbed."

"Don't say that. The police are on their way. My friend, Levi. He's a man of his word. He'll get them here. I know he will."

"It won't be in time." Billy gasped, struggling for breath. "Jacob. The girls. I need you to..."

His eyes drifted close.

"No! Billy! Stay with me!" Jacob leaned down, listening for breaths. He wasn't breathing. Dammitt!

He started compressions.

"Jacob!"

Running feet sounded behind him, the door creaking open.

"Oh my God. Billy!"

He gave Billy a couple of breaths and started. Not an easy task being one-handed.

"Jacob. The police are almost here. And the paramedics, they're right behind me." Levi hurried up behind him. "Come on. Let me take over."

Jacob nodded, stepping back. He watched Levi continue CPR, and moments later the paramedics appeared next to him.

"We've got this."

They took over, and Jacob glanced over at Jacob, then at the girls behind him. They were shaking and crying. "Levi. Are they..."

"Ashleigh's sisters. Yes."

"I need to find Ryan."

"I'm going with you." Levi turned to Callie and Sadie. "Stay here until the police get here, okay?"

Callie nodded. "We're not going anywhere. Billy. He's... he's family."

"Levi."

He glanced up, stumbling back when Sadie rushed toward him, wrapping her arms around him in a tight hug. "Thank you," she whispered. She stepped back, wiping her tears. "Now, go get my sister."

Levi nodded. He glanced at Jacob and they shared a look. A look they'd shared more than once on the football field.

Jacob reached down, grasping the tire iron he'd dropped.

Levi reached for the gun he had in the waistband of his jeans.

"Let's go help our brother and put this damned bastard in the ground.

The door slammed shut nearby, and Ryan swore, slamming his fist against the side of the pit. "Fuck!"

He kicked at the ladder lying on the ground, staring up the sides of the pit. There was no way to climb out. He was stuck.

He leaned back against the dirt wall, rubbing his fingers over his eyes and a cough sounded nearby. He snapped his eyes open, startling, when he saw the dirt on the other side of the pit move, a hand breaking free.

There was someone buried in here and they were alive?

He hurried forward, dropping to his knees. He dug through the dirt as fast as he could. Then his fingers wrapped around a small hand, pulling them free from the dirt.

"Gloria?"

Gloria dropped to the ground, coughing, as dirt spewed from her mouth. She wiped the back of her hand across her mouth, struggling to her feet as she pressed a hand to the wound in her abdomen. "Hello, Ryan."

"Jesus, Gloria. How the hell did you get in here?"

"The bastard threw me in here when I helped Ashleigh escape. Jerked the knife right out of me." She winced again, pulling the T-shirt over her head, and ripping it with her teeth. She lifted the tank top, tying it tightly against the wound. "Hurts like a son of a bitch."

"We need to get you out of here. You need a doctor," Ryan said, wandering around the pit, trying to find some foothold to climb out. He froze, his eyes landing on Marcus hanging from the hook over the pit. "Holy shit."

"I wouldn't feel sorry for him if I were you," Gloria said, stepping up beside him. "He helped the clown get us here."

"What?"

"He was the one helping the clown, Ryan."

"But why?"

"Because he blames the girl's mother's for his mother's death."

"So, it was easy for the clown to manipulate him," Ryan murmured, then he suddenly frowned, thinking back. When he'd been thrown into the pit, the clown had been in front of him. Marcus... well, he was dead. Who the hell had thrown him into the pit? "Damn. They all really had a lot of secrets, didn't they?"

"Yes, they really did."

"Including your mother."

"What?" Gloria looked over at him in confusion.

"She was friends with Mary and her friends too. There's a picture of them together from college."

"And the plot continues to thicken." Gloria sighed, running a hand through her hair. "Just when I think I have something solved, something throws a wrench in it. It's so infuriating! And it's not like I can ask her about it. She doesn't even remember me!"

"I don't think it would make a difference one way or another," Ryan told her. "Because, one way or another, this thing will be all over by the end of tonight." He stared up at Marcus, thinking. "Hey. Do you think we could use that hook to grapple out of the pit?"

"I'd say it's worth a try."

"Damn straight it is." Ryan drew the gun from the small of his back and flicked off the safety. He aimed it, then, pulled the trigger.

The bullet hit the lock holding the chain in place to the rafter above. It rattled, and he pulled the trigger again. It hit the lock again and the chain broke free, dropping toward them.

"Gloria, watch out!"

Ryan wrapped his arm around her, pulling her backward, shielding her body with his as the rafters shook from above. The chain broke free, shattering the wooden rafters above them as it caved and dropped around them.

"Jesus." Gloria coughed, blinking, as the dust whirled around them. "That was a little…"

"Intense?" Ryan asked, as he

made his way through the rubble, pushing wooden boards out of the way until he reached Marcus. He squatted next to him, rolling his body over until he could grab the hook. He jerked it free, blood oozing from the wound.

"Ugh. If I don't see another dead body or pool of blood the rest of my life, I will be a very happy woman," Gloria said from behind him.

Ryan didn't bother responding. He grabbed the chain, walked to the wall of the pit, and tossed it over the top. He gave it a tug, nodding when it didn't move. "I think this is going to work," he said, glancing over at Gloria. "But you can't climb." He glanced at her wounded wrist, then to her abdomen, thinking. "Come on. Climb on my back."

"What? Ryan, I don't..."

"We don't have time to argue, Gloria. Ashleigh's in danger, and you need to get to the hospital. Now, please. Get on my back."

"This is ridiculous. I could climb."

"I am not risking the chance of that wound opening up any more than it already had. Now come on. We're wasting time."

Ryan hunched down, and as soon as her arms wrapped around his neck, he rose. "Don't let go," he said, as he gripped the chain. He placed his foot on the dirt wall, gripping the chain in his hands. He placed one foot up, then another, his arms straining against the chain as he made his way up the wall.

Gloria tightened her grip around his neck. "This is really going to work!" she cried.

"Gloria! I can't breathe!"

"Oops. Sorry!"

She loosened her grip and Ryan pulled himself up another step. Above, he felt the hook shake.

"Oh shit."

The hook flew back, and they both screamed, as they tumbled backward.

Thunk!

A door slammed open, and a moment later, someone grabbed a hold of the chain. Ryan gasped, bracing his hand against the wall, staring above him. Relief immediately washed over him when he saw Jacob and Levi.

"Holy shit! You two have impeccable timing. I thought we were as good as dead!"

"Or at least paralyzed for the rest of our lives," Gloria said, swallowing, as she stared over her shoulder, down at the pit. "Can we get the hell out of here now?"

"Yes. Let's."

They made their way up the rest of the wall, and Levi reached for Gloria. He lifted her onto the ledge, and Ryan climbed out after her, collapsing onto the pavement. He blew out a breath, staring up at the ceiling before taking the hand Jacob offered and climbing to his feet.

"Damn. You two are luck..." Jacob trailed off, his eyes widening when he saw Andrew. "Holy shit!" He hurried across the room, pressing his fingers to his pulse. "It's weak, but he's not dead."

"I'll stay with him," Gloria said, wincing as she rose to her feet. "You boys need to find Ashleigh. He's going to kill her, then he's going to go after the other three. You need to stop him."

"We don't even know where he took her," Ryan said, running a hand over his jaw.

"Through that door," Gloria said, pointing to the door on the other side of the pit. "It leads to the basement. There's a secret room in there. I saw him going in and out of it earlier. He was getting ready." She pressed the other button on the door. A loud roar sounded and they turned as a platform appeared across the pit.

"Whoa..."

"Go. Now!"

Chapter Fifty - Four

Oh. Ouch.

Ashleigh winced, blinking, as she opened her eyes. God, her head was pounding. It was like she'd been in three different car wrecks. Her entire body was aching, and she couldn't feel her arms... her legs...

She turned her head, staring at her hands bound behind her back, and lower to her bound feet.

Damn. He'd gotten her.

"Welcome back, Ashleigh."

She jumped, jerking her head up, as she stared at the man leaning against the wall on the other side of the room. He no longer wore the makeup or the clown costume, and she gasped when she locked eyes with his.

"Oh my God. Vinny?" Her eyes widened, as she stared at him. Her vision cleared, as realization set in. "You're... the clown?"

"Indeed, I am."

"But, why?" Ashleigh asked, tears filling her eyes as she stared at him. "Vinny, I know you! We've worked side by side at the restaurant for three years!"

"And I've been watching you and your friends for even longer," Vinny said, pushing away from the wall and striding toward her. He stopped in front of her, squatting down and lifting the phone in his hand. "You know the funny thing about technology, Ashleigh? They make apps for the most basic things. Like... changing your voice."

He pressed a button, his voice filtering through the air and Ashleigh cringed. "You raped me."

"Indeed, I did."

"But... but why?"

"Oh, Ashleigh, don't you know the answer to that question by now?" Vinny asked, stroking a finger down her cheek. "You needed to suffer. You all did, but what I didn't plan on was enjoying my time with you so much."

"You're sick."

"No. I just know what I like," Vinny said, his fingers trailing down the side of her throat, down her chest, and cupping her breast. He flicked her nipple with his thumb. "And I can't wait to play with you again."

"That'll never happen."

Vinny laughed, rising to his feet and stepping back. "You're wrong," he said, as he paced the room. "You're mine, Ashleigh. And you'll be mine until the day you die."

"Like hell I will," Ashleigh said, lifting her chin and staring at the pictures hanging on the walls. "You knew my father?"

"Very well. He and my father served together," Vinny said, wandering around the room. He stopped in front of a photo of two men and a young boy. "This is me," he said, pointing to the picture. "I was just five years old when their unit got compromised. My father took a bullet right to the spine. It paralyzed him. He told Neil to go, to leave him, but Neil refused. He helped my father get to safety, taking several bullets himself. They were both honorable discharged and were in the hospital for a long time. Your mother knew, but she couldn't have cared less. Said he deserved what he got." He clenched his fist. "I hate that damned woman. She cheated on him. She lied to him. She was his wife. He deserved better."

"And your mother?"

"She died when I was just a baby. While my father was recovering, I went to live with my aunt. It was months before I saw him, but when I did, he wasn't the same man I'd known. He was different. Withdrawn. Depressed. Then I met Neil." He smiled. "Neil came over to the house once he'd been released and together, we would work on making the house accessible for my dad. We built a ramp. We made the shower handicap accessible. We even moved his bedroom downstairs. I spent so much time with him, he eventually became like a second Dad to me. He came and saw us every weekend. Until he didn't." He picked up a small black book from the table. "I never understood why he completely abandoned us, until I received this book five years ago. It details everything your mother and her friends put him through. The abuse. The torture, and finally, the way he died. I knew I had to do something, and then I learned about you and your friends. I thought if I took you, it would bring your mother and Charles out of hiding. But they were determined to keep their secrets. Then I got the idea, that if I could get the four of you to remember, you could hate them as much as I did. Only I didn't realize how much fun I'd have with the four of you. Only, you escaped, and I still hadn't gotten my revenge. I wanted Mary and Charles to suffer. To know that someone knew what they had done. That's when I found MJ and Amelia. It was perfect, and torturing you, well, it was even more fun."

"You are seriously deranged."

"No. I'm as sane as anyone," Vinny said, turning to give her a sinister smile. "And this time, when I'm done with you, you'll die, Ashleigh. It's always been my endgame, Ashleigh. To get rid of anyone connected to that day at the Millers, and that includes you and your friends."

Ashleigh gulped. There was no doubt in her mind that he would do just that. She watched him flip through the journal, glancing around the room, looking for something to help loosen the ropes. She wiggled her hands. The knot was too tight. There was no way she was going to loosen it.

Wait. The lighter!

She suddenly remembered the lighter she'd used to fight off Marcus. It was still in her pocket. She just needed to...

She strained her hand back, reaching her fingers back as far as she could. They snuck into her right, back pocket and her fingers brushed against the lighter. She stretched a little further, her fingers pushing the lighter up and right into her hand.

Yes!

"You know, you have a very different view of my father than I do," Ashleigh said, flipping the lighter in her hand and pushing the lever. "I mean, sure, I remember a nice, genuine man who used to read me bedtime stories every night, but I also remember him as mean and violent. My mother. She had countless bruises from him."

"The bitch deserved it."

"No one deserves to be treated like that. No matter how bad of a person they might be." She frowned. "Vinny. You said the journal was sent to you?" She pressed the flame against the ropes, wincing as the best burnt her.

"Found it on my doorstep." He sniffed. "What the hell is that smell? Is something burning?"

"Yes."

He jerked his head toward her.

"Me."

She ripped free from the ropes, jumping to her feet. He raced forward, and she grabbed the chair, throwing it at him. It hit him square in the chest, and he stumbled back. She lifted the lighter in her hand. "Let it burn."

She lifted the lighter to one of the pictures, setting it on fire. She tossed it on the table.

"No!"

Vinny looked around in horror, as the flame caught, spreading to the other pictures. "I'm going to kill you!" he shouted, lunging toward her.

"You'll have to catch me first."

Ashleigh pivoted on her heel, jerking the door open and racing out of the room. She slammed the door shut behind her, racing down the hallway, and around the corner.

"Come back here!"

The door slammed open, echoing in her ears. She slid to a stop, staring around the basement, her eyes landing on the axe she'd left down here earlier. She raced forward, wrapping her hands around the hammer.

"Ashleigh..."

The panel in front of her slid open and she screamed, stumbling back as the clown appeared in front of her. She fell, the axe falling from her hands. She lunged for it, but the clown beat her to it, kicking the axe out of her reach.

"No!"

She tried to run, but he grabbed her by the hair, jerking her back. She screamed, as her body slammed against the wall. She groaned, her head spinning, as she stared up at him.

"Thought you were going to get away from me, did you?" The clown asked, chuckling as he raised the knife in his hand. He pressed it to her cheek, trailing the sharp edge across her skin before dropping it to her throat. "I told you. I'm going to kill all of you. It's what you deserve after everything your families have done."

"Let her go!"

The door slammed open behind them, running feet sounding. A moment later Ryan, Jacob, and Levi raced into the room, raising their weapons.

"What is this? The three amigos?" Vinny laughed, jerking Ashleigh in front of him, once again pressing the knife against her throat. "You can't save her. She's mine." He started dragging her down the hallway.

"No!" Ryan started forward.

"Nah. Uh. Uh." Vinny grinned at him. "One more move and your girl here is going to drop dead."

"Just shoot him, Ryan," Ashleigh gasped out. "He's going to kill me anyway. Kill him, please. Before he goes after my friends."

Ryan stared at her, then at the knife pressed to her throat. He shook his head, lowering lowered his weapon. "I can't, Ash. I won't put you in any more danger than you already are."

Levi and Jacob nodded, lowering their weapons.

"Good boys. Now, come on, Ashleigh. We have some unfinished business." He dragged her down the hallway, and Ashleigh dug her heels in.

"No."

"What?"

"I said no," Ashleigh said, raising her chin. "I'm not afraid of you anymore, Vinny. You have no control over me anymore." She grabbed his arm, plunging it downward, the knife impaling her through the stomach.

"No!"

"Ashleigh!"

Ashleigh dropped to her knees, reaching for the axe lying on the ground. She swung around, swinging it around hard, and striking him in the stomach.

He stumbled back, and she rose to her feet. "I'm not the one dying here today."

She swung the axe again, and he stumbled back as the blade struck him in the stomach. He laughed, blood oozing from his mouth. "You'll never be free of me."

She raised the axe.

"Police, freeze!"

A dozen police officers raced into the room behind them, and Ashleigh stared down at Vinny. She lifted her head, glancing at the raging fire in the room just behind him.

"You're done, Vinny. I beat you, and you will never, ever hurt anyone else ever again."

A moment later the glass behind them shattered.

"Ashleigh!"

She turned, racing across the room, right into Ryan's arms.

Chapter Fifty - Five

She was safe. She was alive.

Ryan wrapped his arms around Ashleigh, pulling her into his arms, relief flooding him. Seeing her being dragged by that madman, it had taken every ounce of strength he had not to go charging after them.

"I got you," he whispered, pressing a kiss to her temple. "And dammitt, I'm never letting you go. Come on." He wrapped his arm around her, leading her away and through the manor.

"Wait." Ashleigh lifted her head, looking behind her.

"The police will take care of him," Ryan said, glancing back at the flames that had engulfed Vinny just moments ago. "But there's no way in hell he survived that."

"I don't know..."

"There's nothing more you can do. We need to let the police do their jobs, and you, need to get to the hospital."

"You seriously kicked ass back there," Jacob said, as he followed them through the manor.

"It was epic!" Levi added. "The bastard deserved everything he got."

"Levi. Jacob. Thank you." Ashleigh glanced over her shoulder at them as they neared the entrance. "What you did for me. For my sisters..."

"You're essentially family now, Ashleigh," Jacob said, shuffling his feet and jerking a thumb in Ryan's direction. "I mean, if you're certain you want to put up with this bastard."

Ryan threw his head back and laughed.

Ashleigh smiled, turning to look at him. "I don't think he'll be getting rid of me anytime soon."

"Ditto."

Ryan ducked his head, brushing his lips over hers.

"Ah. Yeah. You're welcome." Levi averted his eyes. "I... I'm just going to go... over there."

They ran off and Ryan laughed, shaking his head. He wrapped his arm around her again, leading her out of the manor.

"Ashleigh!"

Callie and Sadie raced across the lawn, engulfing her in a tight hug.

"You're okay!"

"You're alive!"

"Thanks to you two," Ashleigh said, pulling back. She looked between the two of them. "You got to Ryan and got the police here. You saved my life."

"I think we saved each other."

They embraced, and Ashleigh turned, staring across the lawn. It was utter chaos. Police cars were scattered across the lawn, their red and blue lights lighting up the darkness of the night. There were a total of four ambulances, and reporters were everywhere. Across the lawn, she caught sight of Gloria. She was beat up, battered, bloodied, and bruised, yet she was still reporting what happened.

"We got a live one here!"

"Here too!"

She spun around as two stretchers were rolled out of the manor.

"Billy. Andrew." She raced forward, looking at one then the other. "I can't believe you guys are still alive!"

"Can't get rid of us that easily," they said in unison.

They laughed, grinning at one another.

"Hey, Andrew, you were right," Billy told him, lifting the oxygen mask from his face.

"About what?"

"That you'd be a hard one to get rid of."

Andrew grinned. "Guess that makes us brothers now."

"Partners. Brothers." Billy glanced at Ashleigh. "Survivors."

Ashleigh watched as they were loaded up in the ambulances and disappeared into the distance.

"Come on. It's your turn," Ryan said, leading her to one of the nearby ambulances."

Ashleigh sighed, letting him lead her over. She took a seat at the back of the ambulance, letting the paramedic look her over.

"Hey, Cap! We found a body in there!"

Ashleigh glanced over at Captain Vargas, as he stopped next to the ambulance. "Marcus?" she asked.

Captain Vargas shook his head. "No. We already loaded him up. Seems there was another body in that pit. Looks to be much younger. Like twelve or thirteen years old."

Ashleigh gasped. "Could it be..."

Captain Vargas shrugged. "Won't know anything until we bet forensics back." He paused, laying a hand on her shoulder. "I'm glad you're okay, Ashleigh." He turned and walked off.

"Ma'am, I need to get you to the hospital," the paramedic said, as he finished taking her vitals, and applied bandages to her wounds. "You need stitches, and that bullet's still in your shoulder. I'm worried about infection."

Ashleigh nodded. "Okay. Let's go."

She climbed into the ambulance, glancing over at Ryan, the siren blaring loudly as they took off down the road. "Ryan. This isn't over."

Ryan pulled her close. "What do you mean?"

"Vinny didn't steal my mother's journals. Someone else did, and they sent the journal to Vinny. There's someone still out there," she whispered, laying her head on his shoulder. "And they know everything."

Thank you for reading Hunted. Keep an eye out for the next book in the series, Wanted, coming this spring.

Born and raised in the Midwest, Nicole Coverdale writes in several different genres: Mystery, suspense, romance, fantasy, and the paranormal. She is the writer of the urban fantasy series, The Wiccan Way, and the thriller/mystery series, The Randolph Saga.

With several books already mapped out, Nicole spends most of her days on the computer, letting the words flow, but when she's not writing she loves to shop, binge on Netflix or Hulu, cook, bake, and loves nothing more than a good sports game. She loves her Wisconsin sports teams!

Currently, Nicole resides in southern Minnesota with her black lab, Hunter and looks forward to being able to adopt more fur-babies in the future! To learn more about Nicole, follow her on social media and check out her website at www.nicolecoverdale.com

Manufactured by Amazon.ca
Bolton, ON

35805924R00282